THE ARK AND THE EMPIRE

'Accurate history, magic, a diverse cast, intrigue and action, all set in ancient Rome. And Egypt. And did I mention the legionnaires?'
MARY ROBINETTE KOWAL,
HUGO AWARD WINNING AUTHOR

'Breathtaking in scope... A truly inventive epic fantasy-like novel, a massive undertaking that launches a tremendously ambitious series.'
BARNES & NOBLE

'A satisfyingly supernatural back story for the all-too-real final war of the Roman Republic.'
KIRKUS REVIEWS

'Part Indiana Jones, part Game of Thrones, all set against the very real backdrop of the rise of the Roman Empire.'
THE WHEEL OF TIME BLOG

'Beyond the magic, the history and the characters, the novel is relentlessly entertaining.'
SF SIGNAL

'This multipronged tale is dense with action and incident... Grounded in history, mythology, and religion, but not weighed down by them.'
PUBLISHER'S WEEKLY

ALSO BY MICHAEL LIVINGSTON

THE SEABORN CYCLE SERIES
Seaborn
Iceborn
Stormborn

THE SHARDS SERIES
Novellas
The Aegis and the Oasis

Novels
The Ark and the Empire
The Spear and the Storm
The Ring and the Ruin

NON-FICTION
The Killing Ground: A Biography of Thermopylae
Agincourt: Battle of the Scarred King
Origins of the Wheel of Time
Crécy: Battle of Five Kings
Never Greater Slaughter: Brunanburh and the Birth of England
Medieval Warfare: A Reader
The Two Hundred Years War

THE ARK AND THE EMPIRE

MICHAEL LIVINGSTON

An Ad Astra Book

The Ark and the Empire first published as *The Shards of Heaven* in the
United States in 2015 by Doherty Associates / Tor Publishing Group

The Aegis and the Oasis novella first published as *The Temples of the Ark* in 2016

This edition published in the United Kingdom in 2026 by Head of Zeus Ltd,
part of Bloomsbury Publishing Plc

The Ark and the Empire © Michael Livingston, 2015
The Aegis and the Oasis © Michael Livingston, 2016

The moral right of Michael Livingston to be identified
as the author of this work has been asserted in accordance with
the Copyright, Designs and Patents Act of 1988.

All rights reserved. No part of this publication may be: i) reproduced or transmitted
in any form, electronic or mechanical, including photocopying, recording or by
means of any information storage or retrieval system without prior permission in
writing from the publishers; or ii) used or reproduced in any way for the training,
development or operation of artificial intelligence (AI) technologies, including
generative AI technologies. The rights holders expressly reserve this publication from
the text and data mining exception as per Article 4(3) of the Digital Single Market
Directive (EU) 2019/790.

9 7 5 3 1 2 4 6 8

A catalogue record for this book is available from the British Library.

ISBN (PB): 9781035919161; ISBN (EBOOK): 9781035919154

Cover Design: Simon Michele
Typeset by Siliconchips Services Ltd UK
Maps by Rhys Davies

Printed and bound in Great Britain by Clays Ltd, Elcograf S.p.A.

Bloomsbury Publishing Plc
50 Bedford Square, London, WC1B 3DP, UK
Bloomsbury Publishing Ireland Limited,
29 Earlsfort Terrace, Dublin 2, D02 AY28, Ireland

HEAD OF ZEUS LTD
5–8 Hardwick Street
London EC1R 4RG

To find out more about our authors and books visit www.headofzeus.com
For product safety related questions contact productsafety@bloomsbury.com

*For Samuel and Elanor,
who are every reason*

Contents

Preface ... ix
Prologue: The Boy Who Would Rule the World ... 1

PART I: THE TRIDENT OF POSEIDON

1. A Weapon of Many Gods ... 17
2. The Last Quiet Moments ... 28
3. Among the Sons of Caesar ... 41
4. News from Rome ... 59
5. One Must Die ... 70
6. Cleopatra's Daughter ... 83
7. The Scrolls of Thoth ... 91
8. The Librarian's Door ... 101
9. A Show of Power ... 110
10. Calm Before the Storm ... 121

PART II: THE BATTLE OF ACTIUM

11. The Waiting City ... 137
12. Cleopatra's Plan ... 149
13. The Tomb of Alexander ... 160
14. The Traitor ... 171

15. The Great Library	184
16. The Storm of War	196
17. Octavian's Glory	204
18. A Meeting of Minds	212
19. The Hand of an Angry God	229
20. Return to Alexandria	243

PART III: THE FALL OF EGYPT

21. A City Besieged	257
22. The Temple of Serapis	270
23. The Librarian's Choice	285
24. The City Falls	293
25. The Enemy of My Enemy	308
26. The Ark of the Covenant	315
27. One Fatal Mistake	328
28. The End of a Kingdom	342
29. The Power of a Shard	358
30. The Lies of a Scholar	366
Epilogue: The Girl Who Would Fight the World	377
Glossary of Characters	385
Acknowledgements	391

THE AEGIS AND THE OASIS: A SHARDS NOVELLA

A Note to Readers	397
1. The Aegis	401
2. The Oasis	424

Preface

One world's history is another's fantasy. Today we might look upon Zeus and Apollo as wondrous figments of the Greek imagination, but I'm confident Homer felt differently. Indeed, he may well have believed in his history—filled with heroes and gods and goddesses both malevolent and benign—as surely as I believe in the history of George Washington, whom I wager I've met about as often as Homer met Athena.

A story, such as the one that follows, that takes as equal facts the existence of the Trident of Poseidon, the Ark of the Covenant, and the rise to power of Augustus Caesar, therefore, might be entirely history or entirely fantasy—depending on the reader's pleasure and perspective. Know at least that these events and the characters involved in them fit as seamlessly as possible into the timeline of what we think we know of these events. Juba is real. Didymus is real. So, too, are Pullo and Vorenus, Caesarion and Selene, and many of the rest. Actium was real. Alexandria was real.

And maybe, just maybe, so were the Shards.

For the reader's convenience, the following chart reveals the often confusing relationships between the families of Julius Caesar and Cleopatra. Dashed lines represent adoption. Further details may be found in the glossary at the end of this book.

Families of Julius Caesar

```
                    Gaius Julius Caesar
                  ┌─────────┴─────────┐
Cleopatra VII = JULIUS CAESAR    Julia Caesaris m. Marcus Balbus
        │         ┊     │                   │
    CAESARION   Juba II             Atia m. Gaius Octavius
                  └──┬──┘                   │
                OCTAVIAN              Octavia m. Mark Antony
```

and Cleopatra VII

```
     Julius Caesar = CLEOPATRA VII m. Mark Antony
              ┊         │         ┌─────────┴─────────┐
          CAESARION                              Ptolemy Philadelphus
                        └──────┬──────┐
               Juba II m. Cleopatra Selene   Alexander Helios
```

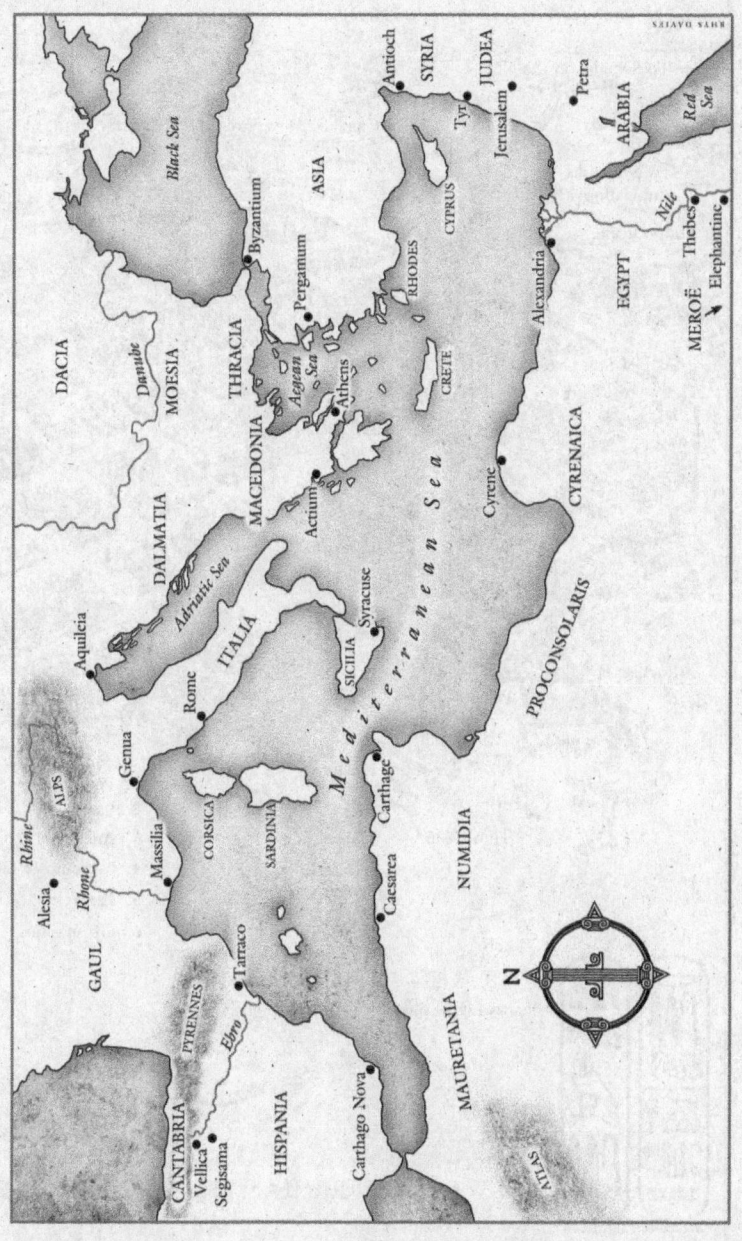

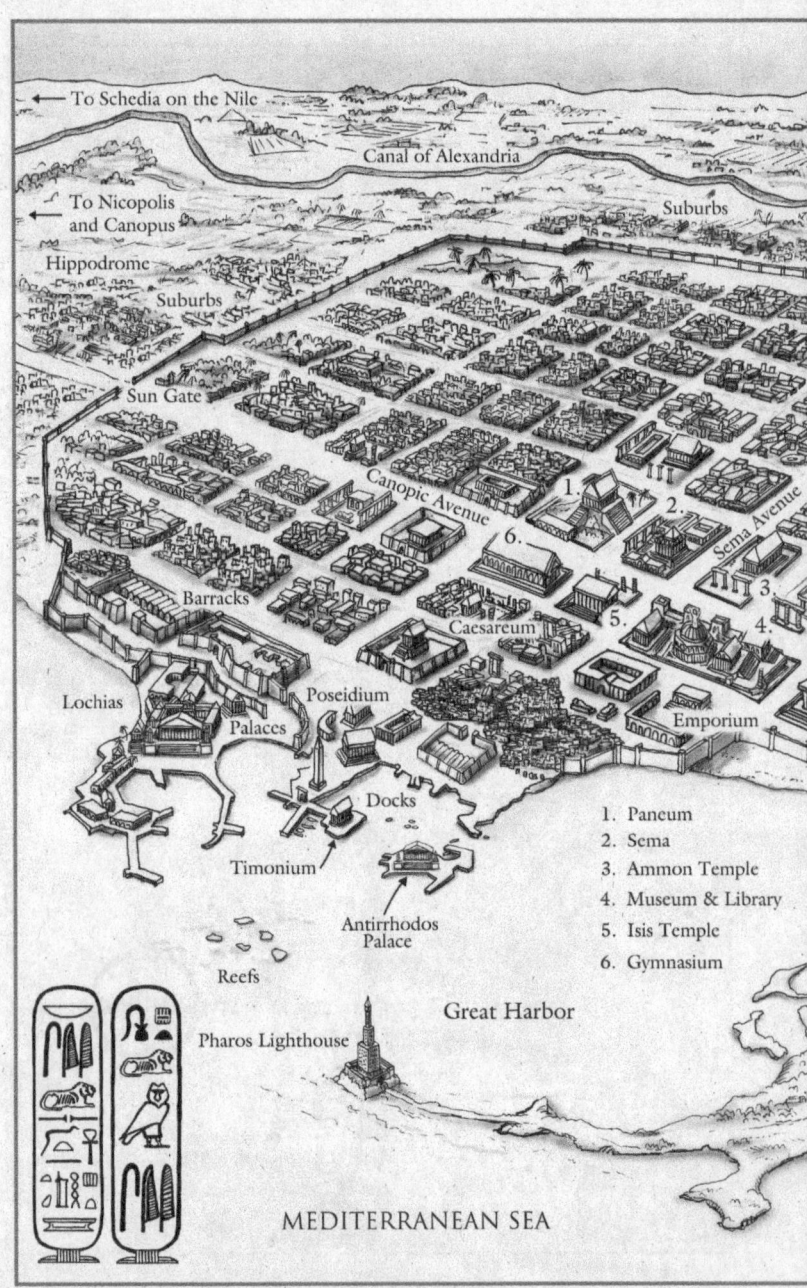

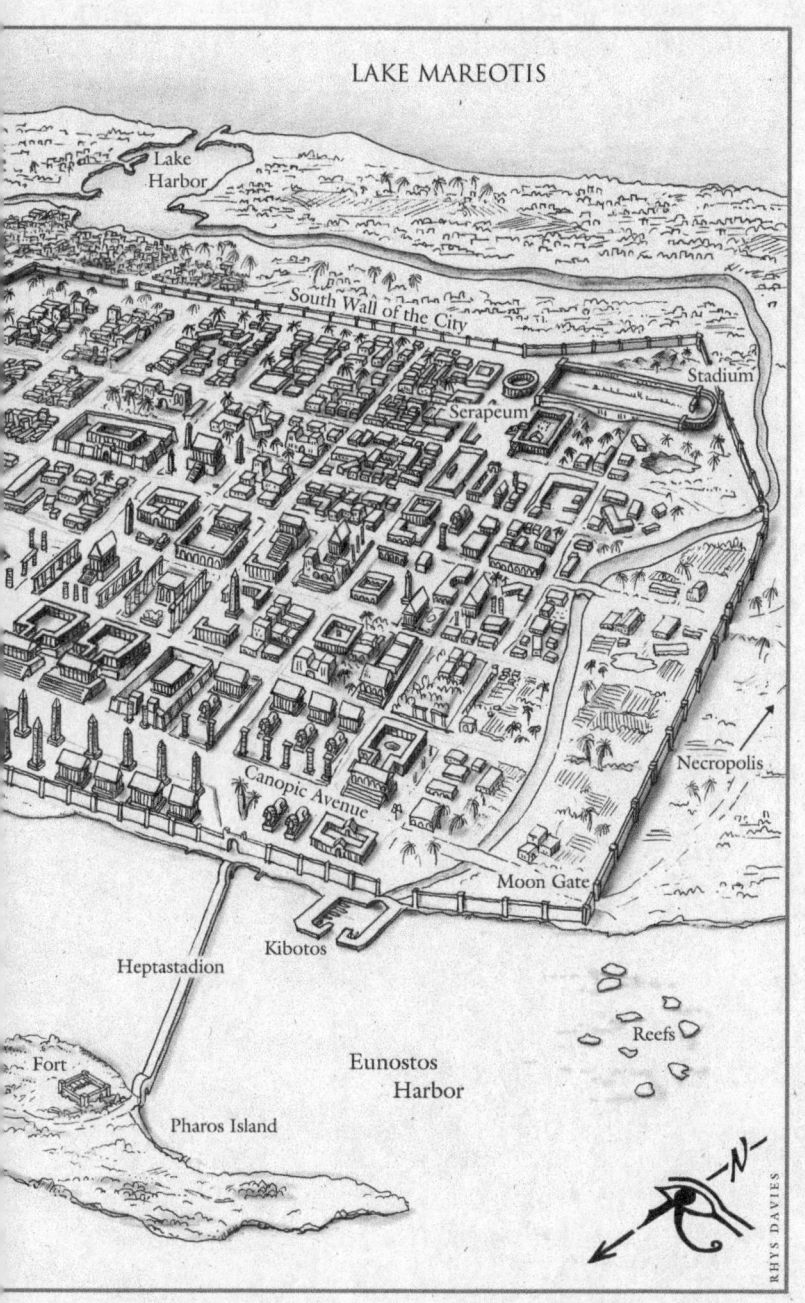

I am all that has been, that is, and that will be. No mortal has yet been able to lift the veil that covers me.

—Inscription on the temple of Neith at Sais, according to Plutarch

Prologue

The Boy Who Would Rule the World

OUTSKIRTS OF ROME, 44 BCE

Hidden amid the shadows outside Caesar's marble-columned villa, the assassin Valerius gazed back across the valley to Rome. Coiled around and upon her seven hills, the Eternal City often seemed like a living thing, her old streets pulsing with life. But now, on this fading day, the city was quiet and still. Her ancient stones, alight with the reds of a setting sun, appeared to be weeping blood. Valerius saw in the image a sign of favor.

The dictator was dead. And the gods approved.

Caesar's blood, he did not doubt, still stained the tiled floor of the east Forum. Pushing his way through the astonished throngs of onlookers after the deed, Valerius had seen for himself the mangled corpse, wrapped in the tattered remains of Caesar's purple robes, and in his mind's eye the thick crimson pooled there was the perfect mirror to the strong light before him now.

Valerius' knife, which he absently turned over in his hands

as he watched Rome's red walls slowly fade to gray, had not been among those that drank of Caesar, and he thought it a pity. The rich senators who'd done the killing were emotional men, ineffective at murder. Even with so many cuts to his body, Caesar had taken some minutes to die. The sprawled trail of blood on the tiles had told the tale. And though Valerius felt no particular love for the would-be emperor, he nevertheless thought it shameful that any man should shake out his last breaths under the eyes of dishonorable men.

Shameful, but little for it: Valerius was under no employ for that killing, and the man who had arranged to hire him only hours afterward would never have wished Caesar dead. Octavian still called the dictator "Uncle Julius" despite all the titles and glories that Caesar had won over his great-nephew's nineteen years. In the streets some citizens were even saying that Caesar had adopted the young man, that Octavian might well be his heir. That was certainly what Octavian seemed to think.

Valerius spit into the vines that gathered about the foot of the villa wall at his back. He knew little of politics himself: he cared for them only insofar as they affected his own movements. Heir or not, adopted son or not, Octavian was his employer now. So Valerius cared only that his employer's beloved uncle was dead and that he had been hired to see that Caesarion, the son of Caesar and Cleopatra, the only blood child of the now-dead dictator, would follow his father to the grave.

As he stopped to think about it, it seemed for a moment odd to Valerius that Octavian should wish the child of Julius such harm. The assassin had never seen the boy, but it was said that, aside from his slightly darker tone of skin and more delicate Egyptian features, Caesarion had every part the striking resemblance to his father. Then again, as heir of Egypt and the only surviving child of Julius Caesar himself, Caesarion did stand in line to inherit the world. And if Octavian thought himself rightful heir to at least part of that world ... well, no price would be too high to see the boy dead.

Not that it really mattered. Octavian's reasons were immaterial in the end. Not like the hundred weight of gold Valerius had been promised for the killing. *That* was material indeed.

Up the hard-packed dirt road from the bridge over the Tiber came the sound of hooves, a punishing gallop of men in fury. Valerius took a deep breath to clear his mind of reasons in order to focus on the simple facts of the task at hand: to get into the villa and end the child's life. With practiced speed he pocketed his blade, fearful of any glint it might give off despite the deep shadows and brush in which he crouched.

The staff emblem rattling above the lead rider showed the markings of Caesar's famed Sixth Legion, and even before they were close enough for the assassin to see the details of the faces of the riders themselves, he knew the man at their center to be Mark Antony: the general was broad-shouldered and handsome in his signet robes, with thick curls of red hair bouncing at every downbeat, and he exuded arrogance and assumptive power with every movement. Even the strong and impassioned way he drove his steed, completely heedless of consequence to the beast, seemed emblematic of the man. If the citizens of Rome knew but one thing about Antony it was that he was full of fire, his eyes never alight on anything but his goal. He'd been Julius Caesar's finest general, perhaps his best friend, and for some reason—Valerius couldn't fathom why—his life had been spared by the conspiratorial senators.

Valerius slowly and methodically stretched some of his tense muscles, grateful for Antony's appearance. He'd counted on an emissary coming to call on the distraught queen of Egypt, but none could be more ideal than Antony. Chaos followed the man like the wake of a passing ship, and his arrival would be sure to send the household into even greater confusion than that which it already labored under, making it far easier for the assassin to complete his work.

Tucked behind the drapes of a momentarily calm foyer, his lungs moving shallow and silent, Valerius listened to the sounds of the villa: servants' feet rushing between rooms, pots and dishes being moved about in the kitchens, the muted sobs of a woman crying, and, very close, the quiet breathing of someone waiting in a nearby doorway. A male someone, by the sound of the breathing. Octavian's contact, he hoped.

Valerius lifted himself to the balls of his feet, floating out from his hiding place. A long, wide swath of torchlight cut across the darkened floor of the foyer, spilling out from the doorway where the man waited, effectively blinding whoever it was to anything moving in the shadows. The assassin glided carefully around the periphery of the room until he stood beside the doorway. Then he took a small rock from his pocket and tossed it lightly out into the open.

The man in the doorway started at the sound of the pebble clattering across the floor, and he took a few hesitant steps into the open. "Hello?" he whispered. His voice cracked. "Is someone—"

The man's quaking voice was frozen by the dull back of the assassin's blade against his throat. Valerius guided him with it, pulling him into the darkness away from the doorway. "Yes," the assassin breathed in his ear. "Someone is here."

"I'm ... I'm ..."

"That's not the code word," Valerius said, pressing the steel against his skin.

The man's body shook in fright, and his neck spasmed before he finally controlled himself enough to remember the arranged sign. "Tiber," he croaked. "Tiber."

Immediately Valerius released and spun Octavian's contact

around to get a good look at him. The man was younger than he'd anticipated, perhaps not even twenty. He had the smooth skin of someone unaccustomed to manual labor and the outdoors, and the tone of his complexion showed he was not Italian stock, though it was also more olive than the deeper tan of Cleopatra and her Egyptian court. A Greek, probably. Or a Cretan.

"I'm Didymus," the man said. "I didn't—"

"Where's the boy?"

"The boy?"

"Little Caesar," Valerius hissed.

A new fear crossed Didymus' face. "Varro said you wanted Cleo—"

The assassin's voice turned low and dangerous. "Octavian will pay you, yes?"

Didymus nodded, his expression numb.

"Pay you well?"

"Yes," Didymus managed.

"Then don't waste my time," Valerius whispered, raising the knife for emphasis. "Where?"

Didymus swallowed carefully, his eyes dark. After a moment he lifted his arm in the direction of the lighted, open doorway. "Through my room, left beyond the curtains. Two rooms down there. Caesarion's is the first."

"Guards?"

"One inside. Abeden. An Alexandrian."

"And the Egyptian whore?" Octavian hadn't ordered it, but Valerius was certain there'd be a substantial bonus if both mother and child died tonight. No one in Rome had approved of Caesar's dalliance with the foreign queen.

The fear in Didymus' face was replaced with something more focused and harsh. Something more like the jealousy of a jilted lover. "Her room's beside his. You'll know it for the moaning."

Valerius nodded, lowered his blade, and padded into Didymus' room. The furnishings were simple enough, but the walls were lined with tables, each stacked tall with scrolls in various states of binding. The traitor was a tutor, he surmised. Probably the boy's. It would explain his hesitation.

The household was still busy at the front of the villa. He could hear Antony bellowing commands, sending the servants scurrying to tend to his horse and to bring wine for his own dust-dried throat. Soon, the assassin imagined, Antony would dispatch one of his legionnaires to fetch Cleopatra.

The assassin doubled his speed as he made his way through the curtained rooms and hallways, keeping to the shadows as much as he could, closing in on the sound of the sobbing woman he now knew for certain to be the queen of Egypt. He encountered no one before he reached Caesarion's door, where he paused to listen for sounds of movement within.

Valerius smiled once more. If the bloodred light of the sunset and the ease of his passage were not surety enough of the gods' blessing on his task, the few noises inside the room would have passed all doubt from his mind. The boy was playing quietly, and from the sound of it Didymus was right about the single guard.

The assassin knocked lightly on the door, then right-palmed his knife. The door cracked, filled with an Egyptian face.

Valerius bowed slightly, kept his voice low and his posture submissive, like a servant's. "The queen requests your presence, Abeden. There's talk of moving the boy." He stood to one side, so as to let the guard pass into the hallway. "I'm instructed to stand at the door in your absence."

The guard glanced back at the room, then stepped out into the hall, pulling the door shut behind him. He turned in the direction of Cleopatra's room. As he did so, Valerius came forward at his back, knife moving in a rapid strike up and into the center of his throat, puncturing his voice box. Then, in a smooth and practiced motion, he pulled the blade back and up and out, severing the vital arteries on the right side of the guard's neck even as his free hand gripped the man's weapon arm and used it as a lever to turn his body and send the bright red spray against the wall, out of sight of the boy's doorway. He pinned the man there for a moment as he shook and gurgled, then he stabbed him once more, this time in the left center of his chest.

The guard sagged, only twitching now, and Valerius let him down to the floor quietly before checking his own body for blood. As he expected, only his knife hand had met with the stain, and this he was quick to wipe clean on the dead guard's tunic. Pocketing the weapon, Valerius dragged the man into a slumped position with his back against the wall. From a distance, he'd look like he was sleeping. Valerius would have liked to hide the body completely, but then he'd need to clean up the blood. And, besides, he planned to be finished with his tasks and fleeing through one window or another in a matter of minutes.

Shaking out his own shoulders and straightening his back, the assassin approached the door, knocked once, opened it, and stepped inside.

The room was modest but not small: perhaps fifteen feet square, with only a single wood-shuttered and curtained window above a well-cushioned bed. Caesarion, the boy who might inherit the world, the three-year-old child he had been sent to kill, was kneeling in the middle of the floor, surrounded by a small toy army: chariots, horses, and warriors. The assassin hadn't been sure what to expect, but he was surprised nonetheless to find the little prince dressed in a simple belted Roman tunic and thong sandals, no different from any three-year-old one might find in a market in the city. Even more surprising, though, was how much he resembled his father: he had dark hair cut round and flat against a strong brow, the prominent nose of the Julii, and, when Caesarion looked up, his dead father's piercing dark brown eyes.

"I'm one of Antony's men," Valerius said, smiling as he did to all children. "We're going to go see your father." Behind his back the assassin carefully pushed the door's bolt into position, locking the room.

Caesarion nodded, and his voice was quiet and even. "See Father," the little boy said.

Valerius took a step forward in the room, nodding solemnly. "That's right. I'm sorry for your loss, my lord."

Little Caesar blinked, then looked down to the wooden figures gathered around him on the floor. His hands moved a Roman chariot forward, knocked over an Egyptian warrior.

Two steps closer. "Your father was a great man. He often won victory over unspeakable odds."

The boy nodded more strongly this time. He picked up the fallen Egyptian warrior, stood it on its feet and then stared, his face blank, at the pieces before him. "I know," he said.

Valerius took another step to stand behind Caesarion, his hand moving stealthily to his pocket to retrieve the warm knife. Slowly, deliberately, he bent at the knees, crouching behind the child and gauging his neck. "I am sorry," he said, and he started to reach forward.

An alarmed shout rang out in the hallway, the hard voice of a man. It froze the assassin's hand as his head turned instinctively toward the locked door and his mind recalled the possible escape routes he'd mapped out beyond the window.

Caesar's son, his own head turning at the shout, saw the assassin's weapon and pushed himself away, scattering toys. He backed into the wall, brandished a wooden play knife in his shaky hands.

Valerius, still crouched with his own knife in hand, was mildly surprised when he looked back to the boy. "You're fast, little one."

"Don't hurt me," Caesarion whimpered.

The assassin stood. In another context, with a man before him instead of a boy, he would have smiled. But not here. No smiles, but no lies either. "I have to."

Caesarion shook his head, swallowed hard. His eyes were dampening, but he didn't cry.

There were answering shouts from within the villa. A sudden crash jolted the locked door, but it held. Valerius found it ironic that Caesar's slaves had kept the house in such good working order that he'd be able to murder the man's son in peace. By the time they breached the door he'd be out the window and on the run, the child dead. Alas that he'd not get the chance at the queen, too. The bonus would have been nice.

"No," Caesarion stammered. "Please ... no."

Valerius settled his knees a little for balance, eyes taking stock of the child's fake knife. The boy couldn't do him any real harm with it, but the assassin didn't intend to take home even a scratch from this assignment.

There was a crash from Cleopatra's room next door, like the toppling of a great table, and the queen's lament turned to sudden screaming. Not seconds later there was another crash, and Cleopatra's voice grew even louder.

Caesarion's wooden weapon trembled more violently in response to his mother's terrified wails, and Valerius took a single step backward, giving himself room for a blade-dodging feint as he charged. He took a breath. Tensed.

Before Valerius could engage, heavy, running footfalls sounded beyond the shuttered window, and he had chance enough only to turn in the direction of the sounds before the wood slats separating the room from the growing night exploded inward as a massive legionnaire came through, tumbling over the bed and into his side.

The two men flailed to the floor together, grunting as splintered wood fell like rain in the little room. Valerius hit the ground first, but he was able to kick his lower body up in continuation of the legionnaire's momentum, sending the far bigger man hurtling against the barred door. The assassin then rolled quickly, recovering his balance even as the dazed legionnaire scrambled to get his feet under him and began pawing for the gladius at his side.

Valerius came forward at him, knife ready in his grip, but before he could strike he screamed and buckled to one knee as Caesarion jammed his little wooden blade into the soft flesh at the back of his right leg. The assassin swung his arm back at the boy instinctively, catching him above the eye with the butt of his knife, sending him sprawling.

Gritting his teeth against the pain, Valerius turned back around in time to see the big legionnaire draw an arm back and forward, pushing a gladius into his belly, just below his rib cage. Gasping against the cold steel in his gut, the assassin still tried to swing his knife, but the legionnaire held fast to his sword with strong hands, and his thick arms flexed as he twisted it in his grip, scratching the blade into bone. Valerius groaned, strained, then dropped his weapon and sank against the killing stroke, watching, helpless and gasping in broken breaths, as the legionnaire stood, wincing from wounds of his own, and pushed forward until the assassin collapsed to his back.

For a few short gasps, Valerius could see nothing but the ceiling, and then the legionnaire returned into his view. The assassin stared in paralyzed shock as the bigger man painfully lifted a foot and planted it on his chest. Valerius heard a crunch that he strangely could not feel as the foot pressed down and the gladius was pulled free with a jerk of the legionnaire's burly arms. Thick warmth washed over the assassin's chest. Then the legionnaire was gone, limping over him and out of view.

"Caesarion," Valerius heard the man say somewhere over his head. "You hurt?"

The child was crying now, and he heard the flex of leather and a grunt.

"There, there," the legionnaire was saying. "All's well, my boy. All's well. You're a brave lad."

Valerius was having a hard time focusing now, but he saw the legionnaire come back into view. With an effort, Valerius turned his head to follow the man as he made his way toward the heavy door, holding the sobbing boy in one massive arm. Someone was pounding on the door—the assassin absently wondered how long that had been going on—and the legionnaire shifted the boy to his hip so he could unbolt it.

The door swung open to a crowded hall. There was a second legionnaire, smaller than the first, who must have been doing the pounding. Mark Antony was beside him, holding back a weeping, panic-stricken Cleopatra. And among the faces gathered behind them he saw Didymus, his Greek complexion gone pale with terror.

"Caesarion!" Cleopatra shouted, rushing forward to take the boy from the bigger legionnaire's arms. By the gods, Valerius suddenly thought, she truly *was* beautiful. He'd heard talk of the queen's beauty, and certainly from afar she had been remarkable enough for him to half-believe the talk that she was part-goddess herself, but seeing her up close he saw the honest truth: she was a woman of flesh and blood, a mother with fears and hopes. And also perhaps the most beautiful creature he'd ever seen.

The smaller legionnaire came forward, too, offering a shoulder to his injured comrade after he handed over the boy, but Antony pushed past them all to kneel before Valerius, filling his fading world with a flushed face and the scents of stale wine. "Who hired you?" the general demanded. His thick fingers rooted in the assassin's tunic, causing the room to shift and bringing Antony's face even closer. "Who let you in?"

Valerius looked to the Greek tutor, but when he tried to

speak it came out as a wet cough. He felt an odd satisfaction to see flecks of red appear on Antony's face. He tried to smile but wasn't sure if the muscles of his face obeyed his mind's command.

"Bah!" Antony said, releasing his grip. The assassin's world unfocused, shook, then came back into clarity. He saw that Antony was standing now, surveying the room. "How'd you get to the window so quickly, Pullo?"

"Broke through the room next door, sir." The battered legionnaire flicked his eyes to Cleopatra in her shift, and he bowed slightly. "Apologies, my lady."

Cleopatra, looking up from stroking her boy's head, seemed to have gathered control of herself. "No apologies, legionnaire," she replied. "I owe you thanks."

Valerius was aware of their voices receding, as if they were moving farther and farther away. It occurred to him that he was dying, a sudden, strange, and fearful thought. He felt his mind bucking and straining against the realization, clamoring to fight on, but his body did little more than tremble in an awkward breath. Even as that part of his mind screamed, another part of him observed his life passing with disinterest. He'd seen this kind of death before, where the blade cut the spine. Less common than the quivering horrors. Strange to experience it now.

"This is the second time I find myself in your debt, Titus Pullo," Cleopatra was saying. Her eyes moved to take in the smaller legionnaire, on whose shoulder the big man now leaned. "And you, Lucius Vorenus."

Through a growing fog of shadow the assassin watched as Antony looked to the two men for explanation. Pullo seemed to blush, and Vorenus in turn gave a shy smile before he spoke: "We brought the lady back to Alexandria before the siege, sir. Before she met Caesar. Was nothing."

"I see," Antony said gruffly. The room was almost gone

now, and the general's words were only a distant whisper as he advised the queen to return to Alexandria.

But Valerius was no longer listening. He was thinking instead of the faces of the dead, of the many shades that would greet him upon the other side. He thought of their anger, of their unslakable thirst for vengeance.

And then the voices in the room faded at last into a still silence, and Valerius saw light—clean, white light—before his eyes. He heard a gentle wind, the sound of water upon a sand-lined shore. The sun shone. Children sang. All times became one time. Valerius reached for his mother's hand. He sat crying in an empty room. He lived. He died. He stood before the throne. And then darkness, an impenetrable and unquenchable black, rose up like a wave and overwhelmed all.

PART I

THE TRIDENT OF POSEIDON

I

A Weapon of Many Gods

NUMIDIA, 32 BCE

Standing at the craggy edge of a ridge that stabbed out into the stormy Mediterranean like a finger pointing north out of Africa—toward Europe, toward Rome—Juba frowned. The last thing the sixteen-year-old wanted to do was to resort to torture.

Sure, he'd read enough about the dark arts of physical pain to be reasonably certain how to go about them. One privilege of being an adopted son of Julius Caesar, after all, had been the possibility of an education bounded only by his own thirsty mind. By the time he'd left Rome a year ago, a tutor had proudly proclaimed him one of the most widely read men in the city—and that was before the old scrolls and tomes Juba had encountered during these many months across the sea in Africa.

Still, the idea of using violence to attain what he wanted didn't appeal to him. He doubted that information wrought from torture could really be of much use. It would be too conflicted. And even more than that, it didn't seem right. It didn't seem, well, Roman.

A hard wind kicked up the cliff-side, bringing with it the smell of brine from the churning waters far below. Gazing down at his arms after the stinging mist had passed over him, Juba noted the little pale droplets clinging to his dark skin. The irony of it further clouded his brooding mind. I'm no Roman, he thought. I'm a Numidian.

Juba heard the sound of someone moving hesitantly down along the narrow, broken path behind him. Even without turning, he could tell it was Quintus. The slave disliked heights. Always had. And now that the years had brought gray to his temples and long lines to his face, loyal Quintus truly hated them. "Yes?" Juba asked.

"It's Laenas, sir. I think he's ... well, growing impatient with the priest. I fear something rash."

Juba nodded. He'd expected as much when he'd left them alone in the old temple. Scar-faced Laenas had proven, time and time again during this past year, that he could be counted on for only two things: to desire coin and to despise those who stood in the way of his getting it. Since Juba had promised him thirty silver denarii if they got the information they were seeking from the Numidian priest, he was bound to be impatient.

Juba turned back from the salty, whipping wind, saw that Quintus was huddled as close to a nearby boulder as he could manage. Despite his own gloomy thoughts, Juba couldn't help but smile at the old slave. Assigned to care for him when he was still just a child living in Caesar's villa, Quintus had grown to be more a father to him than Julius had ever been.

"Very well," Juba said, stepping forward to help his slave back up the path toward the temple. "Let's hope he's willing to talk now."

Cut back into the earth, the old temple dedicated to the pagan goddess Astarte appeared from the outside to be little more than a weather-beaten cluster of stones clinging to the cliffs just below the crest of the bare ridgeline. Quiet. Isolated. Just the sort of place to hide the secrets of ancient gods.

Juba ducked through the clanking wooden door, grateful to be out of the wind and into the relative warmth of the dark, windowless interior. Quintus was quick to follow, the release of his breath signaling his additional relief at being off the precipices outside. "They're still in the back," the slave whispered.

Juba moved quickly through the small, bare antechamber and then through a thick drape into the lamp-lit altar room beyond, its air filled with the heavy scents of spiced incense and moist loam. At its head sat a low stone firepit filled with ash and bones. Behind it, atop a rough-hewn wooden pillar blackened by the fire, sat a small clay statue of a woman, only a little taller than his forearm, perched on a throne and holding a bowl beneath her more than ample breasts. Juba had read of such figurines in his books. It was said that the power of the fertility goddess—and her associated priest, of course—could be seen in the miraculous leaking of milk from the statue, flowing down from her breasts into the bowl.

Juba had studied this particular statue carefully earlier in the day, while they waited for the priest to return from the well in the village. He'd had no trouble finding the small holes bored through the clay nipples into the hollow of her body. He'd even found some flecks of the soft wax plugs that the priest had used to keep her breasts from leaking until the sacrifice burning in the altar below her had melted them.

So much for *this* god, he'd thought.

Juba walked past her now, up the three worn steps of the altar's stone dais, and then down another set of steeper, more roughly hewn steps that led to a low doorway against the back wall. Pushing through the drape there, he entered the last chamber.

The old priest of Astarte, still bound to his simple stool, had fallen over to the damp earthen floor. His nose was running with blood that glistened wetly in the flickering lamplight, and the short but stout Laenas was straddling him, hunched over at the waist, his fist raised for another strike.

"That's enough," Juba said, trying to sound strong, and glad to hear that his voice didn't crack.

Laenas grunted his assent and stood. Juba noticed now that his other hand had been holding a knife, which he quickly slipped back into the folds of his clothing. Its edge did not yet appear wet. "We was just talking," Laenas said over his shoulder.

The priest coughed loudly, a half-retching sound from his gut, and then spat into the dark dirt. Juba had always found it difficult to judge the age of those men older than him, a problem compounded here by the leather-tanned skin of a native Numidian: though it was, Juba could never forget, the tone of his own flesh, it nevertheless appeared foreign to his sight. Still, from the man's wrinkled face, his sparse, white hair, and his thick beard, Juba had guessed him to be in perhaps his seventies, even if his ability to withstand threat—and to manage the long hike to the village for water and supplies—spoke of a younger man, at least in spirit. Looking at him, Juba felt a pang of pity, but not remorse. "Help him up," he said.

Laenas grunted again—the typical depth of his speech—and then stepped around to lift the priest and his stool back into position. It seemed no more difficult for the stout little man than hoisting a sack of wheat. As the old man was lifted upright, Juba saw again the strange symbol on the pendant hanging around his neck: a triangle inscribed, point down, upon a perfect circle. He had seen similar pendants around the necks of some of the men whose information had led him here.

"I'm sorry for that," Juba said, measuring out his words, concentrating on keeping his back straight, his chin high.

"We're all just very anxious to hear what you have to say. Laenas here most of all."

The priest sputtered, his mouth moving, but he said nothing.

Juba sighed and walked over to one of the priest's rickety tables. It had been unceremoniously swept clean, the plates and parchment tumbled to the floor. In their place sat a bundle of bound canvas—substantially bigger, Juba noted with some amusement, than the statue of Astarte in the hall. Juba walked to it and raised his hand to touch the rough cloth, feeling the outline of the broken wooden staff beneath. Where the staff met the wider metal head, the cloth felt warm, and he snatched his fingers away with a start. He swallowed hard, glad his back was turned to the other men in the little room. "Let's start simple," he said, trying to calm his heartbeat. "This staff. This ... trident. How did it come to be here? The priests who pointed me here say it's the Trident of Neptune—or Poseidon, if you prefer. Is that true?"

When the priest said nothing, Juba turned around and saw that he was shaking his head weakly. Standing behind him, Laenas' face appeared to flush, the wide scar across his right cheek a darkening purple in the gloom.

"It's strange, you know," Juba continued, looking back toward the bundle and resisting the urge to touch it this time. "An artifact of the old Greek and Roman gods, here in this place, in the possession of a priest of Astarte. I wonder ... is there something to the idea that Astarte is the same goddess as the Greek Aphrodite, the Roman Venus?"

"I'll not help Rome," the old man croaked.

Juba heard only the briefest rush of movement before the priest gasped, a sound that reminded the young man of a cook tenderizing meat. Juba spun around and saw the old man slumped sideways, grimacing. "Laenas!" he cried out, his voice cracking with the sudden start.

The rugged Roman straightened, his fist coming back

from the priest's side and something like a smirk momentarily passing over his face. "Wasn't having him spitting about Rome," he said.

As if in reply, the priest did, in fact, cough and spit. The blood ran dark streaks into his matted beard.

Whatever else Juba might have expected the priest to utter then—that the Trident wasn't real, that the gods weren't real, maybe that he had money hidden away under a rock somewhere—it wasn't what the old man finally managed to say. "You've your father's eyes."

Juba stared at him, unblinking, his mind and heart racing. The old man held his gaze for a long moment before shutting his own eyes in a grimace of pain. Juba still stared at him, feeling the attention of Quintus and Laenas upon him even as he dared not look at them.

"Lord Juba—" Quintus started.

"Leave us," Juba commanded, cutting off the slave. He flicked his gaze at Laenas just long enough to note the familiar look of disdain on the rough man's face, the same twist of jealousy and disgust he'd seen so often while growing up in Rome as the foreign-born adopted son of Caesar. "Both of you."

"My lord, I—" Quintus said.

Juba silenced him with a wave of his hand. "I said go. Now."

"Very well," Quintus said, bowing deep as he backed toward the doorway. Laenas followed with a predictably dissatisfied grunt.

In seconds, Juba stood alone in the little room with the sagging priest. He took long, deep breaths to steady himself. "You speak the language of Rome well for a Numidian," he said when the sounds of Laenas and Quintus had grown faint.

The old priest licked his lips and swallowed before responding. "I was a slave to Rome, too, once."

"What's your name?"

"Syphax," the old priest said.

"So you knew my father."

Syphax nodded slowly. "I knew the king, yes."

The king, Juba thought. Could it truly be that the old priest, hidden away out here on this lonesome spit of land, was a loyalist to the royal family of Numidia? The lineage of which he alone remained?

"I saw him die," Syphax said.

"What?"

The old priest coughed twice painfully before he regained his composure. "Saw him die on the blade of my master, Marcus Petreius."

Juba staggered backward into the ragged table behind him as if physically struck by the sheer weight of memory and history that flooded into his mind. He'd read the books, sought out every shred of detail he could find on his real father's inglorious end. After Caesar had defeated the Numidian army at Thapsus, Juba's father had fled with the general Petreius, only to be trapped. The histories spoke of how the two men dueled to the death, opting for an honorable end rather than the wrath of Caesar and the horrible, dishonorable Triumph that he would have put them through back in Rome—the Triumph that had thus fallen to his infant son, Prince Juba, first seized and then later adopted by the very man who'd driven his royal father to such a doom.

"No," Juba managed to say. It had only been two months since Juba had knelt, at last, beside the unmarked grave of the true father Caesar had never let him know. His hands gripped the rough wood of the table at his back. "You cannot have."

"I watched them fight at the end," Syphax said. There was no pride in his voice. No power. Only old sorrow. "Petreius was still alive when it was done. As my duty, I ran a blade into his heart."

Juba closed his eyes, tried to imagine the scene as he had so many times in his young life. As ever, his father's face was a blur. Only the darkness of his skin was familiar. But he could picture a younger Syphax there, too, waiting, with a shined and sharpened sword, for either of them to fall. "Yet here you live," Juba said, opening his eyelids to glare fiercely at the priest. "A slave ... you killed your master but didn't follow him."

The priest's jaw quivered, his eyes red and sunk deep into tired sockets. "You're right. I didn't. I promised to fall upon my own sword after it was done. Promised them both. But I didn't."

Juba was just Roman enough to know the depth of Syphax's dishonor on principle. He was just Numidian enough to think the offense against his true father's memory worthy of death. And he was just young enough to act on the impulse of rage that washed over him.

He opened his mouth to call for Laenas.

"But for good reason, Juba!" Syphax cried out in a ragged voice. "I couldn't let them get it. I couldn't!"

The old priest's eyes had a trance-like glaze now, riveted on the bundle of cloth on the table. Juba, despite his rage, decided not to call Laenas just yet. "Tell me of it," he said. "Tell me everything."

Juba stepped around the altar to Astarte, canvas bundle under his arm, and found Quintus and Laenas in the temple's main room, sitting on one of the primitive stone benches. The old slave looked anxious. Laenas just looked sullen. Juba ignored them both for now, walking past them and through the antechamber out into the wind and the smells of the sea, his head too full of thoughts to speak just yet.

Syphax had indeed told him all that he knew. Juba was certain of that. The old man's despair was too great to hold back to the son and heir of Numidia, especially once he knew the secret Juba had kept from everyone but Quintus: that he hated Rome, that he hated his adopted father. He hated them for his real father's death. For the disgrace of the Triumph that was his earliest memory. For everything that Rome had done to his country.

Syphax had told him everything then. He'd told him far more than he could ever have imagined.

The Trident in his hands was indeed the weapon of gods. Poseidon. Neptune. But more than that, it was a weapon of the Jews, whose strange religion Juba knew little about—a fact he intended to remedy as soon as possible with the help of every book he could get his hands on.

And still more: there was an even greater weapon of the gods out there to be found, a weapon of the Jews that might give him the power to accomplish the revenge he'd long hoped to achieve. An ark.

The wooden door to the temple squeaked open and shut. Quintus tentatively shuffled up behind him. "Juba?"

The sixteen-year-old focused his eyes on the distant horizon, where the darkening sea met the darkening sky. Lightning flashed there, silent but threatening.

Syphax didn't have all the answers, but the old priest knew who did. "Thoth knows," he'd said, again and again. The source of the Trident's power, the nature of its strange black stone, the whereabouts of the wondrous ark ... *Thoth knows.*

At first, Juba had thought it was no answer at all. Thoth was an Egyptian god, like the Roman Mercury, a figure who moved between the world of gods and the world of men. A deity of so many faces he seemed to be everything and nothing all at once: god of magic and medicine, god of the dead, god of the moon, god of writing and wisdom, even the founder of civilization itself.

Thoth would naturally know the answers to questions. Yet

Syphax had spoken with a pragmatic earnestness, as if Juba could easily get information from Thoth.

"So where is Thoth?" Juba had asked the priest of Astarte.

And, after some final persuasion, Syphax had answered: "Thoth was in Sais."

Sais, Juba knew, was the cult center for the goddess Neith, the Egyptian counterpart of Astarte, which explained the priest's knowledge. Perhaps it even explained how he'd come to have the Trident. Then he'd caught the nuance in the priest's words. "Was?"

The old priest had smiled grimly, his pale teeth smeared with red. "The Scrolls are in Alexandria."

The truth at last. It wasn't Thoth himself who had the answers, but the legendary Scrolls of Thoth, in which all knowledge, it was said, could be found. And the Scrolls were in Egypt, in the Great Library. Find them and he'd have the power, and the vengeance, that he sought.

"Juba?"

The lightning pulsed again, and beyond the wind and the breaking of waves Juba heard a quiet rumble. Was it from the earlier flashes? Or was it the deep of the sea, calling out for its master? Juba swallowed hard, resisting the temptation to touch the metal head of the Trident in its canvas bundle, to see if it was warmer now. Instead he took a deep breath to clear his mind, to focus on the tasks immediately at hand. He needed to do more research. More than that, he needed money. Getting the Scrolls of Thoth from the Great Library and destroying Rome wasn't going to come cheap, after all, with or without a weapon of the gods. And there was surely no better time to strike than now, with war between Rome and Alexandria threatening to turn the world to chaos.

"We're returning to Rome," he said over his shoulder. "As soon as possible. There are things I need to do there."

"Of course," Quintus said, his voice uncertain. "Laenas wants to know, sir, what about the priest?"

Juba blinked away the beads of salty water that were starting to cling to his eyelashes. What to do about the priest? He was a loyal Numidian, after all, one of the very people Juba was going to save from Rome. Yet he'd abandoned the promise made to Juba's father, no matter his reasons. And, truth be told, he knew far too many things that were best kept secret, even if Juba didn't yet know the fullness of his course. Viewed through the lens of logic, the decision was easy, even if saying it was hard. Juba wondered if his Numidian father had ever felt the same. No doubt his adopted Roman one never had. "Tell Laenas to kill him," he finally managed to say. As the words escaped his lips Juba knew for certain that he would not sleep well this night. He wondered how he would ever sleep soundly again. "Tell him he'll get his thirty coins if he does it quickly."

Quintus hesitated for a moment, a slight stammer his only response. Then Juba heard the sound of the temple door opening and closing again, leaving him alone.

Well, perhaps not alone, Juba corrected himself, watching the approaching storm and wondering whether the gods were real.

2

The Last Quiet Moments

ALEXANDRIA, 32 BCE

Lucius Vorenus, feeling a familiar tiredness in his forty-five-year-old bones, leaned against the sun-bleached stonework atop the old palace wall and peered down into the cleared square of one of the inner courtyards, where Caesarion was practicing his sword work in the fading light of the day. Working against Vorenus' old friend Titus Pullo, the fifteen-year-old co-regent of Egypt had stripped to his loincloth to reveal a body filled out with lean muscle that flexed beneath a sheen of thick sweat—a fact that Vorenus could see did not go unnoticed by the small gathering of the remaining servant girls in the shadows, who whispered between giggling smiles as they watched the young man training. A few months ago there might have been dozens more spectators even in this most private of spaces within the sprawling expanse of red-roofed buildings, pillared arcades, and daunting towers that made up the royal palace, but the threat of Rome had changed all that. For the safety of the royal family, the inner wards of the palace were far emptier these days, even as the city continued to teem with busy life around them.

Vorenus and Pullo had long disagreed about whether it was appropriate to teach Caesarion how to fight in this way. After all, as pharaoh of Egypt, Caesarion was, according to Egyptian rite, the earthly embodiment of the god Horus, and Vorenus thought it might appear inappropriate that a god be trained in the mortal ways of men. While the uneasy peace with Octavian had lasted, Vorenus' opinion had carried the day. But now war seemed increasingly inevitable.

The clash of steel echoed loudly in the little courtyard as Caesarion overreached on a thrust and was promptly disarmed by the experienced Pullo. Vorenus had never known the big man to be patient with anything in his life, but he was loyally so with Caesarion, stooping to pick up the pharaoh's weapon from where it had clattered down amid the red and white tiles. He handed it back to the young man even as he quietly told him where he'd gone wrong.

Though he still felt uneasiness about such martial training for the pharaoh, Vorenus could hardly deny its effectiveness. Caesarion was a gifted and able student, qualities that extended, according to the chief librarian who acted as his tutor, into the intellectual realms as well. Indeed, the Greek Didymus often compared the boy's wide-ranging capabilities to those of his father Julius, who was at once one of Rome's finest generals, orators, politicians, and warriors. Of course, all those involved with the child's upbringing had kept such comparisons out of Caesarion's earshot by mutual and long-standing agreement. He was already the boy who could inherit the world, after all. No sense in giving him even more self-importance.

In the sunny courtyard the two men were in melee once again, dancing across the patterned tiles, and Vorenus turned away from the wall, thinking he might make a surprise inspection of the barracks. This was certainly no time to allow anyone to get complacent, the Roman guardsmen least of all. He didn't get two steps, however, before one of the native guardsmen appeared, hurrying up the stairs from the depths of the palace. "Messengers at the gate, sir," the Egyptian said once he was close. "Requesting entry into the palace."

"So?" Messengers arrived daily, if not hourly, these days—all part of Antony and Cleopatra's efforts to have the most up-to-date information of the events happening around the Mediterranean. War was, after all, in the air, which was also the reason that messengers were never allowed in the palace itself, not unless ... "Wait. Messengers from where?"

The guardsman nodded even as he was starting to beg leave for the disturbance. "Out of Rome, sir. Bearing dispatches for Lord Antony. We thought you'd want to be informed."

Vorenus felt his stomach drop. Such messages could only mean that the whispers of war in the air would soon be the heavy footfalls of war on the ground. "Yes. Thank you. Keep them at the inner gate. I'll be along shortly."

After the Egyptian hastened back down the stairs, Vorenus instinctively raised his head to gaze out across the glittering waters of Alexandria's Great Harbor, toward distant Rome, as if some reflection of the impending doom might be found there. Only the massive height of the Great Lighthouse on Pharos, and the slow-curling smoke of its distant fire, met his eye.

The sound of happy children brought Vorenus' attention once more to the square below. Cleopatra's three youngest—the eight-year-old twins Cleopatra Selene and Alexander Helios, and the littlest one, four-year-old Ptolemy Philadelphus, all fathered by Antony—had appeared from the halls of the bright-stoned palace to cheer their older half-brother as he finished the last of his lessons. Behind them swept Cleopatra herself, her thin gown draped close to her sleek body, the cloth whispering to the steady sway of hips that, even as she neared the age of forty, could still drive men to madness. Her raven-black wig fell in perfect straight drapes against the muscles of her back, its sheen matched only by the oiled, rich tan of her smooth skin. She tousled her eldest son's close-cropped dark hair as the other children gathered around him, then spoke to Pullo.

Pullo, predictably but almost pathetically, still found it difficult to talk in her presence, so it was no surprise that when the queen finished speaking he only gestured, raising an arm to point up to where Vorenus leaned against the wall, watching.

Cleopatra turned, her dark eyes glinting with a promise of unbridled seduction that was, for her, a look of natural habit. Her red-painted lips parted in a weary but thrilling smile. "I'm going to call a council," she said, her voice strong despite the breathless sound of it. "No matter the word from Rome. Antony fears the worst."

No, Vorenus thought: Antony didn't fear the worst, he expected it. For all Vorenus knew of the man, Antony feared nothing. "I'm going now to see to the messengers," he called down. "Pullo can oversee the council preparations."

Cleopatra glanced over to the uncomfortable Pullo, nodded ever so slightly in the sunlight, then floated off into the shadows, children in tow. Caesarion lingered for a moment, uncertain, before a word from Pullo sent him hurrying after her.

Satisfied that Pullo could handle things for at least a little while, Vorenus took a deep breath and strode off to greet the men who might be bringing doom to the doorstep of Egypt.

When Vorenus arrived, the two messengers were dismounting from their horses in the large yard between the massive stone facades of the main hall of the palace and the walls of the royal residences, a public space that remained relatively untouched by the threat of war. Six Egyptian guardsmen stood in a loose ring a respectful distance around the outsiders, and the typical tumult of the yard—a buzzing, dizzying chaos of servants and soldiers, priests and politicians coming and going seemingly everywhere at once—was parting around them with barely a second glance.

The two men, Vorenus saw at once, were unquestionably Roman: their legionnaire uniforms differed from his own only in the amount of road dust upon them. Vorenus therefore greeted them properly as fellow soldiers of Rome, thumping his fist to his chest before bringing it forward in a traditional salute. One man returned the gesture immediately, as if from reflexive instinct. The other man, shorter and stouter than his companion, his right cheek marked with a long, finger-width scar, hesitated for a moment before clumsily returning it.

Vorenus stifled the urge to correct the scar-faced man, reminding himself of how long a road the two men had no doubt just taken. In his early years, long before he and Pullo caught Caesar's eye in Gaul, he, too, had carried dispatches. He could still remember the bone-tiredness of arrival, when all a man wanted was a bath and a bed. "Lucius Vorenus," he said by way of introduction. "Senior centurion of the Sixth Legion of Rome. Welcome to Alexandria."

"Thank you," the first said, apparently the man of rank between them. "We bring news from Rome."

"For Mark Antony, I understand." Vorenus paused while a noisy cart rambled by. "A council is already being gathered to hear it, at the call of Cleopatra."

The messenger swallowed hard, looked down at his filthy traveling gear. "I don't suppose there'll be time…"

"I doubt it," Vorenus said. "They'll not want to wait. We'll see to the horses. And afterward a good meal and a bed."

The man's eyes were tired by more than travel, Vorenus could see. The news they brought was clearly ill. "I understand. Thank you."

"Now," Vorenus said, trying to keep his tone lighter than the sinking feeling in his heart. "Your orders, please."

"Of course," the messenger said, retrieving a small cylinder from his saddlebag.

Vorenus pulled the small slip of parchment from inside the case, taking note of the signatures and seals upon it. "Stertinius of the Seventh Legion," he said, looking up from his reading. The man he'd been talking to nodded and stood a little straighter. "Then that must make you," Vorenus said, glancing back to the paper before turning to the second man, "Laenas."

"That's right." The scarred man's voice had a rough, almost angry quality to it. Parched from the road.

"Not of the Seventh?"

Laenas' brow furrowed for a moment before he simply shook his head.

"You don't talk much."

"Don't have much to say," Laenas growled.

"Just a messenger, then?"

When Laenas only nodded, it was Stertinius who spoke. "Laenas is with Octavian's household," he said. "He was, ah, personally assigned to accompany me, to see the message delivered."

Vorenus felt his face start to frown but forced himself to keep up a professional appearance as he rolled up the orders and pocketed them. "Very well. You'll both need to surrender arms to the guard. And I shouldn't have to tell you that you'll be under close watch in the council."

"Of course," Stertinius said tiredly. "Though I might attend alone."

"Oh?" Vorenus turned to Laenas. "I thought you were personally assigned?"

"To get the message here," he said. "Job's done."

Vorenus was opening his mouth to ask another question—about how such a lazy man got to be so well regarded by

Octavian—when he saw the scholar Didymus walking past, characteristically oblivious to the hectic commotion of the yard moving around him. Vorenus and Pullo had grown to be firm companions with the children's tutor over the years; despite his near-lifetime of service in Egypt, the last dozen years as head of the Great Library in Alexandria, the Greek man shared their sense of outsider status in the ever-bewildering court of Egypt. Vorenus was glad for the friendly face. "A bit far from your books, aren't you, Didymus?" he called.

Out of the corner of his eye, Vorenus thought he saw Laenas' head jerk up at the mention of the Greek scholar's name, but when he turned to look the Roman was only unlashing one of his small saddlebags.

For his part, the scholar turned his direction of travel and approached, pushing back his haphazard, prematurely gray hair to reveal a half-guilty grin. "Difficult to leave my dear Homer behind, but I've time to spend with the children before an early bed."

"You'll have to excuse me," Vorenus said to Stertinius. He nodded to one of the nearby Egyptian guardsmen. "These men will see to your things."

Stertinius saluted, and Vorenus gladly returned it. The Egyptians began to lead them toward the barrack lodgings. Laenas tarried for a moment, fiddling with a buckle on his bags, before he moved slowly after his companion. There was something odd about the scarred man, Vorenus thought, something discomforting. Something that made him glad he wouldn't be attending the council.

Didymus had been watching with a surprised look on his face, as if only now noticing the messengers. "I didn't intend to interrupt," the scholar said. "Though I actually was hoping to run into you."

Vorenus squinted against the red light of the setting sun,

eyeing the receding backs of the Romans. "It's fine, my friend. Messengers from Rome."

The words brought the librarian up short. "From ... Rome?"

Vorenus nodded.

"How much time?"

The scholar's vagueness helped stir Vorenus from his suspicions, and he turned to face his friend. "Until council?"

"No, no. Even lost among my books I've heard the rumors of war. How much time do we have?"

Vorenus knew well that Didymus had few enough friends, keeping to himself either in his rooms at the palace or lost amid the countless rows and stacks of scrolls and books in the ten halls of the city's fabled Library. It surprised him, then, that the scholar would know anything of the war whispers. "And where do you hear such rumors?"

Didymus sighed. "Our young master, actually," he said. "Before we began our reading session this morning."

Of course. Cleopatra knew only too well about the swirling whispers, and she'd surely told Caesarion as part of her recent efforts to involve the young pharaoh more heavily in the affairs of state. Caesarion had been co-regent only in name for so long that it was hard for Vorenus to remember how that relationship, too, was changing. "I'll need to suggest he be less loose with his tongue to nonmilitary personnel," Vorenus said. He started walking toward the columned hall of the palace, away from the bustle of the yard. "No offense implied."

"And none taken," Didymus said with a slight chuckle as he walked alongside. "I've no business in such affairs. Though I do have an interest, as you might imagine."

"As do we all," Vorenus agreed. "The rumors are worrisome."

"And?"

Vorenus took his time thinking about how to answer. If the coming news was as he feared, it would be known all over Alexandria soon enough, despite any attempts to keep the information controlled. "There's no doubt Octavian's forces are moving," he said when they reached the white stone steps of the palace and started to climb them. "They've been making small, fact-finding strikes at Antony's territories in the north. If the war hasn't already begun, it will soon."

They stopped walking when they reached one of the broad, swept walkways that ringed the palace hall. Servants, guards, and even a few early members of the council were starting to make their way inside, passing between the sharp shadows of the tall pillars and the brightly painted statues of god-men that framed its facade. "Do you think we can win?" Didymus asked quietly.

"Antony has almost half of Rome behind him," Vorenus said. "Including both consuls. Much of the east remains loyal to him, including your old homeland."

"We Greeks fear imposition. For all his unpredictability, Antony is a man who respects traditions and makes them his own, as he has here in Egypt. Octavian is a man who would make the world Rome, so to speak."

"He is that," Vorenus agreed. "Ruthless, ambitious, arrogant—but brilliant. We'd underestimate him at our peril."

"You think Octavian will win."

"I don't know," Vorenus said. It was the truth, even if it hurt to say it. "Between Antony and Octavian I can't imagine what any Roman should think."

"Difficult times," the Greek said.

Through the open doors to the palace hall Vorenus could see Pullo, now dressed in his proper uniform, apparently trying to explain something to one of the Egyptian priests. The hulking Roman's face was tight, his shoulders bunched up, and his gestures clipped, yet the priest was prattling on in complaint, clearly oblivious to the fact that he was arguing with a man who was surely fighting the impulse to end the exchange by picking him up and breaking him in two. Vorenus would need to relieve him soon. "You said you'd been hoping to run into me. Surely not to talk of war?"

"No, not at all," the scholar admitted. "Just something came up in my reading with Caesarion today. Thought you might like to know about it. In case he asked."

Vorenus thought about ending the conversation, but a glance back at the doorway revealed that Pullo was finishing up with the priest, who was still in one piece. "Something interesting?"

"We're reading one of his father's works, actually," Didymus said.

"Oh?" Vorenus imagined that he knew as much of such things as Pullo did of politics.

"Caesar's commentary on the Gallic Wars. You're in it."

"Well, I was in the Eleventh Legion then. We were strong in Gaul." Vorenus' voice swelled a little with pride. "I'd be surprised if we weren't mentioned."

A loud trio of court advisors, dressed in gilded opulence, passed by them. Vorenus bowed, but they gave him no notice. Didymus just smiled. "I don't mean the legion, my Roman friend. I mean you."

Vorenus straightened and squinted at the librarian. "Me?"

"You, Lucius Vorenus." Didymus, still smiling, then nodded his head in the direction of the palace hall over Vorenus' shoulder. "And our dear Pullo, too, astonishingly enough."

"Gaul!" Pullo rumbled. "Caesar says we saved the legion, doesn't he? Rightly so!"

Vorenus flinched, surprised by his big friend's sudden presence. Glad for it, though. If there was going to be any talk of Gaul, Pullo was the better man for boasting. Too much of Vorenus' memory was tainted with sorrow.

"Oh, don't get big-headed, my friends," Didymus said. "You're only mentioned once. But I can say with some authority that it is far more space than most men have ever been accorded in the words of Caesar."

"When?" Vorenus asked.

"A battle against the barbarian Nervii."

A spark of recognition widened Vorenus' eyes. "Didn't know Caesar took notice of such things."

"Sounds like few didn't."

Vorenus shrugged, but the growing smile on his face did not disappear. He'd always been proud of what he'd done that day, though it had been a long time since he'd thought of it.

"The two of you were really sworn enemies?" the Greek asked.

"Is that how Caesar described us?" Pullo draped a thick arm over Vorenus' shoulders and jostled him. "No. Not enemies. Competitors, maybe."

"Rivals for influence," Vorenus admitted, shrugging off the bigger man's arm. "We knew each other. Vied for honors. But I spent little of my time thinking about Titus Pullo here. I'm sure he'd say the same."

"Caesar says you broke the lines to prove yourself the better man, Pullo."

"Not at all," Pullo said with a grin. "Was just impatient to get the fight done with. Had a woman back in camp who was frantic for me as a rutting sheep."

The three men shared a laugh. To Vorenus it was like a breath of fresh air, a release from his worries over the council to come. "It actually went well for him at first," he said. "Pullo is a beast in a fight, especially in a blind rage like that. But enough men will stop even an angry boar. The Nervii cut him off, surrounded him, wounded him."

Didymus arched an eyebrow, clearly taking the part of the scholar. "So your enemy—your rival—impetuously charged into the enemy lines, foolishly allowed himself to be surrounded and set up for slaughter, then took what might well have been his mortal wound. Yet you went in to save him anyway?"

"Romans don't leave Romans behind," Pullo said before his friend could answer.

"But surely—"

"We don't leave each other behind," Vorenus repeated. The Greek might not understand it, but it was a principle Romans like he and Pullo knew to their cores. "And, besides, I'd be lying if I said I thought much about it at the time. I don't know if I was even aware that it was Pullo. Just saw a man go down. He needed help, so I went."

"I see," the Greek said thoughtfully.

"That's not how Caesar tells it?" Pullo asked.

"Near enough. He says you didn't want Pullo to outshine you, Vorenus."

Vorenus chuckled again, but more quietly as he thought of Caesar, who'd given him and Pullo so much opportunity for advancement. "He always thought me a more ambitious man than I am."

"Caesar also said that Pullo in turn had to save you."

"Ah, now that *is* true," Pullo said, laughing loud enough to bring annoyed glares from a group of dour-faced priests walking up the steps. "He fought through to me, got me to my feet, and was starting to push me back to the lines when he took a spear in the leg."

"Worst hit I've ever taken," Vorenus said.

"Would've spiked a boar," Pullo agreed. "I'd been hit in my right shoulder, just here. Couldn't raise my arm to fight. He bloody well couldn't walk. So he held the barbarians off while I dragged his sorry ass back to the lines."

"Your action rallied the men."

"It did," Pullo said, puffing up.

"And you became friends."

Pullo's smile was genuine. "We did," the big man said. "A good team. All these years."

Looking over to the doorway of the main hall once more, Vorenus could see that more and more members of the council were gathering: Roman generals, priests with colored robes and painted faces, harried servants of every shade. The reality of what was happening came back, as if someone had placed a sack of grain upon his shoulders. "And, gods willing," he whispered, "more years to come."

"Aye," Pullo said, following his friend's gaze. "Suppose I ought to get back. More folks to get settled. You'll be seeing to the gate before coming in?"

Vorenus nodded. "If you'll be okay in there."

"I'll be fine," Pullo said. He gave a nod to Didymus and a smile to Vorenus before wading back toward the crowding hall.

"I've kept you long enough," Didymus said. "And I have business in the residence. I hope that tonight isn't, well…"

"We'll see," Vorenus said, turning and forcing a smile. "As the saying goes, we're just small fish in a big sea."

"Then let us hope there are no sharks in the water," the scholar said thoughtfully. Before Vorenus could reply, the Greek reached out and shook his hand. "Good luck, anyway," he said. And then he, too, was walking away.

Lucius Vorenus stood for a moment more between his departing friends, trying to clear his mind of troubled thoughts, trying to think of happier times. But no matter how he tried, his memories turned to battle and blood. It was as if war was all he'd ever known.

Sighing in resignation and resolution, he turned and began to march back across the yard to see to the bolting of the gate and the doubling of the guard on the wall.

3

Among the Sons of Caesar

ROME, 32 BCE

Juba and Quintus found Octavian, the most powerful man in Rome, standing over a simple wooden table in his private study, his shoulders hunched as he flipped purposefully among the several maps rolled out over its surface. Though Juba himself looked nothing like Julius Caesar, for obvious reasons, it never ceased to puzzle him that Octavian likewise bore so little resemblance to the man. Almost fifteen years older than Juba, Octavian carried at least some blood of the dictator who'd adopted them both as sons—Julius Caesar was Octavian's great-uncle through his mother's side—yet his build was very slight in comparison to what Juba remembered of the great general's. He was slight in height, too: even as a young man Juba had been aware of Octavian's attempts to appear taller than he was by wearing thick-soled shoes. The great Caesar, it was well known, was a tall man of strong features, and stronger determination.

Octavian had the focus, at least. Even from the distance

of the door, Juba could see that beneath the curls of his dusty blond hair his gray eyes were intense in thought. Around him, in haphazard piles wherever there was room, were hundreds more scrolls and books, representing a mere fraction of the love of knowledge that Octavian and Juba shared. Juba noted that his stepbrother also remained as pale-skinned as ever, another tribute to the love of learning that kept them both indoors more often than not. All that would have to change during the war, of course. Juba wondered if his stepbrother had come to terms with that yet.

"Wine," Juba whispered to Quintus, carefully setting the canvas-wrapped Trident just inside the door. "And two cups. See that we're not otherwise disturbed."

The slave gave him a quick nod, both to acknowledge the request and to wish him luck, then he left, the door shutting behind him with a click. At the noise, Octavian looked up and saw Juba, who smiled and bowed slightly.

"None of that!" Octavian said, striding quickly across the room to embrace his younger stepsibling. "Juba, my brother," he said when they parted, "I am glad to see you."

"And I you," Juba admitted. "I've been gone for too long."

"Just back, then?"

"Made harbor in Ostia this very morning."

"You should've sent couriers ahead from the port." Octavian gestured to the unkempt room. "I'm not exactly prepared for guests."

Juba allowed himself an honest smile, knowing that—unless things had changed in their year apart—his stepbrother had the same small patience for ceremony that he had. "A proper reception could still be arranged, couldn't it?"

Octavian narrowed his eyes, then reached up to tousle Juba's hair. Already at sixteen, Juba was almost his equal in height. "Still a troublemaker, eh? I'd hoped a year out in the world would've cured you of that sort of thing. Well, come in. Sit down."

Juba walked over to one of the benches nearby, carefully setting aside a crooked stack of papers upon it. He tried not to look at the canvas bundle by the door even as it occupied most of his mind. Octavian settled down across from him on the only chair in the room and yawned, rubbing at his eyes.

"You've been busy," Juba said. An obvious thing to say, but it was a place to start.

"Things are moving fast," Octavian said, then his eyes shot open. "Wine! We should toast your return. And you'll be thirsty after—"

Juba held up a hand. "Already on the way. I sent Quintus for it."

"The old fellow survived the trip, did he? Took care of you well?"

"He did. I told him to see us undisturbed."

"Good, good." Octavian paused, sighed. "I'm sorry I didn't think of the wine when you first arrived. Things have just been, well, busy. As you said."

A silence fell between them. Juba felt his gaze begin to slide toward the Trident, but he wasn't yet confident enough to bring it up. No matter how many times he'd rehearsed all this in his mind, when it came to the moment, he felt adrift at sea without oars. He looked over toward the table with its maps. "Is it true about Antony?" he asked. "Did he truly promise all to his children?"

Octavian nodded. Not sadly, not happily. Just assuredly. "He did. Everyone's calling it 'the Donations of Alexandria.' He claimed the whole of the west for himself. Egypt for the pretender. The rest to his children by the whore. By no leave of the Senate, no council of Rome. He would undo the Republic our father fought and died for."

Juba nodded, thinking for a moment of how much, and how little, they shared of their adopted father. "I'd heard it in Numidia, but it's hard to believe."

"There's more, not yet well known," Octavian said. "Some of Antony's lieutenants recently returned to Rome. They told me about Antony's will. I didn't believe what they had to say until the Vestals handed it over and I saw it with my own eyes."

Juba had to blink back his surprise. The Vestals were a holy authority, their temple a literal sanctuary. "How did you—?"

"My guard stormed the temple." Octavian sighed again and waved his hand as if he were pushing away a meddlesome fly rather than centuries of profoundly sacred Roman tradition. "Against decorum, I know. But it was too important, Juba. And the Vestals would not listen to reason. I told them this is about the fate of Rome itself, and isn't that why their temple exists, to protect the city? But they wouldn't hand it over until I forced them."

Juba tried not to blanch at the thought of what Octavian had undone. It might be important, yes, but surely not enough to erode such basic principles, to risk threatening the goddess Vesta? Even as the last question instinctively came to him, Juba's own growing uncertainty about whether such gods even existed surged to the front of his mind. This, too, had changed while he was away. "Well, what of the will?" he asked, trying to keep his thoughts focused. "What did it say?"

"It confirmed the Donations," Octavian said. "And it made clear Antony's plan to be buried with Cleopatra in a mausoleum in Alexandria rather than in Rome."

Despite his wish to appear calm and properly stoic, Juba felt his eyes widen. To prepare to be buried elsewhere was such an affront to Roman sensibilities that he almost didn't believe it could be true—though if anyone was capable of such egotism, it would surely be Antony. "A mausoleum for Antony and Cleopatra? In Alexandria?"

Octavian's head moved up and down slowly. "All true. It's already built."

Juba knew it was an open preference of Egypt over Rome, a betrayal of the Eternal City itself. "There'll be war," he said.

"And you're just in time for it," Octavian said, his voice dispassionate and calm. "I'll read the will before the Senate tonight. It'll be the final undoing. The senators will strip Antony of his titles and declare him a traitor. So, yes. There will be war. Declared against Cleopatra, of course, as a matter of technical detail. Antony will be given the legal option of joining Rome against her."

Silence again as Juba let the finality of it sink in, aware of Octavian's gaze upon him. War. There could hardly be a better time for his own plans than amid the chaos of it. He just needed Octavian's trust. And he knew just how to get it. "Attack Greece first," he said at last. "An attack on his own lands. It'll draw Antony out."

Octavian's face broke into a broad smile, and he let out a laugh. "You always were the smart one," he said. "I plan to do exactly that. So you're with me, then? You're with the Republic?"

"Of course," Juba said, glad he was able to answer the question so quickly. "Why would I not be?"

Octavian started to reply, then seemed to think better of it. "Good," he said. "Very good. You're at the age of military training."

Juba agreed. He'd suspected something like this was coming. He'd planned for it. "I did much reading during my voyage. Caesar's works, of course, as well as a new book by Diodorus—"

"Not everything can be learned in books," Octavian interrupted. "I've learned that to my own sorrow."

"I know," Juba said. "But knowing the mistakes of history can prevent us from repeating them."

"True."

"I'm prepared to begin my physical training, though, if you think that's best." He made sure to meet Octavian's gaze. He hoped his own eyes showed nothing of his conflicted feelings. "It's my duty as a citizen of Rome."

Octavian smiled again. "So it is. But I'll not have you down amongst the rabble, brother. I want you by my side. Antony is the finest field general Rome has." He held up his hand as Juba started to protest. "No. We'd be fools to deny the truth of it. Indeed, I want you by my side to help me maintain the measure of such things. It's easy to grow, well, too assured of oneself. And with Antony we can afford precious few mistakes. I'm going to use every last bit of history you've managed to wedge into that head of yours. It may save the Republic."

"Really does come down to that, doesn't it?"

"Down to what?"

Juba had spoken his thoughts aloud, so it took him a moment to recover himself. "This war, I mean. You and Antony. Republic or dictatorship. Rome or Egypt."

A shadow seemed to pass over Octavian's face. "I think so, brother."

There was a quiet knock at the door, and Quintus entered carrying a pitcher. Another slave, one of Octavian's, followed behind him with a silver tray topped by two goblets. Octavian's face brightened as he stood and turned to face the door. Once his stepbrother's back was turned, Juba quietly let out the air in his lungs, trying to clear his thoughts.

"Ah! The wine!" Octavian was saying. "Yes, yes. Good, Quintus. Bring it here."

Juba saw that Quintus was trying to catch his eye. Not ready to indicate success or failure, Juba avoided the old slave's questioning gaze, instead standing to walk in the opposite direction toward the map table, giving himself more time to think. Behind him he heard his stepbrother hastily clearing off a space on the low table between his chair and Juba's bench. Octavian then took the tray from Quintus, shooing the two slaves off with orders to prepare a quick meal.

Juba stopped walking when he reached the map table. The maps were, indeed, of the Grecian coastline.

"Yes, Imperator," Octavian's servant said as he joined Quintus in hurrying off.

Imperator. One of their adopted father's titles. Only Octavian's full title, Juba knew, was *Imperator Caesar Divi Filius*. His stepbrother had wisely declined to take on some of the titles that had been offered to him, but he'd had no qualms about calling himself the Son of the God they'd made Julius Caesar to be. Would he decline the dictatorship if it was offered? He seemed to think nothing of storming the Vestals' temple, after all. Would he restore the Republic or, as his father had, continue to expand his powers? And what choice was there for Rome in the face of Antony's betrayal?

The door of the room shut once again, leaving them alone. "I'm sorry, but our meal will have to be short tonight," Octavian said. "The Senate is already gathering, I'm sure."

"Of course," Juba said, turning back to him. Octavian was seated, one goblet of wine in his hand and the other held out for him. Juba returned to the table and took it. After he'd sat down, they raised cups and drank.

The wine felt good against Juba's tongue. He'd missed it while he was away. Home or not, there was nothing like true Italian wine to be found in Numidia.

"So your voyage went well?"

"It did," Juba admitted. "Had a chance to do much writing."

"Your book on archaeology?"

Juba nodded as he swallowed another bit of the wine. "Mostly. Though I've been reading about a lot of things lately." He again found himself fighting the urge to look over at the canvas bundle by the door. "Many of the libraries there have very old holdings."

"We should have copies made," Octavian said. "Make them available here."

Juba knew his stepbrother's jealousies at Juba's having the freedom to travel and study abroad. Octavian's own pursuits had been cut off by Julius Caesar's murder, which had forced him into the political arena. "We should," Juba agreed, "when all is done."

Octavian drank down his cup, refilled it, and offered to pour for Juba, who waved him off. "Well, I'm glad you're here," the older man said, leaning back into his chair. "It's good that you're here."

Juba stared at the last of his cup for a few seconds before coming to a decision at last. He swallowed the remainder and let it wash down his nerves. It was now or never, he decided. "You haven't asked me what I've brought," he said.

His elder stepbrother's eyebrow raised, but he seemed otherwise unmoved. "Thought you were waiting for the right moment to tell me. Is this it?"

Juba shrugged. Better to keep things light, he thought. "Could be."

Octavian allowed himself a smile. "Well? Tell me. What have you brought back from your trip, little brother?"

Juba set aside his empty cup, then walked over to retrieve the canvas bundle. Returning, he set it across his lap and couldn't help but notice that the Trident seemed so much heavier than it should be. And warmer. He swallowed hard, took a deep breath.

"One of the first books you gave me was a collection of Homeric hymns," Juba said, his voice a whisper. "Do you remember it?"

Octavian leaned forward, the look of amusement on his face pushed away by Juba's sudden seriousness. "I do. You were nine or ten."

"That's right. The twenty-second hymn: 'And so I sing of Poseidon, the great god, mover of the earth—'"

"'—and of the fruitless sea,'" Octavian said. "I know it."

Juba nodded toward the silver tray on the table between them. "Could you move the wine?"

Octavian did so, barely taking his eyes from the bundle that his stepbrother set down in its place. "Poseidon. Neptune. Mover of earth and sea," Juba continued. His fingers began to unwrap it. "Do you remember how?"

The last of the folds came away, and Juba brought his hands back to rest on his empty lap. The two men stared at the object between them. Its metal surface was rusted in spots, and only a foot of the wooden shaft inserted into its base remained, but the long spearhead of the central head was still intact, like a thick metal arrow, and the spurs of the two points to either side of it were still present even if their tips had long since broken off.

"A trident," Octavian finally said.

Juba had to build the courage to say it. "The Trident of Poseidon. Of Neptune." Octavian did not reply. Juba's focus was still fixed to the trident head on the table, but he didn't need to see his stepbrother's face to know the look upon it. "I didn't want to believe it at first, either," he admitted. "Or I did want to, but I didn't, you know?" He paused to calm his nerves, but still Octavian said nothing. And now that he was speaking about it—the first time he'd spoken to anyone other than Quintus about it—the words were pushing against his throat, yearning to come out. "I'd read the myths. I'd heard the stories. We all have. Neptune cutting islands in two. Neptune raising waves to wreck ships. All with his Trident. All with this."

When Juba finally raised his eyes, he could see the mixture of incredulity and hope on his stepbrother's face. "Juba, I—"

"I know. You don't believe me. I'm young, I got taken in by a trader ... I know." Juba reached for his wine cup, which he'd set down next to him on the bench, and saw that it was empty. He could use the jug, he knew, but that would make too big of a mess. Octavian's half-filled cup, though, would do nicely. "May I?" he asked, reaching for it.

Octavian handed over the cup, his gesture bordering on something like exasperation, and Juba stood, carrying it over to set it down on the floor near the door. He returned, ignoring the confused look on his stepbrother's face, trying to focus his mind as he wrapped his hands around the fragment of wooden shaft and picked it up.

Though it was clearly a trident, it was unlike any other trident that Juba had ever seen, heard, or even read about. Most tridents were simply three metal prongs, or daggers, fixed atop a wooden shaft: sometimes made parallel to one another, but perhaps more often rooted in the same base so that the lateral prongs shot outward at angles from the center one. Their only other differentiations were in whether or not their points were steadily thinning blades, like those atop spears, or flared at the tips, like the heads of arrows.

The design of this arrow-tipped trident in his hands, though battered and broken, was clear enough, and it was strangely different. What was left of the wooden shaft fit into a typical base socket, but everything else about it was odd. The two lateral prongs weren't directed forward at all. Instead, they shot directly out to the side, perpendicular to the main line of the shaft so as to give the whole the look of a cross. Stranger still, there were two serpents, one wrought of bronze and one of copper, that wound their way around the head and down the length of the shaft before they were broken off. Unlike the intertwined snakes on the wand of Mercury, the heads of these twin serpents did not bend inward to the shaft at the top, but instead shot rigidly forward, parallel to the central head, flat-faced and sharp to the point of being prongs themselves. And in the center of it all—atop the socket and acting as a root for the main prongs, framed by the winding bodies of the two snakes—was a blacker-than-black rock that seemed, to Juba's eye, to swallow the very light out of the air. It was this that always seemed—though he was certain it could not be so—to be warm.

Juba forced down his nerves as he shifted his grip so that each hand held the body of one of the two serpents.

He'd only dared to practice with the artifact a few times, but he knew enough to know that his focus was essential. He had to be calm. He had to be confident. He had to reach down within himself, grab hold of something he could not yet define, and then push it outward through the metal in his hands, seeing it all unfold in his mind.

Juba turned to face the goblet on the floor, some five or six paces away. He closed his eyes, focusing on the feel of the metal in his hands. It was cool beneath his skin at first, just finely etched metal scarred by time, but it seemed to grow warm as he held it, as if the serpents were alive. When it did so, Juba let his awareness fall back away from the sensations of scale and form, pushing away the world. Down and into himself, Juba felt at last a kind of quiet solidity with his mind, a certainty of stillness. He grabbed hold of the smallest part of that darkness then drew it up and out through his arms, through his fingers and palms, into the metal beneath his skin. As he did so he pictured the wine in the cup. He *willed* it to move.

The snakes seemed to twitch in his grip as something within him let go. The slightest puff of wind pushed back his hair, like the Trident head itself had exhaled, and as he opened his eyes he saw the goblet of wine fling up off the floor and crash against the door as surely as if he'd strode across the stone and kicked it.

The goblet clattered to a stop, the sound of it echoing in the room. Juba let out his breath, not remembering having held it. The metal beneath his skin still felt warm, but it no longer felt alive.

He shivered.

"By the gods," Octavian whispered.

Juba could only nod. He carefully moved his grip back to the wooden shaft, then set the object once more on its cloth wrappings. Octavian's gaze followed it. "How—?"

"It was in Numidia. Some there called it Nehushtan."

Octavian finally looked up at his far younger stepsibling. "Nehushtan?"

For the second time since they'd sat down to talk, there was a quiet knock on the door. Octavian stared at Juba for several heartbeats. His eyes were intense, but Juba didn't look away. Finally, Octavian rose and walked over toward the door and opened it.

In the light of the hall stood Livia, Octavian's wife, with her hands on the shoulders of a young boy of nine or ten years. It took Juba a moment to recognize the growing lad as Tiberius, her favorite son from a previous marriage. Behind them stood a servant with trays, the legionnaire on guard, and an uncomfortable-looking Quintus, who'd obviously been rebuked for trying to keep the consul's wife and stepson from interrupting the meeting.

"Juba!" said Tiberius. Only Livia's hands on his shoulders seemed to prevent him from rushing into the room.

Juba smiled in honest happiness to see young Tiberius—he'd always liked the boy, even if he did find him prone to a melancholy that he suspected was due to his mother being forced to divorce his father in order to marry Octavian. "Tiberius," he said. "It is good to see you. And you, as well, my lady."

Livia nodded graciously, then turned her eyes to her husband. Something clearly passed between them, as she nodded ever so slightly and started to turn Tiberius away to make room for the servant with the dishes. "As Quintus said, Juba and your father are busy," she said. "You can catch up on his adventures later."

Juba saw the boy's eyes take in the Trident for a moment and widen a little with curiosity before he began trying to protest the departure. It was a feeble effort, though, and he allowed his mother's strong hands to lead him off. Quintus shot Juba a quick look of encouragement before he, too, bowed and hurried off in their wake, no doubt planning to help entertain and distract the boy.

The servant with the trays of food stepped forward. "Your dinner, Imperator," he said. When the man's eyes lowered in deference to Octavian, he spotted the spilled wine at once. Juba noticed that the man swallowed hard. "My lord, was there a problem—?"

Octavian let out a quick, superficial laugh. "No, no. The wine was fine. Just an accident. Can you see to it later?" The servant nodded dumbly, clearly wondering why the Imperator would let the stain sit. "We just don't want to be disturbed right now," Octavian said. "I'll take the food."

There were several bows as the slave handed in a tray and a jug of water. Octavian carefully balanced it all so that no one needed to enter the room. Then, with a quiet word to the legionnaire standing guard, he closed the door.

There was another table, not far from the door, and Juba watched as his stepbrother unceremoniously emptied his arms upon it. "I assume you're not hungry, either?" he asked over his shoulder.

"No," Juba said. "I'm fine."

Octavian nodded, but he didn't shift from his position for perhaps a minute. Juba sat quietly, glad that someone else was lost in thought for a time.

At last, Octavian straightened up and stretched his neck from side to side, cracking it. Then he returned and sat down in his chair, his eyes on the object still set between them. "Poseidon's Trident," he said.

"Or Neptune's, if you prefer," Juba said. "But it's even more complicated than that."

Octavian's eyebrow raised, but he said nothing.

Juba had practiced his next words so often in his mind that they came out easily. "This *is* Poseidon's Trident," he said, absently noting how easily he shifted into the tone of a teacher, even in the face of his powerful older stepbrother. "But that's not all it is. It's also Mercury's wand. And Moses' staff. And Nehushtan. And perhaps even more than that. I still don't know all the possibilities."

Octavian's jaw clenched slightly as he stared at the younger man. "Moses is a Jewish god, no? And I don't know this Nehushtan. Explain."

"They both have to do with the Jews. Moses was a Jewish leader. Not a god, but a powerful man nonetheless. He led his people from Egypt to Judea—so their stories go—and he was said to have possessed a powerful staff blessed by the god of the Jews. It's said among their writings that with his staff he could strike a rock and make it give water."

"The same is said of Neptune and Poseidon," Octavian said quietly. "He did as much in Greece."

"Exactly so," Juba said, nodding vigorously. "It's something I've been thinking about. We accept that Neptune and Poseidon are the same god, yet I wonder if the gods and legends of other peoples are not the same, too."

"Go on."

"Well, it's also said that Moses, with his staff, parted the Red Sea in order for his people to escape Egypt. He controlled the waters with it."

Octavian had the same kind of thoughtful look on his face that Juba fondly remembered from his youth. "So these stories of Moses are stories of Neptune by another name. Or, perhaps, if both are real, then this man somehow got the god's weapon. What of Nehushtan?"

"At one point the god of the Jews afflicted them with poisonous snakes," Juba said. "Strange tale. The god then told

Moses to affix a bronze serpent to a staff and use it to cure those who were faithful to him. They called it Nehushtan." Juba's fingers hovered over the Trident, tracing the broken line of the bronze snake there. "It means 'brazen serpent' in their tongue."

The corner of Octavian's mouth lifted. "Twisted snakes. Like Mercury's wand," he said. "How did you find it?"

"I was searching the old Numidian libraries, and I started to learn about the old religion of the Jews, of which I know far too little. They worship only one father-god now, like our Jupiter, but I don't think it was always so. I think they once worshiped a mother goddess, too, like our Juno. Her name was Asherah. I think she was the same as that which is worshiped in Numidia as Astarte. Anyway, it was among the priests of Asherah that I began to put it all together. And they directed me to an old temple of their faith with many relics. And there I found it."

To Juba's relief Octavian didn't follow any line of questioning about how he'd acquired it from them. "Who knows?" he asked.

"There are two of us now," Juba said.

"Good," Octavian said. He stood, took a few paces back and forth in front of the table. "Good."

Juba didn't reply, letting Octavian pace. Less than a minute passed before there was another light knock on the door.

"The Senate?" Juba asked.

Octavian ignored the query, but he finally stopped pacing. "How well can you control it?" he asked.

Juba had known this particular question was coming, but it was the one thing he'd never decided exactly how he would answer. Unlike some of what he had just said, he opted for plain truth. "You've seen it. I can feel that it's capable of more, but I've been unable to practice while keeping the secret. I need money for space and privacy, for supplies."

"Then you'll have it," Octavian said. "This could be a great weapon in the fight to come, my brother. My personal guard will attend you. We'll give you rooms out at father's villa, and whatever gold you need is yours. Just practice. Get stronger."

Juba swallowed hard when his stepbrother looked back toward the door and the legionnaires who were no doubt waiting outside to take him to the Senate. Juba hadn't realized until just this moment how worried he was that Octavian would claim the Trident for himself. "I will," he said.

The Imperator of Rome threw him a smile, then turned and walked toward the door, his stride seeming more confident with every step. As he reached for the latch, he looked back. "We'll talk later," he said. "After we're at war."

Only when Juba was safely alone did he let his hands begin to shake. "I'm only sixteen," he whispered to the empty room. He was old enough to begin military training, but this was something greater by far.

It seemed so preposterous, so improbable. For all his pride, for all his intellect, for all the privileges that Octavian had just accorded him, for all the innate power in the object that sat before him on the table, Juba still felt like a child playing games in the world of men.

And so much was happening so quickly.

He crossed his arms to quell their shaking and stood up, making his way over to Octavian's table of maps once again.

Greece. The armies would fight there. Thousands would die.

But the real battle, Juba was certain, would be in Egypt. In Alexandria. And no one would know about it. Not even Octavian.

Though there were disadvantages to Juba's youth, there were opportunities, too. A younger man was a more trustworthy man, and so much depended on maintaining Octavian's trust. Without it, he could lose everything. After all, he hadn't told Octavian about the even greater source of power among the ancient Jews, the likes of which he didn't think had a parallel among the whole pantheon of Rome. A power to rival that of Jupiter himself. The seat of God, the Jews called it. The Ark of the Covenant, lost for centuries.

Everything pointed to Alexandria and the Scrolls of Thoth. Find them, and he would find the Ark. Find that, and he would change everything. Numidia, his home, would be free. And he would be, too. His father would at last be avenged. And all that he had been forced to do in the meantime—to play the part of a loyal Roman, even to order the death of that Numidian priest—would be worth the greater good.

He would have to play along with Octavian for now, though. Until he possessed the Scrolls of Thoth, nothing was certain, and even then he would need to use the Scrolls to find the Ark, wherever it was. And he couldn't do it alone.

Still, Juba knew from history that all races were won by single steps. He was young and patient. There was time. He'd won Octavian's trust. He now had the power of Rome at his disposal, so long as he played his cards right. One step was done. Now he could take the next: send someone to acquire the Scrolls and bring them to him.

Juba nodded, as if in agreement with something that had been said, then walked purposefully to the door. His hands had stopped trembling, and in his mind he felt a new calm, as if a storm of worry had blown away from him. Through a crack in the door he summoned Quintus.

First, he decided as he waited for the slave's arrival, he would need Quintus to hire a man to go to Alexandria: a hard and desperate man who would do whatever it took to earn the large reward that Juba would offer with Octavian's money. Laenas, he was certain, would fit the bill quite nicely.

Second, he would need to write a letter of introduction to the keeper of the Great Library, the one man who surely knew where the Scrolls were kept. If Juba's teacher Varro was to be believed, the Greek scholar was a man who'd worked for Octavian before. And even if not, promises of power and Octavian's money could go a long way toward persuading him.

Third, he thought with a smile, he would need to track down a good woodworker. After all, if the Trident of Poseidon was once more going to be wielded on earth, it was going to need some repairing.

4

News from Rome

ALEXANDRIA, 32 BCE

Vorenus could see that the road-weary Stertinius, the Roman messenger to the Egyptian court, appeared even more exhausted as he stood in the middle of the tall-columned council chamber of Alexandria, facing the high-stepped dais where Cleopatra and her freshly bathed son sat in gilded wood chairs, their ornate headdresses framed by firelight. Beside them, in a chair only slightly less opulent, sat Cleopatra's lover, Antony, his eyes dark and brooding beneath his gray-tinged curls of red hair, his jaw tense as he stared at the messenger. The vizier and at least a dozen high priests of various Egyptian gods and goddesses were arrayed about the marble dais and the rug-covered stones at its feet, their paint-enveloped eyes warily judging the poor, dust-covered soldier standing uneasily in their midst. Interspersed among them all were dozens of Roman officers and soldiers under Antony's command.

One of the last to enter the hall, Vorenus took careful note of the full crowd, unable to shake his continuing feeling of anxiety about the security of the royal family.

Pullo, he saw, was standing with a small group of Romans a few paces behind Antony's seat, looking nearly as miserable as the road-beaten soldier waiting to make his report—Vorenus knew only too well how uncomfortable such official proceedings made him. Pullo was a man of deeds, not words, and though he was rarely called upon to speak at such occasions, the mere thought that it might happen often left him almost paralyzed with fear. Vorenus swung around the gathering crowd to reach him, observing the number and names of the guards on duty—their distance from the royals, their armaments—and approached his friend from behind. "Care to make a speech?" he asked when he got close.

The big man started a little at Vorenus' voice, but there was genuine relief in his eyes when he moved aside to let Vorenus stand beside him. "Not me," he said quietly. "I'd rather screw a Gallic whore."

"You *have* screwed a Gallic whore," Vorenus whispered. "Twice, as I recall."

"Only proves my desperation. I'd rather do it a third time than be in charge. You're the smart one. It's your job."

Vorenus gripped his comrade by the upper arm for a moment then stepped forward to stand directly behind Antony's seat.

It was one of the first times he'd seen both Caesarion and his mother in the elaborately formal, dynastic garb that was meant to give them the appearance of Egyptian deities. He noted how uncomfortable the young man seemed to be, trying to stare straight ahead, expressionless as the statues outside the hall. Cleopatra, on the other hand, managed the guise perfectly. Her own expressionless face conveyed whatever emotion one desired to see in it, and her luminous eyes took in everything and nothing all at once. Not for the first time Vorenus felt his own foreignness in this land very sharply.

When at last the final priests had arrived, the queen raised her hand in a call for silence that was almost instantly followed. The vizier stepped forward, bowing to the co-regents before turning to address the gathered court with a series of titles and salutations meant to convey the majesty of the Ptolemaic dynasty.

Vorenus ignored it all until the vizier made a half-bow in Antony's direction, clearly providing him the floor to deal with the messenger. Antony in turn gave the vizier a terse nod and then stood, his still-thick muscles hulking beneath the fine cloth that was gathered in pleats about his shoulders.

The messenger came rigidly to attention, bringing his right fist to his chest and then pressing his arm out, fingers extended and palm down in a salute. "Rome eternal," he said.

Antony's posture was less formal, the snap of his arm less brisk as he returned the salute. Vorenus felt his own jaw tighten, not surprised by Antony's air of arrogance but certainly not approving of it. "Rome eternal," Antony said, his voice at once absent and gruffly commanding. He took a step down closer to Stertinius, his footfalls heavy. "What news, soldier?"

The messenger's eyes seemed to sink even further in his tired face. "Octavian's forces are preparing to sail from eastern Italy, sir."

Whispers broke out across the gathered crowd, but Cleopatra and her son made no reaction. Antony raised a broad hand to keep the focus on himself. "Under Agrippa's command?"

Stertinius just nodded.

"What's his target?"

"Greece, sir."

The muscles of Antony's jaw pulsated in and out. "Where in Greece?"

"I don't know, sir."

"*No* one knows? North? South?"

The messenger shook his head.

"Why now?" Antony asked. Vorenus saw Cleopatra's shoulders tense slightly. Probably she thought the question below Antony's status. Why now? Because Octavian thought he could win. He thought he had an advantage. But Vorenus knew Antony. Though his tongue was too often faster than his mind—ruled by his passions as he was—Antony's thoughts were undoubtedly upon the next step: What advantage did Octavian think he had? "And how many ships?" Antony continued, his eyes narrowing.

"I'm uncertain, my lord. Hundreds."

"How many hundreds? One hundred? Two hundred? Three? Surely, you worthless—"

"Six hundred, maybe," the legionnaire sputtered.

Antony looked like he'd been slapped. "Six?"

"Agrippa's full fleet, sir. And everything Rome can spare. Octavian is gathering his armies, too, in the east." Stertinius swallowed hard. "He's ... he's even conscripted new legions, sir, to replace those at your side. 'Rome should have a loyal Sixth,' is what they say he said."

Vorenus felt anger rise in his chest and could imagine the rage on Pullo's face without turning to look at him. There were no truer Romans than they. Who else could speak of having given more for their country?

"He's created another Sixth?" Antony's voice was incredulous, spacing out each of the words as if to let them sink in.

"Yes, sir."

It was a proclamation of exile, of final and irreparable separation, and the few Romans in the council chamber all knew it. Antony looked back at Vorenus, the general's face momentarily twisted in a look of horrified shock. Vorenus, for all his own rage, tried to focus in on Antony's face, willing him to stay calm, to think clearly.

Antony seemed to understand the message, and he let his

anger pass into a kind of levity, smiling as he turned back to the messenger and the gathered council. "I remember, when I was young, that a man once stole my sword," he said, his voice booming. Vorenus knew the tone well, from boisterous jests over countless tankards of wine. "It was a fine gladius, the likes of which I thought could never be found again, and I despaired to go to battle without it. But a blacksmith traveling with the legion heard of my troubles and offered to make me another, just like the one I lost. Loyal to his word, the blade he made looked the same as the one I lost—only better, I thought, because it was shiny and new. But when I took it to battle, it cracked on the first stroke against the edge of a shield. I learned then that nothing can replace what is tried and true." He paused for a moment, to be sure he had the attention of the council. "Let him make a new Sixth. Let him make a new Antony. He'll find the original far superior!"

There was a shout of determined agreement from the Roman officers and soldiers in the crowded room. Vorenus, too, felt a puff of pride in his chest, though it seemed little enough to contrast the news that he'd been exiled from his homeland.

"What of the man who stole your old sword?" one of the younger Roman officers called from the back of the chamber.

"I had him crucified." Antony laughed. "But not before I used my old friend to cut his balls off and feed them to dogs. I look forward to doing the same to Octavian!"

There were more shouts of riotous agreement from the Romans, though many of the Egyptians looked disgusted. Vorenus just felt old and tired.

Stertinius noticeably took no part in the revelry, looking more and more uncomfortable as it died down. Antony, who'd been cheering on his officers, at last took notice and motioned for silence. "What more, legionnaire?"

"Octavian—" The soldier's voice caught, then he bowed

again as if to excuse what he was duty-bound to report. "Octavian raided the temple of the Vestal Virgins, sir."

What was left of the smile on Antony's face fell away at once. "He ... *raided* the temple?"

Stertinius closed his eyes as his mouth worked over the words before he could speak them. Vorenus wondered if he was saying a prayer for someone's soul. Octavian's, for such a desecration? His own, for fear of Antony? "He ... he forced them to hand over your will," the man finally muttered.

Antony stared. Vorenus noted that while the general's face was suddenly unreadable, Cleopatra had actually leaned forward slightly.

"Octavian said it confirmed the, uh, Donations. And that it said you'd be buried with Cleopatra—" the soldier's eyes flew open and fixed on her for a moment—"I'm sorry. The queen, my lady."

An uncomfortable silence fell over the chamber. Vorenus heard the soft rasp of leather armor as one of the Romans in the crowd shifted his weight from one foot to the other.

Antony's face was hard again by the time he spoke. "Yes. So?"

The messenger's face was a contorted mixture of hope and despair. His voice, when he found it, was tinged with pleading. "We're all lost, sir," he said. "The Senate's declared war on Egypt."

Like the breaking of a wave that roars as it crests, the soldier's words shattered the silence of the chamber. All at once, it seemed, everyone was talking.

The co-regents sat impassive in the resulting cacophony, silently listening as one advisor or priest after another shouted out to address them with portents of the gods or opinions about Rome. Antony moved back and forth from the majestic seats atop the dais to the tired messenger at its feet, seething anger. After a minute, he dismissed the shaken Stertinius, who gratefully took his hurried leave. In his wake, other Roman officers converged on the general, anxious to make status reports.

Whatever the course of the debate to come, Vorenus knew his part would be measured only in the aftermath, not in the decision-making itself. As such, he had little interest in remaining to stay and listen to the din. Slipping to the back of the raucous crowd, he made his way between glyph-inscribed columns to a short passage flanked by guards. Nodding to them both, he followed the hallway to a broad balcony looking out across the city.

The noise was still buzzing out here, but it was quiet enough for thoughts. Quiet enough for regrets.

Beyond the palace walls, Alexandria was a pool of torch-lit windows in stone facades—winking and glittering beneath a cloudless, half-moon sky—bounded by the black of water. It was beautiful—he'd always thought so—but it wasn't home. It wasn't Rome.

Vorenus breathed deep of the cooler air carried up from the water, trying to clear his head.

Replacement legions? Was he really no longer a Roman? Why had he come here if not for Rome? If not for Caesar and for all he'd meant to do? And didn't Octavian claim to be fighting for Caesar, too? Didn't that make Octavian's fight his fight?

Yet to storm the temple of the Vestals ...

Vorenus shook his head in the half-dark. It was hard to imagine such sacrilege, even if it did uncover Antony's betrayal of Rome. And betrayal was what it was, without doubt. The Donations were bad enough, promising Roman lands to Egyptian royalty—he'd told Antony it wasn't a good idea—but to abandon Rome for burial in Alexandria was a slap in the face of all that they'd ever fought for. All that Caesar had ever fought for.

Was it not for Caesar that he and Pullo had fought and bled in Gaul? Was it not for him that they'd left their legion to come to Egypt so long ago? Was it not for his memory that they'd agreed to return here, to protect his son?

Vorenus blinked out at the lights blinking back.

Caesarion. A young man. But a good man, Vorenus was sure. Honest, respectful, intelligent, and strong. Truly Caesar's son.

Then again, fighting for Caesarion meant fighting Rome. How could he do that?

"Mind some company?"

Vorenus didn't need to turn to recognize his old friend Pullo. "Please."

The big man joined Vorenus in leaning against the wall, gazing out at the city that had so strangely enwrapped their lives. "It's getting a bit heated in there," he said.

Vorenus nodded. "Any indication of the wind?" Not that it mattered. Duty was duty. Or should be. Had been, at least.

"Antony's angry."

That brought an honest smile to Vorenus' face. "When is he not?" he asked.

Pullo's own smile was grim. "He'll go to Greece to lead the defense. The only question is whether Egypt will go with him."

Vorenus let the air out of his lungs and was suddenly struck by the memory of his breath rising into the winter-grayed skies of Gaul, above snowfields strewn with stains of red amid leafless trees. How often had he thought he'd left war behind, only to find it at his heels? And for Rome. *Always* it had been for Rome.

"I don't like this fight," Pullo said.

"Have you liked any?"

"Sure. I guess. I mean, I liked smashing heads in Gaul. And our fight here in Egypt." Pullo's voice grew wistful. "That was a piece of work, you must admit. One legion surrounded but holding back the tide. Nine months—"

"I was here," Vorenus whispered.

"Well, you know. Some fights are good fights. But Romans against Romans…"

"Apparently we're not Romans anymore, Pullo. Didn't you hear?"

"Bah." Pullo spat out into the night. "They said the same of Caesar once, didn't they?"

True. But was this the same? The people loved Caesar, but he knew they didn't feel the same for Antony. And fewer still loved Caesarion, the foreign prince for whose sake Antony claimed to be fighting. "I just don't know anymore," Vorenus muttered.

"Antony should go to Rome. It's what Caesar would've done."

Vorenus shook his head. "When Caesar crossed the Rubicon he did so as a liberator, not a conqueror. You know that as well as I. But Antony … as soon as he cast his lot with Egypt he became like a foreigner to the people. Attacking Octavian in Italy would only make him look worse."

Pullo frowned. "I just don't like this fight," he repeated. "Antony or Octavian. Isn't much of a choice, is it?"

"It's not our choice to make, Pullo," Vorenus said, struck by the honest truth of it. "We cast our lot when we came to Egypt, I think. Octavian would have our heads if he could. I think our fate is Caesarion's."

Pullo said nothing for a long time. "Well, I don't understand why they can't just live in peace," he finally said. "Octavian can keep the west; Antony can keep the east. Just like it's been."

Vorenus smiled at his friend's naive optimism and was starting to reply when he saw, out of the corner of his eye, a shape move among the shadows inside the palace, along the base of the inner wall. Staring after it, he thought through the rotation of the guards, trying to recall whether any had business there at this time of the night. He felt a sinking in the pit of his stomach.

"I mean, I guess there's the problem that Antony proclaimed Caesarion to be his father's only true heir," Pullo continued.

"Pullo," Vorenus whispered, eyes still fixed below.

"I guess that means Octavian lied about Caesar's will, about how Caesar had meant for *him* to be his heir. That can't make Octavian too happy, being called a liar and all."

"Pullo—"

"But I still don't understand why Octavian needs to attack—"

"Pullo!" Vorenus said, his voice rising to a hushed shout.

"What?" the big man asked, seemingly annoyed with having lost his impressive chain of thought.

"The guard," Vorenus said. "Call them out quietly. Don't let anyone in or out of the council chambers. Lock the gates. Then take a strong contingent toward the northeast quarters, checking for intruders."

Pullo just stood, looking confused. "Why?"

"Just move!"

Pullo blinked, actually snapped to attention, and then rumbled off, his hulking form blocking the interior light in the seconds before he vanished inside.

Vorenus turned back, trying to catch sight of the figure again among the various pockets of shadows within the confines of the palace's thick walls. When he failed to find it, Vorenus looked down over the balcony. The stone wall was sloped below him, not unlike the sides of the massive pyramids up the Nile. Farther down, the smooth surface disappeared into the black shapes of a garden shaded by palm trees. He could make his way back through the commotion, he knew, back through the winding stairs and rooms, but the straightest line would be the fastest.

Taking one more look to memorize the place where he'd last seen the intruder, Vorenus stepped up onto the edge of the stonework. His knees ached, and his aging back seemed to groan from the anticipation of what was to come, but duty was duty. No matter how old he got. No matter who that damn Octavian thought he was.

With a final glance at the moon, Vorenus dropped down into the dark.

5

One Must Die

ROME, 32 BCE

Three weeks after he'd brought the Trident of Poseidon to Rome, two weeks after he'd used Octavian's coffers to send Laenas to Alexandria, Juba left the Forum and began walking the paved streets west through the colorful stone labyrinth of Rome, down toward the Tiber and Caesar's family villa beyond it. He wore civilian clothes, the sash and symbols of his estate left behind, and he tried, as he made his way through the winding streets between painted and columned estates, brick-walled inns, and the fluttering awnings of open shop windows, to imagine that he was an ordinary sixteen-year-old citizen of the Eternal City with few enough cares in the world.

But for all his appearance as a common, if foreign-born, man, Juba couldn't feel common in his mind. He was most uncommon. He had a chance to grasp the very power of the gods—if gods there were.

He'd thought much on that particular question since he'd found the Trident in Numidia: If Neptune and Poseidon were one, if their weapon could, in turn, belong to Moses, if Thoth and Mercury and Hermes could be the same god ... was it possible that *all* the deities of the world were reflections of the same, single, united god? And, even more difficult to consider, if the man Moses could be so much like Neptune, was it possible that Neptune had been a man, too? Might it be possible that there were no gods at all, just men made divine in the memories of other men? Juba's adopted father, Julius Caesar, after all, had been declared an immortal god after his very mortal, very human murder.

That there might be no gods at all was a troubling thought, but it was also a thrilling one. It was an old adage that the clothes made the man. Wear the sash of office, as Juba had just an hour earlier in the Senate strategy sessions, and the people would treat you as an officer. Perhaps it was also true, then, that the weapons made the god.

Walking back to practice once more with the Trident of Poseidon, Juba considered this conclusion a point of much interest.

Coming around the fruit stalls of a shop on a blind corner, lost in his thoughts of gods and men, Juba barely had time to look up and see the legionnaire on horseback bearing down the street before he was upon him. Juba gasped and dove to the right to avoid getting hit. His body crashed into a stand of apples beneath a faded green awning, sending some clattering to the stone pavement, and the churning legs of the beast just barely missed him.

A messenger, Juba could see. Probably carrying dispatches from the port, updates on the enormous undertaking of sending the legions to Greece.

As Juba stared after the departing horse, the shopkeeper reached for a sawgrass switch and brought it down on his hand. "You ass!"

Juba recoiled in pain, startled. He saw the apples on the

ground and instinctively began bending to pick them up. "Citizen, I—"

The switch came down again, with more force this time. "Keep your filthy hands off, slave!"

Juba staggered back into the flow of pedestrians that was moving in the soldier's wake and let it carry him away from the cursing shopkeeper.

Slave. How often had he been called that in this, his supposed home? He, an adopted son of Caesar himself, weighed and judged at a glance.

A just god, Juba thought, would change things, make them better. That things only seemed to get worse, in fact, might be proof that no just gods existed, perhaps no gods at all.

Juba felt a grin crossing his face even as he massaged the welt on his dark-skinned hand. If there were no gods to fix things, he'd just have to do it himself.

The villa beyond the Tiber that had once been Julius Caesar's now belonged to his adopted son, Octavian, and it was there that Juba had been given the most secure space they could think of in which to practice using the Trident of Poseidon. The compound had been breached just once that Juba had ever heard, and that on the day that Caesar died. But since falling to Octavian's hands, its walls had been built higher and stronger over the years, and a squad of praetorian guards—Octavian's loyal personal bodyguard—had been permanently assigned to protect its grounds. Juba and Quintus had been given rooms there, and a pavilion had been erected in its private garden to conceal Juba's work from outside eyes. No one, not even Quintus, was supposed to know what was going on within.

Juba entered the quiet villa in good spirits, glad that he'd had time after the morning's meeting to walk the streets of

Rome. He'd often done so to clear his head, especially enjoying the dirtier, more traditional markets beyond the walls of the city, where the shopkeepers practiced their trades in the old ways that had been passed down from generation to generation. He felt especially at home amid the small knots of smithies that were dotted here and there amid the tangled sea of traders. The men who labored in them were a hard lot: hunchbacked from tending their fires, arms corded thick with muscle from swinging their tools, hearing partly gone from the constant crash and ring of metal, and skin permanently blackened—darker than his—from the soot. But they were an honest, hardworking lot. They were, Juba had always thought, the best of Rome. No surprise, then, that so many of them were, like him, from the provinces: either lured to Rome by the vast hordes of wealth that ebbed and flowed in and out of the Eternal City or brought there in chains as slaves who managed to win freedom enough to ply a trade. Walking among them helped remind him why Rome had to be stopped. This morning's encounter with the horseman and shopkeeper had underscored the matter even further, so he was anxious to begin practicing, to begin feeling the power of the Trident, to imagine once more the still-greater power of the Ark, which he hoped would be his in time.

The villa was customarily calm, a place of sanctuary for the family, away from the bustle of the city. Moving through its halls, Juba couldn't help but think of the happy times he'd spent here in his childhood, when he was too young to know the truth of the world. Slaves passed by him as he walked, their heads down and spirits broken as they carried linens or trays of food from one place to another. He heard yelling from one doorway, and the sound of a switch falling on a slave who hadn't done her duty properly.

Juba winced to hear the blows and the muffled screams, and he absently rubbed his hand. It made no sense that some people were born to hold the switch and others were born to feel it. Quintus, he knew, was a good man, as good a man as most of the free citizens he'd ever met. It made no sense.

I'll set him free, he thought. Once I'm free of Rome.

With no breeze this morning, the large tent in the garden stood as still as if it were built of stone. Beyond it, standing beside one of the statues near the wall, Juba could see a lone praetorian watching the rear of it, but there was no one else in sight. In his caution, Octavian had encouraged the guards to keep not only the servants but also themselves away from the tent. Juba, still smiling to himself, strode up to the tent and lifted the heavy flap to step inside.

To his surprise, the tent was not empty.

The low, makeshift wall along the back of the tent was there, of course, as were the numerous pots and jars and pitchers he'd practiced flinging against it. The three heavy barrels were there, too: sources for the water to fill the items, as well as objects for him to try moving when he felt he had the strength. All this was as he had expected. What he'd not anticipated was to find Quintus facedown on the grass floor, shaking like a man in a fit.

Juba ran to the old slave, kneeling to roll him over to his side. Only then did he see that Quintus was holding on to the Trident, that he'd only miraculously not managed to fall upon one of its points.

Quintus had whites for eyes, and Juba clutched his shoulders, trying to wake him. The slave just shook, his fingers squeezing so hard into the metal skin of the twin bronze and copper snakes that the bones of his knuckles stood out grotesquely beneath his skin. Finally Juba gripped with his right hand the newly polished ash staff that they'd had fashioned to hold the Trident head. With his left hand he grabbed the prominent arrow-topped central point—near the blacker-than-black stone at the center of the uniquely shaped artifact, but not touching it—and then he twisted and pulled, straining until he'd wrested the Trident out of the old man's hands.

Quintus at once let out a long breath like a sigh, and his body relaxed back into the sun-starved grass. The blades crinkled beneath his weight. His lungs seemed to rise and fall more easily, and his eyes closed as if he was sleeping.

Juba set the Trident aside and then tried to wake his old friend, tugging more gently at his shoulders than he had before.

The slave's eyes fluttered, opened, and then focused. "Juba," he croaked.

"What happened? What were you doing?"

Quintus was pale, but the look of guilt in his eyes was more pained than anything his exhausted body could communicate. "I'm ... I'm sorry. Didn't want to but he ... he made me try."

"What? Who?"

"Him," Quintus managed to say, peering back behind Juba.

Juba turned his head and saw that he and Quintus were far from alone. Positioned around the inside of the tent, tucked away in the shadowed corners near the flap at its center, were four members of the praetorian guard who'd evidently been standing at attention the whole time, watching the slave convulse. And in front of the flap stood Octavian himself. "Hello, Juba," he said.

Juba tried to still the hard, angry beating of his heart as he laid Quintus back down. "You must have come down on horse, brother, riding hard."

Octavian's face was tight. "And you must have taken your time walking. Daydreaming through the markets again?"

Juba agreed as nonchalantly as he could, given the questions surging through his mind. Was Octavian having him followed? For how long? Did he know about Laenas and Alexandria?

"I see you've decided to have the wooden staff replaced," Octavian said, his eyes moving over to the Trident in the grass.

"I did," Juba said. There was no sense in denying the plain truth.

"And you chose a craftsman by the river for it?"

Juba had, in fact, found a woodworker down in the traditional markets: an older man, wrinkled but still sturdy, regarded as one of the most able at his craft even among his competitors. He was also a man who, much to their annoyance, refused to divulge any of the secrets of his trade to younger men. When Juba had given him the task of shaping the wooden shaft, he'd encouraged this tendency toward silence by paying him twice what the work should have cost, with another payment on completion. "I thought it safest to find a man where it would be least expected," Juba said carefully. "In the old market, down among the rabble ... none would think to look down there for something like this."

"I did."

Juba started to reply, then reconsidered. Beside him, he heard Quintus finally regain movement and push himself to his elbows, away from Octavian.

The Imperator sighed, shook his head as he stepped slowly forward. "Well? May I see it?"

"Of course," Juba said, pointedly not looking at Quintus as he lifted the Trident from the ground and stood. He carried it carefully in his hands, like an offering, the few steps it took to reach his adopted brother.

"Remarkable work," Octavian said, though his hands remained at his sides and he leaned back slightly when Juba got close.

"It is," Juba agreed, trying to make his gratitude clear. "Beautiful work by a master woodworker."

"A master woodworker," Octavian repeated. "You paid him well?"

"Very," Juba said. He tried to meet Octavian's eyes, but he found it difficult to do so. "To keep his silence."

"Silence is important," Octavian said.

"I agree," Juba said quickly. "Absolutely."

Octavian smiled gratefully, as if they'd come to an understanding. "I'm glad to hear it. I'm glad we can agree on the need for secrecy in this, well, business," he said.

Juba nodded, tried to show his calm by lowering the Trident he held out in his hands. He wanted to look back at Quintus, but was afraid to do so.

"You've been practicing?" Octavian asked.

"Every moment I can," Juba said.

"Every moment but those in which you've wandered in the market, offering the Trident to the view of woodworkers."

The artifact slipped slightly under Juba's fingers, but he caught it again. "All but those, yes. And I never walk long, naturally, I—"

Octavian held up his hand, cutting off his younger stepbrother. "Of course not, Juba. I know you wouldn't toy with the future of Rome like that."

Juba had to build the courage to look up and meet Octavian's gaze. "I need time away to regain my strength," he said. "Working the Trident is ... taxing."

Octavian's face fell soft with pity. "Taxing? If you are ill I have the finest doctors of the Republic at my whim, dear brother. If you're tense I can bring the most beautiful girls to your bath, to your chamber, perhaps?"

"No, no." Juba felt the heat of his anxiety flush his cheeks, and he hoped it would seem that his primary concern was embarrassment before the guards. "It's hard for me to admit— you know how proud I am, my brother—but it's nothing so, well, physical."

Juba's attempt to wrest some control of the situation from Octavian seemed to work, as his stepbrother didn't respond immediately. "Explain."

Juba let his eyes pass over the praetorians with obvious concern.

"They can be trusted, Juba. Speak freely."

"Well, it takes a kind of inner effort to work it." Juba felt his heartbeat calming in his chest as he wove his way into honest truth. "I cannot sustain it yet for any length of time. It's like tapping into a cistern. There's only so much in there before you must wait for it to be replenished. I'm trying to learn how to make it last longer, Octavian, but I'm not there yet. My walks help me get ready."

Something like genuine concern appeared on Octavian's face while Juba spoke. "You're better now, then?"

Juba thrust his chin forward slightly, head up and strong, as if trying to stand like a man before the older, bigger guards. "I am."

"I'm heartened to hear it," Octavian said. He walked up to the younger man and put his arm around him. The two of them started moving toward the front of the tent. "You've clearly thought things through."

"I've tried."

They were nearing the flap. Octavian stopped abruptly. "Then you ought to have thought, dear Juba, about what attention it would have brought that poor woodworker to have garnered such a windfall. You ought to have thought about the fact that I'd have no choice but to have him killed."

Killed? Juba swallowed hard, felt certain he could hear his own heart beating in his ears. That old man was dead?

"And you ought to have thought especially about the consequences of lying to me."

Juba knew what happened to those who betrayed Rome. If Octavian knew the truth of his plans, if he knew about the

Ark and Alexandria, the best he could hope for was a quick death—though the cross, he knew, was far more likely, far more in keeping with Octavian's style. Or being thrown from the Tarpeian Rock, screaming the seconds to his death on the crushing stones below. As his mind wailed in terror, Juba concentrated on appearing shocked at the accusation. "Lying?"

"You told me that none knew of the Trident but you and me."

"The staff was broken. And he didn't know what it was—"

"Not the woodworker. That was a small matter, brother. I'm speaking of this slave, who's not just known of the Trident but helped you practice with it."

Juba turned instinctively to look at Quintus, who'd now managed to lift himself to his knees. He was staring at them tiredly, his chest heaving. The old man said nothing but shook his head from side to side.

"He's a slave," Juba said. "I didn't think he mattered."

Even as the words came out, Juba regretted them. The body of Quintus—his old friend, the closest thing to a real father that he'd ever had—sagged, and his face trembled.

Octavian stared down at the old man as if looking at a beast of burden. "I suppose you're right, of course," he said. "Which is why I didn't feel bad asking him to try to use the Trident himself."

"But why—?" Even as he started to ask the question, Juba knew the answer.

"To see if just anyone can use it," Octavian said, voice objective with logic. "I wasn't about to try it myself, you understand. Or to subject one of the guards to it. Goodness, no. You saw what it did to him: if you hadn't walked in when you had, he would've died. I don't want to lose a good man like that."

The full truth of Octavian's thinking struck Juba hard in the gut. "But a slave isn't a man," he whispered.

"Precisely so," Octavian said, pride puffing his voice as if he'd just led a prized student to a proper conclusion.

Quintus knelt, swaying slightly—in grief or exhaustion, Juba couldn't tell. He imagined the slave's heart breaking.

"And, since we can't have him talking, either," Octavian continued as he turned to the praetorian to his right, "kill him."

The guard didn't hesitate. His nod was almost imperceptible, but within a heartbeat he had pulled his gladius free with an effortless, smooth movement and was stepping forward. Quintus at last moved, coughing out assurances of his silence as survival instinct staggered him to his feet and he tried to retreat toward the back of the tent. He tripped, fell to a knee, and then the guard was there, his arm coming back along his side in perfect thrusting form. The old man knelt, tears running clean paths across his dirty skin as his eyes pleaded with the impassive killer. Juba felt paralyzed, knowing he could do nothing without bringing further suspicion upon himself but also knowing he couldn't just stand by and watch Quintus die. Caught between terrors, he shut his eyes.

"Wait."

Octavian's voice was not loud, but when Juba opened his eyes again he saw that the praetorian was as motionless as a statue before his old friend, who'd raised his arms to shield his face.

"Return to your position, praetorian."

The guardsman sheathed his blade as smoothly as he'd removed it and strode back to take his place by the others. The fact that he'd almost murdered a man in cold blood didn't seem to register on his face.

Juba felt himself breathe again. The old man's arms fell away from his face and something like hope appeared in his eyes.

"You said you agreed with the need for silence," Octavian said to his younger stepbrother. "'Absolutely,' you said. An interesting choice of words. But a good one. The need for silence *is* absolute." Octavian's eyes narrowed. "*You* do it."

Juba blinked, his mind racing. "Do—?"

Octavian smiled gently. "Be not so innocent with me, little brother. You know quite well what I mean. What is necessary here, what absolute silence demands." His head tilted toward the slave. "Kill him."

"I'm unarmed," Juba said, holding out against hope.

Octavian's smile only grew. "Oh, but you do have a weapon." His arm still around his stepbrother's shoulder, he turned him around so that he was squared up to the old man. Then the Imperator of Rome looked down at the Trident in his hands. "No need to blunt the points. Move his blood."

Move his blood? Juba stared for a moment, uncomprehending. Then, with horror, the realization of what he was being asked to do washed over him. He knew with full certainty, just as he'd known he could knock over the cup of wine in Octavian's office, that he could reach out, feel the flow of blood in his old friend's body, and stop it: with the power of the Trident he could seize up the stream of life in the man's veins and kill him. Juba could even see Quintus' dead eyes, wide and frozen, in his mind. But he couldn't really do it, could he? "But, brother, I—"

"Don't tell me you're tired. You're rested. You said so yourself. Now. You can move wine and barrels of water. Move blood."

Quintus suddenly looked like a caged beast, his eyes a mix of terror and confusion. His gaze at last met and locked on Juba's, and the awareness that they each had a choice to make passed between them. Juba had to choose whether he would kill his old friend. Quintus had to choose whether he would reveal Juba's secrets to Octavian.

The slave smiled and began to pull air into his lungs. He opened his mouth as if to speak.

Before he could change his mind, Juba closed his eyes and tried to push the face of his old friend out of his thoughts. Then—forcing himself to keep down the heaving of his stomach, to keep in the tears of his eyes—he raised the gleaming Trident, held tight to the two snakes, and felt the metal beneath his flesh grow warm.

Speed, he thought. Do it quickly. For his friendship. For his silence.

6

Cleopatra's Daughter

ALEXANDRIA, 32 BCE

Cleopatra Selene couldn't sleep. It wasn't just that they were staying in the noisier old palace on Lochias while workers installed new statues at their home on the harbor island of Antirhodos that kept her awake. They'd moved back and forth between the royal palaces enough to make each feel as much like home as the other. No, it was the feeling that she was being left out that she didn't like. She knew there was a big meeting in the council chambers, not far away. She'd heard her mother talking about it in the square that afternoon: a messenger, news from Rome.

Rome. Lying in bed, the eight-year-old mouthed the word into the darkness, holding the sound of it out, like a long, slow exhalation. *Rome.*

In her dreams it was a golden place, more opulent than even fair Alexandria. Its streets shone in the light of a kinder sun. Its people laughed in their many-colored clothes: happy, peaceful, content. For what else could the peoples of the world aspire to be than citizens of Rome? Did not her own father want more than anything to return to Rome, his home? Was that not what his fight was about? He often told her and her brothers that most Romans were loyal to his cause. Most Romans would love them. It was only a scant few—wicked men, like Octavian—who denied the true spirit of Rome, the spirit of the great Julius Caesar, which survived in her stepbrother, Caesarion.

What news had the messenger brought? Her mother had said her father feared the worst. Probably something to do with Octavian, then. Most bad news seemed to be tied to him.

War, perhaps. Selene knew all the servants expected it would come to that eventually. She overheard them talking about it when they didn't know she was listening or didn't care—how, they thought, could a girl understand? It was a lot like the attitudes of those the servants served, who gave little thought to the submissive men and women pouring their drinks as they discussed the fates of nations. Selene had seen it often enough to feel certain that she'd be more careful when she was queen.

The messenger must have brought news that Octavian had declared war, she decided. They were probably debating what to do about it even now. Maps were being drawn up. Plans were being made. Tempers were flaring, and faces were getting red.

Selene rolled over in her sheets. It wasn't fair that she couldn't be there. Just because she was a girl didn't mean she couldn't understand things. Couldn't they look at her mother and see that?

Not that her twin brother, Helios, would be there, either. But at least *he* was getting extra lessons with their teacher, Didymus, meeting for tutoring sessions after she'd gone to bed. That wasn't fair, either.

Selene looked toward the darkness outside the window, wondering what time it was. Not too late, certainly. Perhaps Helios and Didymus were still in session.

She swung her legs out of the bed and pushed on her sandals. There was a thin haze of sand dust on the stone floor, and her feet made little *shush-shush* noises when she stood.

Selene cringed, listening hard to hear whether or not her movements had awoken one of the chamber servants. When she heard nothing but snoring, she stepped back out of the sandals and set her bare feet on the floor. It was cold, but it was quiet. Then, pulling a shift over her head, she started to tiptoe across the room, toward the hall and the greater palace beyond.

There were normally at least two guards that she could see from the door to her chambers, but peeking out into the lamp-lit hallway, Selene saw none. Apparently, most had been pulled away to the council chambers. The fact that even the guards—the guards!—knew more about what was happening did not do much to improve her mood, but she was glad, at least, that it would make moving through the complex easier.

Her brother's chambers were just down the hall, so Selene didn't have far to go. She padded between the pools of flickering light, checked for guards around the one corner she had to turn, and quickly reached her brother's door. Leaning against the wood, she listened and heard the steady voice of Didymus.

She'd hoped she could just listen to the lesson from outside. Over the years she'd listened in on many conversations through closed palace doors, after all. But their voices were more muted than most. And there was the chance, too, that a guard would actually show up, and he'd undoubtedly send her back to bed with stern warnings and exasperated looks, and then she'd hear about it in the morning.

Selene's little fingers pulled open the door as quietly as she could manage. It was dark inside, and she realized why it was she couldn't hear them from out in the hall: they'd pulled thick curtains across the corner of her brother's chambers that served as a study. Even this close, their voices were muted.

Selene shut the door, then tried to make her way closer in the black, trying to place her bare feet on quiet places. But it was too dark, and her foot hit a wooden staff that was leaning against the wall, sending it to the ground with a clatter. The curtain parted quickly, casting the light of a lit brazier across her, and the back-lit head of Didymus appeared.

"Selene," he said. She could only see the silhouette of him, but his voice was only partly disapproving. "I think you're supposed to be in bed, my lady."

Selene's twin brother pulled back on another of the curtains, peeking around their teacher. "What?"

"I'm sorry," Selene said. She tried to look bashful and forlorn all at once. With care, she picked up the staff—it was the tutor's walking staff, she could see now—and set it back against the wall. "I was in bed. I just ... I couldn't sleep is all."

Didymus sighed, then he held the curtains open for her. "No sense leaving you there now," the Greek said. "And no sense sending you back if you're already sneaking about."

Selene tried to contain her smile and to ignore her brother's scowl as she stepped past their tutor and into the little study area. The brazier was in the middle of the space, and there were a few scrolls half-rolled on a table against the wall. Didymus sat back down on a chair and motioned for Selene to take another on the opposite side of the brazier. The three of them, she noticed, made a sort of triangle around the brass tripod, so each of them could see the other's face.

"We were talking of Rome," Didymus said.

Selene's eyes lit up, and she leaned forward. "I was just thinking about Rome," she said.

Helios huffed. "I bet you weren't thinking about Hannibal's tactics."

Selene glared, started to say something, but Didymus cut her off. "More snapping and you're *both* off to bed." His pale blue eyes fixed on each of the two children in turn until they both lowered their gazes and relaxed their shoulders. "Good," he said. "So. Why were you thinking about Rome, Selene?"

"That's what they're talking about, isn't it? In the council chambers? That's what Mother said."

"I suppose she did," Didymus agreed. "I suppose they are."

"It must be a very nice place," Selene said, her voice quiet.

Helios smiled deviously. "Selene loves Rome. She wants to be a Roman."

"I do not!" Selene startled herself with how loud her voice was in the quiet space.

Didymus motioned for her to lower her voice, shot a glare at Helios. "Rome is a city of wonders," he said. "It's true. But to be Roman isn't everything."

"You're not Roman," Helios said. "You're Greek."

Selene wasn't sure if Helios was being mean or being nice. It bothered her sometimes that she could have such trouble reading her own twin. Didymus, for his part, just nodded. "I am. But I've spent a lot of time in Rome. And I've known many Romans in my time. Rome isn't so glorious, and its people not so pure, as they may seem in dreams."

Selene furrowed her brow. "But Father..."

"We make ideals out of our memories," Didymus said, raising thin fingers to rub at his eyes. "Antony—your father—imagines a city that doesn't really exist. We're all this way. I remember a Greece far greater than it is. If you left Alexandria, you'd recall it with far more fondness than you have for it now. Rome? Rome is a place where no one can be trusted. Where nothing is what it seems." His eyes were on the flickering brazier between them. "And not just Rome. The world is like that, children. Sooner or later, we all learn it."

Everyone was silent for a few moments, and Selene found herself watching her brother. Like their Greek teacher, he was staring down at the glowing brass. Her twin had always been more sickly than she was—weaker, thinner, more prone to illness—but tonight he looked almost normal, she decided. The shadows under his eyes seemed less dark, and his cheeks appeared less hollow. When his eyes rose, he saw her, too, and he actually smiled. "Except us," he said. There was a kind of pride in his voice. He looked over to their teacher. "And you."

Didymus looked up from the light and smiled tiredly. His pale eyes took in them both. "You are indeed some of the best, most honest people I've ever met," he said. "Rome would be fortunate to have any of you."

Selene imagined being queen of Rome for a moment before she shook the silliness of the thought away: if any of them would rule Rome, it would be their elder half-brother, Caesarion. He was, after all, Caesar's son. If they won the war to come, it would be he who ruled the streets of her dreams. "Do you think we'll win, Didymus?"

"Win? We're not even at war yet."

Selene frowned, but it was Helios who spoke. "We will be."

Didymus shrugged. "Perhaps. Perhaps not. It isn't for us to decide."

Selene had once overheard some of the servants talking about what had happened to the king of Gaul after he'd been defeated by Julius Caesar. "What's a Triumph?"

Didymus' eyebrows raised. "A Triumph? Where did you hear about that?"

"I heard that's what Caesar did to Vercingetorix."

Didymus chewed on his lip for a moment, thinking. "It's a parade in Rome, meant to honor a military commander for a great victory."

Selene's eyes narrowed. "They take the defeated king on it, too?"

"Yes."

"What happens to him?"

"Children, I—"

"Vercingetorix was publicly strangled during the Triumph,

Selene," Helios said quietly. "So was Jugurtha after the fall of Numidia."

Didymus glared at the boy, but he didn't disagree.

"She needs to know," Helios whispered.

"Strangled?" Visions of their father and Caesarion suddenly flashed into Selene's mind. "But why—"

"Not always," Didymus said quickly. "And not everyone. The kings of Numidia and Gaul, it's true. But it isn't always that way. And it's not something we need to be concerned about. We're not at war yet." He tried to smile. "Besides, you're too young to think on such things. Both of you."

"It's not fair," Selene whispered. Young or not, girl or not, it wasn't as if she'd be spared the results. So why wouldn't anyone let her take part?

"No, I suppose it is not," Didymus admitted. "But no one here is bound for a Triumph, anyway. If it comes to war, Antony and Caesarion will win. And we'll be safe here in Alexandria. Rome is a place of danger, but not Egypt. There's no place more secure. Our dear Vorenus sees to that."

The mention of Vorenus cast a moment of happiness into the gloom. "I think it's neat Vorenus knew Caesar," Helios said hopefully.

Didymus agreed, his long thin hair bouncing in the flickering light. "I'll tell you what. Caesarion and I found something about that today in our readings. If you'll promise to go right to sleep afterward, we can go look at it."

Helios yawned, then coughed lightly. Selene hoped he wasn't getting sick again. "Not me," he said. "I'm tired. Can I see it tomorrow?"

"Sure," Didymus said. "Of course." He stood, slowly, groaning as if against the weight of age. "I'll wish you a restful night, then, Helios. Selene? Let's take you back to your room."

"Can't I see it now?"

"You promise to go to sleep afterward?"

Selene nodded vigorously, excited to know something before her brother did. "I will. Promise."

"Fine. You'll have to walk slow with me, though. My legs are more accustomed to sedation than yours, I'm afraid."

Selene retrieved the teacher's staff, and they walked together down the hall in silence, taking care not to disturb those in sleep. Selene walked respectfully behind him, her mind a confused swirl of Roman gold and blood, glories and triumphs.

So lost was she in her thoughts that she walked into Didymus when he stopped at his door. He looked down at her with a sigh, shaking his head, but she could see the hint of amusement in his eyes. Selene bowed her head apologetically, took two steps backward to give him plenty of space. Didymus appeared to think about saying something but opted to maintain the silence of the hallways and instead just rolled his eyes before reaching out with his left hand and opening the door.

He'd shuffled halfway inside, moving his staff from his right hand to his left so he could hold the door open for her, when someone spoke from within. "Do not cry out, librarian," the voice said.

Didymus froze in place for a long heartbeat. Then his right hand, now free, slowly lowered until it was near Selene's level, palm downward, fingers outstretched in a sign to be silent and still. "Who's there?" he asked. "What are you looking for?"

"You," said the voice. It was a man. Someone Selene was sure she didn't recognize. His voice sounded Roman, like Pullo's, but even rougher. "Please, come in. I've been expecting you."

Selene, confused, watched as Didymus started to move, even slower than he usually did. His eyes never turned in her direction, but his thin-fingered hand twitched at her.

Away, it said. *Run.*

7

The Scrolls of Thoth

ALEXANDRIA, 32 BCE

The voice came from the shadows in the corner of the ransacked room. Didymus' mind flashed through possibilities of escape, of alarm. He opted for none of them. Anything might put the girl at risk. "Who's there?" he asked, trying to infuse his voice with a strength and authority that he knew he lacked. His eyes passed across the overturned chest, the scattered scrolls. Whoever it was had been searching for something, clearly. "What are you looking for?"

A scar-faced man, one of the Roman messengers Didymus had seen in the busy yard, stepped out of the dark. His hand held a short, bare dagger, and his gaze rested on Didymus with a kind of indifference—as if he were another object in the room rather than a human being. Didymus had seen such a look only once before, but he recognized the signs at once, in a flood of memory so sharp, so brutally painful, that he actually felt his stomach twist in revulsion.

"You," the assassin said. "Please, come in. I've been expecting you."

Didymus had to fight the urge to look to Selene, to scream at her to run. It would be foolish. If the man knew she was there she would never outrun him. The scholar's right hand was still outside the door frame, though, so he motioned with it—once, twice—flicking his wrist as sharply as he could manage without moving the parts of his arm visible to the room, to the assassin. *Get away, girl*, he shouted in his mind, hoping to will her away. *Go!*

And then he stepped into the room, his hand reaching back for the door to shut it, to put one more barrier between the killer and the eight-year-old daughter of Cleopatra.

Selene was smarter than most people gave her credit for, he knew. Surely she understood. Surely she was already on her way down the hall. If not finding the nearest guard, at least sneaking back to her chambers, back to her room. Back to her innocent dreams of Rome.

"So," Didymus said. "You come for me?" It surprised him how little concern he felt for himself as he asked the question. Even against the prospect of his own death, his greater concern was for the girl.

That he'd not always been so self-sacrificing, so caring for the children of Cleopatra, was the sickening thought he had to fight to keep at bay.

The assassin smiled, almost apologetically. "Not for you, no. Not for anyone unless it need be." He pulled the blade back to a sheath at his side, tilted his head toward the simple wooden bench under the window. "Please, librarian. Sit."

Didymus thought once more about whether he should raise the alarm—but he would be a dead man, he was sure, before help could possibly arrive. Most of the guards had been pulled away to the council chambers in the nearby royal court. Better, then, to find out whatever he could. Perhaps he could still be of use to his friends, even once-treacherous as he was.

Besides, he abruptly realized, the assassin hadn't identified him as the children's tutor. Perhaps it had nothing to do with them. "You called me 'librarian,'" Didymus said, making his way over to the bench, trying not to step on the scattered contents of the room: his drafts of a volume on Aristarchus' recension of Homer's *Iliad*, which would take days to put back in order. What, he wondered, could the man have possibly been looking for? "And it looks as if you're in search of something. A book, perhaps?"

"Yes. A book. And not just any book will do."

"Of course." Didymus allowed his voice to swing toward patronizing. He gestured toward the scattered debris as he sat down. "Though it seems you're confused. I'm the librarian, but this isn't the Great Library."

The assassin's smile was thin. "My mistake," he said. "But I think only you know where it is. It's an important book. Important enough I thought you might keep it here."

The Greek's mind raced, wondering what volume could be important enough for someone to send a killer to procure it. But it was useless. The Royal Library held countless volumes that could be priceless to someone. Nothing, after all, was more precious than knowledge. He sighed. "What book?"

The scar-faced Roman fished from the folds of his clothing a small sealed letter. "A scroll," he said, handing it over to Didymus. "Maybe a set of them. Very important. Very unique."

Didymus looked at the red-wax seal and felt his heart skip a beat. It was Octavian's. The same as he'd seen on the letter from Varro some dozen years earlier, the letter promising him Senate support for the position of librarian if he aided the man sent by Octavian to kill Cleopatra—or so Didymus had foolishly thought.

All at once the memory of that night broke through the barriers of his mind, and he was there once more. Nineteen years old again. Walking the halls of Caesar's villa as if in a dream. Certain it couldn't be real. Certain he hadn't just told Octavian's assassin where to find the boy. Certain he'd wake up any moment. Half-driven to insanity by his youthful yearnings for Cleopatra—a yearning churned to anger at her clear lack of interest in the young Athenian scholar hired to tutor her children—he'd agreed to help the conspirators kill her. But not the boy. Not the innocent boy. Surely it was a dream. Surely he'd never spoken those words.

But then Cleopatra's moans turned to screams, cutting through his daze. A banging began. A horrible, hollow banging that reverberated through the villa: the sound, he would soon discover, of a legionnaire named Vorenus pounding against the barred wooden door to Caesarion's room. Didymus ran toward the sounds, the horror of what he'd done suddenly real. Quick as he was, Cleopatra and Antony were there already, the queen half-collapsed in her soon-to-be-lover's arms. Vorenus, his face red, was throwing his shoulder, his body, again and again and again into the unyielding barrier. Against the wall, slumped like a discarded sack of wheat, lay one of Caesarion's guards, his throat slit because Didymus had told the assassin where to find him. There were shouts and crashes from within, Cleopatra's high-pitched wail from without. And then a moment of terrible, awful quiet before the door suddenly came open to reveal a massive veteran Roman legionnaire—Pullo—holding the frightened boy in his arms. And beyond him, bleeding out on the floor of the little bedroom that Didymus had almost made the child's tomb, the assassin himself. They looked into each other's eyes—assassin and traitor—and in that moment everything that Didymus had thought he'd wanted died. His desire for power. His foolish desire for Cleopatra. If Antony had pulled Didymus' name from the lips of the dying assassin, he would have met his inevitable death without sorrow. More than that, he would have welcomed it.

Even now, sitting in his littered room, holding the sealed letter, he wondered if it would have been better if he had died that night. It would have been easier than living with the guilt of knowing that he'd been the one to betray the boy he'd taught for all these years. Far easier.

But, then, he'd grown to love the boy as his own. He'd done all he could for him, and for the other children, too, when they came along. That had to be worth something, didn't it? Nothing could make up for what he'd done, nothing could make it right, but the world was a better place for him having been in it since then, wasn't it?

"Librarian?"

Didymus blinked himself back to the present, smiled grimly at the assassin. "I'm sorry," he said. "I was just thinking it had been a long time since I'd seen the seal of Octavian."

As soon as the name escaped his lips, Didymus heard a sound from the hallway outside the room. It was muted by the wood, but clear enough to the scholar: Selene had just choked off her own involuntary gasp.

The assassin heard it, too, but he didn't recognize it at once. His head turned in the direction of the door, and he rose up to the balls of his feet as he took a step toward it.

Selene! Didymus cleared his throat and kicked at one of the scrolls on the floor with his toe. It made a kind of scuffing sound, somewhat like the girl's half-gasp. "You picked a good night to come, my Roman friend," Didymus said, his voice louder than it had been. "The guards are all in the council."

The assassin froze, confused by the Greek's familiar address and the origin of the sounds he'd heard. "Yes, I know."

"Of course you do," Didymus said as he grunted and cracked open the seal. Again his foot pushed a scroll, and he was relieved to hear it make a sound almost perfectly attuned to Selene's. "A clever way to slip past the guard."

The assassin's eyes narrowed, suspicious, and he didn't answer. But he didn't take another step toward the door, either.

Didymus let out his breath slowly, fighting to appear at ease. He looked down at the letter, concentrating to keep his hands from shaking as they unwrapped it, then let his eyes pass over the whole of it to calm his nerves.

Octavian's seal meant it was from someone close to the family of the Julii, if not from Octavian himself. That the vellum was fresh, not scraped and reused, certainly pointed to a man of some position, too. And the formal Latin script meant an educated man. The handwriting was neat and even, unhurried and precise. Probably from a young man, then, or a middle-aged one at the latest. Not Varro this time. Someone much younger, but with a calm mind, thinking clear, practiced thoughts.

Didymus nodded, feeling his own mind at last beginning to calm itself. Only then did he raise his eyes to the greeting at the top of the page and begin to read.

Juba.

Unexpected, certainly. Didymus paused to consider all he knew about the young man. A year older than Caesarion. That would make him sixteen, nearing the age when Roman nobles would begin their military training. Like Octavian, an adopted son of Julius Caesar. His father, the king of Numidia, had killed himself when the boy was two, refusing to be paraded through Rome in another of Caesar's Triumphs. The child Juba, his only son and heir, had taken his place instead, before Caesar had made a show of adopting the boy. Unexpected, but interesting.

Didymus took a moment to look up at the deliverer of the letter. The man was watching him impassively, and Didymus wondered if he knew that he worked not for the Imperator Octavian but for his foreign-born, youthful adopted brother.

Youthful but ambitious, Didymus corrected himself. As for his ambition, his reason to write a careful letter to the librarian of Alexandria, sealed under the imperatorial wax of Octavian ...

Didymus read on.

It wasn't a long letter, but even so it took the scholar several minutes of starting and stopping to get through it.

The Scrolls of Thoth.

Didymus couldn't imagine more shocking words to be written on the page. He kept reading the words again and again to be certain they were there.

The Scrolls of Thoth.

The scholar's mouth felt suddenly dry. The Scrolls of Thoth, the most powerful book imaginable, the secrets of the god of wisdom supposedly inscribed by the hand of Thoth himself. A book with the incantations Thoth taught Isis to resurrect her husband, Osiris. A book that would reveal the secrets of the universe to whoever held it. A book long sought by pharaohs and scholars alike: here said to rest in seven nested boxes, watched over by an immortal serpent, buried beneath the deepest depths of the Nile, there said to be hidden in a secret crypt under Thoth's own city, Hermopolis. A legend. A dream.

The Scrolls of Thoth.

And, in return, Juba promised the release of Greece from Roman control. The return of freedom to Didymus' homeland. The end of more than a century under foreign oppression. The return to glory the likes of which they'd not seen since the days of great Alexander, who even now rested in his golden coffin in the splendid mausoleum not an hour's walk from where Didymus sat.

The Scrolls of Thoth.

The parchment trembled in the scholar's hands, and he had to close his eyes against the frightening weight of it all. "I can't," he whispered.

"Not what I want to hear."

"I can't give it to you," Didymus said. He opened his eyes, hoped their dampness wouldn't show in the dim light. "I don't care how much you need it."

"Oh, but you see, *I* don't need it, librarian. It's our employer who needs it."

"Our?"

"Yes, *our*. You're not one to forget favors, are you?"

"I try to remember my friends."

"I'm pleased to hear of it. Octavian will be pleased, too."

"Octavian. I've not worked for Octavian for years."

The assassin shook his head sadly, as if disapproving of a delinquent student. "Isn't what I was told. You do answer to the title 'librarian,' yes? Head librarian of the greatest library in the world? I'm not one for books myself, but—"

"And I'm not a man for games."

"No, but you are a man for sale."

The finality of it cut so close to Didymus' soul that he actually leaned back as if recoiling from a strike. "But ... I..."

The assassin pulled from his pocket a second note. "You're a tutor to the royal family. Our employer has tutors, too. One of them is Marcus Terentius Varro. An old friend of yours, yes?"

Didymus just stared, knowing what was coming even as he prayed that it would not.

"I have here a letter from Varro himself, testifying that he helped arrange for you to be librarian here. All for the death of the Egyptian pretender. And the whore mother, too, if possible."

"Enough," Didymus croaked, voice weak.

The assassin looked up from the page, the corners of his mouth turned up in a look of abusive amusement. "It seems you've been working for Octavian all along, *librarian*. No reason to stop now. Your other option is for this little note here to find its way to the royal family. And that just wouldn't do at all, would it?"

Didymus swallowed hard, fighting to keep their faces out of his mind. "I can't."

"You're offered fair payment?"

Greece. Home. Freedom. Alexander's glory. "Yes."

The assassin moved slightly, and Didymus saw that he was reaching for his weapon again. "I've no payment to give, but I can offer pain."

Didymus felt his heart race. "Kill me and you've nothing to take back," he blurted out.

"No," the assassin admitted. "But there's much pain on this side of death." He took a step forward, his hand curling around the hilt exposed at his side.

"Do you know what this asks me to give you?" Didymus asked quickly.

The assassin paused, left the blade in its sheath. "A book," he said.

"Not just any book."

The assassin smiled, let go of the weapon completely. "So you know it."

"Of course."

"Good," the assassin said. He motioned with his hand toward the door. "Take me to it."

Didymus didn't move. "I told you. I can't." Didymus sighed, the image of Alexander's golden coffin shimmering away from his mind like a mirage on the horizon. "I can't, because I don't think it exists."

"Our employer believes it does," the assassin said. "Says it's in the Royal Library. You're the librarian."

"And I know every volume in its halls. It's not there. I don't think it ever existed."

The assassin, just two steps away, cocked his head slightly, gauging the Greek for long moments. "You're telling the truth," he finally said.

The scholar's eyes were locked on the Roman's face. "I've no reason to lie," he said, disturbed by how true it was now.

"No, you don't," the assassin admitted.

Didymus was certain the relief must be apparent on his face. He looked down at the letter in his hands, swallowed hard. "I just don't know where it is."

"I know. So you don't have a reason to live, either," the assassin said, pulling his blade free with a metallic ring.

The sound of it snapped Didymus' eyes back up, and he instinctively tried to stand, to jump away from the bared blade. But his feet slipped on the scattered drafts of his book, sending papyrus and vellum skittering out into the air even as he flailed backward and struck the back of his skull on the stone ledge beneath the window.

For a moment the room was a spinning haze of manuscripts floating in the moonlight, a slow-time dance through which the blade in the assassin's hand moved gracefully, like a metal hawk angling against the wind, glinting hungrily. Didymus thought he cried out, but there was no sound. He tried to move, but darkness descended over his mind like a falling curtain.

Then, all at once, the doorway behind the assassin burst open. And light—blinding light—flooded the room.

8

The Librarian's Door

ALEXANDRIA, 32 BCE

Vorenus regretted letting go of the balcony railing almost as soon as he began sliding down the steadily sloping stone face of the palace wall. Distances were deceptive in the dark: despite his familiarity with the complex, the garden beneath him seemed to be much farther down than he anticipated. And he was picking up speed faster than he thought he would.

Not to mention that he wasn't as young as he used to be.

He reached out, pressed the leather vambrace strapped to his forearm against the stone. Its metal buckles sent out a flicking trail of sparks in his wake, but it did little to slow his pace.

Vorenus brought his other arm over his face as he hit the first whipping fronds of the tall palms that grew close to the wall. The space of a heartbeat followed before he crashed into the softer leaves of the tended plants below, his legs buckling instinctively and the air leaving his lungs even as he kicked forward and rolled across the hard earth.

He came to rest against the low wall bounding the little garden, and for a moment all he could do was stare at the slow wisps of cloud crossing over the moon above. His right hip throbbed in protest of the exertion. The ribs on his left side positively ached. And he could feel the sting of more scratches than he cared to imagine. He had slid more than four floors along the building. He'd done stupider things in his life, but not many.

Too damn old, Vorenus thought. If he didn't feel the urgency of danger, and if he didn't know that it would hurt too much, he would have laughed at his own foolish mortality. Instead, he painfully pulled himself to his feet, the air only beginning to return to his lungs.

Not bothering to dust himself off, Vorenus started south along the stone path through the garden at an easy trot, speeding up as he caught his wind, his head on a swivel to get his bearings and his mind determinedly pushing away the pain of his fall. The figure he'd seen from the balcony had been moving inward from the main walls, toward the residential areas south of the palace. Cleopatra and Caesarion were safe, he was sure: there were more than enough guards in the council chambers, and Pullo would see to it that everything was secured quickly.

No, it was the children that Vorenus kept thinking about: Cleopatra's younger children by Antony. The twins Selene and Helios, and little Philadelphus. With the council bringing an increase of guards at the palace, there would be no better time to strike at the youngest members of the royal family. Vorenus stole a glance off to his left, where the island of Antirhodos sat low in the harbor. He should have been more forceful about insisting that the family stay in residence at their palace there. He'd been foolish to allow Cleopatra to have her way about moving them all while the new addition was built. Foolish.

Fighting the urge to damn himself for the danger, Vorenus pulled out his gladius and set off at a run.

He'd just entered the main hall of the residential complex, just started making his way toward the quarter where the twins and young Ptolemy would be sleeping, when Selene's hushed shout froze him in his tracks. "Vorenus!"

He turned, lowering his blade slightly so as not to frighten the girl. Selene was looking out from behind the half-open doorway leading not to her hallway, but his own. She looked deeply frightened.

Taking a quick glance to left and right, Vorenus padded over, kneeling to make her feel more at ease. "Selene," he whispered. "What are you—"

"Didymus' room," she stammered. "Rome. Rome."

"Slow down." Vorenus took her slight shoulders in his hands as if to steady her. "Deep breath. Now. What's in Didymus' room?"

Selene's eyes were wide. "A man," she said. "From Octavian."

Vorenus stood, started to tell her to stay where she was. But then he realized that he didn't know if the man was still in Didymus' room. And surely there'd be no reason for the man to go to the librarian's room aside from attempting to use him to get to the children. So her safety had to be his first priority. He couldn't protect her here.

By the gods, where's Pullo?

"Okay," he said, getting his bearings again. "Stay close. We're going to go help Didymus. If I tell you to, though, I want you to run, okay? Doesn't matter why. Just run, as fast as you can, for the council chambers. Don't look back. Got it?"

Selene nodded vigorously. It wasn't much of a plan, Vorenus knew, but at least it was something. And, gods willing, some of the other guards would arrive soon.

Didymus' room wasn't far down the hall. Fortunate, since Vorenus took every step as another reason to curse himself for leaving so few guards in the residential areas, for not insisting that the family stay in the much more secure palace on Antirhodos.

When they got close to the librarian's room, Vorenus tried to push his guilt back out of his mind to focus on the moment. He crept forward cautiously, his gladius drawn and ready, while with his spare hand he pushed Selene as far back as she was willing to go. At the door, he leaned his ear against the wood.

Nothing. He wondered if he was too late, if Octavian's assassin had already come and gone, leaving Didymus dead in his wake. Or perhaps he was forcing the librarian to lead him to the children's rooms.

Vorenus was just starting to pull away when he heard the Greek's voice within. "I can't," Didymus said.

"Not what I want to hear," another voice replied. Selene was right: he did sound Roman. And vaguely familiar.

Laenas.

Vorenus listened with increasing silent rage as the assassin revealed Didymus' role in the assassination attempt on Caesarion's life, the near-murder of that innocent child that set him and Pullo on the path to this place, this time: cast out by Rome, enemies of the very state they desired so much to serve.

Didymus! If Vorenus wasn't hearing it for himself, he would never have believed it.

And what were these Scrolls of Thoth that the assassin's employer was after? Why were they so important?

"I just don't know where it is," he heard the Greek reply to the assassin's questioning.

"I know," Laenas said. "So you don't have a reason to live, either."

Vorenus heard, unmistakably, the metallic glide of a blade being drawn. He envisioned, in the eye of his mind, the scar-faced Roman moving in for a strike.

As he had many years before, wading into the thick of the barbarians in Gaul to rescue his wounded rival, Pullo, Vorenus acted without thinking. That Didymus had once betrayed the royal family—that even now he might be willing to sell them all to Octavian if he actually had access to the Scrolls—didn't cross his mind in the moments after he heard Laenas pull a blade.

The door wasn't the thickest wood, and it wasn't barred. With a single step back and one head-lowered shoulder-thrust forward, Vorenus was able to splinter the latch and charge into the room amid the flood of light from the fires in the hallway.

It would have been over quickly, the assassin run through the back, quivering out his final moments on Vorenus' weapon, except for the scattered manuscripts on the stone floor of the room. As it was, Vorenus took two strides into the librarian's chambers—left, right—and then felt his third step push out from beneath him just as he was planting it for the final strike. His right knee buckled as his left foot shot forward and his left hand shot down to the ground as he fell into a slide through the papers.

Laenas, a younger man, had catlike reflexes. Startled at first, he recovered quickly after Vorenus slipped and lost the advantage of surprise. Light on his feet, the assassin altered the aim of his arm in mid-swing. Originally intending his strike for the Greek Didymus—who was sprawled out now against the stone wall just below the window—he spun on his feet, bringing the blade around and down in a wide swath.

Vorenus saw the strike, but a moment too late. As it was, he had to drop his own sword in order not to stab himself as he curled down into his slide, ducking and rolling onto his side as he passed by the assassin. He felt the wind of the blade stroke pass inches from his head. He saw, as he rolled, the wide, dazed eyes of the traitor he'd once called his friend a moment before he, too, crumpled into the wall beneath the window, his boots planted hard on the stone and his knees bent to take out the speed of his impact.

The effort of the assassin's strike had spun him around momentarily, and he had to be careful to avoid slipping on the papers. By the time Laenas had turned back around, Vorenus had already kicked out of his crouch, recoiling his body back across the floor and into the assassin's legs. The two men fell, grunting, into a flurry of manuscripts, and the sound of the assassin's dagger clattering away across the stone rang loud in the little room.

Through the rain of papers in the dim light, Vorenus saw his own sword on the ground between them and he kicked his way forward, lunging for it. Laenas, fallen to his stomach, saw it, too, and he flung his foot out in that direction, sending it skittering noisily back toward the open doorway. Vorenus growled—out of frustration, out of pain—and grabbed the Roman's foot instead. One hand on the toe, one on the heel, he twisted as hard as he could manage, as if he might wrench the appendage off. It didn't come loose, but he was pleased to hear a pop. Laenas screamed, pulled himself toward Vorenus, and swung his free foot downward with savage ferocity, the heel crunching wetly into the older man's nose and cheek.

Vorenus cried out in a gasp that brought up the taste of iron, but he didn't let go. Instead, he twisted even harder, rolling his own body like a barrel so that the next strike, if it came, would hit the back of his head.

It did, but Vorenus was ready. His vision swam for a moment, but he held fast, and his own feet, somehow, found firm grip on a bare spot on the floor. Pulling down on the assassin's foot even as he pushed up with his own, he flung himself on top of the younger man and slammed his fist down into the side of his head. Laenas responded with a blind, upward jab of his elbow that struck Vorenus in the stomach. Vorenus coughed the air out of his lungs but still managed to raise up his other fist and bring it down into the man's scar-twisted mouth. Teeth splintered inward.

The assassin's jaw clenched, biting hard into one of Vorenus' fingers. Somehow he'd managed to pull a short knife with his other hand, and he swung it up as best he could. Vorenus twisted away and managed to avoid the worst of it, but even so he felt the searing wet of a slash across his ribs. Another strike wouldn't miss, he was sure. Another strike would take his gut.

With one hand Vorenus grabbed the sweat-slicked back of the assassin's skull while his other took hold of his jaw. Keeping his weight as far forward on his body as he could, he yanked up on the man's head. Then, with the full force of his remaining strength, he slammed it down into the floor.

Snapping bones cracked loudly over the grunts of the two struggling men. The assassin's legs bucked hard, and his body convulsed once, twice, before it fell still. Then only the muscles of his scarred cheek seemed to twitch, shimmering in the moonlight.

Vorenus rolled off of him, gasping as he flopped down to the floor. He pushed himself back a few feet, somehow caught motion out of the corner of his eye.

It was Selene, framed by the backlight in the doorway. She was holding his fallen gladius in her hand, and he could not see her face.

"Sword," he coughed out, raising his hand toward her. Bits of sticky papyrus clung to his arm, dangling strangely.

Selene took a step backward, hesitated, then came forward in a rush to hand him the blade.

Even close, Vorenus couldn't see her face, but he was certain she'd been crying. He tried to smile reassuringly, hoping that his mouth wasn't full of blood. "It's okay, Selene. It's okay now." And then, because he didn't want her to watch and couldn't think of what else to tell her, he said: "Go get Pullo."

Selene's mouth opened as if she wanted to say something, but it closed again and she backed partway out of the room before turning and hurrying away out of sight.

Vorenus felt pain from seemingly every part of his body threatening to overrun his senses.

Not yet, he told himself. Just a little longer.

He staggered to his knees, forced to close his eyes hard against the screaming of his nerves as he did so. For several heartbeats he teetered there before he steadied himself enough to stand and open his eyes again.

Laenas was still alive, but his limbs were stilled. His head, though, was trembling slightly. Vorenus saw that the man's eyes, though wide in shock, managed to focus on him. Something like agreement passed between them.

"May the gods welcome you," Vorenus said. Then, as quickly and efficiently as he could, he placed the point of his gladius above the man's heart and pressed downward until the tip bit the solid floor.

The glint in the man's eyes softened, and his trembling stopped. Vorenus pulled the blade free.

Didymus had returned to his senses during the fight, managing to back himself toward the corner away from the melee. He was sitting with his back against the wall, his knees drawn up in front of him, holding his head. His eyes were rooted on the dead assassin, and the look on his face was one of sheer horror.

Vorenus stepped over the body, limped over to stand in front of him. He raised his sword like an outstretched finger pointing at the librarian's soul. The gore on it was shining as it drew toward the point and dripped down onto the strewn papers. "Now," he said. "Give me one good reason not to send you with him."

For several seconds Didymus made no reply. Then his eyes blinked, raised up from the corpse. "I've none."

"I heard," Vorenus said. He felt his stomach rising in an urge to vomit and knew it wasn't for the sight of the blood or the pain in his aged body. "How could you?"

Didymus shook his head dully. "Just finish it," he said. "Be quick."

"Vorenus?" Pullo said.

Vorenus turned back toward the hallway, saw Pullo filling the doorway, his shoulders touching both sides of the frame. The sword in his hand was slowly lowering as he took in the scene. At his other side he held Selene in one massive arm, the girl huddled against his chest and looking back over her shoulder, through her hair, at Vorenus and her teacher.

Seeing her, Vorenus lowered his sword, too, and tried to smile again. "Pullo," he said, his voice cracking with pain. "Need to see to Heli—"

"He's fine. Philadelphus, too," Pullo said. His eyes were riveted on Didymus. "What's going on, Vorenus?"

Vorenus swallowed hard, looked back to the traitor. "Just one reason," he whispered.

Didymus had been staring at Pullo and Selene, too. When his gaze returned to Vorenus, his eyes were full of tears. "I'd die for her," he said.

Vorenus let out a breath that he didn't know he'd been holding. Pain, too long held at bay, rushed forward into his skull. He leaned over against the wall. "Didymus hit his head, Pullo." The wall under his weight seemed like it was falling away. He leaned further toward it. "Needs help."

"Vorenus, I think you—" he heard Pullo say, but then he was falling over to the floor, or the floor was rising up to meet him. And Didymus, his old friend, was reaching out to catch him.

9

A Show of Power

NEAR SICILY, 32 BCE

A week out of Portus Julius, Juba stood near the prow of Octavian's massive quinquereme, watching the undulating waters of the sea slip under the iron ram at the front of the wooden hull as the hundreds of men rowing beneath her deck labored to pull them all closer and closer to Greece. He'd been on oar-driven ships before, but never one of this size: there were three hundred oarsmen belowdecks rhythmically moving 184 oars in three stacked rows. Their steady back-and-forth thumped like the pulse of a heart in the wood, a constant beat that Juba was only now beginning to be able to ignore. There were close to a hundred legionary marines milling about on board, too, spending most of their time lounging on deck, obsessively tending to their gear and trading boisterous, often uncouth stories.

The wide quinquereme, Juba knew, could hold far more men-at-arms. The dozens of vessels spread out on the sea around them—mostly smaller triremes and biremes—were certainly loaded to overflowing. Their ship's lesser load was no doubt due to having the Imperator on board, which also dictated the presence of a dozen of the impassive praetorian guards who accompanied Octavian everywhere these days, and whose watchful gaze Juba had come more and more to fear.

Though never speaking the threat aloud, Octavian's intentions were clear: Juba no longer had his freedom, and he was fortunate to still have his life. Octavian had never been a man given to trust others, nor was he a man quick to forgive those who'd betrayed that trust. And even when he forgave, he was—once wronged—a man who without question never forgot. That Juba had survived losing Octavian's trust was something that he'd spent the better part of the weeks since Quintus' death thinking about.

If nothing else, reflecting on Octavian's motives helped keep his mind from the memories of that afternoon: the sound of the screaming, the sight of the spasms, the smell of the surging blood.

Juba shook his head, focusing his senses once more on the wide sea. So why had Octavian spared him? It was certain that Octavian still didn't know how far Juba had betrayed him. He didn't know about Alexandria and the Scrolls of Thoth, about his search for the Ark of the Covenant. Perhaps he still wanted to think the best of his young stepbrother, never believing that little Juba could be as two-faced as Janus, the god of beginnings and endings.

Juba suspected, too, that his continued existence was proof that Octavian had not managed to use the Trident himself. The Imperator of Rome had kept the weapon under his own control—for mutual safekeeping, he insisted—ever since he'd forced Juba to use its powers to rip the helpless, innocent slave into red shreds of flesh. Octavian had been attentive to Juba's actions then, just as he'd been on each occasion that they'd met and he'd asked Juba to practice the Trident's control. Without doubt, he was seeking the secret that made it come alive in the younger man's hands, the secret that kept Quintus from being able to do it. The secret that kept Octavian, perhaps, from doing it himself.

Refusing to use the Trident in front of Octavian was not an option, of course. After all, Juba's ability to use it might well be the one reason he was still alive. So at best he could only try to provide false leads for Octavian's search: flexing his muscles this way or that, whispering gibberish beneath his breath as the power began to flow up and out, or entwining his fingers just so as they wrapped around the metallic snakes of the staff. Each trick, each twist, gave Octavian another bit of information to consider if he ever attempted to master the device. And so Juba bought time. It wasn't much, and it couldn't last forever, but it was time nonetheless. Time to think. Time to plan. Time to hope for good news from Alexandria, to hope the Scrolls would soon be in his possession, the greater power of the Ark soon to follow.

A dark shape was moving beneath the water in front of their rolling wake, and Juba raised his hand to his eyes to see it clearly. He'd seen something similar when he'd set sail for Numidia, and he remembered thinking, in youthful wonderment only months gone, that it might be the hand of Triton come to crush them all. But then, as now, it was only a dolphin. Looking out into the sea, he saw it break the surface, its smooth gray back glimmering as it lunged in and out of their artificial wave in an exuberant dance. Watching it, Juba was reminded once more that not everything was what it seemed. Triton's merciless hand or a frolicking dolphin: the truth was known only when it was exposed.

Not unlike Octavian.

Not unlike him.

The other men on board saw the dolphin now, too, and a

great cry of elation went up. Such beasts, it seemed, were a sign of good fortune on their voyage.

Standing apart from the men who cluttered the rail to cheer the jumping, diving dolphin, Juba looked back along the length of the quinquereme and saw Octavian moving in his direction. No real soldier himself, the Imperator nevertheless moved easily among the veteran fighters. Juba could see that he'd adopted the mantle of Caesar's power well. Even the grizzled men seemed to accept him.

"How are you, brother?" Octavian asked when he was close. His smile was the same warm, friendly smile he'd had when Juba was just an excitable child, the same smile he'd had when he'd asked Juba to move the slave's blood. Not everything was what it seemed.

"Well enough," Juba said, trying to sound as if he meant it. "I think I'm starting to get my sea legs under me."

A couple marines standing nearby chuckled—Juba's seasickness in the early days of their voyage had been a source of much amusement to the more seasoned soldiers—but they were quick to catch themselves. With nods to Octavian, they backed away from the prow, leaving the two adopted sons of Caesar alone.

"I'm glad," Octavian said. He leaned against the vacated rail. "I've missed your input with the other generals."

"I don't want to disappoint you," Juba said, meaning every word. "I do wonder, though, what useful plans can be made when we know nothing yet of where our battle will be fought. We drive for Greece, I know, but the ground where we will fight there isn't yet known."

Octavian let out a little laugh. "This is why I miss you, Juba. As I told you back in Rome: I need you to keep me in check with reality. You see the truth of it in a way these old soldiers do not. You see the truth of it just like our father did."

The compliment was so unexpected, stated so matter-of-factly, that Juba's head actually turned. "Like Caesar?"

Octavian smiled, but his eyes didn't leave the sea. He appeared to be looking at a bireme nearby, a much smaller vessel. "You're too young to remember how he thought. It's one thing to read of his mind, it was quite another to see it. Always one step ahead. Seeking answers to questions not yet asked. Asking questions not yet considered. Whatever else he was, whatever else people might have thought of him, there was no doubting he was brilliant. And, yes, you remind me of him in that way."

Juba thought a long time before he replied. "I don't know what to say."

"Say nothing, for it's only the truth. These generals ponder and debate this tactic and that decision when no facts are known, when the ground, as you say, is undetermined."

"If it is to be ground," Juba said.

Octavian looked over at the younger man. "What do you mean?"

"Well, Antony is the finest general Rome has—or had. You said so yourself, remember? And with Egypt added to his legions, he may even have the bigger army."

"One reason we're moving for Greece so quickly. Before he can gather himself."

"Of course. But I wonder if this is enough to undo his advantages." Juba paused before taking the calculated plunge. "I wonder if we might be better off to keep the fight on the waves."

Octavian stared at Juba for a long moment. "Antony will have bigger ships."

"Yes, but ours will be faster, and we should have more of them. Speed and numbers beat size."

Octavian frowned a little. "The Roman way is to fight on land."

Juba shrugged, seeing it all unfold before his mind's eye. "That, too, will probably come. But there's no reason to fight Antony at his strongest. Force him to fight on the water first. And even then sit back. Refuse to give battle at close quarters." Juba paused to lean a bit farther over the rail, gesturing to the iron ram cutting through the water just beneath the quinquereme's prow. "Antony will try to ram us down, no doubt. It was the Carthaginian way, it's been our way: build up speed to cave in the side of the enemy's vessel and send him to the depths. Like you said, he has bigger ships. It's precisely what he'll try to do. But most of our ships will be like that little ship out there. Biremes or triremes. So we use our maneuverability to get out of the way, to stand back and rain fire from afar. Only when he's weak should we close in and go for the kill. We use our advantage."

Octavian's frown had gradually turned to a grin as Juba talked. When the younger man was done, Octavian's eyes were sparkling with delight. "You'd make our father proud," he said.

Juba's smile was more sheepish. "Well, it's just an idea, anyway."

"No, it's a great idea," Octavian reassured him. "As you said, 'use our advantage.'"

Juba agreed. "Leave nothing to chance," he said.

Octavian's smile grew even wider, and his gaze returned to the little bireme cutting the waters about a stadium away. "Our every advantage, no?"

Something about his stepbrother's smile, his tone, and his unbridled enthusiasm, made Juba's heart stop cold. He said nothing.

"Yes. Every advantage," Octavian repeated, as if Juba had agreed. "You said you're feeling better now, didn't you?"

Juba had to force himself not to bite his own lip. "Not perfect. But better."

"Excellent." Octavian pushed himself away from the rail, took two steps toward the rear of the ship, and gestured to someone.

It took Juba a moment or two to spy the recipient of the signal, but soon enough there was no doubt: five of Octavian's personal praetorian guardsmen were moving forward, one man surrounded by four. Even from nearly the full length of the ship, Juba could see that the man in the middle was carrying the shrouded bundle of the Trident in his arms. The sight of it, so welcome once, now made him want to weep.

Octavian whispered something to the praetorians after he took the Trident. At once the five men took up positions immediately surrounding the two adopted sons of Caesar. As Juba watched, more praetorians—raised by some unseen signal—came forward to join them. It took Juba the better part of a minute before he realized what they were doing.

"Why are they shielding us from view?" he asked.

Octavian was carefully unwrapping the Trident, and Juba noted that the cloth was not wrapped in the same way as when he himself had last finished using it. He wondered if Octavian had indeed tried to use it. "We want to keep our secrecy, do we not?"

"Of course," Juba said, unable to shake the sinking feeling in his stomach.

When the Trident was finally revealed beneath the bright sun, Juba took in his breath instinctively. The metal sparkled in the light: gold, bronze, and silver. And among it all was the blacker-than-black stone in its casing, its darkness lending even more brilliance to the surrounding metalwork. The woodworker's repair work, Juba thought grimly, was beyond description. The staff shined.

Octavian, too, gazed at it longingly, a look that Juba had no doubt had been repeated often over the past few weeks. At length the Imperator handed the Trident over to Juba, only hesitating a moment before letting it go. "So," he said. "Cups, jars, barrels. Child's play, I should think."

Juba nodded dumbly, forcing his mind to cease inserting other words into his stepbrother's list. *Quintus. Man. Body. Blood.*

"Neptune is the god of the sea. This, his domain. This, his Trident." Octavian chuckled quietly, as if thinking of an old joke. "Assuming he doesn't appear to snatch it away, let's see what it can do, shall we?"

Juba looked from the gleaming metal Trident to the long stretches of surrounding sea, littered with rowing vessels like so many insects crawling upon the water. His feeling of dread, though he would not have believed it possible, grew deeper. "I don't—"

Octavian clapped him on the back, forcing him to square up to the railing and the sea beyond. The little bireme bobbed in front of them. "So coy," he said. "Yet so keen on the best strategies of war. It's a strange mix, brother."

Juba feigned ignorance of his meaning, wondering if he'd really felt the Trident wiggle in anticipation beneath his hands.

Octavian leaned over his shoulder, arm outstretched as if they were on the hunt and he was eyeing a hare in the brush. His finger lined up perfectly with the exact center of the bireme, causing Juba to swallow hard. "Let's see you sink it," he said. His voice was calm, as if the bireme, with its six dozen rowers working belowdecks and its forty-odd legionary marines atop it, were just another barrel. "A rising wave, perhaps? Or the opening of the sea? It's up to you."

Juba locked his eyes on the bireme to avoid looking at Octavian, to avoid glancing around at the entrapping praetorian guard. Even so, he tried to keep his eyes unfocused, to keep from seeing the individual men moving on the distant deck, the faces as they talked and laughed under the warm Mediterranean sun. *No*, his mind screamed. *No*.

Octavian had leaned back, was watching with sharp interest. "Use your imagination, lad. I'm sure you've thought about it."

Juba's fists tightened on the wooden staff to keep from shaking. That he had indeed thought about it was something he still couldn't admit to himself. How could Octavian have known? "I—"

"We need to know if it works. As a matter of strategy. Imagine being able to drown Antony and that Egyptian whore Cleopatra," Octavian said, almost spitting the names of his enemies. "Imagine ending it all at once, in one wall of your power. Saving Rome. Saving the lives of these thousands of other men. Perhaps my own. Perhaps *your* own."

Juba wasn't sure if it was a threat or not, but everything in his being told him to treat it as one. "But, Octavian, I don't think—"

"Oh, but I think you can," Octavian said. "And you will. Now."

Juba swallowed hard, felt his head nodding agreement over the cries of his conscience. His hands, too, seemed to be moving of their own accord—turning the wooden staff until the head of the Trident was square to his shoulders and he could see, between the coils of the entwined snakes, the rhythmically surging bireme. And its men.

Dear gods, Juba thought, for a moment forgetting his own doubts about their existence. Its men. With wives and children. With dreams. Men looking to the blue sky. Men laughing with their friends. Men who couldn't imagine that the sixteen-year-old standing at the prow of Octavian's quinquereme held the power to end it all.

Juba's hands moved out to hold the weapon by the undulating snakes. He swallowed, whispered something without breath—not nonsense this time, but a silent prayer for their souls. For his own.

His muscles flexed. His jaw clenched. He closed his eyes. He felt the warming metal scales beneath his fingers and palms.

Down, deep down within himself, he found the stillness, the darkness. He opened himself to it, pulling it up and up and out until he felt the power like his own pulse, heavy in his chest, pressing against his ears.

Breathing carefully to keep his mind still, to keep the world and the thoughts away, he slowly opened his eyes and focused on the water between the vessels. He imagined his hands dipping into it, like a water-filled basin. He imagined lifting the water up and forward. He *willed* it.

The water rose, almost imperceptibly at first. But Juba felt it. In his mind, in his arms. In his soul. But not enough. He needed more. More power.

He dug deeper into the black, deeper into the stillness. The water rose, just out beyond the sweeping oars, like the wake of an unseen vessel: a rolling ridge easily keeping pace with their passage.

Still more.

Juba's knuckles grew white. His arms quaked. His throat constricted as if he gagged on something.

Then, all at once, the ocean before them erupted in a geyser wall. The sound of the sea ripping apart and up broke like thunder across the sky, a sound like the roar of Triton sounding his conch-shell horn. Many men dropped instinctively to the wooden decks of their ships, fearful that the wrath of Juno was upon them. Others only stared as the angry hand of a god pulled the frothing sea above the empty masts of Octavian's quinquereme and then slapped it away with a second crack of terrible noise.

A wind rushed against Octavian's ship, rocking it backward and forward like a child's toy. The few men still standing scattered, gripping what they could while the decks bucked and rocked.

Juba, lost in the darkness of his power, fell backward, his head hitting something hard that was not wood. The impact rattled him back up and into himself, into a world of screams beneath the still-blue sky, of angry waves fluttering out across the sea.

Juba's face was wet—seawater? tears? blood?—but it was the shaking of his body that concerned him. He could feel it like a distant thing, as if the whole of him was numb. One of the praetorians, he realized, had broken his fall. He could feel the man moving beneath his head.

A face appeared over his own. A face mixed with concern and elation. Octavian's face.

"Get him below," he said. "Blankets. Wine. Wait."

Something tugged at Juba's distant arms, and he realized it was Octavian, pulling at the Trident that must still be in his hands. He blinked his eyes into movement and saw Octavian pry open his still-clenching fingers and pull the Trident away. As he did so, the black stone rattled.

Octavian froze. Then, just as strong arms began to lift Juba into the air, the Imperator shook the Trident again. The stone was clearly moving in the spaces between it and its metal casing. Octavian's eyes went wide, moved to fix his gaze upon Juba's.

But then the world was moving, too, and Octavian fell away from Juba's sight. All he could see was the ragged sea beyond the rail, and the scattered fragments of the shattered bireme floating amid the bodies.

Juba closed his eyes.

10

Calm Before the Storm

ALEXANDRIA, 32 BCE

Even before Vorenus opened his eyes, one thought was clear in his waking mind: everything hurt. His head, his shoulders, his ribs, his legs. By the gods, even his toes hurt.

His eyes came open slowly—because the right one felt swollen and tender, because he hadn't the energy to open them fast—and his surroundings blurred into focus.

It wasn't much. A little room of desert stone, scarred black here and there from the flames of lamps that even now glowed quietly. There were two chests against the wall, two simple chairs, a few hooks for clothes, and two beds, including his own, crammed into the space. The other bed was empty. Everything was cast in the half-dark orange of the lamps. The air was heavy with spicy incense.

Noise came to him then. Voices beyond the door, too distant to make out. Footsteps marching somewhere far away.

The sound of footsteps closer to the door made a kind of

dull echo through the stone, and Vorenus looked over to see the door creak open. The sounds of the outside world grew louder for a moment—the moans of Egyptian priests, the ringing of iron—before the door shut once again and Pullo was standing there, his huge form filling the little room, a smile on his face.

"Ah, good," the big man said. "You're awake. I feared you a dead man. Thought they'd put you in wrappings, make a mummy of you."

Vorenus instinctively tried to rise, to show his good health, but at once his body rebelled. He moaned, laid back down flat.

"Not so fast," Pullo said. He leaned over in the dim and flickering light, pressing a big hand to Vorenus' less-bandaged shoulder. "You're only out of the fever, my brother, not out of the woods."

Vorenus squinted against the pain, was glad to feel it recede enough for him to talk. "Where—?"

Pullo let go of his shoulder, but he didn't move away. "Temple of Asclepius."

"Priests of healing?"

"Aye. Cleopatra's own."

Vorenus tried to take in a deep breath and cringed as his ribs rejected the notion. While he resorted to shallow breaths, he occupied his mind with sorting out what was going on. "How long?"

"A little over a day. Not long."

Vorenus was glad the fever hadn't gone longer. He'd seen men in a fever for days at a time. Sometimes, even if it broke, they were not the men they'd once been. "Good," he said. He stretched his legs out a bit, felt a warm ache in his muscles. "When can I go?"

"Not for me to say. Perhaps—" Pullo broke off and stood straight, looking to the door.

As if in response, the door came open again. The old man

who stepped through was not one Vorenus recognized. A Greek, almost certainly, wearing the same kind of linen wrappings as Didymus usually did—

"Didymus!" Vorenus gasped, his eyes wide in remembrance. He tried to raise his hands to get Pullo's attention. The pain was searing. "Didymus worked—"

Pullo looked down, once more placed his big hand on Vorenus' shoulder, to keep him from rising. "For Octavian. I know," he whispered.

Hearing Pullo say it somehow made it more real than it had been in his fevered dreams, and Vorenus felt raw emotion bubbling in his chest. Didymus, their old friend. All these years. He'd sold Caesarion—young, innocent Caesarion—to Octavian. For money. For power. For *books*. The reason they'd spent these many years in Egypt. The reason they were now outcast by Rome, the very thing they'd bled for all this time. Didymus, by the gods. Didymus.

Vorenus realized he was clenching his teeth, so he forced himself to relax. "Is he dead?"

"Not now, brother," Pullo said. He looked back to the slow-moving old man, who'd managed to close the door and was shuffling to the bedside, leaning heavily on a staff. Pullo bowed his head slightly, a proud and boyish smile on his face. "Told you he'd be fine, priest," he said.

The old man grunted, pushed himself past the massive man. "Awake, then?" he asked Vorenus.

Vorenus nodded. "Yes, sir. Can I go?"

"You may not," the priest said.

"He looks fine," Pullo said. "Believe me, I've seen the ugly bastard much—"

"One of us is the high priest of the god of healing, Titus Pullo," the old man said, his voice surprisingly strong and firm as he cut him off. "Is it you?"

"Well, no. I was just saying that—"

"One of us knows the rites of Imhotep and the ancient ways of Asclepius. Is it you?"

"No."

"Then be quiet."

The priest leaned over Vorenus. One of his wrinkled hands came up to pull at the skin around Vorenus' eyes. Then he held the back of his hand to the younger man's forehead. Vorenus noticed that he smelled of fertile earth.

The old man mumbled something in a language Vorenus could not understand, then he lifted his staff over the bed. It was a straight rod of wood, entwined with a solitary serpent—it looked to Vorenus' eye like a rat snake—cast of bronze. Moving the snake-wrapped staff back and forth above the sheets, the priest closed his eyes and recited more prayers. Vorenus closed his own eyes, too, trying to hear the words in his mind, to take them in as if they were the healing power of the gods themselves. Even if he couldn't understand them, they felt comforting. They made the pain feel less real.

When the priest's intonations were finished, Vorenus opened his eyes to see that the old man had returned the staff to his side and was looking at him plainly. "So. The fever is broken. Good. How are you feeling?"

"Tired. Sore. But alive," Vorenus said. "Thanks to Asclepius, I take it."

Pullo, who put little stock in such things as gods and priests and healers, made a quiet scoffing sound, but the old man ignored it. "Or Imhotep, if you prefer," he said. "We accept either name here. You've tired us all out in our labors to speed your recovery, though, Lucius Vorenus."

"I thank you, priest," Vorenus said. "I can offer—"

"There'll be no payment," said another voice in the room. Vorenus hadn't heard the door open, but as his eyes followed the old man's turning he saw Caesarion, leaning against the open door frame, arms folded across his chest. "It's taken care of," he said.

The young man looked even older than Vorenus remembered. He'd always been mature for his age, but there was a fresh worldliness in his eyes now. And his movements were more self-assured, as if he were more comfortable in his own skin than he had been before. Vorenus wondered what else had happened since he'd been asleep. "My lord," he said, trying again to rise.

It was the priest this time, rather than Pullo, who gently pushed him back into the sheets. "So I understand," the priest said to the young pharaoh. He pushed his snake-wrapped staff out to brace himself as he bowed deeply.

"It is I who should give you such courtesy, dear priest," Caesarion said, uncrossing his arms and coming forward to help the priest rise. "You've saved my friend."

"Not my help. The help of the gods. But I don't think he needed much of it, at any rate." The old man turned back to Vorenus. "I think he's a hard man to kill, this one."

"He is that," said Pullo from the corner.

"How long until he's up and about?" Caesarion asked.

The priest shrugged. "Another day or two and he should be moving. The worst of the danger has passed. It is only pain and the possibility of opening up his wounds now. A few weeks and he'll be fine."

A few weeks? Vorenus groaned.

"Good," Caesarion said. "That should be in time."

In time? Vorenus looked questioningly to Pullo, but the big man wasn't paying attention.

"I'll leave you, my lord," the old priest said to Caesarion. He looked to Pullo as he headed toward the door. "Don't push him now," he said, waggling a bony finger as if talking to an unruly child. "He still needs his rest."

Pullo's smile dampened so slightly that few other than Vorenus would have noticed. "Of course."

"Thank you, noble priest," Caesarion said, stepping aside to let the old man pass. "We won't be long with him."

The priest mumbled something as he hobbled out of the room, his staff clicking on the stone. When he was gone, Caesarion shut the door quietly. Pullo grabbed the two chairs and brought them up beside the bed, offering one to the son of Caesar as he took the other himself. Caesarion nodded to the big man gratefully and sat down, his shoulders slumping in tiredness. "Glad to see you up," the young pharaoh said.

Vorenus managed to turn his body to better face the two men. "Me, too. Thank you, my lord."

Caesarion sighed, but his smile was genuine. "Must everyone thank me when I owe them? First the priest, now you. We're all in *your* debt, Lucius Vorenus. If not for you ... well, you did your work well."

The image of Selene, cradled in Pullo's arms, staring as he prepared to kill her teacher, returned to Vorenus' mind. "So the children—?"

"There was only the one man, and you took care of him," Pullo said.

"My sister is scared, but fine," Caesarion added. Not for the first time Vorenus noted how easily the boy—the man— accepted Antony's children as his own family. He wondered why Octavian could not act the same.

"Was my fault," Vorenus said. "Had a bad feeling about Laenas when I met him. I should've insisted on a return to the palace at Antirhodos."

"Even if you had, my mother wouldn't have listened," Caesarion said. "She wants no one back on the island until all the workmen have finished. Did you know she's raised a statue of me there now? Right beside hers, looking like Horus. Massive thing. She means to surprise me with it, but you can see it from the docks. The head alone is taller than my leg."

"Quite an honor, Lord Pharaoh," Vorenus said.

"No, it isn't, Vorenus. You know I'm not a god, no matter how many statues my mother puts up. No matter what headdress I wear or what scepter I hold. No matter what the people think. I'm not Horus."

"What about Caesar?" Vorenus asked.

Pullo leaned forward, nodding. "He was deified, what, two years after his death? Makes you the son of god, does it not?"

"People like to think of the gods being like us," Caesarion said. "That's all. That's why they made my father a god. It makes them comfortable."

"Don't let your mother hear that," Pullo said. "Isis ... Venus ... I think she likes being divine."

"It's because she's afraid of growing old," Caesarion said. "Of losing her beauty. Of dying."

Vorenus shifted a little, felt the sharp pain of the wound in his side. "I'm afraid to die," he said. "I don't think I'm a god."

"No, but you worship them," Caesarion said. "Dutifully. Always have."

"The gods are not to be trifled with."

"He's been saying that to me for years," Pullo said, light laughter in his voice.

"Yes," Vorenus said, trying but failing to sound stern. "And I hope one day you'll listen."

"Bah!" Pullo pushed away at the air as if swatting away invisible bugs. "The gods have done little enough for me. I don't believe in them. Present company excluded, of course."

Caesarion rolled his eyes. "The fact that I'm not a god has nothing to do with the existence of any other god. Look at Vorenus here, healed by the power of the priests."

"Nonsense." Pullo patted Vorenus' leg through the sheets, ignoring his friend's wincing. "He's simply too strong to go."

"No," Vorenus said. "When that priest prayed, when he waved that staff over me, I felt something. The gods have power, my brother. I hope you'll see it one day, before it's too late." It was tiring to talk, but it also felt good. In some small way it helped to push the pain out of his mind.

Before Pullo could reply, Caesarion leaned forward toward the big man. "Look at it this way. You're alive, aren't you? After all your battles? All your fights? You're a good fighter, Titus Pullo, and a good teacher of the arts of war—for which I'm thankful—but skill alone will not serve in battle. You've told me as much. So how have you survived if not by the will of the gods?"

Pullo frowned. "Luck, I suppose."

Caesarion wouldn't let it go. "Do you fear death?"

"I suppose so. But death is death."

"For what, then, is the city of the dead here in Alexandria?"

"For the families left behind," Pullo replied. "There's nothing else there but offerings to rotting corpses."

"No crossings of the Nile? No Elysian Fields?"

"I've never seen them," Pullo said, voice defiant. "Nor do I know any who has."

"Must you see to believe?"

"Yes."

Vorenus coughed a little, wincing, but the pain subsided quickly. "You believe nothing you can't see, touch, feel?"

"That's right," Pullo said.

Vorenus smiled. "What of Britain, then?"

Pullo's brow furrowed. "What of it?"

"I think he's asking whether you believe in Britain," Caesarion said. There was a mischievous light in his eyes.

"Of course I believe in Britain."

"But you've never seen it, have you?" Caesarion smiled. "Never touched it?"

"No, but it's a place. It's there on the maps."

"Didymus has shown me many maps that have the realms of the dead upon them."

"And Alexander looked for them, I know," Pullo said. "But look at him now, in that crystal coffin in the Mausoleum. Dead. I've known men who served in Britain. We were near enough to it ourselves, Vorenus and me. But I don't know anyone who's really lived after death, if you know what I mean."

Vorenus closed his eyes to think, and the others fell silent until he opened them again. "Caesarion," he finally said, looking over at the young ruler. "About Didymus ... you need to know something."

Caesarion held up his hand—a royal gesture, Vorenus noted. "I know. I read the assassin's letter."

"You know?"

The tiredness, which had disappeared from the young man's shoulders as they'd bantered, was back. "Much has happened while you were asleep."

Pullo agreed but said nothing.

"You said something about me getting better 'in time,'" Vorenus said.

"So I did," Caesarion said with a smile, but the look in his eyes was grim.

"In time for what?"

"To take a ship," Caesarion replied.

"A ship?"

"A ship north," Pullo said. Any trace of a smile on his face was gone.

North. That could mean only one thing. "War," Vorenus said quietly. "And Egypt?"

"My mother is going herself," Caesarion said. "I'm to stay here in Alexandria in her absence."

"Cleopatra herself?"

"Antony didn't want her to go, you know," Pullo said. "But Publius Canidius convinced him to let her. I think he must have owed her a favor or something, and she called it in. She's taking the whole fleet, Vorenus."

The whole fleet? That would mean hundreds of vessels. Thousands of men. Tens of thousands.

"It's true, Vorenus," Caesarion said. "And you'll need to go with her. You and Pullo both. Your first priority is the protection of my mother—and Antony, of course."

Something in the young man's tone caught in Vorenus' ear. "You don't approve?"

Caesarion stood, paced in the small space behind his chair for a few moments. "I'm not the general Antony is," he said.

"Experience isn't wisdom," Vorenus said, trying hard to lock the young man's eyes with his own.

"That's truth enough," Pullo muttered.

Caesarion took a deep breath, let it out as he sat back down. "He is Antony."

"And you're pharaoh."

"As is my mother. And Antony has her ear. I'm just a boy." He rubbed tiredly at his eyes with his fingers, tried to stretch out his neck. "But to your question: no, I do not approve. I've told them so. Antony ignored me. Mother, well, she believes Antony is Osiris on earth, that he's invincible."

"Our young king here thinks we're better off defending Alexandria," Pullo said.

"It's far more secure than foreign Greece," Caesarion said, rising once more to pace. "Let Octavian have Greece. Let him keep Rome. Let him have all the world. Without the grains of Egypt he will in the end have nothing. With Antony's legions and Egypt's armies here, Octavian cannot force us to trade. He would, in the end, have to negotiate. Victory lies in waiting for peace, not in rushing off for war."

Vorenus smiled at the young man's logic, futile though it was. "Too long-term," he said. "Antony thinks only in tomorrows."

Caesarion stopped pacing. "I know. And that's why you

both need to go with them to Greece. They won't listen to reason now, but perhaps they will when the need comes." He seemed to gather himself. "And even if he won't, perhaps she will."

Vorenus blinked. He looked to Pullo, saw that his face was blank as he stared at the young man. They were sworn legionnaires of Rome. Antony was their superior. "I don't—"

Caesarion met Vorenus' eyes. "I'm not asking you to betray him, not asking you to betray your oaths to the legion. I'm just asking you to think about all that's at stake. To think, like you said, long-term. And then to follow your good heart. That's all."

Vorenus saw that Pullo was looking to him now, confusion on the big man's face. He felt a new pain in his hip and shifted again in the sheets, his mind racing. "We'll do what we can," he finally said.

"It's all I can ask," Caesarion said. He came back around to sit in his chair. "I'll take my sister and brothers to Antirhodos once the fleet has sailed, if we haven't moved there already. We'll be safer there in your absence. When Didymus needs—"

"He's not dead?"

"No."

"I thought Antony…"

"If he knew, yes," Pullo said, leaning forward in his chair. "He doesn't. Neither does Cleopatra or the kids. Only the two of us and little Horus here."

Caesarion ignored the jab this time. "Once you were in the hands of the physicians, Didymus himself took me and Pullo back to his room. He produced the assassin's papers. He denied nothing and revealed everything."

So that was where the new worldliness in Caesarion's eyes had come from, Vorenus thought. "You didn't tell," he said to Pullo. It was bordering on treachery not to report it to their superior officer.

The big man's cheeks, already toned orange by the light of the lamps and stone, appeared to darken. "Antony would've killed him. You know that. And we both know Didymus. No matter what he did back then, he's a different man now."

It was true. Vorenus had spared him, too, hadn't he?

"Besides," Caesarion said, "we need Didymus alive. If this Juba is really seeking the Scrolls of Thoth, Didymus is our best shot at finding them first. We can't let them fall into their hands."

Vorenus was getting tired, but he didn't want to stop talking. He needed to understand what was going on. "I heard Didymus say he didn't think they existed."

Caesarion nodded. "So he told the assassin. But he is, nevertheless, unsure. He's already combing through the oldest records of the Library, looking for information."

"All this for some scrolls?" Vorenus had been to the Great Library once. It was filled with scrolls. There were thousands of them. Perhaps thousands of thousands. Vorenus wondered if a man in one lifetime could count them all.

"You don't know what they are," Caesarion said. "Thoth is the Egyptian god of wisdom, the mind of the gods themselves, you might say. Thoth gave us writing. He gave us civilization. Laws. Numbers. Thought. The calendar. He's said to have set the very stars in their places. When Osiris was dismembered, it was Thoth who taught Isis the incantations to raise him from the dead. Without his words, it's said, the gods themselves might not exist."

"So he wrote a book?" Pullo, apparently, had not yet heard of this, either.

"More than just a book," Caesarion said. "The legend is that he poured the fullness of his wisdom into the Scrolls. Secrets known only to the gods. Secrets known not even to them. Magic and power we cannot imagine. It's said that if you read the first page of the book you'll be able to enchant the sky, the earth, the abyss, the mountain, and the sea. That you'll understand the language of the birds in the air, the beasts of the earth, the fishes of the sea. If you read the second page, you become immortal, and you'll behold the great shapes of the gods that are hidden. That power must be what Juba is after. If it does indeed exist, if it's here in Alexandria, we must find it before him."

Silence fell over the room. Vorenus rolled to his back and stared at the ceiling. Pullo leaned back in his chair.

"So," Caesarion said at last, "while you're off to Greece, Didymus and I will be in the Library."

"All the answers to all the questions," Vorenus whispered. "What if you actually find it?"

"We'll know if Pullo is wrong about the gods."

"You'd use it?"

Vorenus turned his head, saw that Caesarion's face was hard in the lamplight. "I'd like to think I could use it to preserve Egypt," Caesarion said. "But then I think I'd be just like them."

Vorenus nodded. A smarter man than any of them, he thought. "So what will you do?" he asked.

"The only thing I think I could do," the boy-king said. "Destroy it. We're not meant to know the mind of the gods."

PART II

THE BATTLE OF ACTIUM

11

The Waiting City

ALEXANDRIA, 31 BCE

Caesarion stood on the paving stones near the edge of the little harbor on Antirhodos, looking north and trying to ignore the two massive statues behind him—statues of him and his mother, the co-regents of Egypt, styled as gods. Though the gray granite structures were meant to welcome newly arrived visitors to the royal island, they did nothing but make the young man uneasy.

The rising sun was still out of sight behind the tall edifices of walls and palaces and temples on the peninsula of Lochias, but Caesarion knew its approach from the warming glow on the east side of the great Pharos lighthouse at the head of the harbor. That broad, sky-reaching expanse of stone was alight in red and white, broken only by the crisp shadows of architectural arches and windows. Atop the towering structure six crystal windows lensed the night's simmering watch fire to an eerie glow against the dawn light. Looking out over the harbor this morning, toward that mountainous pillar at its mouth, Caesarion tried not to think about the fate of his family and friends—his armies and perhaps his kingdom—far to the north across the inland sea in Greece.

The fleet had sailed with pomp and optimism enough. Caesarion remembered how Antony, standing tall at the prow of one of the finest Roman quinqueremes in his fleet, looked strange to be once more in the garb of a Roman general. He remembered, too, how Cleopatra sat in golden light amid the luxurious pillows of her chair beneath the shadowed canopies of silk that covered the rear deck of her massive catamaran. He remembered how the people all along the docks cheered, how they'd lined the breakwaters, flags waving in color, voices raised in song, to see the ships depart. Watching it all happen from atop the palace walls on Lochias, bedecked in the finest god-mimicking headdress his mother's vast wealth could procure, Caesarion had sat impassive as a rock—glad, for once, that he was not meant to show emotion. He'd held the gilded wood scepter upright, unmoving, until the last of the vessels, riding waves and goodwill, had entered the open sea. Then he'd left his throne, handed the scepter and the headdress to the safekeeping of priests and guards, wiped his face of the stifling paint upon it, and marched directly to the great hall of the palace, to the gathered commanders of the tiny remnant of an army his mother and Antony had left him. Within an hour of the fleet's departure, he'd begun preparations for the defense of the city. And half a day later, when those plans were at last done, when he was certain that they all knew their tasks, he'd led his half-siblings to the plain, unadorned boat that was waiting to take them to Antirhodos, where the workmen were still completing repairs to the palace—including the damnable statue of himself.

Caesarion yawned, rubbed at eyes that were thankfully free of dark paint. Though he knew his mother wouldn't have approved of his actions on the day of her departure, he knew that disapproval would be nothing compared with what she would think of his actions in the intervening months. He'd secured the royal isle as quickly as he could, leaving some of the workmen's labors unfinished, keeping the family's presence there as quiet as he could manage. Any emissaries seeking an audience with the ruling house of Egypt were made to await his presence at the Lochian palace on the mainland, the stewards there making whatever excuses they could manage until a boat—quietly dispatched and quietly returned—had brought the young pharaoh from the secure island. Worse in his mother's mind, he imagined, would be the fact that he rarely allowed himself to be fitted with the symbols of his station for any meeting, preferring instead to appear as the man that he believed himself to be. Only once since her departure had he accepted the full regalia and adulation of his supposed divinity: earlier in the year during the festivities held to celebrate the tricentennial of the city's founding by Alexander the Great. He'd abandoned, too, the almost weekly, exorbitant parades through the city that his mother had been fond of making, her heavy throne-chair carried on the bent backs of slaves, her hands equally ready to order a whipping or to throw coins at the adoring masses. Instead, his occasional trips to the city—his destination almost invariably the Great Library and Didymus—had been quiet affairs, in disguise as a simple scholar, accompanied by one or two of the loyal Egyptian guardsmen, similarly attired.

Caesarion glanced over to the man who would accompany him this morning: Khenti, the head of the palace's Egyptian guards. Of average height but stoutly muscular, Khenti often reminded him of a shortened, more deeply tanned Pullo—though only in physical appearance. Where Pullo was a man to take little in life seriously, Khenti didn't seem to possess any sense of humor at all. Stern duty defined him. Even now, on this beautiful morning, he appeared to take no notice of the beauty of the warming light on the stones, the soft flashing of reflections on the harbor. Instead, his eyes stared straight ahead, seemingly aimed at nothing. Not for the first time this early hour Caesarion regretted that the guardchief had volunteered to accompany him on this outing: Khenti looked nothing like an academic despite his scholarly clothes. No one working at the Library, Caesarion was sure, could possibly stand so stiffly perpendicular. If it wasn't for the soft breeze brushing the man's clothes and dark hair, he would have appeared to be another statue. "You really do need to relax," Caesarion said to him. "No one will think you a scholar."

"I am not," Khenti said, his Greek formal and well pronounced, though tinged by his native Egyptian accent.

"I know, but that's not the point. We want to appear to work there. To not raise suspicion."

"Yes. I understand, sir," Khenti said, though he remained unchanged in his stance.

Caesarion thought about pushing the matter but decided against it. He'd got what he deserved, after all: he hadn't had to agree to Khenti's request for the duty. The guardchief had many other jobs, after all, and he'd just finished overseeing the night watch when the message from Didymus arrived. Surely the man was tired, even if he showed no ill effects of it at the moment. Caesarion had been so surprised by his request that he'd agreed to it immediately, without thinking. He had no one to blame for the company but himself.

"You don't really have to go this morning," he tried.

"I know, sir."

"You were on watch yourself last night, yes?"

"Yes, sir."

"You're not too tired?"

"No, sir."

Caesarion knew his mother would approve of this kind

of empty exchange—it wasn't the place of mortals like Khenti, after all, to make meaningful conversation with their superiors.

Realizing he was frowning, Caesarion shifted his face to a smile and called up the Egyptian language he'd been learning in his spare time, the better to understand his subjects. "So why are you here, Khenti?" he asked, doing his best to mimic the general accent of the men as he'd heard it, listening unseen to their banter in the guard barracks.

Khenti blinked at the sudden shift of language, and his gaze actually flicked up and down over the pharaoh for a moment, as if sizing him up. "It seemed best," he said in Greek.

"You're worried about something," Caesarion said, keeping up his Egyptian, hoping his inflection was the proper conversational tone in the somewhat unfamiliar language. "Why? Do you know something I do not?"

Khenti thought for a moment, then turned to square up his shoulders with the co-regent of Egypt. His eyes were downcast. "My lord Horus," he said, at last speaking in his native tongue, "you know there is nothing hidden from you."

Caesarion felt like rolling his eyes, but he didn't out of deference to the older man's beliefs. "My dear Khenti, you know I'm not Horus. I'm just a man. Just like you. As much is hidden from me as it is from any other man. Perhaps more, if those who serve me will not speak freely their thoughts, their suspicions."

Khenti's gaze at last met the young man's, though Caesarion could not read the emotions that might be roiling behind his dark eyes. "I am sorry if I have offended my pharaoh," he said. "What would you know?"

"Why are you here this morning?"

"Would you have me speak in Egyptian? Or in Greek, as a scholar?"

There was, Caesarion thought, the slightest hint of a smile

in the corners of Khenti's eyes—though he couldn't be sure. "Egyptian for now. I can use the practice."

"Very well, my pharaoh." Khenti took a deep breath, a sight that struck Caesarion as notable, as if he hadn't seen the thick-formed man breathe before this morning. "It's rumored in the palace that the Greek teacher has not always been kind to my lord. It is said that he's *odji*."

"*Odji?*" The Egyptian word was one Caesarion did not know.

"Wrong," Khenti said in Greek. "Wicked."

"I see. And who says this?"

Khenti shrugged, returning smoothly to Egyptian. "It's rumored among the guard. I don't know where it started, Lord Pharaoh, though I've ensured that it has not passed beyond my men."

"And so?"

"Begging your forgiveness, my pharaoh, I think it is true what is said of the Greek Didymus. I do not trust him."

"He hasn't harmed me when I've journeyed to see him before. What makes you think it will be different this time?"

Khenti's face betrayed a hint of a frown, and Caesarion wondered if it was disappointment that his pharaoh did not see things as clearly as he did. "He has not called on our lord Hor—... on my pharaoh in two turns of the moon," he said. "I'm told he's been away, in Sais. And his message now is unexpected, and begging haste."

"You think he's been up to no good while he's been in Sais."

"I think it best to accompany you," Khenti replied, looking back in the direction of the island's small palace.

Caesarion's gaze followed the guardchief's, and he saw his half-sister and -brothers running down the stone steps toward them. Their tending nurse, Kemse, a black-skinned slave from Kush, the land south of Egypt along the distant reaches of the upper Nile, was running behind them, panting. They'd clearly given her the slip. "Caesarion!" Selene called.

"I think I'm not the only one," Khenti said in formal Greek, and then he was rigid as a statue once more as the children approached.

It didn't surprise Caesarion to see that Selene was in the lead. Though a twin to her brother Helios, the nine-year-old girl had increasingly taken charge among the younger siblings over the past year, exerting herself in the same kind of headstrong manner as her absent mother—never against her older half-brother, thankfully, but there was no doubt who was in charge among her and the younger siblings.

The three children skittered to a stop in front of Caesarion. Though not adorned with such gold and finery as they had worn in the Lochian palaces in previous years, they nevertheless exuded a sense of wealth and the privilege that came from it: finely woven and clean, unmarred linens, delicate bracelets, fresh-washed hair, and a softness of flesh that had never known labor. Caesarion had actually considered some remedy to the last of these separations between the royal family and their subjects. He himself was proud of the calluses on his hands and feet that he'd developed from the weapon training that he'd continued even in the absence of Pullo. Even so, he couldn't bring himself to force labor upon them. They were too young. And they'd already suffered so much, being confined to this little island, bereft of the god-worshiping treatments they'd known before their mother had left. At least the health of young Helios seemed to have improved after the move. Perhaps the air over the harbor was cleaner.

"What brings you out here this fine morning?" Caesarion asked. "Aren't you supposed to be studying?"

Kemse came huffing up behind them, bowing so quickly and low she couldn't catch her wind. "Apologies ... Lord Pharaoh ... I ... they..."

"We want to come with you," Selene said. The jut of her chin up and out was more than was necessary to look up at her taller half-brother. "You're going to the city, aren't you?"

"I am," Caesarion replied, waving away Kemse's still-stuttering concerns. "I have some business there."

"We'll help," Selene said. She looked over to Helios and knotted her brow.

"That's right," her twin brother said at the prompting. "We'll help."

Caesarion smiled. "I don't think you'd enjoy it. I'm going to check on the defensive works." They'd accompanied him on one of his trips to do just that, a month earlier. The experience had bored them nearly to tears. "You know how much fun *that* is." He sighed.

"No, you're not," little Philadelphus blurted out. Kemse gasped sharply, and Selene turned to shoot her little brother a glance that bore daggers. The boy wilted for a moment before hardening his face in defiance at her. "Well, he's not. You said."

Caesarion chuckled, tousled Selene's lustrous dark hair to cool her emotions. A quick look at Kemse told the slave woman not to think about scolding the little boy. "Ah, you've found me out, have you, little ones?"

"You're going to the Library," Helios said. "To see Didymus. We want to see him, too."

"I am," Caesarion admitted. He looked to Philadelphus as he gently corrected him: "Though I will be seeing to the defensive works beforehand." *Because the news from the north is not good*, he didn't say.

"We miss Didymus," Selene said. "We haven't seen him since ... well, it just isn't fair."

Not for the first time Caesarion wondered how much the children—especially Selene, who'd been so close to the events of that fateful night—knew about the assassination attempt a year earlier. Did they know Didymus had once betrayed their mother? Did they know how close he'd come to betraying them all? Not that he himself even had time to think much on such questions. If Antony and his mother failed—and the latest information he had made that possibility seem more than likely—he had a kingdom to save. These children's lives to save. Not to mention his own. "No, it isn't fair," he confessed. "And I'm sorry for it."

"You mean we can't go?" Selene's voice, playing at a regal bearing moments earlier, had fallen into a whine.

Caesarion shook his head, but before he could say anything Khenti cleared his throat. "The boat arrives, Lord Pharaoh," the guardchief said, nodding toward the harbor. "We should go."

Alexander the Great, the supposed god-man child of Zeus himself, the conqueror of the known world whose preserved corpse—still wearing his bronze breastplate—lay on display in a crystal coffin in the great mausoleum in the center of the city he had founded and named for himself, had done well in choosing Alexandria's location three centuries earlier. Every Alexandrian knew the story of how the Macedonian king, after defeating the Persians controlling Egypt and being welcomed by the native people as a liberator and savior, was said to have aspired to found a city to carry on his name, a city built out of nothing, a city planned to the last detail with the finest infrastructure of sewers, streets, and deep underground aqueducts that engineers could devise. One night, the stories told, he had a dream of an old man of hoary locks who called out to him, reciting from the fourth book of Homer's *Odyssey*: "Now there is an island in the surging sea in front of Egypt, and men call it Pharos, distant as far as a hollow ship runs in a whole day when the shrill wind blows fair behind her. Therein is a harbor with good anchorage." Alexander traveled to the island—where the Great Lighthouse of Pharos now stood—and saw at once that Homer was not only a fine poet, but an admirable architect. The island did indeed protect a fine harbor on the Mediterranean. And the mainland beside the harbor, where the city itself would be built, was a level and narrow sandstone spur separating the sea and the large inland lake Mareotis, which provided abundant fresh water, fish, and, perhaps most important, canal access to the Nile and the rich interior of Egypt. Even more favorable to Alexander's disposition was the suitability of the location for long-term defense. Since direct attacks by sea posed tremendous difficulties, Alexandria was, in essence, a city with only two natural approaches for any attacking army: northeast and southwest along the constricted strip of land between waters.

In the three centuries since the city had been founded, the generations of Macedonian rulers—self-styled as proper Egyptian pharaohs, Caesarion was sure, only in order to better control their native subjects—had not forgotten the natural defensive advantages of their position, though to Caesarion's mind they'd nevertheless grown complacent in strengthening the place. The city had achieved world-spanning fame and glory, fed by an unparalleled prosperity in trade between the Nile and the Mediterranean. But Alexandria's enormous wealth had more often gone into the construction of great palaces and temples, the Great Lighthouse, the famed Library that was aided in its growth by the wide swaths of papyrus marshes around Lake Mareotis, the bigger and longer canals connecting lake and sea, city and river, the new harbors on the many waters, or the great seven-stadium-long causeway connecting the mainland to Pharos Island. The walls of the great city, so carefully planned out by Alexander, had served more often as barriers to its outspreading growth than as bulwarks essential to its survival. So it was to the city's walls that Caesarion had focused most of his energies in the past months.

As he'd told the children, his first order of business, despite the Greek scholar's note calling for urgency, was to sail southwest through the Great Harbor, past the shipyards and the temples beyond them, up to the Heptastadion itself. The massive causeway connecting the mainland and Pharos had been cleverly designed: splitting Homer's natural anchorage into two distinct harbors—the Great Harbor itself and the less-famed Eunostos Harbor to the west—the Heptastadion was broken in two places by wooden bridges that not only served to allow water traffic to pass between the harbors but also could be burned in the case of an attempted land assault from Pharos. Caesarion and Khenti passed under the mainland-side bridge this morning, one of the oldest structures in the city, and they both examined the workings as best they could from beneath.

Alexander had built enormous water systems under Alexandria, deep canals that could be as wide as the streets that ran through the city above them. Caesarion saw the grate-covered spillway of one of the largest of them emptying out in the shadows just below the bridge. The little-used drain was flanked by twin weathered ledges of stone, each served both as a base for the massive wooden supports of the bridge above and as a platform to use the locked iron gates that allowed access to the undercity. At Caesarion's order, large clay jars had been placed alongside the seabird nests amid the wooden bridge supports rooted at each platform, and more were set just inside each of the gates. The jars would all be filled with a highly explosive concoction of oils and minerals, Caesarion knew, and he was glad to see that they were in place: if an attacker took Pharos he could order the bridge removed in what would surely be a frightening and deadly conflagration.

Caesarion and Khenti had paid the boatman to carry them along the southern coast of the city as far as Kibotos, the box-shaped harbor that men had cut into the sandstone at the mouth of the river that ran between Mareotis and the sea. The boatman, knowing only that his two clients were paying in good coin and were well enough connected to be allowed to set foot on the royal island, did as he was instructed, keeping as close to the breakwaters as he could. There were hundreds of boats on the sea here: trading boats moving out toward the open sea, early morning fishing boats coming in from the same, and barges of grain moving down the river to Kibotos, where their goods were being transferred to bigger, oceangoing vessels. Everywhere there was motion, including, Caesarion noted with pleasure, along the walls framing Kibotos and passing south toward the western Necropolis, the great City of the Dead beyond the walls of Alexandria. As he had ordered, workmen were strengthening the fortifications there.

Assured that his instructions were being carried out as intended, Caesarion whispered to Khenti, who passed word in Egyptian to the boatman to take them ashore at Kibotos. The Navalia docks on the Great Harbor side of the Heptastadion were far closer to the Library, but Caesarion was confident that anyone trying to follow their little boat this morning would quickly lose it in the bustle of activity at Kibotos. One couldn't be too careful.

Besides, with the increasingly dire news from the north, it would do him good to walk the wide, busy streets of his city again, thinking of simpler times, simpler fates.

And thinking, too, about what to do with Didymus in the end.

12

Cleopatra's Plan

ACTIUM, 31 BCE

Even here, on the relatively higher ground where Mark Antony had established his advanced base, Vorenus breathed in air that was rotten with death, seemingly held down beneath a clouded, starless sky. It was the stench of malaria, of thousands of men dead or dying, mixed with the thick heaviness of smoke that may or may not have been from the burning of wood. Trudging up the muddy road to the top of the hillock where Antony's sprawling headquarters had been erected, knowing that tonight their fates might well be decided, Vorenus tried not to smell it as he took stock of the situation in his own mind.

They'd had some 22,000 men—mostly legionary marines—when they'd first taken up their position on the Actium Promontory to face Octavian's armies on the northern side of the Gulf of Ambracia. Twenty-two thousand men, over five hundred warships, and a substantial portion of Egypt's treasury as a war chest, held in the largest of Cleopatra's own vessels on the water. There was hope, given Antony's excellence as a land commander, that the war would be hastily concluded. And since they outmanned Octavian by several thousand men, the hope was high on their side.

Vorenus stepped aside as two hollow-cheeked men came down the path, pulling a handcart. Three emaciated, slack gray faces stared out from the back, shaking in lifeless motion to the bounce of the wheels. Three more Roman dead from the malaria or the starvation or the despair—it was getting harder to tell the man-killer these days.

Vorenus watched them without emotion, without surprise. He'd seen too much of war to have much hope for anyone's future in the field. There were too many unknowns in the mud, in the blood. Too many factors that no one could foresee.

Octavian's refusal to engage them, for instance. Who could have imagined it? The armies had faced each other across the narrow opening to the Gulf of Ambracia for most of a few months now, yet despite the occasional minor skirmish they'd never met in battle. Antony had sent challenges. Octavian had refused them. Antony ordered his forces to build a bridge across the mouth of the gulf to bring his men up to this advanced position, on the same ground as his adversary. Octavian had just fallen back to the strong defensive positions he'd been building to the north. Fallen back and waited in quiet confidence.

And for good reason, they now knew. In a surprise attack, Octavian's admiral, Agrippa, had struck to their south, attacking the western Peloponnese with several hundred war galleys and close to ten thousand marines. He'd cut off their line of retreat and their line of supplies, effectively trapping them here at Actium amid the swamps and the bugs and the slaughtering disease.

Vorenus had not been alone in asking Antony to attack Octavian en masse as soon as they'd built the bridge. There was a chance, they thought then, of overrunning the enemy position before Octavian's camp and defenses were in order. They would push them back to their ships or die trying.

But Antony—confident, boisterous, arrogant Antony—had refused the advice. He'd sent personal challenges to Octavian. He called on Octavian's honor, on Octavian's manhood. The adopted son of Caesar met all with silence or simple refusal, content to hold tight the knot of the noose he'd settled around them: armies to north and south, and his more numerous fleet of ships—now that Agrippa's vessels had rejoined them—settled just out to sea, blockading the gulf. They were trapped, like a fox run to a blind alley.

Vorenus felt his jaw clenching as he watched the cart rumble away in the dark, and he forced himself to take a deep breath, to relax as much as he could. Not thinking, he nearly choked on the thick stench that rolled into his lungs.

Coughing the air out again, he shook his doubts away and started to walk once more up the hill. It wasn't his duty to question, he reminded himself. It was his duty to obey.

It was just death, after all.

Antony's pavilion had more in common with a Roman villa than it did with the ragged tents that most of his men—eight men crowded to a shelter—had made their homes these months. The general's quarters were solidly built: the cloth walls were framed square and taut with wooden bracing, the roof was tall and peaked by thick, stable poles crowned with flags that tonight hung unmoving in the still air, and the floor they encased was planked, perhaps the most rare but welcome of luxuries in an army camp.

The tendrils of smoke drifting from the roof venting and the slivers of light pooling out through gaps in the tent's heavy sheets of cloth hinted at the brightness of the interior, so Vorenus squinted his eyes as he approached. Aside from the many lamps that would no doubt be lit within the tent, after all, he knew the light would be amplified by reflections from the gilded furnishings and other signs of opulence befitting the de facto throne room of Antony and the queen of Egypt. Sure enough, when the legionnaires on guard pulled aside the entrance flaps to admit Vorenus, he seemed for a moment to be stepping into the sun itself as he blinked away the shock of leaving night for bright noontime day. Only through the practiced steps of memory was he able to negotiate stepping up onto the wooden floor and out of the way of the quickly closed flaps without stumbling or running into the legionnaire guards posted just inside.

As the interior slowly contrasted out of the light, Vorenus saw with relief that he was not the last to arrive. Insteius and Caius Sosius were already there, standing over a table in the center of the room on which was spread a rolled-out map of Actium and the positions of the various forces on either side, but the third of their remaining Roman commanders, Delius, had not yet arrived. Neither had Antony nor Cleopatra graced them with their own presences.

Not comfortable enough to approach the map table, and knowing it would tell him little he did not already know about the enemy that had enveloped them, Vorenus made his way across the rug-covered planks to a triumphal-weapons rack beneath a decorative legionary standard. Insteius acknowledged him with a curt nod, but the two generals otherwise ignored him, whispering over the map.

Vorenus abruptly realized that at least some of the lamp oil burning in the room must be scented: the stench of decay was only just perceptible beyond a sweeter smell that reminded him of distant spring, of flowers and the memory of meadows.

The flaps moved again and a half-dozen lesser commanders, men he was certain would stay silent as flies on the wall through the meeting, entered and took up places on the opposite wall, trying to look self-assured. New to their positions of rank, Vorenus knew. Death and desertion tended to do that to an army.

Behind them, to his delight, came Titus Pullo, who was forced to duck low to step through into the light. The big man blinked once, twice, and then caught sight of Vorenus. He smiled—as only Pullo could in such conditions—and walked over to join his old friend.

"So," Vorenus said, "you finally straightened out the watch, did you?"

"Had to knock a few heads together. But it's settled now—for all the good it'll do."

Vorenus nodded. They both knew the watch was little more than a formality, really. Octavian was content to let starvation and disease take a toll far worse than his legionnaires could manage. The men knew it, too, and they had grown increasingly hostile to standing guard through the night. But duty was duty. Even when it made no sense.

"Vorenus?"

"Hmm?" Vorenus blinked up at his friend. "Sorry, I was thinking about something."

"I asked if you'd seen Antony and Cleopatra," Pullo repeated.

"I suspect they're still in back," Vorenus said, motioning to the cloth drapes that led out to the sleeping quarters the two shared. "Probably waiting to make an entrance."

"Glad I'm not too late, then," Pullo said. He was still smiling, but it was a grim expression, and there was a deep tiredness in his eyes.

They were simply too old for this, Vorenus knew. A couple of weathered men, far beyond their usefulness. It had been almost three decades since they'd sworn allegiance to the eagles of the legions. How was it that they were now fighting men who were children back when the two of them were hacking apart the barbarians alongside Julius Caesar? And how was it that they were fighting a son of Caesar? What had become of the world? It was like he'd fallen asleep one day and awoken in a different life.

The flaps at the entrance shifted again, and the last of the remaining generals, Delius, stepped through. He was wearing his full armor of breastplate and greaves, all neatly shined and gleaming in the lamplight. In the crook of his arm he held his formal bronze helm, its horsehair mane neatly combed for presentation. He took in the room slowly, barely betraying sensitivity to the stark light, before he strode up to the map table and set the fresh-polished helm upon it. Face hard, he leaned forward to stare at the maps before he whispered something to his two colleagues. Vorenus saw in their faces a hint of displeasure despite their efforts to remain calm.

"It's true, then," Pullo whispered.

"What's true?"

"Walking here I heard a rumor that another of the magistrates failed to report for duty."

Vorenus frowned. "That leaves three?"

"Aye," Pullo said.

The sound of movement from within the bedchambers ceased the whispers in the room, and the guarding legionnaires reached out to pull aside the cloth doorway for the general. Antony, too impatient for such things, pushed through ahead of them, leaving the men grasping at the folds to keep them from falling back on the graceful Cleopatra, who glided straight-backed into the room in the wake of his pounding strides. Unlike the queen's, Antony's face was easily read: his cheeks were flushed with anger and frustration—perhaps, too, with wine—and his eyes flashed like a caged tiger's despite the circles beneath them. The men in the room snapped to attention, saluting crisply as he settled into the heavy chair one step above the floor. "Reports," he commanded.

Insteius and Caius Sosius exchanged glances before looking to Delius, but the third commander didn't acknowledge them. He was staring, features taut, as Cleopatra moved around to stand behind Antony's chair, her hips swaying beneath her fine linens and her wrists twisting to clink the ornate bracelets that wound around them like thin gold snakes.

Insteius swallowed hard before bringing his full attention to Antony. "My lord," he said, "Delius brings word that another consular magistrate has failed to report. We've only three remaining."

Antony didn't blink. "Malaria?"

Insteius shook his head. "No, my lord. He's gone to Octavian."

Defection had been occurring in massive numbers in the past week as men from all levels of the army went to Octavian's side. One more reason he was content to wait them out. The loss of any man was difficult for a commander, Vorenus knew, but losing a high-ranking man like a consular magistrate was a heavy blow indeed.

"The cause of this treachery?" Antony asked.

Insteius started to say something, but his jaw froze. Instead, it was Delius who spoke out, his voice strong and firm, coldly impassive. "You've asked the men to fight the son of a god for an Egyptian sorceress. Or so such men are saying," he added.

Antony's face darkened with blood, his eyes burning even more fiercely as he glared at Delius. "A sorceress, you say?"

"*They* say, my lord," Delius replied evenly. "I ... *we* ... believe that the queen's presence is, more than any other, the cause of the defections."

Cords were twitching in Antony's neck, and the muscles of his arms and legs seemed to be bunching as if he intended to throw himself down on his commanders, to throttle them with his bare hands. Before he could move, however, the long smooth fingers of Cleopatra draped over his shoulder, gently restraining him to his chair. "They believe a woman on the battlefield is"—her painted lips parted sensuously, seemed to work around the word in Latin that she was searching for—"improper?"

Vorenus noted that Insteius and Caius Sosius seemed embarrassed to look at the queen. Delius, however, remained as he was: proud in his armor, eyes firm and certain. "Yes, my lady. *Improper* is the word. War is man's work."

"War is man's work," Cleopatra said. She stepped around Antony and paced back and forth before the men. Vorenus, watching her sinuous movements, was reminded of something, though at the moment he couldn't place the image. "Do the men not realize their work would be difficult without the weapons they need to slay their enemies, the armor to deter their foes, the ships to bring them to their destination? Or is it that they have forgotten that all these things are bought with Egypt's coin? *My* coin?"

"Begging my lord's pardon, I think the men know all too well the influence of the queen of Egypt."

"The influence?" Antony rose, his temper ready to break again, but Cleopatra, passing before him, quelled him with a smile and brush of her fingertips across his wide chest.

"Yes, my love. They fear I've seized power over you. That you're not yourself. That I'm a ... sorceress, was it? Yes. A sorceress. And you, dear Antony, are subject to my spell." There was a dangerous undercurrent to the mirth in her voice, the seductive smile on her face.

A snake, Vorenus suddenly realized. She reminded him of a beautiful but deadly snake.

"It matters not, of course," Cleopatra continued. She'd returned to her place behind Antony, who'd calmed enough to sit back down. "Lost men are lost. What matters now is tomorrow. Does it not, Delius?"

"The lady speaks true," Delius said. He looked back down to the maps on the table. "We can wait no longer. Between disease and defection, the time to act is now. We should begin our withdrawal south, fighting through Agrippa's men on land as best we can. We'll lose men, but without—"

"No," Antony interrupted.

Delius blinked, his focus still on the map. Insteius and Caius Sosius appeared unsure where to look among the polished figure of their colleague, the seething general on his throne, and the slyly smiling queen behind it. In the end, Vorenus observed, they opted to look at each other. The lesser leadership in the tent tried to fade into the background of the cloth walls. Pullo just stared, looking tired.

"My lord, we cannot stay," Delius said. "Each day Octavian's opportunities grow. We didn't strike when we first had the chance here. We didn't retreat when it was clear all advantage to this position was lost. We cannot stay now."

"I agree," Antony said.

Delius looked up, something like hope on his face. "Well, since we cannot push north through Octavian's force—not now, not after these months of loss and entrenchment—we have no option but to move south and—"

"There," Antony said, cutting him off. "That's where you're wrong. We do have another option." He stood and barreled down to the maps, thrusting a thick finger into the sea just west of their position.

All three of his commanders were around the table now, staring. Cleopatra, too, had come down to the table and was resting her right hand between Antony's shoulder blades, her fingertips reaching up to spiral in the ends of his curly hair. Delius shook his head slowly, disbelievingly, but it was Insteius who spoke. "With the disease and the ... losses, my lord, we cannot outfit many of our ships. And even at full complement, we are outnumbered against Octavian on the water. Our men are tired and hungry, his rested and full."

Insteius didn't say it, but Vorenus was certain that he was also thinking about the same additional fact they all had in mind: Octavian had Agrippa commanding his navy, the greatest admiral in Rome. Antony, on the other hand, was a man for the land, not the sea.

Antony at last released his finger from the table. "You would have us retreat by land?"

"Yes," Delius said. "We would. All of us. South out of Actium. The army Agrippa landed is small and scattered. Enough to cut supplies, but not to stop the full might of this army, even hobbled as it is. We push south out of Actium, down the coastline—"

"And leave my ships here to rot?" Cleopatra asked. "My treasury for the plunder of that cold fish Octavian?"

"There's no retreat by sea, my lord," Delius said to Antony, ignoring Cleopatra. His finger traced the coastline extending west away from the base of the Actium Peninsula, on which their main camp was situated, resting finally on Leucas, an island separated from the mainland of Greece by a sliver of water shallow enough to be forded on foot during low tide. Vorenus had looked out to the island often these months, wishing Didymus had been around to see it: his old friend had a profound interest in Homer, and it was rumored that Leucas had been the Ithaca to which Odysseus so long sought to return. "The wind is running north to south this time of year. So any flight by sea means rowing west, right through Octavian and Agrippa's navy, right through the teeth of it, all the way out west of the island. Only then could we raise sail and escape. Better to go south by land."

"Go south," Antony said. "To where?"

"To fight another day," Insteius said.

"No." Antony shook his head firmly. "To die another day, someplace else. Without Cleopatra's ships our only hope would be to run our way out of Greece. And even if we manage it, where do we run? Through Thrace? Across the Bosporus and Bithynia, Cappadocia and Syria? And what will remain of Alexandria when we return, panting and sweating after our rather long run?"

Cleopatra's face was tight, but Vorenus didn't think anyone but him was looking at her.

"You still have friends in the east," Delius said. "Forget Alexandria. Forget Egypt."

"Forget Egypt?" Antony shook with fresh rage and raised a fist as if to strike the man. He brought it down, instead, on the map table. Vorenus felt the blow reverberate through the wooden planks beneath his feet. "My *children* are in Alexandria, you worthless sack of shit," he spat.

Delius' jaw clenched, but he lowered his eyes. "I beg your pardon, my lord. I spoke unthinkingly."

Antony's arm trembled as he pulled his fist back off the table. Vorenus half-expected to see a dent where it had landed. "There is no option," the general said firmly. "There is no choice. That coward Octavian, these coward defectors, this godsforsaken land ... there's no choice."

Antony turned on his heel, chest heaving for control of his emotions as he walked back to his chair and sat down. Cleopatra remained beside the table. "The plan is simple," she said, ignoring Delius' refusal to watch as her elegant hands traced lines on the maps, the fates of thousands. "We attack tomorrow."

13

The Tomb of Alexander

ALEXANDRIA, 31 BCE

Getting out of the palace hadn't been difficult. She was, after all, a queen and the daughter of a god. If she wanted to go for a walk outside along the water, if she wanted to look out over the harbor at the busy world around them, who would stop her? Kemse had tried to keep her inside anyway, but Selene knew the old woman couldn't force her to stay. So despite the anxious looks from Helios and Philadelphus—which were mostly looks of envy, Selene was sure—she'd left the palace for the second time that morning. It hadn't been difficult at all.

No, the hard part had been finding a way to the city. It wasn't far to go, of course, especially off the southern tip of Antirhodos, but she wasn't about to swim. The currents there were said to be far too strong to be easily crossed. And, even if she could somehow do so, it wouldn't be … proper, she was sure.

Unlike Caesarion, she couldn't order up a boat, despite the

handful of gold coins she'd nabbed before leaving the palace. She might be a queen, but Caesarion was a king, and he'd told them to stay on the island. The guards, Selene knew, would faithfully obey his command and prevent her from leaving if they knew she was trying to do so.

She'd been thinking about the difficulty of the problem, chewing her lip in both concentration and frustration, when she'd seen the little shipping barge pull into the island's harbor. It came a few times each week, bringing in full crates of fresh supplies for the royal family and taking out empty ones. The attention of the workmen had been on their labors. The attention of the guards had been on ensuring that no one set foot on the royal island. Between them, no one took notice of the nine-year-old girl—wearing a slave's shawl for a cloak—who'd ducked from pillar to pillar, then crate to crate before she slipped aboard the barge, tucked behind some already-placed empty boxes. And no one noticed when she slipped back off again, half an hour later, when the boat tied off along the buzzing docks near the temple to Poseidon.

Standing now at the edge of the docks, the noisy city stretching out before her, Selene took a moment to glance back across the water toward Antirhodos. She couldn't see it at first, there were too many men in the way: slaves and dockmen laboring under loads, tradesmen and merchants shouting, sailors laughing. She started moving a little to the side, to find a sightline back to the island, but she didn't look where she was going. A barebacked laborer, sweating despite the early hour of the morning, strode hard through the crowd and clipped her shoulder, sending her sprawling down onto the wood. She gasped, feeling pain in her hand and shocked that someone would treat her thus. "Out of the way, girl," the man grumbled, never looking back.

Selene stood quickly, spinning to glare at the man and instinctively wanting to order his arrest, but he was already receding into the seething crowds. Suddenly remembering her intention to hide, though, Selene lowered her head and looked from side to side this time as she moved out to the edge of the dock, away from the thick of the pressing flow of men. There was a sliver of wood in her palm, and she gritted her teeth as she worked it out with the fingernails of her other hand. A little bubble of blood welled up and trembled, bright red against her smooth and clean skin, before she wiped it away on Kemse's shawl. Then she looked back to the island at last.

Antirhodos was quiet. The red-roofed and white-walled royal palace gleamed peacefully amid the greens and browns of trees and gardens, and the few guards she could make out among the pink granite columns of the long east-west colonnade were standing at ease. Selene felt a pang of sadness—at first for the anxiety that Kemse would feel, but after that for the fact that they'd not yet noticed her absence—but she smiled nonetheless. If they hadn't noticed her missing yet, then she had all the more time to cut through the tumbling Emporium, which stretched along the water's edge from the Poseidium to the Navalia docks. She'd find a street south and make her way to the intersection of the Sema and Canopic avenues, the city's two great streets, where Alexander's mausoleum and the Museum and Library stood.

Selene turned back to the city, to the sprawling maze of stores and carts and banners and people that was the long Emporium of Alexandria. She took a deep breath, reminding herself that the hard part was getting off the island. Then she started walking.

The assault on her senses was immediate and filled her with wonder. To her eyes came the bolts of bright fabrics held forth by a dyer, the headless little animals held up for sale by a butcher, the strangely clad foreigners from every land. To her ears came a thousand voices from as many cities—talking, cursing, chanting, singing, or roaring with laughter—a rumbling of carts, an elephant's trumpet, and a ringing of hammers that echoed up from smoky shadows. To her nose came the scents of meat and men, of sweets and filth, and, everywhere, spices upon spices.

Selene tried to keep her head down and her shoulders up as she walked against the tide of sights and sounds and smells. She tried to walk straight away from the docks and the water, into the heart of the city itself. But unlike the easy grid laid about by Alexander for the boulevards of his namesake city, the little alleys and pathways in the Emporium were a confusing maze with no sensible organization, as if it had all been jumbled out against the shore. Twice Selene had noticed the crowds thinning and thought she'd made it out—only to realize that she'd somehow circled back to another spot on the shoreline and had to start over again.

On her third attempt, turning right where she'd gone left, left where she'd gone right, she was pleased to see the crowds thinning out again—but this time, the street below her feet was rising upward and simultaneously widening before it abruptly opened up into one of the wide, perfectly straight and paved streets of Alexander's design: a hundred paces wide, built atop an intricate network of aqueducts and sewers that she'd once heard her mother describing as the city beneath the city. Selene had never been down there, but it nevertheless had a hold on her imagination. Even walking now, she wondered if a person standing in the waters somewhere below her—and she was certain that people lived down there, probably hiding from someone or something—could hear her steps as they echoed down through the stones. They probably could, she decided. They could probably even tell by the lack of weight in her steps that she was just a girl.

Not just a girl, she corrected herself. A queen.

Her steps faltered then, and she nearly tripped. Would they care that she was a queen? Or would they only take her for a helpless girl, and do things to her that men did with girls? Or, worse yet, would they care that she was a queen but hate her for it? Would they take her away and parade her through a Triumph like Helios and Didymus had talked about? Would they strangle her then?

Pulling her stolen shawl close, Selene hurried her steps onward, deeper into Alexandria.

No sewer-people attacked her, and by the time she'd turned west along the Canopic Way, mingling with the streams of people and chariots and wagons, Selene was feeling more confident and relaxed. No one was giving the little girl in the slave's shawl the slightest second glance. No one knew who she was. And, unlike at the docks, she felt a kind of relief in the fact.

It helped that she also knew exactly where she was now. Two hundred paces wide, the Canopic Way was the longest, broadest, and most famed of Alexandria's streets, running from the Sun Gate on the east side of the city to the Moon Gate on the west, from the road to the city of Schedia on the Nile to the pathways and gardens of the City of the Dead. The parades her mother had enjoyed holding—like the parade after Antony had made everyone in the family kings and queens by donating so many lands to her and Helios and Philadelphus and Caesarion—were always held on the Canopic Way or its north-south counterpart, the Sema Avenue. She'd been carried down these wide streets in litters, on elephant-mounted platforms, in boats on wheels, pulled by slaves. She knew them well. Still, she'd never *walked* one before, and she thought it was interesting how different it was from the ground.

Her meandering path through the Emporium had taken her a little farther east than she'd intended, a fact made clear when she walked past the beautiful porticoes lining the gymnasium, more than a stadium in length. The home of athletes stood beside the Canopic Way, however, so she needed only to turn right and continue walking to reach her destination.

Everything seemed much bigger from the ground, without the pressing throngs of cheering people. The Canopic Way was busy with all manner of traffic on foot, horse, litter, or chariot, but it was wide enough still to seem relatively open. Buildings, too, seemed larger.

Selene didn't feel hurried as she walked down the street between the high walls of buildings fronted by columns, arches, hanging banners, and statues of gods and goddesses, kings and queens. A few of the statues were of her brother Caesarion, she noted with a smile. He would hate that.

There weren't any statues of her yet.

The heart of Alexandria, without question, was the great plaza of the intersecting main avenues that Selene soon saw opening up before her. Here, on the four corners of the plaza, surrounded by magnificent minor palaces, temples, theaters, and gardens, stood four massive structures. The first, which she began to pass on her right, was the grandest of the city's resplendent temples to the goddess Isis—to her mother, Selene supposed. The second, to her left across the Canopic Way, was the pyramid-topped mausoleum of Alexander the Great, where the body of the mighty conqueror was displayed in a crystal coffin. Opposite these structures, on the other side of the plaza, stood the imposing temple to Zeus-Ammon on her left—fitting, Selene always thought, given that this two-horned god was supposed to have been Alexander's father—and the enormous complex of the Museum on her right. It was in the latter, amid the many structures dedicated to the Muses, that she would find the Great Library, Didymus, and her stepbrother.

But because she had time, and because she was enjoying seeing the city from the perspective of her people, she didn't walk directly to the grounds of the Museum. Instead, she carefully dodged across the busy Canopic Way, feeling bolder and more grown-up with each step, and then bounced up the swept granite steps, between high pillars and the trinket men plying their wares there, and into the gaping shadowed mouth of the mausoleum.

Alexander's resting place was quiet this early in the morning. Other than the echoes of a few distant footsteps inside, and the quickly receding noise of the city outside, she heard nothing as she passed through the scores of pillars of the great gallery. She'd walked the length of this hall many times before, but always there were crowds to wade through, duties to perform. She'd never actually slowed down to look at anything. Doing so now, she saw that the pillars were wrapped with scenes carved in intricate, meticulous relief. Here she saw Alexander solving the riddle of the Gordian knot by cutting it apart with his sword. There she saw him on horseback during the battle of Issus.

Farther on, close to the end of the gallery, she stopped beside one of the last columns, one showing Alexander in distant India. Walking around the pillar, the tales of his adventures in that strange, far-off land wound out before her sight: the defeat of Porus, the refusal of his army to continue east toward the unknown edge of the world, the terrible battle in which Alexander was struck with a spear arrow in the chest. The wound was so grave, so deep, that his men thought it might kill the man they thought was the son of the father-god: it was said that it gushed red and frothed like water when the iron point was pulled free. Selene remembered how in the stories Alexander had looked down on his surgeon's finger pushing cotton into the hole to staunch the bleeding and smiled at the faces around him. "Behold: it is blood, my men, not the ichor of a god," he'd said.

Somehow, Alexander had recovered. He always did. Despite his many wounds, despite his insistence on being at the front of the line in so many battles, he was invincible. Like a living Achilles, Didymus had once told her and Helios, certainly not unable to be wounded, but just as surely incapable of dying from his wounds. It took poison to kill him in the end.

It was the best way for the conqueror to die, her mother had told her once. The best way for any king or queen to die. Not bloody. Not hard. And poison left the body whole, so that it could reign in the afterlife among the gods.

Selene left the pillar and passed through the narrow portal between the great gallery and the central chamber of the mausoleum itself: a square space wrought of dark stone, sided by free-standing, life-size white marble statues of Alexander and the Ptolemaic dynasty he'd founded in Egypt, her ancestors. Three hallways, at the moment sealed shut by wood and iron, branched off from this four-sided chamber, leading to the tombs of those men and women. In the middle of the chamber, surrounded by the seemingly glowing figures, Alexander's crystal coffin sat atop three polished white marble steps that gleamed in the light from the tiny arched windows that stood just beneath the pyramidal roof of the chamber. Selene noticed that this morning, in the bright light of a clear day, the light pouring through those arches blurred out the supports between them, giving the roof the appearance of floating. So, too, the marble dais seemed to be set apart: white marble on dark stone, with the clean crystal shape at its summit sending rainbows of color out against the walls and floor.

Alexander's body hadn't always been on display in such a coffin, she knew. For days after he'd died, the Egyptian priests whom he'd asked to tend to his remains had refused to work on the body. He was no mortal, they said. And indeed his body did not rot. But for his stilled chest, he appeared to be sleeping. Only when a week had passed did they reluctantly agree to perform their rites of death. And when they were done his corpse was placed in two nested sarcophagi made of thick gold. That's how they had come to Alexandria from the far east. And that's where they had stayed for generations. Until her great-grandfather, short on money, had melted them down to help pay for a mercenary army.

The people of Alexandria had killed him for that. His statue was around here somewhere. As her mother's would be. And as Caesarion's would be one day. Maybe even hers.

There were three other people in the chamber when she entered. One, a woman, knelt on one of the steps, paying respect to the body. And two men stood near one of the statues in the shadows, watching the woman and whispering to one another. Priests or quiet guards, she imagined. None of them paid Selene any mind. None of them knew that the little girl in the slave's shawl might one day take her place among the statues in this sacred room.

For all the times she'd been in the mausoleum, paying her respects to the man who'd given their family the power that it now held, she'd never looked closely at the body. The thought of death disturbed her, more than she cared to admit, even if she was fascinated by adventurous stories of battle in strange lands.

But not today. Today she felt grown-up. Today she would look.

Selene pulled Kemse's shawl close and tried to keep her breathing slow and even as she climbed the steps to approach the crystal coffin. The body, she saw, was smaller than she would have imagined. For all the stories of his power, Alexander was no giant. Probably no bigger than Vorenus, she thought. Pullo would have looked down on him.

Alexander's body rested beneath the glass on luxurious pillows in his royal red cape, and she was surprised to see that the man looked, as the priests had observed hundreds of years before, like he was merely sleeping. At times she'd seen other corpses in this mausoleum—those of her ancestors in the extended hallways, occasionally ritually rewrapped in ceremonial fashion—and always those mummified remains had appeared dried up, shriveled and hollow, with skin like old leather when it appeared from beneath the linens. Not Alexander. His skin looked as she imagined it did on the battlefields of his life: if not soft at least strong and real. He still bore color in his cheeks, lashes on his closed eyes, and his muscles were taut, as if he were ready to rise for battle at a moment's notice. The leather of his sandals and the wrappings winding up to the greaves on his lower legs appeared more aged than the dead man wearing them. And his hands, crossed over his chest, still seemed to grip the sword that lay vertical over his body. Taking it all in, Selene wondered if the priests who oversaw the tombs here opened the coffin to somehow maintain his appearance of preservation, or if his preservation was a sign that he was truly divine, despite the fact of his death. Certainly it was no wonder that the people still held him so, and that this room, even more than the street-formed plaza outside or the ornate palaces on Lochias, was the true heart of the city.

Not everything within the coffin was as well preserved as the conqueror, though. The sword in his hands bore spots of brown, and the exquisitely formed bronze breastplate under his crossed arms gleamed only dully where the sunlight danced across it. Strange, she thought, that the priests would not shine the metal. How it would shine and glow if they did! Like fire, she imagined. Like glorious fire.

Then, looking closer, she saw that parts of the breastplate still *did* appear to be freshly shined. Not much, but along the side, amid the shapes of muscle and images of beasts and battle cast into the metal, there were thin lines of burnished bronze visible, like thin, branching tendrils. Like vines.

No, she thought, tracing them with her eyes. Not vines. Veins.

His crossed arms and the sword obscured much of the armor, but she could see enough of it to tell where the veins were leading: to a single central spot in the middle of his chest. And visible there, right under his hands, was the edge of something dark. Something very dark and black, mounted into the metal: a flat stone the color of thick oil that seemed to swallow the light even as it fed the veins of still-polished bronze.

Selene shivered, feeling suddenly cold. She'd been leaning forward and she stood straight now on the step beside the body, pulling the shawl even closer.

It hadn't felt cold when she came in here. She backed down a step, forced herself not to look at the other people in the chamber. It must have been warmer outside on the street, she decided. And she'd spent enough time in here as it was. She needed to get to the Library.

Moving away carefully, Selene turned her back to the crystal coffin only once she had reached the floor of the chamber, whose stones no longer seemed so dark.

14

The Traitor

ACTIUM, 31 BCE

The starless, oppressive sky above Octavian's encampment matched Juba's mood as he sat on the uncomfortably squat wooden stool, pushing a stick through the dirt between his feet and generally trying to ignore the two praetorian guards on the other side of the fire. The praetorians, Octavian had insisted, were there to ensure Juba's comfort—and indeed they did tend to such matters as the building of fires and the many chores of camp maintenance that were second nature to campaign veterans such as themselves but were acts quite foreign to a young man who'd grown up huddled among books in the household of Caesar. That's not why they were there, though. Not really. He knew that. They were there to guard him.

The two men slept in shifts so that one was always awake to keep an eye on him, and they showed little interest in him beyond their duty of protecting him and keeping him ready to attend to Octavian and the real generals at a moment's notice.

Even after months of working with the serious military

men, Juba knew they didn't respect him. He remained, in their eyes, a dark-skinned foreign upstart. He'd never fought in battle. He'd never even swung his sword outside of practice swings at wooden dummies. He had no wealth to his name, no men to bring to the fight, no reason at all to be in the camp. Yet he was. And he was not only allowed a sizable tent—small though it was in comparison to those of Octavian and the field generals themselves—but he was also allowed to attend the most high-level meetings, where his voice was held equal with any in the army.

No, not equal, Juba thought, actually allowing himself a smile as he drew a caricature of a large-breasted woman in the dirt. More than equal. His voice, more often than not, carried Octavian's mind.

This protracted stalemate with Antony, for instance, was Juba's idea. As he'd told Octavian that day at sea—another day of many he was fast trying to forget—they would be foolish to engage Antony on land. That was Antony's strength. Combining his own Roman legions with Cleopatra's soldiers, he'd arrived in Greece with more men. And even Octavian, as ambitious and arrogant as he was, admitted that Antony was the finest general between their two camps—a finer general, perhaps, than even the now-divine Caesar had been. Octavian's military generals had insisted on a fight nevertheless, especially as Antony began sending his letters attacking their personal honor in light of their refusal to fight.

That they had refused at all, that they'd instead done their best to contain Antony's army without engaging it, was in complete accordance with Juba's designs. "Choke him from a distance," he'd said in one of their early councils, summing up his plan. And, despite the angry insistence of the generals, Octavian had agreed, correctly surmising that defection would further ravage Antony's numbers as hunger and the disease that inevitably followed close quarters took their toll. Thus, the longer they waited, the more they swayed even the advantage of sheer numbers on land to their side.

It was a good plan. And there was no doubt it was working. What had begun as a trickle of men crossing the lines from Antony's camp to Octavian's had, in the past week, turned into a nearly constant flow. The defectors were often near to starving, and at times already succumbing to the illnesses that bred in the bad air of the surrounded Roman-Egyptian camp.

Scuttling his vulgar drawing to keep the praetorians from seeing it, Juba peered up and out over the perfect lines of tents in the encampment toward Antony's forces. Antony's main base was across the gulf of Ambracia at Actium, but after he'd built his bridge across the gulf's opening he'd established an advance camp not a mile distant from their own. Looking out across the dark distance between them, Juba saw fewer watchfires on Antony's side: yet one more sign of the flagging morale among his men. And one more sign, too, that it wouldn't be long before the generals would again call for battle. Antony is weak, they'd say. Attack now, while there's still honor to be had!

Juba frowned, returned to drawing shapes in the dirt. Battle was the last thing he wanted. And not just because he thought it tactically prudent to keep their forces out of the fray: more than once Octavian had made it clear that, if it came to a fight, Juba could be made to use the Trident. Octavian hadn't managed to use it himself, but after their tests—Juba shuddered despite the warmth of the flickering fire—it was clear that Juba could use it effectively in a fight, whether sinking ships or maybe even freezing a line of men in their tracks.

Not that they wanted to use the Trident exclusively. It could detract from Octavian's glory, after all. And Juba, despite his practice, could only manage so much use of it before his strength gave out.

And then there was the issue of the stone, the black stone so carefully embedded in the head of the Trident between the winding snakes along the shaft. Though he'd managed little research on the Trident before they left for this campaign—by the gods, he missed his books!—the strange stone was the obvious source of the object's power. What it was, or how it worked, he didn't know, but it was the stone that somehow generated the Trident's power to move water. And using it—again, through means he did not yet understand—was draining that power. The stone had physically shrunk through its many uses in Juba's hands. Not much, but enough to worry both adopted sons of the divine Caesar: Octavian because he viewed the Trident as a secret weapon in his fight to unify the Mediterranean under Rome's control, and Juba because he viewed the Trident as his one secret weapon in his fight to avenge his father and his homeland—and not incidentally, as his one chance to stay alive.

As for Juba's own, more personal plans, they were not going well. He didn't have to look any farther than to the two praetorians across the fire to see that. He was, for all intents and purposes, under Octavian's control, his every move watched. The Trident was under lock and key in Octavian's tent. And Laenas, whom he'd dispatched to Alexandria to procure the Scrolls, which would lead to an even greater source of power—the Ark of the god of the Jews—had disappeared without a word. He could only be presumed dead, and any opportunity to send another man had long since disappeared, too.

Feeling a restless tiredness, Juba stood and tossed his stick into the fire. Though young, he'd increasingly felt a kind of weariness in his legs, something he'd begun noticing more and more since his return to Rome from Numidia. That this coincided with his increased usage of the Trident—of the black stone—had not been lost on his mind, hard though he tried not to think about it: whenever he did, he imagined leeches, grown fat on blood. The only thing that seemed to help was movement, so without direction he left the tent and began to walk, stretching his legs despite the uncertain looks of the other men in the camp. He didn't have to look behind him to know that at least one of the praetorians had stood, too, and was following.

He'd left the main camp and was halfway down the road toward the busy harbor that Octavian's admiral, Agrippa, had constructed along the coastline beaches, when a messenger arrived, panting. Though the young man appeared to be close to Juba's own age, and Juba held no formal rank or command, he nevertheless bowed deep and stammered out apologies for disturbing him on his walk. Only then did he pass along the word that Octavian—"the Lord Caesar, Son of the God"—had requested his immediate presence in council.

Juba looked toward the sea with longing, then nodded, turned, and began to trudge back to the camp, wondering what was so important that it couldn't wait until morning.

Even at this late hour, Octavian's spacious tent was a hive of activity, with a nearly constant flow of messengers bringing in reports and taking out dispatches. It truly was the headquarters for the campaign: all activity in the army spread out from this one central location, just as the actions of a body grew out from the mind. So when Juba entered the tent to find a flurry of comings and goings, of snapped salutes and creased papers, with the indefatigable Octavian explaining three different things to four or five attentive men at once, his first thought was that nothing was out of the ordinary. Even the pockets of higher-ranking generals scattered through the space, focused on their engagement of myriad duties as they carried out the administration of the tens of thousands of men at their disposal, seemed no different than they had on any of the dozens of times Juba had been in the Imperator's tent. Why, he wondered, had he been summoned?

It was only then, as he looked around the room for an explanation, that he found the obvious cause of his summons: a man standing at rigid attention not far from the tent's flaps. He wore the full battle dress of a general, as if he intended to take the field immediately: his armor flashed in the lamplight, and his horsehair helm was tucked perfectly in the crook of his arm. Only the inevitable splashes of mud on his greaves marred the perfection of his presentation. He might well, Juba imagined, be standing before the people of Rome in a Triumph—except that there was, Juba noticed as he took the measure of the man, a hollowness to his eyes. A man standing not in triumph, Juba decided, but defeat.

Octavian at last noticed Juba's entrance, and after a few final dispatches he ordered the tent cleared for council. In less than a minute, the only men remaining in the tent—and they were all men, of course, a fact that Juba knew was a point of pride for Octavian's soldiers as they looked across the lines toward Antony and his Egyptian queen—were Octavian, five of his highest-ranking commanders, the brilliantly dressed general Juba didn't recognize, and Juba himself, who tried to ignore the heated glares that three of Octavian's commanders shot in his direction. Bad enough that he was allowed to be present, but clearly Octavian had held up the council until his arrival.

There was no throne as such in the tent: Octavian preferred to sit at a simple chair—not so simple as the stool in Juba's tent, but simple nonetheless—that was positioned behind the central map table. The chairs of his commanders stood along the sides of the table, so that their war councils had, to Juba's eye, the appearance of a small dinner gathering. Octavian had been standing off to the side of the room when Juba had entered, and he let out his breath now in a long, tired sigh that seemed too dramatic to be real. Then he walked over to stand behind his place at the table, the rest of the men following suit. Juba's place was, as ever, just to Octavian's left. He walked to the spot without looking at the other generals and stood along with them in silence, waiting for Octavian's next move. Juba hoped it was an order to sit down.

"I'm sorry we've kept you waiting, Delius," Octavian said to the newcomer once everyone was in position. He gestured to the opposite end of the table, where a seat was left open.

Juba thought on the man's name a moment before connecting all the threads: one of Antony's top generals.

Delius approached the designated seat, but he did not sit down. His back straight, his chin raised in a sign of pride belied by his eyes, he thumped his free hand to his chest and then thrust it out in a formal salute. Octavian, his face serious, returned the salute crisply—another of the many small things he did for which the common men loved him.

"Thank you for receiving me so late, sir," Delius said.

Octavian smiled warmly. "It's no trouble at all." He gestured toward the tent flaps. "As you can see, we were still quite awake and at work. There's truly no better time. I regret only that our fires have already grown cold. All I can offer you is some fine Roman wine, fresh from the vineyards of home."

It was a subtle aggression, Juba knew. Antony's forces had been cut off from their supply lines for long enough that the thought of good drink ought to make the most self-controlled man salivate. A few of the other generals grinned. Juba just watched Delius.

The general's only reaction was a knowing, tired smile. "My thanks to you, Imperator," he said, emphasizing the title. "Perhaps later, if you will allow me."

Octavian nodded. "Please, sit," he said.

Juba wouldn't have thought it possible, but Delius' back grew even straighter. "I prefer to stand."

Gods!, Juba thought, but then Octavian was shrugging and sitting down himself. The other generals followed suit, and Juba gratefully took his chair.

"So," Octavian said, leaning forward to rest his forearms on the table. "To what do we owe the presence of so high-level an emissary, Delius? Has Antony sent you to call for my surrender?"

Once more there were smiles around the table. A couple of the generals laughed quietly, trying not to show disrespect but finding it difficult: Antony had so often called for their surrender that it had become a sort of joke between them.

"No, my lord," Delius said. "I believe he is done doing so."

"Another call on my honor to fight him man to man, then?"

"No, Imperator. I come of my own accord."

The sniggers of the generals ceased at once, as surely as someone snuffing a candle. Octavian's smile disappeared and his eyes narrowed probingly. "Of your own?"

Delius opened his mouth as if he meant to say something more, but his jaw froze, trembled for a moment, then clamped shut. With careful, deliberate movements, he withdrew the helm from the crook of his arm and set it before him as if on display. A half-breath later, he gripped the ornate handle of the gladius at his hip and unsheathed it in a smooth motion before setting it down beside the helm. His jaw was so tight with emotion that Juba wondered if he might crack his teeth.

Octavian pushed back his chair to stand, his own back straightening to match Delius' upright posture.

"I give you my sword," Delius said. "And my life, should you wish it. It is forfeit." His eyes glanced down to his bare blade, the edge shining in the flickering light. "I would have fallen on it already, but I wanted—"

"No such talk," Octavian said, interrupting him. With

quick strides he came around the table to stand face-to-face with the older general. "We'll have no talk of suicides here, my friend."

Delius had the look of a man on the verge of weeping. "I have fought Rome. My honor—"

Octavian shook his head. "Your honor is intact. You did what you thought was right. Nothing more. Come, Delius," he said, offering his hand. "Let us be strong in friendship now."

Delius hesitated only a moment before he took Octavian's hand and gripped it firmly. The Imperator of Rome smiled kindly and leaned forward to embrace the distraught man.

"You did your duty," Octavian said. "There's no shame in that. Just as there is no shame in doing your duty now that your path is clear." They separated, and Octavian held him by the shoulders, looking hard into his face. "I forgive you, Delius, and I welcome you to my council. Please, sit. Take your proper place."

Octavian let him go, spun to address the tent flap. "Wine!" he shouted. "Seven cups for my council!"

There was instant movement from outside the tent, the sound of feet moving in response to the command. Octavian turned back to the table, his smile genuine.

Delius had not moved. He seemed more in control, more at peace than he had been. "Lord Imperator," the general said. "There is something more."

Octavian's eyebrow arched upward. "Oh? What more?"

"News," Delius said. "Antony attacks tomorrow."

Several of the commanders around the table gasped, and they began to talk all at once. A soldier appearing at the door with wine was quickly waved away.

"Silence!" Octavian said, marching around to stand at his place once more, leaning over the map spread out before them. His gaze passed across the various representative blocks of wood upon it, signifying the latest information on troop numbers and placements. "He's too weak," he said. Then he looked up to Delius. "Does he mean to try and break out south?"

Delius' jaw clenched again, in obvious anger this time. "No, despite my advice that he do so."

Octavian bobbed his head in positive agreement. "It is sound advice, sir. We are too strong on this front."

"He means to attack by sea," Delius said.

A couple of the commanders started to speak again, but Octavian's raised hand silenced them. "Go on," he said.

"It is Cleopatra's plan, I believe," Delius said, his distaste for her palpable. "In the morning they will attack your fleet in two waves, hoping to destroy you on the sea since you'll not fight on land. Barring improbable victory, they hope to break your lines and make it to the open water beyond the isle of Leucas. From there they will hoist sail and flee for Alexandria."

There was silence for a moment as Agrippa, Octavian's admiral, moved representative blocks off the Actium shoreline and into the gulf. "Three and one?" he asked, eyes narrowed in concentration.

Delius looked confused for a moment, then nodded in understanding. "Yes. Antony will divide his fleet into four relatively equal parts: the first wave will have three commanders, the second only one." Agrippa began separating the pieces accordingly. The other men watched. "Heavier ships in back, including the treasury," Delius said, leaning over the table to correct him. "Cleopatra herself will command the second wave. The first will be centered on Insteius, with Caius Sosius to the south. Antony will lead the north flank."

Agrippa moved some more pieces around, creating an open-backed rectangle of ships framing the entrance to the gulf like a squared-off wave. Behind it, Cleopatra's fleet was a single line. He placed little flags amid the pieces, marking the place of the commanders. Once Delius indicated his agreement with the representation, the admiral began arranging their own fleets in a larger, encompassing crescent-moon shape, framing Antony's forces.

"Not a bad plan," Agrippa said, with the slightest hint of approval in his voice, like an artist studying another's work. "The wind will be north to south. Antony surely hopes to burst against it with a hard row, then roll up our own north flank, pushing us south against Leucas. It's not a bad plan at all, given what they have to work with."

A knowing smile had been working its way across Octavian's mouth. "Then Agrippa and I shall command our north flank," he said. "The south is yours, Marcus Lurius. And to you goes the center, Lucius Arruntius." Two of the commanders nodded, seemed to puff up a bit. "Agrippa will work out the rest of the placements, but we must have a mind to our overall strategy."

Lucius frowned. "Strategy, my lord? It is a naval engagement. Ranged weapons once they can reach: archers, ballistae, flame pots. Once we close in, we ram them as best we can manage, then board and fight." He looked around the table, saw approving nods from the other generals. "Right?"

Octavian, still smiling, sat down in his chair and steepled his fingers to his lips. Delius at last sat, too. "That is traditional, yes," Octavian said. "But have you a better idea, Juba?"

All eyes turned to the forgotten seventeen-year-old at the table, none kind. Juba swallowed hard, shocked to be thrust to the center of attention. He wanted to shrink down and disappear. "I ... I don't know—"

"No, you don't," Lucius said. "How could you—"

"I think you do," Octavian said, ignoring Lucius. "Indeed, we talked about just this, I recall. Not two weeks after we put to sea. You told me you thought it best *not* to engage in such a situation."

"Not to engage?" Lucius guffawed, but the few who joined him did so nervously. Delius just stared.

When Octavian still looked expectant, Juba at last managed to gather himself. "Lord Delius," he said, hoping his voice wouldn't crack, "am I right that Antony has lost too many men to outfit his full fleet?"

Delius agreed. "He'll likely burn the rest tonight. A few dozen, perhaps."

Agrippa leaned out and made a few adjustments to the pieces on the map.

"And Antony's men are weak, are they not? Lack of food and good water? There's talk of much bad air in the camp."

Delius nodded once more.

"Then, no, I don't think we should engage them," Juba said.

Lucius looked incredulous. "But they'll be even weaker than we thought! We'll have more ships, stronger men—"

"I don't think that's the boy's point," Agrippa said, still staring at the map and ignoring Lucius' animosity. "Antony's right flank, the one he himself will command, must row against the wind to reach us. His men are already weak. The farther we make him row, the more tired they'll be. If we back off, we'll have more time to riddle his decks."

"And have ours riddled, too," Lucius added, frowning.

"More than that," Juba said, feeling a growing confidence. "It's no secret that Antony's Egyptian ships are bigger, better than ours."

Several of the commanders seemed instinctively ready to defend their Roman-built craft over those of their foreign counterparts, but Agrippa was already once again agreeing. "Without question. Say what you will about that Egyptian witch, but she's rich."

Octavian laughed, and most of the commanders joined in, glad for the break in tension. Delius smiled, too, but noted that Octavian's ships were smaller and faster.

"Antony has raw power, we have maneuverability and endurance," Juba said. "Let's use our advantage on sea, just as we have here on land."

No one objected to Juba's characterization of their current strategy as a model to be followed, a silence that he took for a begrudging admission that his plan to choke Antony out had been a success. The affirmation, small though it was, gave Juba something to hold on to even as the thought of a battle on the waves—where the Trident would be most effective, most likely to be used—gnawed at his despairing soul.

"What do you think?" Octavian said abruptly, addressing Delius.

Delius was staring at Juba, who found it difficult to meet the older man's gaze. "I think you have even more strength than Antony can know," he said.

"Ah," said Octavian, smiling and clapping Juba suddenly on the back. "You have no idea."

15

The Great Library

ALEXANDRIA, 31 BCE

By the time Selene had hurried across the wide plaza where the two great streets of Alexandria met, the sun was nearing midmorning. Whether from the warmth of its rays or her physical distance from the mausoleum and the body and armor of Alexander, the girl had managed to put the feeling of cold behind her even before she entered the sprawling complex of the Museum. A series of buildings dedicated to the Muses, the complex had been a place of wonder for Selene even before she knew about the glories of the Great Library: the complex was filled with a staggering array of theaters, temples, observatories, lecture halls, dining halls, living quarters, and a broad walkway where scholars and artists from around the world conversed as they strolled. A place where study and sculpture, song and painting came together to erupt in the flowering of human possibility, the Museum was, for a young girl of Selene's wide curiosities, a place of dreams.

And that was before she was allowed to see the Great Library.

Built of white marble and stone, the Library sat in the middle of the Museum like the physical embodiment of the flowering within the complex: a six-sided, multitiered building crowned with a magnificent cupola that was itself mounted by a gleaming gold statue of a man holding aloft a scroll, opened to the heavens. Just the sight of it stirred her soul when she was Philadelphus' age. Now that she was older and knew what was within those six walls, under that exquisite dome, she had even more cause for thrill as her feet carried her through the gardens and pathways of the grounds toward its imposing shape.

Scrolls. Such simple things. She'd laughed about it when Didymus had first told them about the Library: so much care for some papyrus harvested from Lake Mareotis, carefully prepared and rolled into long sheets, then covered with writing. So silly. But she'd soon learned the power of the knowledge in those scrolls, and in the collection in her city. The Great Library, it was said, had been started by one of Aristotle's students at the very birth of Alexandria, and it had early on incorporated Aristotle's own library. Fitting, everyone thought, given that the philosopher had been Alexander's tutor in Greece. The growing wealth of Alexandria funneled into the institution, and the generations of rulers had given the librarians as much support as they could manage. Didymus had described to her and Helios how ships entering the harbor were searched for writings of any kind, which were summarily seized and taken to a series of warehouses nearer the docks. There the scrolls were read by young scholars, and any worth adding to the collection were transferred to scriptoria, where trained scribes efficiently copied them out. Only then were the texts returned to their original owners. Thus, their Greek teacher explained, the Great Library had quickly become the largest repository of knowledge in the world, so big that its collection couldn't be housed in one building. In addition to the buildings on the docks, the city's scrolls were also held in some of the catacombs in the city and in the small library behind the walls of the royal palace on Lochias, where the children took most of their lessons. It was on hearing, during one of their lessons, that the Royal Library paled in comparison to the central collection held at the Great Library in the Museum that Selene had first demanded to be taken to see the building that loomed before her this morning. It had not disappointed then, and it would not disappoint now, she was sure.

If the Muse-inspired men and women on the grounds thought it odd to see a little girl in a slave's shawl hurrying through the Museum alone, they said nothing. And certainly Selene gave her appearance little thought until she'd entered the fountain-adorned plaza surrounding the building and was approaching the wide, pillar-framed steps of the east-facing entrance to the Great Library itself. Then, seeing the scholars of the Muses standing watch beside the heavy iron doors, she abruptly stopped walking and stood on the paved walkway under the shade of a palm, wondering how she was going to get in. They wouldn't just let some girl off the street into the Library, would they? Probably not, she decided. And if they didn't, should she tell them who she was? Or would they take her back to Antirhodos before she got a chance to see Didymus again, to find out whatever Caesarion was finding out?

"You look as astonished as I am," said a male voice beside her.

Selene, startled from her own thoughts, turned to see a young man sitting on a bench just a few feet away, under the shade of the same tree. His body was facing toward the Library, but he'd turned his head to look over at her. He was a handsome young man, she could see, about Caesarion's age, and his smile was strikingly warm and kind. He was not, however, anyone she knew, so she hastily started to walk away.

"I'm sorry," the young man said. "I didn't mean to scare you."

Selene turned quickly—too quickly, in fact, as the slave's shawl slipped from her grip and fell open for a moment, exposing hints of her more luxurious linens beneath. She hastily pulled it closed, hoping he'd seen nothing. She felt safer on the grounds of the Museum than she did at Lochias, but she still didn't feel totally safe. "I'm not scared," she said, trying to maintain her composure even as she tried not to appear too royal. It was difficult to do. Talking so close to someone, she wondered if her soft skin and fine hair would give her away, too. Why hadn't she thought of that?

The man squinted an eye at her in what seemed to her a kind of mock appraisal. "Ah," he concluded. "I can see you're not. So you're here for the Library?"

"Yes," she said, biting her desire to scold him about minding his own business.

"Me, too," he said, as if she'd asked him the same question. "It's hard to work up the courage to go in there, though. I had to sit down here for a bit to think about it. And besides," he said, glancing up at the sun, "I was early, and it's a nice day."

"It's not that scary," Selene said without thinking.

"Oh? You've been in there before?" He paused, then laughed a little. "What am I saying? A clever girl like you, of course you have. Lots of times, I bet."

His accent was a little different from most of those she heard on a regular basis. Not Egyptian, certainly. But not Greek or Roman, either. Nor was his appearance easy to place in any of those cultures: he was dressed in simple, well-used traveling robes, wearing the cloth wrapping atop his head that she'd seen on some of the desert people who had made occasional calls to the court. He had the scraggly beginnings of a beard, and lightly curled locks drifted down from his temples, much longer than the rest of his hair. A strange young man, but he held himself well, Selene thought. Self-assured and satisfied. Not rich, but not poor. A bit better than common, she decided, but probably of little importance. "I've been inside a few times." She shrugged.

The young man chewed on his lip for a moment, thinking. Then his eyes brightened. "Say, I've got an idea. You've been in there before, right? And I need a boost of confidence to get in. How about we go in together?"

"I don't think—"

The young man stood, stretching his arms high before relaxing and seeming to shake himself out with a smile. He was, Selene saw, about the same height as Caesarion. And though he didn't appear to be as strong as her half-brother, and his eyes were not the same deep brown, she thought he could pass for Caesarion's full-blood brother if he trimmed back his hair. She'd seen that kind of hair before, but she couldn't remember where. "Plus, you'll never get in alone," he said when he was done.

"I won't?"

"Nope. You need to have business in the Library. Or be in the company of someone important. You know, like royalty or something."

Selene felt her throat swallow. "Well," she said, "I do have business. I'm going to see the chief librarian."

She wouldn't have thought it possible, but the young man's face brightened even more. "Is that so? I'm here to see Didymus, too. Not to worry, though: I'll let you go first. I'm sure your business is more important than mine. Shall we?"

The young man started walking toward the Library. He didn't seem hurried, but she had to move her legs quickly to catch up.

"My name is Jacob," he said as they walked.

"Oh," Selene said, trying to decide whether she really should be walking with the odd young man. He seemed friendly enough, but was it proper? Then again, what if he was right about not being able to get in otherwise?

She was still mulling it over when they started mounting the wide, smooth steps. One of the scholars stopped chatting with a companion and approached them. He was a very young man, perhaps even younger than Jacob, though she found it tough to tell. Unlike the guards she was accustomed to at the palace, he seemed far more casual than deadly. "On what business?" he asked.

Jacob's smile never left him as he retrieved a folded letter from his robes. "We're here to meet with Didymus," he said.

The scholar took the letter, started to unfold it. "From the Jewish Quarter?"

"Nearby, yes," Jacob said.

Jewish Quarter? Selene looked over her companion again. A substantial number of Jews lived in the eastern portion of the city, said to be the largest community of them outside of their homelands to the north and east. She'd never had occasion to tour their quarter—it had built up around what once had been an eastern necropolis to rival the City of the Dead to their west—but from time to time she'd seen some of the Jewish leaders in court. They'd always been old men, speaking carefully, with long, full beards and full heads of hair. That's where she'd seen Jacob's oddly long locks of hair before, though. She just hadn't recognized him for a Jew without the long beard.

The scholar started to read Jacob's letter. "Summoned by Bronze Guts himself, eh?"

Another scholar standing guard let out a small laugh, and Jacob looked down at Selene with a quizzically arched eyebrow, but they said nothing.

The scholar looked up from the letter, then glanced to Selene. "Doesn't name two people."

"It should," Jacob said. "This is my—"

"Sister," Selene blurted out.

The scholar started to say something, then appeared confused as he looked back and forth between them. "I ... um..."

"In the faith," Jacob said, still smiling, still calm. "Didymus had wanted to talk to her, too, since she's converting to the contemplative life."

Becoming a Jew? Selene glared at Jacob, wanting to stomp his foot or order his seizure for such an improper—

"Ah, good," the scholar said as he turned and opened the door for them. The heavy portal opened slowly, and Selene's anger washed up against her thrill at gaining entrance. She thought she could smell the scrolls already. The hundreds of thousands of scrolls. The knowledge. The power. "So, you're looking for Bronze Guts, are you?" The scholar grinned as he led the way inside. "He's popular this morning."

"I'm sorry," Jacob said. "'Bronze Guts'?"

"What? Oh, it's something we call him. He's tireless, you know. Works right through meals. Never takes breaks. We figure his bowels aren't real."

"Ah. I see." When the scholar looked away for a moment, Jacob made a disgusted face at Selene, causing her to suppress a giggle.

The entry hall took up an entire side of the six-sided building. There were offices here, and a few more guards visible in the shadows, but mostly Selene was focused on the five thick pillars on each side of the narrow reflecting pool that ran down its center. The ten pillars, she knew, represented the ten halls of knowledge within the structure itself: two to each wing on the remaining sides of the building, filled with scrolls. The scholar walked briskly, clearly intent on his duties, and soon they entered the main hall of the Library itself.

The six-sided main hall was open all the way to the high top of its dome, and Selene felt a cool chill to the air as she entered that reminded her unkindly of Alexander's mausoleum. But the similarities to that place of death ended there. The Library was light and open while the tomb had been dark and oppressive. Unlike the shadowed pyramid floating above a single line of small windows, here large portals for light dotted the top of the dome, streaming the sun into a space built of pleasantly bright stones. The sets of doors surrounding the sides were not locked barriers between tombs but held open to a steady flow of busy scholars and servants moving between the halls with scrolls and wax tablets in their hands. Three staircases rose around the walls in a kind of spiral, connecting the three tall levels of the main hall, and the chill of the air was due not to some silly feeling of fear, Selene knew, but from the gentle cascading of the entry hall's reflecting pool as it tumbled down three steps to the floor of the hall—the same elevation as the outside plaza, she surmised—where it entered a larger, round pool in the middle of the space. Men were sitting on curved stone benches around the rippling waters, chatting amicably, and she couldn't help but smile.

The scholar led them out to the edge of the pool and gestured to one of the benches. "Didymus is busy with another guest at the moment," he said. "A gentleman named Nebi. We'll need to wait here until he sends a summons. My name is Cleomedes, and I can answer any questions in the meantime."

Nebi? Wasn't Didymus supposed to be meeting with Caesarion? Nebi was an Egyptian name, Selene was sure. It meant "panther," didn't it? Her shoulders slumped a little, not only because she wouldn't see Didymus right away, but also because she might have missed the chance to impress Caesarion with her ability to move through the city so freely.

Jacob's own attitude, she noticed, hadn't changed at all. She wondered if that look of pleasant satisfaction was frozen on his face. "Of course," he said. "We understand."

Cleomedes nodded politely then started to step toward the

end of the bench. He didn't get two steps before Jacob caught his arm.

"So Didymus is in his office right now with his other meeting?" He gestured to one of the doors on the second floor above the entry hall behind them. "That's just up there, right?"

"No," the scholar said. "The chief librarian's office is on the third floor. Those are the lecture rooms and the scriptorium."

"That's right. I remember now," Jacob said, shaking his head in embarrassment, the long locks of hair hanging from his temples bouncing. "I'd forgotten. End of the hall, right?"

"Yes, but we'll need to wait here," Cleomedes repeated.

"Of course." Then, before the scholar could sit down, Jacob had walked past him, gesturing toward the halls opposite the entry and Didymus' office. "I've always wondered why there are ten halls. Is it to sort the books somehow?"

Cleomedes stepped up to stand to Jacob's right. "Exactly. Based on Aristotle's divisions of knowledge. So that's Mathematics over there."

"Ah, I see. Labeled above the doorway. So that's Medicine?" He pointed past the scholar, causing the man to turn his head away. As soon as he did, Jacob quickly caught Selene's eye and winked, nodding in a crisp gesture toward the stairs behind her.

Selene just stared. Was he telling her to go? Was that why he asked about the office?

Cleomedes confirmed the medicine hall, then started to look back to Selene. Jacob laughed a little, throwing his arm around the scholar's shoulder and sweeping his arm forward to distract his attention. "So many books, you'd need some organization like that! They say you've got a copy of everything ever written here. Is that true?"

"I don't know about everything," Cleomedes said, nevertheless looking smug. "But close to it. Name something," he dared.

Jacob's face screwed up in dramatic thought, keeping the scholar's attention. Selene took a step backward.

"Okay ... well, how about Artapanus?"

Cleomedes almost laughed. "Artapanus? Wrote a history, right? *Concerning the Jews?*"

"That's right," Jacob said, appearing impressed. Selene took another two tentative steps in the direction of the nearest stairway.

"You'll need to do better than that for a challenge," Cleomedes said. "We have Artapanus' own copy. In fact, Didymus himself has been reading it of late."

"Is that so? Artapanus' own copy?" Jacob started walking in the opposite direction from the retreating girl. "You have a lot of originals here, I imagine," he was saying. "Do you have anything in Aristotle's hand?"

The young scholar was laughing again in his pride, but Selene stopped listening to their conversation. She turned, as quietly as she could, and hurried over to the wide stairwell. Three middle-aged scholars, engaged in deep conversation about circles and someone named Eratosthenes, were just starting to make their way up and she stepped into their wake, hiding as best she could manage behind them, keeping her head low and trying not to bring attention to herself.

The scholars departed the stairway on the second floor, leaving the stairway clear to the third floor, so Selene pulled her linen dress away from her ankles to run up the rest of the way. At the top she glanced down to the floor of the main hall one last time—just catching a glimpse of Jacob as he led the young scholar over and into one of the open doorways—before she turned and headed through her own double set of doors, into the hall where she hoped to find Didymus.

The third-floor main hallway, like the entry hallway two floors below it, was lined with pillars. Between them were a series of doors, a few half open to reveal tables and piles of scrolls with the occasional scholar or priest in concentration among them. A single door stood at the end of the hall, shut. Selene stepped up to it lightly, hearing voices from within. She leaned forward to listen, trying to make them out.

"How long, then?" It was her Greek teacher's voice, no doubt. She smiled.

"Not long at all," she heard Caesarion reply. "The battle may already be done. And not for the best, I fear."

Selene's smile grew. Caesarion must be going by the name Nebi, she decided, to keep his visit quiet. He thought he was so clever. Wouldn't he be surprised to find out she could—

"Selene," said a familiar deep voice behind her.

A part of her instinct told her to run, but it was the other half of her instinct—the royal one—that she obeyed. She withdrew from the door and stood straight, head held high and face controlled as she turned to face Khenti. The dark-skinned head of the guards stepped out from the shadows behind the nearest pillar, his face impassive. She silently cursed herself for not being more careful. He'd gone out with Caesarion this morning, so she should have expected that he would be around. She should have looked. "Guardchief," she said with a curt nod. "Pleasant to see you here."

Khenti's eyes narrowed and he frowned slightly. "I imagine so," he said. Then, before she could reply, he looked over his shoulder down the line of pillars toward the main hall and spoke something in Egyptian. She wasn't as comfortable in the language as Caesarion was, so it took her a moment to translate it to Greek in her mind. "I'll watch her from here," he'd said.

Silently, like ghosts, two more Egyptian palace guards melted out from the shadows behind pillars and bowed first to her, then to him. Selene just stared. Palace guards? Had they been following her this whole time? How long—?

"If you will, Shushu," Khenti said to one of them, still in

Egyptian, "inform Kemse that the young queen is safe and sound." Khenti's gaze returned to Selene. "And that she's looking forward to returning the shawl she stole. She's quite sorry for the trouble she's caused this morning."

Selene smiled politely, the best she could manage in her shock. The other guards bowed once more to the two of them before they filed out in silence.

"So you've been busy," Khenti said quietly, returning to addressing her in Greek.

Selene shrugged. What business was it of his?

"The world is an unfriendly place," he said. "You shouldn't be out alone."

Selene considered a few curses before settling on the proper thing to say. "I wasn't alone," she said, eyes flicking to where the guards had departed.

Khenti's frown broke into a hint of a smile. "That's true," he said. "Still, in the future, it would make our lives much easier if Your Majesty would follow directions, impressed though we are by your obvious ingenuity. One of the supply ferries?"

"Of course," she said, as if it were the most obvious thing to have done. How did he know that?

"Clever," he said. "But, please, no more. I'll ask Lord Horus to give you and your brothers more liberty. Just please don't sneak off, my lady. There are too many people who want you dead."

Dead? "Why would anyone want—"

"Dead, Selene," he repeated. "It seems the world is coming—the war is coming—whether we're ready or not. Perhaps it's time you understood that."

Before she could reply, Khenti had stepped forward and was reaching past her to knock on the door.

16

The Storm of War

ACTIUM, 31 BCE

Dawn on the day of the attack had brought dark clouds, a bad omen made worse when they began to burn the ships whose rowers were either dead in the burial pits or had defected across the lines. Watching the thick black plumes of smoke rising to meet the storm-promising sky, Vorenus had felt a sorrowful resignation to death that had surprised him. Death didn't frighten him overmuch—he had done his due diligence to honor the gods, even on this gods-doomed day—but he was accustomed to feeling a kind of bloodlust take over his mind when battle approached. It was something he and Pullo, even when they were young and thought themselves rivals, always knew they had in common.

But not today.

Perhaps he was just getting old. Or perhaps he was too close to the truth to convince himself that they stood any chance of victory. Whatever the cause, he'd been certain as he'd watched the sun rise that it was the last dawn he'd see.

Though he had lived to see noon, nothing in the half-day of slaughter had yet convinced him that anything but death awaited him today.

Keeping his stance wide on the salt-slick, heaving deck of Antony's flagship, Vorenus peered north through the sheeting rain, trying to ascertain the status of Octavian's vessels. There were close to a thousand ships on the water today. The numbers were on Octavian's side, though not by much. And his fleet was mostly biremes and triremes, smaller ships than their own flotilla of four hundred or so heavy quad- and quinqueremes. The size difference was substantial: it would take little more than a single strike from the triple-beaked bronze ram at the head of one of their massive ships to sink a trireme. The even smaller biremes would likely be blown into splinters.

If only they could catch them.

Octavian, as he had on land, was refusing to give fight. He'd begun the morning far off from the shoreline, not moving in for the battle. Then, when at last Antony gave the frustrated order around noon to head forward into the storm, into Octavian's lines, Caesar's adopted son had given way, backrowing out of reach of their wave-plowing rams.

Not out of reach of each side's ranged weapons, though: the blood of the day so far—and there had been much of it—had been wrought through the air. Archers' volleys that pinned men to the decks and made pincushions of their side-curved shields. Great iron bolts shot across the waters that could cut through two men at a time. Skull-size stones launched from deck-mounted ballistae that could blow men to pieces. Greased firepots of oil that made a mockery of the rain, vaulting through the air to explode on the decks in infernal heat. Even now Vorenus could see, like parodies of lighthouses on the water, ships burning on both sides—though there were more among their own lines. Bigger ships made for bigger targets. It was astonishing luck that the flagship had suffered only minor burns about the deck.

Though Antony had for a time paced about the ship, raving about cowardice and dishonor, Octavian's tactic was clear and sensible: he was going to let Antony's men row and row until they were to the point of exhaustion or death before he attacked. The rowers were the heart of the ship, after all. Indeed, on clear days, with their rhythm beating steady and sure, Vorenus had often closed his eyes and imagined himself standing atop the hollow heart of a great giant swimming in the sea. But weakened by disease and hunger, sick from the pitching waves, and forced to row harder and longer than they were meant to, the rowers at the heart of these giants were fading fast. Vorenus could see it in the increasingly erratic lift and stroke of their long oars, and he could feel it in the chaotic shouts that echoed up from belowdecks. Octavian, he was certain, was seeing it, too. They wouldn't have long to wait now.

He looked over to his right, where Pullo was standing tall and unfazed by the weather or the arrow that had managed to pierce his shield far enough to rip into his bracing shoulder. He was kicking his feet to snap the shafts of other arrows that had landed around him, trying to keep his balance as the storm-stirred seas pitched against the massive vessel. Over the past few hours they'd found that the hundreds, if not thousands, of iron points embedded in the deck made for a useful addition in the wet, shifting conditions: their shaftless necks were welcome points of traction and grip when one's feet were inclined to slide out along the wood.

On the other hand, Vorenus had noted more than once, they were also hell on one's knees when fresh volleys came down and the legionnaires hunkered beneath their large rectangular shields.

"They still backing off?" Pullo asked, voice betraying only moderate interest.

Vorenus nodded. Their thinning squadron of archers still alive on deck fitted arrows and launched a fresh salvo up into the gray sky. Red shields flipped up and overlapped into traditional tortoise formation on the deck of one of Octavian's smaller ships nearby, and Vorenus saw a few of the shields cave away as arrows slipped through the gaps and found targets. Never enough, though. It was only a matter of time. He could only hope that Cleopatra would do the right thing when that time came. He'd managed only a few moments to talk with her in private after the generals had met during the night, and she'd seemed none too eager to hear his advice, but perhaps something of what he'd said had sunk in. There was no way of knowing now, and not for the first time he wondered if they should have stayed with Cleopatra instead of Antony. But, then, it was one betrayal to speak against his commander and quite another to act against him. Let Cleopatra do what she would now. He would stand and die where duty called.

"Some hits?" Pullo's eyes weren't what they once were. Another sign that they were both too damn old for the young men's business of battle.

"A few," he said.

"Good," Pullo said, looking satisfied. "It's a good day to die."

"Is it?"

"Good as any other, I suppose," Pullo said.

"*Testudo!*" shouted a legionnaire closer to the bow of their ship. At once trained reflexes kicked in and the men closed ranks, raising their shields and collapsing in on one another, left knees to ground, shields braced against their right arms and shoulders. Vorenus, as he had been more times than he could count in his life, was beside Pullo. And not ten paces away he could see the familiar battle armor of Antony, characteristically fighting alongside his common men. Vorenus turned to say something to Pullo but promptly forgot what it was when the legionnaire in front of them dry-heaved spittle onto the deck.

"I was thinking," Pullo said calmly, "I rather prefer fighting on land."

Because of the sounds of storm and waves and beating oars, the high buzzing whistle of the volley came only moments before the arrows fell among them like murderous iron rain. Vorenus' shield bucked back against his tired frame as if struck with repeated blows of a smith's hammer. Fresh shafts slipped through cracks in their shield wall, blindly burying themselves in wood or flesh with a rumble of splinters and screams.

Vorenus opened his eyes, not having realized he'd closed them, and saw a shaft quivering in the wood between his legs. A matching, fractured hole in his shield—just below his arm—showed where it had come through.

"Well, that was close, eh?" Pullo chuckled. "Not that you use your tackle much anyway these days."

They'd only started to stand and lower their shields, the spent shafts upon them clattering down to land amid the debris and bodies, when another legionnaire near the head of the ship raised his arm to the sky: "*Testu—*"

Vorenus had time to see an arrow rip out the back of the man's neck, but not time to see him fall. His own shield was up too quick for that.

Again the angry hammering. Again the screams. A man not far to his left took an arrow down the back of his spine and dropped his shield, falling forward with a terrible shriek before that cry, too, was silenced in the wave of arrows.

When it passed they stood or cried, threw up or tended to the wounded as circumstances fit. Vorenus looked across the momentarily chaotic deck for Antony and couldn't see him at first. Then, at last, he saw him looking off through the waves to their right. "Ballistae!" the general was shouting, his arm outstretched in the storm. "Archers!"

Vorenus turned and saw first the bronze ram folding open the frothing water, then the trireme behind it, oars driving hard and fast. Through the rain and the splash of waves, Vorenus saw that the men at the trireme's forward ballistae had mounted iron bolts and lowered their sight to the line of the flagship's deck.

Pullo was staring, too. "Holy—"

Vorenus dove into his old friend's back, slamming him down to the deck just as the ballistae released. He felt the rip of the wind as the iron bolts passed through the space above them, heard the bolts cutting into the men who hadn't reacted as quickly.

Antony was directing their own ballistae to return fire, and the archers were already doing so at will, needing no directions at this point, but they weren't going to stop the vessel now.

"Ram right!" Antony shouted.

The men scuttled across the deck, trying to stay low as the distance between the two ships rapidly shrank and the air above the deck rails grew thick with missiles. Vorenus and Pullo moved, too, until they were huddled against the deck railing opposite the impact point. Pullo was panting, and Vorenus saw that he was holding his hand to a red spot on his stomach.

"You threw me on a broken one, you son of a bitch." The big man laughed. "Knew you'd get me one day."

The trireme hit and the deck lurched. One second they were crouched against the rail, Pullo holding out two bloodied fingers and smiling in the rain, and the next second they were ten feet away, tumbled against friends alive and dead. Wood was still flipping through the air. A new source of screams arose belowdecks.

Antony already had archers up, and they were firing down at the smaller ship even as roped grappling irons flipped over the deck railing and found grip in whatever or whoever they could. Vorenus groaned as he rolled to a crouch, feeling assorted pains across his torso but not wanting to see if anything had broken his skin. Pullo knelt beside him, his gladius already in hand. If the wound in his belly was serious, he wasn't showing it.

Vorenus pulled his sword, too, and focused on the grappling hooks. Any rowers surviving below ought to be trying to get anyone climbing the sides with spear thrusts through the ports, but he doubted many would do so.

It surprised him that the trireme was trying to board them so quickly. He'd expected it to try to sink them with several ramming thrusts before they attempted to storm the deck. Someone, he surmised, must have recognized Antony. They knew this was the flagship, and who could forego the honor of killing the man they believed to be the cause of the war?

"Ram left!" Antony cried out, and this time Vorenus didn't have time to look before the world lurched again as a second ship rammed them on the opposite side, sending the men sprawling up against the deck rails they'd braced against seconds before.

He and Pullo scooted upright, leaning the backs of their heads against the low wood wall of the shaking railing. A grappling hook clanged over the side, landing between them and then pulling back quickly to slam its iron spikes into the railing just between their heads. Vorenus, amid the screams of men and the raging sea, ceased holding his death at arm's length and embraced it. He began to laugh, and Pullo laughed, too.

Antony was gathering up the archers in a squadron at the bow of the boat, even as portions of his guard formed up around him. The ranged volleys from other ships had stopped now that Octavian's men were preparing to board them, but Vorenus was quite certain that their situation had not improved. The ocean waters roiled beneath the three bound ships, crashing their hulls into one another and lifting the bronze rams pierced in the flagship's side up and down with a sound like great millstones smashing.

On the opposite side of the deck, the first of Octavian's men were coming up over the side. Titus Pullo and Lucius Vorenus, side by side and laughing, rushed to meet them.

17

Octavian's Glory

ACTIUM, 31 BCE

From atop a covered siege tower raised above the deck of the Imperator's flagship, Juba watched the battle unfold with a growing feeling of unease. His stomach was already twisted and knotted from the pitch and roll of the storm-troubled waves, both amplified by his height above the water, but he knew that his sense of dread was more than mere seasickness or even the fear of death. Octavian, he was certain, was going to make him use the Trident of Poseidon again.

This highest level of the tower was scarcely populated. Aside from himself, the only men standing with Octavian were six praetorian guards, the traitorous general Delius, and a signal-man with flags, relaying the Imperator's messages to the fleet. A few arrows had slipped around the edges of the metal roof above them and lay broken underfoot. And a long chest, containing the Trident itself, was strapped to the rear wall nearest the ladder. All else on the platform was spray and rain and the echo of shouts from the common men on the decks far below them.

This flagship was one of their few relatively large vessels, and Octavian had arranged for it to be centered in the mass of their northern flank, facing Antony's personal assault. A long line of smaller, faster, and—Octavian had noted this in particular during their planning the previous night—more expendable triremes lay before them, stretched out into the waves and weather and taking the brunt of the attack so far. Just at the edge of his sight to their left, Juba could see another of these larger, hulking ships in the storm: the quinquereme with Agrippa aboard. As he watched, one of its tall ballistae launched a rock big enough to be seen through the thick rain as it hurtled skyward.

If Octavian was bothered by the pitching sea, he didn't show it. He stood, stance wide and arms on the railing, swiveling his gaze to take in the unfolding events of the battle. Not far away a firepot exploded on the deck of one of their triremes, scattering men in silent flames.

"See how that ship's oars grow sloppy," Octavian said to Juba, ignoring the fire to point to one of Antony's nearby Egyptian-built ships. Its rowers were clearly no longer in rhythm, some moving forward while others pulled back. With many of its legs thus tangled, others completely stilled and hanging limp in the water, the great bug of a thing appeared to be wounded, only limping its way toward them under the heavy onslaught of archers and ballistae.

"It won't be long now," Juba said, not certain what event he was referring to but hoping against despair that it would be a victory without use of the Trident.

"No," agreed Octavian, eyes still scanning the horizon. "Not long."

"The Imperator's plan has been a fine one," Delius said, his voice steady and cold, betraying no emotion as he watched Octavian surgically destroy the men he'd called friends and comrades.

Octavian just nodded, and Juba watched his adopted brother's lips move in little whispers, as if he were working over a problem in his mind, debating with himself as he calculated the next move in his game. The fire on the trireme started to spread, a nearby bireme steering close to take on evacuees.

"No sign?" the Imperator asked over his shoulder, his gaze elsewhere.

For the better part of the last hour, Octavian had been sending some of the smaller ships forward in feinted attacks. His aim was twofold, he said. First, the little charges forced Antony's rowers to break rhythm as they attempted to maneuver their hulking vessels to counter the threats, and this could only serve to tire the men further. Second, and perhaps more important, each would-be attack gained information about the fleet facing them. And Octavian hoped to acquire one piece of information most of all: "Antony," he'd told them again and again. "Give me Antony."

The signalman's own gaze was skipping among the ships around them, looking for messages. "Nothing certain, sir," he said. "Agrippa does report ranged engagement with a heavy ship forward of his position."

Octavian's gaze was still out on the water. "He must be close. He'd be near the center if he's on this flank."

"He is," Delius said.

"I believe you," Octavian said. The slightest hint of a frown creased the corners of his eyes as he stared out into the storm toward his admiral's big ship. "Signal Agrippa. Two triremes forward. See if it's Antony."

Even as the signalman began the message, Octavian turned his back to the water to address the older general behind him. "Delius, I want proof this war is over. Proof that Rome is whole again. I want Antony on this ship today. Alive. Rome depends upon it."

Delius, still wearing the polished finery in which he had

appeared before them the night before, saluted. "It shall be done, Caesar."

Caesar. Juba chewed on the word. A family name, of course. But increasingly a title, a claim to power in its own right. Would Caesar himself have approved?

"Very good," Octavian said. "Pass word down to the decks: all ready to row. We'll push soon."

The ship swayed. Delius went down the ladder. The rain fell. The men below shouted their readiness to attack. After a time, Delius returned. Minutes passed.

"Message from Agrippa, sir," the signalman finally said, breaking into a smile. "It's Antony's flagship, sir, right where you thought."

"Good." Octavian's own smile was almost imperceptible. "Forward to the position, Delius. You'll lead the boarding party. And send word to the fleet: all ships forward." He took a deep breath, but for all the calmness in his voice he could have been talking about the weather. "This ends now."

The praetorians grinned. Delius snapped to a salute then slid down the ladder once more. The signalman relayed the Imperator's commands with earnest excitement, and a great, growing cry went up into the storm.

The steady beat of the oars began.

"Come stand beside me, Juba," Octavian said.

Juba came to the railing of the tower, trying not to think about the last time he stood thus next to Octavian on the sea. Around them, the fleet was moving forward. Their own path began to turn, angling toward Agrippa's ship in the distance. "Yes, brother?"

"Does it bother you that the men call me 'Caesar'?"

"No," Juba said with as much confidence as he could muster. "It's your name by right of inheritance."

"Then it's your name, too, is it not?"

"No. Well, yes, but I'm undeserving of it."

"Ah, but you've Caesar's mind for the strategy of war," Octavian said. He swept out an arm across the closer ships moving into position, the more distant ones in flames, the rising and falling swarms of missiles, the storm and the waves dotted with the drowning and the drowned. "This whole campaign is a testament to it."

Juba thought through different responses, abandoned them all. In the end, he tried to change the subject. "Why send Delius to take Antony?"

"I need to know his loyalties. If he turns to stand alongside Antony in the end, he'll be cut down." A volley of arrows rained down on the ship, the men below them raising their shields in tortoise formations. Octavian didn't move. He was relaxed and unflinching as the bolts rattled down on the roof above their heads and fell, harmless, to the deck. "If he remains loyal to me, he may prevent Antony from taking full honor of victory from me."

Their big ship was moving fast now, cutting a diagonal line across the engaging fleets, driving hard for the presumed location of Antony's flagship. Everywhere he looked, Juba saw men dying in the rain. From his campaign. "Full honor?" he asked distractedly.

"By preventing me from taking him back to Rome in chains, to face the Triumph I *will* be owed." Octavian's face brightened momentarily, and he looked over to Juba as if he'd just thought of something interesting. "By killing himself, brother, like your blood father did to avoid Caesar's rightful triumph."

Juba blinked, trying to keep down a surge of rage. "Of course," he managed to say.

"Antony is just the sort to do it, I'm certain. Trapped, he'll fall on his sword before he'll face Rome's justice." Octavian's jaw was hard as he returned his gaze out toward the approaching ships. "I'd rather lose him to the waves," he said.

Out of the storm the shape of a massive quinquereme

emerged, its deck a chaos of men in combat. Two triremes were already engaged with Antony's vessel. As their own vessel approached from the western side, Juba could see that the second of them had just followed the first in successfully ramming the flagship's flank: its bronze ram was buried in a splintered wound in the ship's side, and its marines were starting to climb grapple lines to heave themselves into the melee on Antony's deck. Through a momentary pause in the misty sprays Juba could see that Antony's rowers were thrusting spears through their oar ports, trying to stab the legionnaires as they climbed. There was still a strong defensive knot of men on the flagship's deck—presumably where Antony was—but even through the distance and distraction it was clear that the addition of the second trireme's men would quickly overpower the defenders. If Antony was still alive, Juba thought, he would be overwhelmed by either Agrippa's men or his own blade soon enough.

"No," Octavian rasped, seeing it, too. Juba watched his knuckles whitening on the rail.

The signalman spoke up from behind them. "Agrippa's ordered a full assault—"

Octavian spun on the signalman, his face red with rage. "I can see that," he said, biting off each word. "Go below. Tell Delius to brace for impact."

"Sir, from here I can—"

"Go. Now."

The signalman's gaze instinctively flashed to the ornate gladius at the Imperator's side, momentarily paralyzed by his confusion. Four of the praetorians, Juba could see, already had hands on their own weapons. Two of them were silently moving behind the young man. The signalman, wide-eyed and trembling, swallowed and bowed hastily before he turned and sped down the ladder as fast as his limbs could manage.

Octavian's torso was heaving, his head lowered like a cornered bull's. "Get it," he snapped to one of the praetorians.

Though no one had spoken about the long chest—no one had even seen it opened in weeks—the praetorians atop the siege tower did not have to ask what it was that Octavian wanted. Two praetorians moved with efficiency, unlocking the chest and pulling free the cloth-wrapped Trident of the god of the sea.

Juba, watching them, felt as if he'd stepped out of his own body, as if he were watching all this unfold from somewhere else, as if he was not about to unleash the power of the gods upon the men—Antony's and Octavian's—on the ships in front of them.

"Agrippa's not getting my glory," Octavian said, his voice disturbingly quiet. "Nor is Antony. Better that the hand of a god take them all."

One of the praetorians pressed the Trident into Juba's hands. The metal-enwrapped staff gleamed against the background gray of storm and sea: the three sharp arrow points, the wide central casing, the twisting, sinuous snakes—everything but the chillingly black stone. Juba held it distantly, his hands wrapped around the polished wood of its staff.

Octavian stepped behind him, wrapped his own hands over his adopted brother's shoulders. He gripped the bones there tightly, making Juba wince as he was turned toward the sea, toward the water and the ships beyond. "Do it," the newest Caesar whispered. "We'll storm what remains. We'll have our victory. *Rome* will have its victory. No one can blame us for this war when they know that the gods themselves support us, when they see that the gods have turned against Antony and destroyed him. Feel it, brother. Now. For Rome. Destroy them all."

Octavian's hands squeezed so hard into his skin that Juba had to close his eyes against the pain, close his eyes against the horror that was about to unfold.

Down into the stillness he sank: deep down within himself, away from the nightmare and the helplessness. Down, out of the storm and into the black quiet, where he felt, behind the shadowed silence, the pulsing beat of his heart and the desire to one day be free.

Juba's hands moved to the metal. The metal grew warm. Then he opened his eyes, and the screaming began.

18

A Meeting of Minds

ALEXANDRIA, 31 BCE

Caesarion, sitting with his back to the door, was in the middle of explaining to Didymus how little time they might have before Rome's armies arrived at the gates of Alexandria when he heard Khenti's voice outside, speaking his half-sister's name.

Holding up his hand to keep Didymus from saying anything more himself, Caesarion stood and moved quietly to the door, listening in as the guardchief scolded Selene as best a man of such relative status could.

Caesarion sighed, shaking his head a little to himself. Selene had always been headstrong. Far more than her brothers. Philadelphus was probably too young for much mischief at this point, but there was certainly a difference between Selene and her twin brother, Helios. Perhaps it was due to the boy's seemingly constant bouts with illness, but he'd never been the kind of child to fight authority. Selene, though ... Selene felt it was her right, if not her duty, to push back against anything that threatened to hold her down. She was like their mother, Caesarion supposed. For good and ill.

It was impressive that she'd made her way to the Library. He had to give her credit for that. If it were not for Khenti's well-trained palace guards—far better trained than they'd been a year ago under Khenti's executed predecessor—she truly would have made it here alone.

Caesarion winced as he heard Khenti telling the girl how the world meant her harm, and how it was time she understood the fact. It was true, even if he wished it were not. He'd tried too hard to keep his half-siblings in the dark about the realities they were facing. Of course they didn't understand his urgency about keeping them on Antirhodos. They didn't know how desperate the war was, how unpopular they might be with the people. They knew nothing about the forces that were arrayed against them.

Khenti knocked on the door three times, then paused before adding two more. A signal of no danger at the door.

Caesarion took a deep breath, collecting his thoughts, before he moved the bolt on the door and opened it to the hallway. He didn't pretend to be surprised to see Selene standing there, Kemse's shawl around her head and shoulders doing surprisingly little to cover her royally groomed skin and hair, her sea-green dress of rich linen, her expensive sandals, her scents of perfume and oils—and her face reddened with shame.

"Thank you, Khenti," he said, not addressing Selene and allowing her to squirm for a bit longer. "You've seen to contacting Kemse?"

"Yes, Lord Horus."

Caesarion winced again, but he didn't bother to correct Khenti for once more attributing the god-name to him. Such habits were hard to break, he knew. And what was worship of the gods if not a habit? "Very good," he said, finally looking down to his half-sister. "Been wandering the city this morning, Selene?"

Selene pulled off the shawl with a small huff before she walked into the room, her still-narrow hips managing a sway not unlike her mother's as she entered Didymus' office. Though still a girl, she was beginning to blossom. Sibling or not, he could recognize that. She would be an extraordinarily beautiful woman in the years to come. And then she'd be ready for some royal marriage—if any of them actually lived long enough for it.

The Greek teacher rose and bowed from behind his cluttered desk. "My lady Selene," he said as Caesarion shut the door and rebolted it.

"Didymus," Selene said, smiling and dropping all pretenses to walk quickly around the obstacles of the room to wrap her arms around his down-leaning neck.

"It's been too long," he said. The scholar hugged her back, but Caesarion could see the pain in his eyes, the look of uncertainty: Didymus still hadn't forgiven himself for his long-ago betrayal of the family.

Selene, too, seemed uncertain despite her enthusiasm, Caesarion noticed. Her embrace of the scholar was more stilted than it had once been. His own fault, he thought. He'd not involved her in things as he should have. He'd coddled her like the little girl she was fast outgrowing, and even she was becoming aware of it now. Khenti was right. It was wake-up time, like it or not. Caesarion cleared a stool for her near his own chair after they pulled apart. "You should sit down and rest for a minute, Selene," he said. "You've been walking a lot today."

Selene hoisted herself up. Caesarion stayed standing, and Didymus did the same.

"I suppose you heard we were just talking about the war," Caesarion said. "I'd been telling Didymus about the latest news from the north and my plans."

Selene's face lit up. "There's news?"

"There is, Selene. But I don't know that you should stay to hear it."

Selene's eyes flashed with hurt. "Why not?"

"Well, you did just sneak away, against my orders, trying to *spy* on us," Caesarion said, trying to sound stern. "That doesn't make you quite trustworthy, does it?"

Selene started to say something in anger, then caught herself and clenched her jaw on the emotion.

"Caesarion is right," Didymus said. "We must have secrecy over what we discuss here."

"I *can* be trusted," Selene said, her hurt feelings just barely straining her voice. "Just no one's ever let me prove it."

Caesarion knew she was right. As Khenti said: it was past time that she understood the dangers she faced. But, even so, could she be trusted? Especially after today?

"Besides," she said, looking down at her dress and smoothing it with her hands, "I've never told anyone what I know about you."

"About me?" Caesarion asked, surprised.

"No," Selene said. Her voice was quiet and eyes still downcast. "About Didymus. About back in Rome."

Didymus crumpled down into his chair, a look on his face as if he'd been kicked in the gut.

After a few moments of silence, Caesarion managed to gasp out, "How—?"

"I heard it. With Didymus and that man. I didn't hear much, but I heard that. I've known, and I didn't tell."

"Oh, Selene," Didymus said. "I don't know what to say."

When Selene at last looked up at him, her eyes were wet but her face stoic. "There's nothing to say. It can't be changed. And it doesn't matter now: you refused to betray us again." She took a deep breath, turned her bright eyes to Caesarion. "I've never told anyone. Not even Helios. I *can* be trusted."

Caesarion was uncertain what more he could say. He looked over to Didymus for a sign, but the Greek scholar's face was sunken, as if he'd fallen back into himself. "I'm sorry we never told you," he finally said.

"I understand why, though," Selene said. "I just ... I think I'm old enough now."

"You are," Caesarion agreed, hoping it was true. He sat down, letting out a long sigh as he did so. He rubbed at his eyes for a moment to clear his thoughts. Then, realizing there was no easy way to begin, he laid out the facts: "The news from the north, as I was telling Didymus, is dire. Our army has been trapped by Octavian at a place called Actium, in Greece, with no clear way out. Our men are starving to death, riddled by disease, and defecting to Rome in large numbers. It's probably only a matter of time until they're defeated."

Whatever smile of success Selene had upon her face went out like a light, and for a few seconds she blinked too often as Caesarion watched her. Quickly, though, her face moved to a stoic impassivity, just as their mother had taught them to do in times of emotion. Gods and goddesses weren't meant to feel emotion, after all. It wouldn't do for the public image. "Surely my father—" she started to say.

Caesarion shook his head. "Not this time."

The girl swallowed hard, gave the slightest nod. "And what now?"

Caesarion started to say something, then decided against it. What to tell her? That Antony and Cleopatra, if they lived, would probably be captured, paraded through Rome in a Triumph? And if not captured, pursued home in frightful defeat to await their doom here? Caesarion knew that he himself would be a dead man if he fell into Octavian's arms—as Caesar's blood child he was, after all, the greatest threat to Octavian's ambitions—but what would await Antony's children? Would they die, too? Or would Octavian marry them into his family, subsuming the threat? To whom would Selene go? Who would claim this beautiful little girl, raping her in a victory bed that was too terrible for Caesarion to imagine?

"We don't know," Didymus said, breaking Caesarion's dark thoughts with a weak but steady voice. "Peace with Octavian? More war? We don't know. We need to be prepared for anything."

Selene nodded, her jaw clenching again despite her stoic face. For a long minute no one spoke, and her gaze seemed to be far away. "It must be kept quiet," she said at last, talking to no one in particular.

"Yes," Caesarion said. "We cannot have panic. Even if they are defeated—today? tomorrow? we don't know when—we'll send word to the citizens of victory. There will be rumors—we can't prevent that—but it will buy us some time. Meanwhile I'm redoubling the work on the walls and defenses." He sighed. "It's all we can do right now."

Didymus agreed, seeming to recover his wits. "Anything more would look like desperation, which you cannot afford."

"But this isn't why you're here," Selene said to Caesarion. "It was Didymus who called *you* with news, wasn't it?"

Didymus smiled grimly. "You always were clever," he said.

"Too clever sometimes," Caesarion said, trying his best to smile, too. "I believe Didymus had some news for us, too. News from his latest travels?" He tilted his head toward their Greek teacher, giving him permission to speak freely.

"Of course," Didymus said, but he then appeared unsure where to begin.

"The man sent after Didymus a year ago had a letter from Rome," Caesarion started, noticing but ignoring Selene's shiver at the memory of that night. "Only it wasn't from Octavian. It was from a man named Juba, a Numidian adopted into Caesar's own family. He wanted Didymus to give him the Scrolls of Thoth."

"Scrolls of Thoth?"

"Yes," Didymus said, his voice sounding stronger as he entered the conversation on familiar turf. "A legendary book of the god Thoth, into which he poured the knowledge and power of the gods themselves. It doesn't exist."

Caesarion raised an eyebrow, uncertain if he felt relief or not. "Oh? You know this for a fact now?"

Didymus nodded, but his eyes were troubled. "Well, it doesn't exist in the way Juba is thinking. Not on earth, anyway."

"I don't understand," Caesarion said.

"Nor do I," Selene agreed.

"Well, it's ... complicated," Didymus said. "I don't really understand it all myself. Not the way I'd like to. But I'll explain what I can, as I can. And I've asked another scholar to come to the Library this morning to join us. I think he'll be able to shed some, ah, unique light on the facts of the matter. He actually should have been here by now. He's coming from the Jewish Quarter."

Selene took in her breath abruptly. "Oh," she said. "I think I met him."

"Really?" The Greek scholar looked surprised. "He's here?"

Caesarion, shaking away the urge to wonder at how his half-sister had come to know an important Jewish scholar, rose and went to the door, opening it quietly. Khenti melted out of the shadows in response. Caesarion kept his voice low out of instinct. "There's a Jewish scholar in the Library," he said. "He's supposed to come see Didymus."

"Yes. He came with young Selene, my lord."

He really needed to find out how that happened. She was indeed full of surprises today. "Can you see that he comes to join us?"

"At once, sir," Khenti said, bowing before he strode quickly down the hall.

Caesarion shut the door, turned back to the room. Selene, he noticed, seemed to be blushing slightly. "So you came to the Library with this scholar?"

The girl's face reddened a bit more. "I met him outside," she said. "He said he was coming here, and so we came in together."

"Begging your pardon, lady Selene," Didymus said, "but you need to be wary of the company you keep beyond the palace."

Selene huffed and rolled her eyes. "I was fine. He reminded me of you," she said, looking over to Caesarion.

Confusion spread on Didymus' face, gradually twisting into a look of fright. "He looked like Caesarion? That's not—"

Khenti's knock at the door cut off the scholar, who froze, half-leaned over his desk, staring at Caesarion with concern. Selene just appeared flushed.

Caesarion held out a hand to still the scholar—not that it was necessary, given his position—and then moved to open the door from behind it, so that he stood between the door and the girl and could put his whole body into a push against the wood if needed. Trying to appear relaxed for Selene's sake—there might be nothing afoot, after all—he unobtrusively patted his side to reassure himself of the little blade there. Then, nodding to Didymus, he opened the door and looked around it.

Khenti was there, looking rock-solid as ever. With him was a young man about Caesarion's own height and age, dressed in simple robes. He was, Caesarion could see, clearly a Jew: sparsely bearded, but with long curled locks of hair hanging from his temples. In his hands he held a simple cloth-wrap hat, and he was smiling. "Pharaoh," he said, bowing. "It's pleasant to see you so far from the palaces."

Caesarion, seeing no danger, opened the door enough to let the young man enter. Khenti followed, stepping to the side just after he entered, to stand beside the door as Caesarion shut it. The guardchief was clearly uncertain about the newcomer.

Didymus, still standing at his desk, appeared more confused than ever, but before any of them could speak, the young Jew had turned to Selene and bowed again. "My lady Selene," he said.

Selene's upper lip tucked in slightly in a pout. "You knew who I was, Jacob?"

The man grinned but didn't reply, straightening to stand before Didymus. "I'm sorry my father could not come in reply to your letter," he said, drawing a summons from his robes and handing it to the flustered scholar. "He's ill, and he sent me in his stead."

Didymus took the letter, opened it, saw that it was indeed the one he'd sent. "Joachim is your father?"

"He is. My name is Jacob."

"I see," Didymus said. He blinked, seeming to remember himself. There was a second chair, like Caesarion's, tucked away in the corner of the little office, and the scholar gestured to it. "Please, do sit down. We were just getting started."

Caesarion moved his own seat closer to Selene's stool to make room for Jacob as he pulled the extra chair out and into position in front of the scholar's desk. Khenti remained standing, quickly fading into the woodwork.

When he sat down, Jacob had a pleasant smile on his face, as if remembering a joke. "To what do we humble Jews owe the pleasure of being called to a meeting of such powerful folk? Something to do with the impending defeat of our beloved ruler at Actium?"

Didymus seemed much more in control of himself as they all settled into their seats, only the twitch of his eyebrow betraying his surprise that the young Jew was so well informed of the situation to the north. "Only partially," the scholar said. "Your father holds a well-deserved reputation as the finest living Jewish scholar in Alexandria. A student of history, I know. I wanted his particular experience to confirm, and perhaps clarify, a few bits of, ah, unique history we were going to discuss today."

"I see," Jacob said, his voice serious despite the hint of bemusement on his face. "Well, I shall do what I can in his place. He's taught me well, I assure you. Perhaps only my younger sister knows my father's work better than I." He looked over to Selene and Caesarion, winking gently at the girl. "One never suspects how much they truly know, of course."

Selene laughed lightly, and Caesarion felt that what tension had been in the room had melted away. He decided he liked Jacob, young though the man was.

Didymus leaned back in his chair. Caesarion, too, settled into his seat, noticing that Selene, still pouting a little that she'd been so easily identified on her morning's travels, did the same. "Octavian, as you know, will probably defeat our armies sooner rather than later," Didymus said. "While this is a concern for us all, it isn't directly the matter at hand. What brings us together is the fact that a man at Octavian's side, a Numidian named Juba, is trying to acquire the Scrolls of Thoth. Do you know them?"

From the corner of his eye Caesarion thought he saw the smile on Jacob's face flicker for a moment. "I do. An old legend. The pagan god Thoth was supposed to have put his powers into them. They're not real, you know."

"You sound sure," Didymus said.

Caesarion kept his face impassive, feeling quite suddenly that there was a dance going on between the Jew and the scholar, and that he himself didn't know the steps.

"Thoth isn't real," Jacob said.

"Of course." Didymus smiled. "The belief in one god is a central tenet of your faith, isn't it?"

"'Hear, O Israel, the Lord your God is one,'" Jacob said, the tone in his voice clearly identifying the phrase as memorized doctrine. He shrugged. "God alone is God. There is no Thoth, so he can have no scrolls."

"So no gods but your own exist?"

"I could not be a Jew and believe otherwise," Jacob said, before he nodded slightly toward Caesarion. "Begging your forgiveness, Pharaoh Horus."

Caesarion felt a sudden heat in his face as his trained impassivity failed him. Certain that the emotion showed, he embraced the loss of control and tried to turn it to his advantage in whatever game was being played. "I no more believe myself divine than I believe you don't know that there's truth behind the legend of the Scrolls, Thoth or not."

Jacob's smile broadened even as his eyes narrowed in measurement. "I misjudged you, lord Caesarion. My apologies."

"Accepted. Things are not often what they seem, my friend. Octavian's armies would seem our biggest threat, for instance, but Juba's goals are not to be misjudged, either." That he himself didn't understand Juba's goals didn't matter to his point, he figured. Besides, Didymus seemed ready to reveal them. "It's just important that we be honest with one another here."

"So it is," Didymus said. "Juba wrote me a letter, Jacob, asking me to acquire the Scrolls for him. He was certain, for reasons I did not then know, that they were here in Alexandria. Here. In the Library."

"You would think they would've been cataloged," Jacob said wryly.

Didymus grinned. "Indeed so. I didn't know anything about the Scrolls other than their legend, yet Juba's certainty about them was disturbing."

"I told you: they don't exist."

"Not in the way Juba is thinking, no. But that was one of the last things I found out."

"Didymus began research on the subject at once," Caesarion said.

"I did," the scholar agreed, "starting with trying to trace where Juba might have learned what information he had. It took me some months, but I was eventually able to retrace his steps from Egypt to Numidia. It seems the young man—a stepson of Caesar, just like Octavian, and near to your own ages, in fact—had taken an interest in objects of ancient power, objects associated with the gods, like Poseidon's Trident. And he had a man here in Alexandria looking for the Scrolls of Thoth."

Seeing the memory of that night, of that assassin, beginning to overtake his friend, Caesarion moved himself in his chair noisily, bringing Jacob's attention in his direction and giving the scholar a chance to compose himself. "As Didymus said, though, we didn't know why he was looking for the Scrolls here."

"But you do now," Jacob said.

Thankfully, the scholar had once more regained his academic bearing. "I think so, yes. I believe he heard of the rumors that the Scrolls were in Sais."

"The center for the cult of Neith," Caesarion said, thinking aloud as he heard the news. "The Egyptian form of the goddess Astarte."

Didymus looked positively proud. "Exactly so. Most of its holdings have been brought here, which is probably why Juba assumed the Scrolls were here, too."

"But they're not," Selene said from her stool, seemingly eager to take part in the unfolding conversation.

"Absolutely not," Didymus said, smiling over at her. "As Jacob said, they don't exist at all."

"Then everything is okay," Selene said.

The scholar's smile was that of a caring, loving father. It was, Caesarion noted with regret, the kind of smile she had seen far too rarely from Mark Antony. "I wish that it were. But in the past months of retracing his steps I've learned much about the books that Juba was reading, the questions he was asking. And I know the rumors of what else was once in Sais, what it is that he's really after. It's something far bigger and far more real." Didymus paused for a moment, taking a deep breath as he turned back to focus on Jacob. "I'm almost certain that Juba is seeking the Ark of the Covenant."

Caesarion was sure he saw something dark pass across Jacob's face, but the Jew's face was quick to recover its calm. "So you wish to know of the Ark," Jacob said.

Didymus nodded. "From what I've read—many of the same texts that Juba has—it's an object of almost unparalleled power," he said. "Associated with a prophet of your people, yes? Moses?"

"That's right," Jacob said. He seemed to be speaking more carefully than he had been before. "In the Torah—the sacred text of the Jews—it's said to have been built in accordance with God's own instructions, spoken to Moses in the wilderness. It is called the strength of God. It housed the stone tablets of our Law, and its power was enough to destroy the walls of Jericho at a word."

"But it's actually older than Moses, isn't it?" Didymus asked. His eyes were piercing with a need to get at the truth. "The physical ark itself, I mean. That's where Thoth and Sais come in."

Jacob said nothing for several seconds, staring across the table at the scholar. Finally he blinked and leaned back deeply into his own chair, all traces of mirth erased from his face. "Few alive know of such things," he said. His voice was quiet, almost dangerous. "It's meant to stay that way."

"We're only interested in the truth," Caesarion said, suddenly aware that Khenti had faded out of the background and was standing closer to the young Jew than he was before.

"Not all truth is meant to be revealed," Jacob said, still focusing on Didymus.

"So much of the story already is," the scholar replied. "Most of it is all there, in the old books, waiting to be read."

"You've been reading Artapanus and Manetho."

"I have. They reveal much. As do others. But not all. And we need to know all we can."

Jacob's eyes narrowed thoughtfully for a moment. "There's an inscription at the temple of Neith at Sais. Did you see it in your travels? 'I am all that has been, that is, and that will be. No mortal has yet been able to lift the veil that covers me.' So it is with God, my friends. Man is not meant to know everything."

"I think you're wrong," Caesarion said, unable to contain himself.

Jacob turned in his chair. "Do you?"

"Each gain in knowledge is progress toward perfecting what we can of this world." Even as he said it, Caesarion remembered his promise to Vorenus that he would destroy the Scrolls of Thoth if he found them. Were the secrets of the Ark so different? Its power less dangerous?

"So it seems to you," Jacob said. "And perhaps even to all of us here in this room, or even in this Library, where men seek knowledge as others do religion. But certainly all knowledge isn't meant for all men." His smile suddenly returned. "Or would you have the knowledge of Egypt's coming defeat shared immediately with your people? This afternoon, perhaps?"

Caesarion started to say something more, then thought better of it. Instead, Didymus spoke: "It's true that the responsibility of knowledge is not something to be taken lightly. Not everyone is ready for the truth about their world, or even about themselves. But it doesn't follow that the truth should be hidden away forever. It must be passed on until the world is ready to receive it. That is, I believe, what your particular family has been helping to do for generations. It's why I wanted to meet your father, to talk with him. I think there may be times when the circle of those asked to harbor the truth must grow, for the greater good."

"What makes you think this is one of those times?"

Didymus took a deep breath. "Because I think I know what Octavian might be able to achieve, what Juba must be working to achieve for him. I know the danger. I've learned about the Shards of Heaven."

Jacob visibly cringed, but he said nothing.

Selene was perched on the edge of her stool. "Shards of Heaven?"

Didymus didn't look away from the young Jew. "If I can learn what I have, Juba can learn it, too. Octavian can learn it. What then? Do you think he'll not pursue them? Not just God's power, but God Himself, Jacob."

The Jew's face fell as the scholar spoke, lending him the look of a man defeated. "Tell me what you know," he finally said.

"And start at the beginning," Caesarion said, realizing he, too, had moved to the edge of his seat as the tension in the room had grown.

"I'll explain what I can," Didymus said. "And perhaps it's best to begin at the beginning. What do you believe about the gods, Caesarion?"

Caesarion leaned back a bit, conscious of Selene's presence in the room. Though he'd spoken with Didymus about such things, he'd never done so in the girl's presence. "I'm unsure in my belief in the traditional gods."

"None of them?" Selene asked.

"Perhaps not none," Caesarion said. "But if there are divine beings, I think there is only one, just as Jacob's people believe." It was the honest truth, even if he suspected it wasn't what she wanted to hear.

"But isn't Mother—"

"Parents aren't always right about all things, even if they mean well. Just like half-brothers," Caesarion said. "They're not wrong about all things, either. But we do have to think for ourselves, Selene, and I think that the concept of divinity can mean there's only one God, as the Jews believe, or perhaps none."

"Why perhaps none?" Didymus asked.

Caesarion frowned. "The Jews define God as all-powerful and good. It's hard to believe in such a God when there's such evil in the world."

"Ah, the problem of old Epicurus." The scholar smiled knowingly. "Either God wants to abolish evil and cannot, or he can abolish it but does not desire to do so. If he wants to abolish it but cannot, he is impotent. If he can abolish it but does not desire to do so, he is unjust. If God can abolish evil, and truly desires to do so, why then is there evil in the world?"

"Exactly," Caesarion said. "If evil exists, then a good, all-powerful God cannot exist."

"Is there no reason to believe such a God exists nonetheless? What about Aristotle?"

"Aristotle?" Caesarion had to think a moment to recall what the scholar was getting at. "Oh, the prime mover."

"What's the prime mover?" Selene asked.

"An argument about the nature of all creation," Didymus said, "but it can be taken for an argument about the existence of a creating God. Aristotle reckoned that all events have causes. All things that move do so because something else moved them. In other words, everything has a beginning. So, too, with creation itself. Something outside of it—outside of time, outside of the world—must have caused it. Something must have set the first movement in motion. A prime mover. God. That's stretching the philosopher a bit, but it works."

"Oh," said Selene, brow furrowing.

"It's a good argument," Caesarion said. "But it says nothing about a god's goodness. And there's no way to know for certain that creation has a beginning point. Maybe it has always been. I mean, if you can say that God doesn't have a beginning, you might as well be able to say the same thing about creation."

"All religions say otherwise," Didymus observed.

"All religions could be wrong," Caesarion said, feeling frustrated. Selene gasped a little at his response, but he ignored it. "And besides, what does this have to do with these Shards of Heaven?"

"Because it's all about God," Jacob said, his voice small. "Everything leads back to Him."

It was the response of a man of faith, but Caesarion didn't dismiss it out of hand. "Please," he said, "explain this to me."

"Well, unless I'm wrong," Didymus said, "creation *did* have a beginning. God was indeed Aristotle's prime mover. This God created everything, and I believe He was, in our sense of the word, good."

"*Was?*" Selene asked.

"Well, I think that's the reason evil exists in the world," Didymus said. "God is dead."

19

The Hand of an Angry God

ACTIUM, 31 BCE

Pullo, his long strides quickly closing the distance across the deck, was the first to engage Octavian's men. Running to catch up, Vorenus watched as his old friend rushed forward into the rail-breaching tide, gladius flashing. The first man Pullo met fell trying to hold his guts in—a task he failed to achieve when his body hit the deck—and the second man had just stepped onto the flagship when Pullo met him with his shoulder lowered, bull-rushing him backward into the railing he'd just crossed. The man's feet caught on the boards of the deck, and his back arched obscenely before snapping with a loud crack. The upper half of his body fell away, dangling limply over the side, but Pullo was already off of him, spinning sideways, gladius wide and wet in the rain, diving into the next line of boarders.

Then Vorenus was among them, too. He deflected an attacker's sword into the deck before impaling him on his own blade, and all around him were the sounds of screams and war-crazed shouts. His gladius stuck for a moment in the shaking body of the dying man, and another man, coming up over the side, raised his weapon in glee, prepared to swing for Vorenus' exposed head.

Vorenus' blade had passed cleanly through the man's body, so he did the only thing that came to his mind: he threw himself and the dead man forward, running the bloodied point of the gladius into the would-be assailant and then rolling past them both as the now sticky-wet deck pitched atop another wave. His gladius pulled free with his momentum and he slid into the center mast of the flagship.

Pullo was there, and from the look of his blade he'd just finished off another of Octavian's men. He looked down at Vorenus with a quick smile of greeting, but he offered no hand before he squared his shoulders to two men facing him and let out a roar. He would kill them both, Vorenus was sure. It was a good day to die.

Vorenus got to his feet and headed back into the fray. Antony's archers had abandoned their bows in favor of short swords for the close quarters, and they were entirely engaged with the enemy. Bloodied bodies were falling like leaves onto the deck, and Vorenus hoped that the majority of them were from the other side.

Looking around, he could see that the second trireme that had rammed them was bringing men over the side now, too. Beyond it, in the haze of the rain and waves, still more vessels were moving, circling like vultures around a kill.

Vorenus got to his feet and spun to take on the newcomers, adjusting his balance to keep from falling in the pitch and roll of the stormy sea. The tied-off grappling irons were making it worse, he could tell, catching tight to jolt the ships as each wave passed under. More than once in the ensuing bloody seconds and minutes he was knocked to his knees by the tightening ropes and the slick, rain-soaked surface beneath his feet. A few times it seemed that every man was felled by the shifting deck, and the melee paused for a moment while friend and foe alike got back onto their feet. But still they fought on, killing and being killed. Vorenus took a cut across his left forearm blocking a swing meant for his gut. He earned another slash on his right thigh from a man lying along the side railing that he'd thought was dead.

He was preparing to put the latter finally to rest when the sea itself seemed to groan: a low and long yawning that froze his strike and made him stare out into the rain. The waters over the side—he blinked to believe it—were, like a falling tide, receding away to the north, racing in smooth waves toward Octavian's ships. Even the rain appeared to be slanting back in that direction, as if Neptune himself stood somewhere out in the fog beyond Octavian's fleet, drawing in his breath. Yet the stormy northern wind was still pushing against them, as if water and air worked against one another.

The other men aboard the flagship, moments earlier committed to each other's deaths, had ceased fighting, too. Antony, surrounded by loyal men near the prow, had turned to stare. So did they all.

"By the gods," one of Octavian's nearby marines gasped.

"What's—" started another.

Like a sudden exhalation, matched with an echoing boom that reverberated in Vorenus' chest, the rain came back against them, faster than even the hard wind itself, stinging like a thousand tiny arrows.

And behind the rain came the roar of an angry god.

Some men stood where they were, transfixed. Some walked forward against the gale, trying to see. Vorenus, without thinking, sheathed his gladius and dove away from it all toward the center mast of the flagship. His hands scrabbled to find holds among the coils of rope there, winding lines tight to his forearms and lowering his head as he braced for the impact. He didn't need to look up to see the wave rushing toward them. He could feel it in his bones: a terrible, awesome power bent on their destruction.

It hit like a thunderbolt from the hand of Jupiter himself, bursting into the three interconnected ships with a world-quaking power Vorenus could not have imagined. As the instant of the impact stretched out, the noise of fierce destruction was everywhere all at once around him—wood ripping, men screeching, limbs snapping—until Vorenus heard nothing at all and had to shut his eyes against the pain as his body flapped against his grip, pulling the rope into the flesh of his forearms as the water roiled over him. His heart pounded in his chest like a trapped beast eager to flee. Everything churned around him—up, down, in, out—and when he screamed he was uncertain if any noise left his throat.

Sound returned with a disturbed rush of wind. His scream popped out into the air, bubbling the seawater clinging to his face. He felt as if he were hanging in suspension for a moment, then his stomach was in his throat as he felt himself falling.

The flagship struck the water with a crash, and Vorenus smashed into the deck a moment later. He felt something snap in his left arm. And then the wave was gone. The rain was falling in natural sheets. The lean and lurch of the deck returned to the mere bucking of the storm. Vorenus rolled to his side, taking a deep breath and coughing out the sting of saltwater, but smiling in momentary gratitude to be alive as air returned to his lungs.

The flagship rumbled beneath him, and over the sound of the roiling waves Vorenus heard the mad rush of water pouring into space.

"The hooks!" Antony's voice shouted over the storm. "Cut the hooks! Cut it loose!"

Vorenus frantically unwound the rope from around his forearms, trying to ignore the wide welts along the inside of them where the rope had burned into skin not covered by his bracers. He felt confident that his left arm had indeed broken, but by a miracle it had been a clean break and the bones hadn't shifted. The bracer was helping to hold it in place. For the moment his hand still worked, painful though it was.

He got to his feet as quickly as he could, even as he felt the deck of the flagship begin to lean to port, in the direction of the second ramming trireme. He looked up and saw Antony amid a small knot of surviving men along the opposite, high side of the ship near the railing, gesturing wildly back the other way. "Cut it loose!"

Vorenus' head turned to follow Antony's fingers—too slow, he thought, as his senses slowly returned—and he saw that the snapped-off mast of the second trireme was slipping out of sight over the railing. The deck, moments earlier cluttered with men and bodies and debris, had been swept clean of all but the embedded arrow points that Vorenus used to stagger down the side-sloping wet wood to the railing.

The wave had ripped the second trireme in half, as if it were a child's plaything. Bodies, twisted and torn, lay scattered about in the waves. Few of them were moving. The forward half of the trireme was still attached to the flagship by its grappling lines, and the water was fast swallowing it, pulling the ropes tight and tugging the side of the flagship down. As it did so, more and more water was surging through the hole that the trireme had punched in their ship's side. Now that he knew the rumbling belowdecks for what it was, he could hear behind it the screaming from the throats of the rowers who'd survived. How many, he wondered, dozens? Hundreds?

The deck canted further with a sound of cracking and moaning wood, and Vorenus had to grab the rail to keep his balance. His head at last cleared through its daze and he drew his blade.

"Jump for it!" he heard Antony shouting to the men on the

other side of the ship, and he imagined them scrambling over the side, trying to jump across to the first ramming trireme, which must have survived the wave.

A grappling hook was buried in the railing right in front of him, and Vorenus cut at its knot, watching the line flip over the side with a snap. There was a momentary pause in the tilting, but too many other lines held them to the sinking ship. Looking fore and aft he could see at least half a dozen more straining at the wood, pulling them down. The deck pitched over a few degrees more.

One of Octavian's men appeared at the railing, his eyes wide with terror and shock. Two of the hooks were within striking distance for him.

"Cut the ropes!" Vorenus screamed at him. "Cut us loose!"

The man looked at the grappling irons and the tightened ropes attached to them, then looked at the bloodied sword in his hand, then back to Vorenus.

"Cut them!" Vorenus yelled again, then turned his back to the man to run forward to the next line and slash it. One more line held closer to the bow, and he cut that, too, before turning back toward the rear of the ship. Octavian's man was hacking at one of the lines, but he was too scared and shaking to connect properly with the rope. It was frayed, but it held. "Cut it!" Vorenus yelled and began running.

The starboard side of the deck pitched up into the air as the bound-up remains of the trireme slipped fully into the water at last. The man screamed and dropped his sword in the lurch. The tilting sped up, and Vorenus' footfalls started to come down in the crack between rail and deck, his good arm desperately swinging the gladius at the ropes as they did so. He cut two, but only half-severed two others before he ran into his enemy.

"Climb to starboard!" Vorenus shouted, shoving him toward the skyward side of the deck. "Go!"

They began scrambling, trying to claw their way up the wet deck, but even with the arrow points as holds it was too slick. Time and again they slid back to the railing and to the ever-nearing water, their hands bloodied from the splintered wood. The other man began to cry.

The splash of the waves beneath them was loud, and the larger ones were now crashing over the flagship's railing and into their legs. The water was very cold.

Vorenus pushed the man along the railing to midship, where the main mast stuck out of the deck at an angle growing frighteningly close to parallel with the choppy waters. The sails had partly unfolded from above, dangling at the tops of the waves, and their rope lines swung about in the wind. Sheathing his gladius, Vorenus grabbed one of the lines and began climbing, bellowing at Octavian's man to follow. The line ran to the mast, and Vorenus was able to swing himself up onto it despite his increasingly useless left arm. The other man began to scream horribly, and Vorenus straddled the round wood for a moment to look back down at him.

The tilting of the flagship had sent a rope netting sliding down into the man, and his foot was caught, wrapped tightly in the mesh. He was pulling as hard as he could, but the foot would not come loose. The railing had sunk into the waters now, and the waves were breaking against the floor of the deck. He was halfway up to his knees in the frigid sea, the breakers striking him in the torso, and still they were sinking. His scream was piercing.

Vorenus grabbed a line dangling down from the masthead and quickly wrapped it around his right forearm before allowing himself to spin around the mast, hanging with his legs wrapped around the damp wood and his right arm extended behind him. He reached out toward the trapped man with his left arm. "Take my hand!" he yelled.

The water was up to the man's knees, and he flailed wildly for long seconds before their hands finally met.

"Don't let go!" the man shrieked. The water was breaking at his chest. Vorenus pulled as hard as he could manage, screaming in agony as the break in his arm stretched out against the muscles trying to keep the bones in place. His legs slipped, but they held.

The water seemed to yawn and open to take the man in. Vorenus pulled as hard as he could, but the man was held too fast. "Don't leave me!" he shouted, the pitch of his voice high as the cold took his chest and constricted his lungs.

The draft of water was pulling the man away from Vorenus, their grips straining. The rope wrapped around his outstretched right forearm began to burn and tear the flesh from friction, adding new welts to those he'd already received. He felt liquid running up his shoulder from the wrist, and it felt thicker than the rest of the rainwater covering his body. Octavian's man screamed desperately, but the waters were too strong, and the waves began to crash over his head. Vorenus heard the muting of the man's voice as he began to swallow water, and then the sea at last pulled them apart.

Vorenus watched the thrashing of the man's arms in the water for only a heartbeat before he pulled himself upright on the mast and tried to reach the other side of the ship, where Antony and the others had gone.

He couldn't make it. His left hand alternatively screamed in pain and went numb, the fingers unable to work individually, and the deck was too steep and wet for him to make it one-handed. Vorenus sat for a moment on the mast, seawater stinging his eyes, the sound of the drowning man very close in his ears, before he chose a course of action. The mast was slick, but it was at least out of the water. Using the line leading to the masthead to help pull himself along, he began to shimmy up the wood and out into the space above the sea.

The yard—a heavy crossbeam normally mounted horizontal to the mast to secure the top of the sail—was angled strangely, but it had somehow remained intact in the punishing wave. Vorenus had nearly reached it when he looked back and could see over the side of the flagship to the other trireme. The grapple lines connecting it to the flagship had been cut, and its ram had pulled free from their side as the flagship had rotated, but it was still tantalizingly close. The battle yet raged there, as if the unnatural wave had never struck, and men lay like sacks of supplies across the deck amid the flurry of bloody activity. Antony was there among them, hacking in furious rage. He'd managed to rally his men to him on the enemy deck. At least six of them, Vorenus could see, had somehow maintained holds on their shields through the chaos—or found some close at hand, he supposed—and Antony's makeshift force was advancing across the trireme's deck behind their shield wall in trained legionnaire formation. The numbers of Octavian's men had clearly been obliterated by the wave, and Vorenus could see that it was possible—just possible—that Antony and his men might actually win the ship.

Pullo! Vorenus thought with a jolt. Where was Pullo? Not on the deck of the trireme with Antony. Vorenus would have been able to recognize his old friend even from the distance in a storm.

Vorenus started to look out to the bodies on the sea, to the few arms still waving for rescue, when the mast beneath him creaked and shook.

No, he thought, looking up. Not—

The strangely angled yard above him shuddered, rocking free of the mast. Lashings began to snap, one at a time, as if an invisible hand were counting them off: *one, two, three ...*

Vorenus cursed. Half his mind told him to give up at last, but the other half insisted that he was going to make it through this, rescue Pullo from wherever he was hiding, and then explain to the sacrilegious old bastard that *this* was exactly why he believed in the gods. The possibility that Pullo might be dead was spared only the most passing thought before it was swept aside by the final crack. And then the wide beam, as wide as the great flagship itself, came loose and fell.

Vorenus scrambled his feet against the mast, searching for purchase even as he tried to tighten the tired grip of his right hand on the masthead line. He had time only to roll the rope once, twice, three times around his forearm—he'd have no skin at all on the inside of it before long, he thought—before the yard was bouncing and twisting down, crashing and catching through ropes, the sail unbound now and adding its own madness to the falling tumble. His feet caught on the wood an instant before it all struck and he kicked off, swinging out of the way and into the rain.

The world spun. The sailcloth slapped against his outstretched arm. But the yard missed him, coming down into the water with a splash and at last breaking the grappling lines that he'd only managed to half-sever.

Just reaching the end of his swing, Vorenus had time only to smile before the flagship, finally released of the weight of the drowned trireme, abruptly rocked back toward upright, whipping him up through the air.

Vorenus saw the flagship's deck passing below him. Then he saw the storm-dark sky. Then he lost his grip entirely, the rope burning its way loose of his arm, and he fell, screaming obscenities at the gods, down into the frothing sea.

The cold water momentarily paralyzed him, squeezing the remaining wind out of his lungs and preventing him from taking in more even when he bobbed up to the surface amid the waves. He would not float long, he knew. His armor was weighing him down, and as its leathers soaked in the sea he could feel it all pulling him lower—like Neptune's own hands. As soon as the frigid shock of the impact let go, Vorenus took a deep breath and frantically began trying to unfasten the straps and binds of the armor, even as the weight took him back under. When the last of them came loose, his lungs were burning. He kicked his legs wildly toward the light above, breaking the surface to gulp down the salty air, his teeth chattering and his eyes scanning for help.

The other trireme, he thought. It must be near. I must have landed—

He spun in the water, saw the boat not an oar's length away. Glad for the numbing cold on his arm, he started swimming, screaming for Antony.

In response, a face—enemy? friend? did it matter?—appeared at the railing and saw him. Seconds later, a rope was flung over the railing, the frayed, chopped-off end landing only a few feet from him.

Grasping the line with shaking hands, Vorenus held on, his last ounce of strength threatening to fail him. "Just don't let go," he shouted, to both his savior and himself. "Don't let go!"

Neither of them did. The man on the trireme pulled. Vorenus kicked. And then he was rising out of the bone-chilling water, the man gripping his soaked clothes and using them to pull him up and over the railing.

Vorenus fell to the blood-splattered deck, shivering violently. His rescuer stepped away, looking for a blanket, for something to put over his shoulders and his bleeding arm. Vorenus coughed and retched, his vision rattling along with his teeth, but then he looked up and saw—unmistakably, undeniably—the big shape of a man that could only be Pullo exiting the trap that led to the rowers' hold.

"Vorenus!" Pullo shouted, seeing him at the same time and rushing forward. "Antony! It's Vorenus!"

Vorenus could see blood smeared across his friend's face and chest when he got close, but the big man looked happy enough. He was still alive, by the gods. And the fight on the trireme's deck was over: Antony and his men had indeed somehow taken it.

"Pullo, dammit," Vorenus muttered as Pullo helped him to his knees. "This is why I believe—"

"You need a surgeon," Pullo said, frowning as he examined the rope-mauled arm. "Why do you always get hurt more than me?"

"Glad you made it," Antony said, striding into Vorenus' field of vision. The thick curls of the general's hair were sodden with more than water, and his eyes were heavily dark with sorrow despite the confident smile on his face. "We've lost too many—though we've taken a ship, eh, lads?"

A faint, tired cheer went up on the deck.

Vorenus shook his head. "Go," he said.

Antony's face froze. "What?"

Pullo had his arm around his back now and lifted him to his feet. When Vorenus couldn't seem able to stand, the big man just held him there. "Cleopatra," Vorenus managed to say.

Antony's face turned away, toward the south, as if he might see something in the storm. "Go send her a message? We've lost our signalman, Vorenus. But she knows to enter the fight late: the second wave."

Vorenus shook his head, more vigorously for the sudden memory of the ungodly—or was it godly?—wave that had nearly killed them all. Octavian's other ships, the ones he'd seen circling. They must have been driven back by the wave, but they'd return. Vultures always came back. They didn't have time. "No," he said, concentrating to keep his voice steady despite the cold. Someone threw a blanket over his shoulders—a good feeling despite the weight. "She won't come."

Antony's face whipped around to face him again. "How do you—"

"I told her to run," Vorenus said, knowing there was no

time for pleasantries about it. "If things turned bad. Told her to run. Break free."

Antony's face grew red, a crimson of anger. "What?"

"The children," Vorenus croaked. "Alexandria."

"You told her to run? To *leave* me?"

"We need ... catch up. Keep flying Octavian's flag. Push hard for the south. There's a chance—"

Antony recoiled as if he'd been slapped. "Flee the field?"

"Fight another day," Vorenus said. "Get the children—"

"You coward," Antony growled, his fist pulling back to strike.

Vorenus cringed at the impending blow, but he lacked the strength to move, only standing because Pullo's big left arm supported him. So when Antony began to swing, it was Pullo who stopped it, his free right hand coming forward in a quick punch that caught Antony squarely on the cheek and spun him around and down to the deck like a dropped sack of wheat.

"Pullo!" Vorenus gasped. "You can't ... oh gods..."

Pullo hoisted Vorenus up a little straighter, moving some of the weight over his hip. "Bah!" he said. "I never really liked taking orders from him anyway. Let's get back to Alexandria, shall we?"

Without waiting for a response from Vorenus, Pullo turned around to face the stunned squadron of fellow legionnaires gathered around them. "We're going south," he said. "You heard Vorenus: keep up the enemy's colors. Keep up the appearance. We're just a lowly trireme limping after the enemy, got it?"

The legionnaires, much to Vorenus' shock, saluted and began carrying out Pullo's instructions. The one who'd brought the blanket for Vorenus paused, looking uncertainly down at Antony's unconscious form. "Sir, what should we do with, um—"

"Pullo," Vorenus whispered. "We can't—"

"Get him out of the rain, for one thing," Pullo said. "He'll be in a bad enough mood when he wakes up. No sense adding a cold to it. Let's take him below with Vorenus here. It smells to the highest heaven down there with all those blasted rowers, but it's warm and relatively dry."

Vorenus tried to help as much as he could, but Pullo still had to half-carry him down the trap while three other men carefully brought Antony along. The hold stank—they always did—but Vorenus was glad that Pullo was right about the warmth. And there were a few open rowing benches near the front. The bodies on the floor beside them attested to what Pullo had done to ensure control over the captured rowers. Vorenus ignored the dead, broken men as his comrades stretched him and Antony out on the wooden seats.

"Pullo," Vorenus said after the other legionnaires had moved away to take positions between them and their prisoner rowers. "Do you know what you've done? At best you'll be dismissed from the legion."

The big man smiled, nodded. "Just didn't think today was a good day to die after all," he said.

Vorenus started to say something more, but Pullo had already turned to the rowers, his voice reverberating between the walls as he boomed orders on his way back toward the trap. "You call this speed? My one-armed grandmother can turn an oar quicker than you lot! Faster! Faster! You two," he said to a couple of the watching legionnaires, "tell them to keep rowing for all they're worth or I'll come down and bust another head or two."

The two legionnaires saluted as he passed by. The third looked expectant. "Me, sir?"

Pullo stopped at the base of the ladder, his first foot two steps high upon it. "With me, son. There's sails to get ready. We've got a queen to catch!"

20

Return to Alexandria

ALEXANDRIA, 31 BCE

Caesarion sat like a statue upon the throne atop the walls of the Lochian palace, the royal scepter upright in his hand, unfocused eyes stylized with black paint, the tall crown of a pharaoh perched atop his freshly shaved head. While his mother had been away he'd enjoyed the freedom to grow out his hair, but now that she was returning, he'd shaved it back to his scalp in accordance with custom. He would become annoyed with the practice, he knew, but for now, with the heat of the high sun adding to the heaviness of the crown, he was glad for the lack of additional weight on his head. Even with slaves steadily waving palm fronds around them, the air was dreadfully stifling. Helios, whose health had taken another downturn in the past week, had been too weak to handle it, so Caesarion had sent the grateful boy back to the cooler shade, along with the useless slaves and the rest of the platform party. Only Selene and Vorenus remained close to him now.

For his part, Vorenus refused a seat, preferring to stand between the two remaining thrones despite the obvious discomfort of the wounds he wouldn't acknowledge. "It's hard to believe," the old soldier said as another cheer went up from the throngs of people surrounding the harbor.

Caesarion wanted to nod, but he didn't dare do so with the tall crown on his head. There were thousands upon thousands of people in sight; seemingly the whole of the city had turned out for Antony and Cleopatra's triumphant return. The wide surface of the harbor itself was awash with bright swaths of bobbing color where the cheering people had thrown flowers into the sea—to carpet the victors' path home. It was, indeed, hard to believe. "They'll know the truth soon," Caesarion said. "The truth will come out."

"It's known in whispers already," Vorenus said. "News always flies ahead of the army." He'd been back only a day—the stolen Roman trireme acting as a forward ship to inform the city of the pending return—and Caesarion was still having a hard time growing accustomed to the new tiredness in the older man's voice. Much had changed in the months they were apart. He wondered if Vorenus felt the same way.

"We've tried to keep it quiet," Selene said, her voice stoic. That, too, seemed to have changed, Caesarion noted. Especially after what they'd learned from Didymus and Jacob. His half-sister seemed more and more a woman in a girl's body, even if that, too, was changing. Sitting here now her upright bearing might as well be their shared mother's as she sat in regal, divine impassivity and watched the lie unfolding below them. "But it won't last."

Caesarion made a sound of agreement. "The traders already know of the defeat, and of Octavian's movements east, cutting off our allies one by one. We've bought them off as best we can, but it's only a matter of time." From the corner of his eye, Caesarion saw Vorenus shift on his feet, and he thought he saw him wince. "Please," he said, "I'll have a chair brought up."

Vorenus shook his head, visibly stiffened. "Wouldn't be proper," he said.

Caesarion let out a careful sigh, not breaking his impassive expression. Moving his eyes alone, he saw that Cleopatra's massive flagship was crawling past the mountain-like lighthouse at the head of the harbor. The ship's oars were in careful, patient time, and its decks were alight with gold and metals that shined in the sun. He had to fight back a smile. His mother had always been good at theater.

The glinting of the ship hurt his eyes and he had to look away, not for the first time cursing the fact that they'd not had clouds this day.

"Tell me again about the wave," Caesarion said. "The one that destroyed the ships."

"Like the wrath of a god," Vorenus said. "Unnatural. Like Neptune's anger unleashed."

"Poseidon's," Selene said.

"If you like, my lady," Vorenus said. "I've never seen anything like it."

Poseidon's Trident, Caesarion thought, sensing that Selene was thinking the same thing. Didymus said Juba was looking for it.

"Some of the men are saying Octavian has the gods on his side," Vorenus said.

"I think not," Caesarion said. "I think Didymus is right: there's only one God. Didymus thinks He's dead. Jacob thinks He's just fallen silent. Either way, He has nothing to do with creation anymore."

"You think this wave has something to do with this man Juba?" Vorenus asked.

"It might," Caesarion said, glad that Vorenus didn't ask whether he agreed with Didymus or Jacob. "He was looking for Poseidon's Trident. Perhaps he has it. That's not the biggest worry, though." Since they'd found this moment of quiet solitude during the celebrations, Caesarion had been slowly explaining to Vorenus what they had learned in Didymus' office. It helped to explain it to someone, he thought. And he trusted no one more than Vorenus. If anything needed to be done because of it all, Vorenus would be the man he'd call upon. It would've been Pullo, too, if he hadn't been forced to remove the big man from his service when he'd arrived in Alexandria in chains. Better removed from service, though, than the public execution Antony had intended him to carry out. Caesarion hoped that Antony would accept Caesarion's decision to exile the big soldier into Didymus' care instead. He was just too good a man to lose. And he'd saved Caesarion's life back in Rome, after all. It was only fair to return the favor.

"You said something about the real threat being the Ark, and the possibility that Juba wants the 'real' Scrolls of Thoth, since they're not what Didymus had originally thought," Vorenus said, not bothering to cover up his obvious confusion.

Caesarion actually cracked a smile before he remembered to erase the emotion from his face. The slow approach of his mother's ship—during which he'd need to remain here—seemed interminable. "It's all very confusing," he admitted. "Jacob and Didymus had to explain things three or four different ways before we understood it all. I'll try to explain if you'll concede to a stool."

Vorenus agreed, and a flick of Caesarion's wrist brought a slave scampering out onto the wall to receive the order to procure suitable seating for Vorenus.

"Imagine trying to describe the Pharos lighthouse," Caesarion said after the slave was beyond earshot once more. "On the ground it has a length and width, but of course it has a height, too. To describe it you'd need at least those three things. But that's not enough, is it?"

"I don't understand your meaning, sir," Vorenus said.

"Well, the lighthouse changes over time, doesn't it? Our grandfather replaced the statue of Poseidon at its top. That surely changed its height. And reinforcement at the base has changed its width, too."

"So you need to state the time at which you're describing it. I see."

"Yes. Time."

"Fair enough." Vorenus' voice didn't sound entirely understanding, but Caesarion knew the old soldier well enough to know that he wouldn't continue the conversation if he wasn't interested.

"Didymus brought all this up when he suggested that we try to imagine one God, the creator of it all. God must, if He exists, live outside time. Above it, if you will, seeing everything that's below just as easily as we can see a rock on the floor."

"Makes sense, I suppose."

Caesarion heard the slave returning with a stool for the old soldier, though he couldn't turn his head to observe whether it was a suitable one; the slave placed it, as was proper, just behind the line of the two thrones. Only by straining his eyes could he see the haze of Vorenus settling into a sitting position. Then the slave retreated, the shuffle of cloth indicating deep bows of reverence. Caesarion only barely contained the urge to roll his eyes.

"Tell him about the angels," Selene said when the slave had disappeared into the distance and it was safe to talk once more.

"Angels?" Vorenus asked.

"It's a term from the Jews," Caesarion said. "But we found it useful to talk in terms of that religion. It was easier that way with Jacob there. Angels are beings that are like gods to men, but are nevertheless creations of God, like us. They're even supposed to appear like men, though of great beauty and strength. Like perfect beings."

"There's something like this in other faiths," Vorenus said thoughtfully.

"I imagine so," Caesarion said. "If there's any truth in faith, Didymus pointed out, most religions should have at least a glimpse of it. We think these angels were among God's first creations. They accompanied God and acted like His agents in the realms below Him—though you understand that 'below' is not accurate in a literal sense. Wherever God lives surrounds all of creation, in the same way a man on the first floor of the Pharos lighthouse is surrounded by the room around him, the vast height above him, and the passing of time that encompasses that in turn."

"It is, as you say, confusing," Vorenus said, sounding amused despite the tiredness in his voice. "But I think I follow. These ... angels would be like a guard assigned to one level of the lighthouse, who cannot guard the whole forever."

Caesarion hadn't thought about it that way, but he decided the analogy fit fairly well—though he again managed to avoid nodding. "Just so, Vorenus. Now imagine that God lives at the highest realm of creation, and from there He can see everything. As Didymus explained it, for Him, past, present, and future would all be the same. So from His perspective nothing below Him would have free will. The only way for anyone to have free will, in other words, would be for them to be like God. Yet without free will God's creation wouldn't be truly alive. So He decided to give part of Himself to some of His creatures. This part, we think, is our soul. It is what then exists beyond our deaths, journeying up through the realms to that highest place where God dwells: the gift of true life, imparted through the gift of death, for only in knowing true loss can a being truly know love. At least that's how Jacob explained it. The point is that God gave us the opportunity to become one with His eternity, to have the free will to live and love as we chose."

"Because God alone is capable of free will," Selene said. Her voice sounded distant to Caesarion, and he longed to look at her. "So the soul is a portion of God."

"I think I understand," Vorenus said. "And you believe this is true?"

"You know me," Caesarion said. "I'm stubborn about anything. But this makes some sense. We're all gods in the sense that we all have free will. We do as we wish."

"And this one God just watches? Just sits and lets people kill each other?"

"It doesn't seem so," Caesarion admitted. "What happened isn't exactly clear—Didymus didn't know for sure, and Jacob either didn't know or wasn't telling—but there was some kind of dispute among God's angels about God's desire to give us free will. Some of the angels may have refused because they did not want to see man become greater than they were. Some may have objected because they didn't want to lose God."

The flagship of Egypt was close enough now to see the two figures lounged in luxury upon its deck, surrounded by wealth and slaves. Cleopatra and Antony were dressed as the victorious gods they pretended to be. Antony waved and smiled as the people ashore cheered and the men below the vessels deck pushed and pulled the long dipping and lifting oars. Cleopatra might as well have been made of rock.

"But God's will couldn't be denied," Caesarion continued, his voice sounding rehearsed even to his own ears. "The only way to make us truly free was to unmake Himself. So God sat upon His silver throne, and in a surge of power He destroyed Himself, unleashing what Didymus called the breath of God, which instilled true life in those creatures ready to receive it. The rest of God's great powers—the powers He'd used to create us all—were infused into His throne, which turned to broken stones of impenetrable darkness. And where He had sat upon it, all that remained was a book, the real book behind the legend of the Scrolls of Thoth. God, Jacob says, created of Himself a Book of Life and Death, containing the fullness of His knowledge. It is said to be the most powerful object in existence, and it remains in the Heaven where God resided, protected by the angels who forever mourn God's sacrifice."

"What of the angels who were against it?" Vorenus asked.

"Eventually, war broke out among them all," Caesarion replied. "They were divided over what they believed God's plans were for creation. There were some, it seems, who desired to destroy man. In order to defeat these angels who had fallen away from God's will, another group of angels used some of those power-filled fragments of God's throne to create a gate down through the dimensions. In a terrible cataclysm, Jacob said that an angel named Michael, leading the loyal angels, forced the defiant angels into the void. Gehenna, Jacob called it. Hades is another term, I think. Some call it Hell. After the war was over, after the Fallen angels were banished, the loyal angels, who called themselves the Vested, determined that they'd try to unite all the pieces of God's seat, to bring the powers of God together in order to find the God they'd lost."

"They tried to remake God?"

Caesarion's shoulders raised to shrug before his mind overrode the instinct. He slowly lowered them back into position. "Jacob said as much. I don't know how that would happen. Whatever they tried failed, though: the throne shattered across creation, and these pieces of God's strength—the Shards of Heaven—have fallen here, where they remain sources of enormous power."

New cheers went up, and Caesarion could see that the surviving ships of the fleet that had left with such high hopes were entering the inner harbor. He tried not to think about the wives and children who would count the ships and find that too few had returned, that the ships of their loved ones were gone to the deep.

"There's proof of this in the stories of these Jews?" Vorenus asked.

"Some, but not all. Didymus found traces of the story in many places. It seems the truth was scattered in men's memories, the details of what happened only available in bits and pieces that now need to be cobbled together. It's like a big puzzle, with some pieces missing and others we cannot understand. I'm sure we don't even know the half of it all still."

"You believe it, though?"

Vorenus sounded, Caesarion thought, hopeful. He wanted to turn and look at him, but his mother's ship was close enough now that she would see his fault for sure. Caesarion could see Antony very clearly now. The great general was still waving and smiling, but his eyes were sunken, and his smile was hollow. He looked ... broken. Defeated. One of Cleopatra's hands was draped over his elbow, clinging tightly to him. He wondered to whom she was giving strength. "I think I do," he finally said.

"I see," Vorenus said. "And this truth is what Juba was seeking?"

"Juba was looking for the Scrolls of Thoth, but whatever that book is, it is unreachable in Heaven. Only stories about it are here on this earth, whispers that survive in legends. What's important here and now are instead those Shards of Heaven, those fragments of God's power that made it here, to earth, to us. The first one arrived more than twenty-five centuries ago. That Shard has a special power to control earth and stone. It was used to build many great structures of the ancient world. Didymus thinks maybe this First Shard was taken to Sais during the Hyksos invasions of Egypt."

"The Hyksos?"

"It doesn't matter," Caesarion said. "It only explains how the Shard became associated with Sais."

The flagship was turning into the royal dock below the wall. The cheers were very loud. Antony stood and smiled up at him, and Caesarion fought the urge to smile back.

"So is that Shard the Ark you're worried about?" Vorenus asked. "The one you want to keep from Octavian and this Juba man of his? I thought that it was an object of the Jews."

"It became that, yes," Caesarion said once his stepfather turned away to greet the servants and dignitaries lining the dock. Little Philadelphus was down among them, waving happily to his parents. When Cleopatra stood and actually waved back to her little boy, Caesarion was so surprised that he had to collect himself for a moment before he could answer Vorenus' question. "Thirteen centuries ago, Pharaoh Amenhotep's eldest son was named Thutmose," he said, working hard to recall all the names Jacob and Didymus had given him. "His name means 'Son of Thoth' in the native tongue. He was the crown prince of Egypt, and he led the armies of the kingdom against the people of Kush, the kingdom up the Nile. He defeated them by marrying a Kushite princess named Tharbis. Perhaps through her influence, or through some other, Thutmose revolted against the religion of many gods held sacred in Egypt, and against his father. Somewhere, somehow, he acquired the Second Shard, which has power over water. He built a staff to hold it, to avoid touching it directly. He became, it is said, a Jew, and his name is known to that people as Moses. He returned to Egypt and took the First Shard from Sais, and he built a kind of box to hold it, which is what the Jews call the Ark of the Covenant. Thutmose took the two Shards and used them to cross the Red Sea and journey toward Judea, escaping Egypt and his father. The Jews who followed him established a kingdom there."

Vorenus made a sound of uncertainty in the back of his throat. "I know something of the Jews, but I know nothing about them having such great powers."

Below them, a causeway was being drawn out from the deck of the ship to the dock. Cleopatra and Antony were standing now arm in arm as they started toward it. "Jacob didn't want to admit the truth that Thutmose and Moses were one and the same," Caesarion said, "or that the Ark derived its powers from a Shard, but he did so under the questions of Didymus. He couldn't deny the truth. For the same reason, he admitted that the Ark is no longer with the Jews in Jerusalem. It hasn't been for many hundreds of years."

It surprised Caesarion that Antony wasn't barking orders as soon as he set foot on the docks. Had the defeat so crushed him?

"So where is the Ark now?" Vorenus asked.

"We don't know," Caesarion conceded, letting his frustration with the fact show in his voice.

"The Jew didn't know?"

"Jacob admitted, as Didymus had already discovered, that he's descended from those who removed the Ark from Jerusalem," Caesarion said. "But he insisted that he didn't know the exact whereabouts of it now. How the Second Shard got into Juba's hands he didn't know, either, though he was very insistent that we cannot allow him and Octavian to get hold of the First."

"Why?" Vorenus asked. "I've seen enough of the power of the Second Shard—as you call it—to think it the hand of a god. What difference a bit more?"

"This is the crux of it, Vorenus. The Shards are the result of the attempt to remake God, remember? If a man were to gather them together once more, he might be able to reach Heaven. He might even succeed where they failed and become God."

Cleopatra and Antony disappeared from sight below them, and Caesarion heard the sounds of servants and priests approaching to take him and Selene to meet their parents. He felt like throwing his damnable scepter at the priests, but he knew, with regret, that he'd just hand it over.

"A gate to Heaven," Vorenus said, his voice quiet.

"Or down to Hell," Selene whispered.

PART III

THE FALL OF EGYPT

21

A City Besieged

ALEXANDRIA, 30 BCE

It was after midnight when Vorenus left the battlefield and marched his remaining men back through the tall gates into beleaguered Alexandria. The cool air of the dark, breathed in between chapped and broken lips, was a welcome respite from the midsummer heat of the field that had hung heavy about the men as their battle had raged on long after the sunset. Vorenus drank it into his lungs gratefully, careful not to use his nose to do so. He had no interest in the stench of sweat and blood that they'd be bringing back from the day's work.

They'd won a victory, Vorenus knew, and he smiled tiredly as his numb legs carried him past the war-worn stone walls and the few remaining guards. Not that it would matter in the end, but Antony—outnumbered two to one and without a navy or even a cavalry following the mass defections of the past month's siege—had been brilliant. Old Caesar had said no one could best the man on land, and he'd been right. Everyone knew that Octavian had thought he'd strike the final blow this day, that he'd enter the city with the rising sun, triumphant in the defeat of Egypt, but he'd lost. Antony had outfoxed him, bought them all more time.

For what, Vorenus didn't know. There was no question that Alexandria would fall: Octavian's navy—bigger now after the mass defection—had blockaded the Great Harbor and even Lake Mareotis and the canal access to the Nile; and Octavian's armies had cut them off from both east and west, closing Alexandria in an unbreakable vise. Their defeat was only a matter of time, even if they had more of it now.

No matter, Vorenus thought, his smile spreading as a soft breeze pushed down the road and brushed over him. He was alive.

Without an order to do so, but without an order not to, the legionnaires behind him began to disperse as the column paced its slow way east up the wide Canopic Way toward the heart of the city. Vorenus listened to them stumbling away into the quiet dark: here in groups of two or three into a tavern or brothel, there in a whole company heading off down one of the side streets toward the main barracks close to the Lochian palaces.

It was tradition that the army's march should take them through the center of town, past Alexander's tomb, before turning north along the Sema Avenue and circling back to the barracks, but he wasn't about to begrudge his weary men the relief of a quicker return to beds and blissful sleep. And it wasn't as if the people of the city were lining the parade path: Alexandria was silent as the grave it was near to becoming, the people locked into their homes in hope that the storm of looting to come would pass them by.

Ahead, in the gloom, Vorenus saw the figure of Antony atop one of their few remaining horses: his back was straight, his head held high in pride despite the city's lack of praise for this day's good work, but Vorenus knew it was just a show.

Though he remained as brilliant in battle as ever, the general had been a broken man ever since Actium. In the weeks after their return to Egypt, as the extent of Octavian's enormous victory became clear, he and Cleopatra had at first tried to arrange a fleet of ships on the Red Sea to take them to India. When those ships were burned by once-loyal vassals who capitulated to Octavian's rule, Antony had built himself a rich hermit's home out on the harbor, at the end of a jetty between Antirhodos and Lochias: he named it the Timonium, in honor of the man-hater Timon of Athens, and there he secluded himself, turning his back on the world that had turned its back on him. Cleopatra had mourned, and Octavian had crept closer. Only Caesarion had kept the state together then. Even now, coaxed into leading the city's defense by his beloved queen, Antony was a shell of the man he'd once been.

Gradually, as he walked, Vorenus became aware of the various pains in his body. There were muscle aches and strains in abundance, of course, and the cap of his right knee had been cut badly. The fingers of his left hand somehow ached despite their numbness—a lingering testament to what he'd been through at Actium—but more pressing was the seething burning sensation ripping through his right forearm, which had never really healed after being rope-flayed in that sea battle. He could see the striated lines of scars leading to his wrist had opened up again and were festering red, weeping blood. He'd need to clean them out soon, he decided.

A large contingent of men behind him stumbled off into the dark as they passed the gymnasium on their right. It was a fairly straight path to the barracks from here, but Vorenus did not follow them himself. Like Antony, he was determined to see the parade through despite the gloom of midnight. He didn't even turn to watch them go. Instead, he turned his eyes away, off to his left, to the wooded gardens surrounding the conical, treed hill of the grotto dedicated to the Greek god

Pan, which was only visible as a rising blackness against the sky. Faunus, Vorenus grew up calling him: goat-man god of shepherds and fields, music and glen. Once, when he was a young legionnaire in Gaul, Vorenus had trapped a brace of rabbits and slit the throat of one over a tree-surrounded stone, offering it to the hairy god in thanks.

Vorenus let out a long sigh, wondering when he stopped believing like that. How many times had he defended the gods to the laughing, mocking Pullo? He'd been more enemy than friend to the giant of a man those days back in Gaul, but he could imagine what Pullo's reaction would have been to the sacrifice of the rabbit. "A waste of a good meal," Pullo would have said, annoyed. "There's good meat there, and I don't see any goat-men around to eat it." And then he'd try to take the still-warm creature, and Vorenus would have had to snatch it back, lecturing him about the folly of denying the gods and of taking what was rightfully theirs.

"Even if you don't feel certain in your soul," he might've told Pullo, "it's safer to at least act like you believe in the gods. If the gods exist, they'll be pleased; if the gods don't exist, you're no worse off for pretending they do."

"Except I'm hungry," Pullo would have replied. "And since none of your gods are about to feed me, I need to take care of it myself. Give me the damn rabbit."

Vorenus imagined himself standing between Pullo and the sacrificed creature, holding up the remaining one. "The gods did feed us," he would have said.

Then the big man would have looked at the little wiggling creature and laughed. "There are *two* of us, Vorenus. And two rabbits! Praise the gods, Greek and Roman! Don't offend them, brother: give me the other one!"

Vorenus allowed himself a grin, lost in his thoughts. It *was* how the conversation would have gone, wasn't it? They'd said much the same to each other over the years, had they not?

Not anymore, though. With Pullo cast out from the legion—only by the mercy of Caesarion allowed a job as a personal guard assigned to protect Didymus at the Great Library—they saw each other only rarely these days, and when they did, their talk never turned to such serious matters. Vorenus didn't doubt that Pullo had probably sensed the change in him. And since Pullo surely knew about the Shards of Heaven now, about the one God and His death—or His exiled silence, which Vorenus figured amounted to the same thing in the end—his old friend probably knew the reason why. That they'd not discussed it was only because Pullo, that great man-killer in battle, was too kind to point out that he'd been right all along. Pan, Faunus ... no matter the name; there was no god but God, and He wasn't listening anymore. That rabbit had indeed been wasted.

Vorenus felt his stomach growl at the thought, and if not for the pains in his arm, his legs, and even his heart, he might have laughed.

The palace, Vorenus noted at once, was far quieter than he would have expected. It was customary for some celebration to have been arranged for Antony's return, with Cleopatra dressed in her finest linens and jewels to hail her beloved, but not this night. This night it seemed no one was waiting for them.

Vorenus could see Antony's disappointment. Even broken-spirited as he was, the general's dark-circled eyes betrayed his sorrow at missing his wife's welcoming embrace as he strode up the wide steps and entered the main hall. Only Vorenus was with him now. The rest were settling into their quarters in the barracks outside or, in less happy circumstance, recovering from their wounds under the guidance of the Asclepian priests that Vorenus had grown to know so well given his own injuries.

The braziers in the hall were only sparsely lit, giving the space a dim aura between pools of flickering heat. In one of those rough circles of light, not far from the passageway leading to the balcony from which Vorenus had jumped some two years earlier, two men stood in whispered conversation: Khenti, the Egyptian chief of the palace guards, and Caesarion. A few slaves and minor priests shuffled elsewhere in the shadows, but the hall was otherwise mournfully silent and empty.

"A poor welcome," Antony said to Caesarion when they grew close, his booming voice echoing loudly off the stones in the empty chamber. The sudden sound of it seemed to startle even the general. When he next spoke it was in a more hushed voice. "A poor welcome indeed."

Caesarion, appearing to Vorenus' eyes at once so much older than his seventeen years and yet still the child he'd taught to play games in the courtyard, nodded. "It is. I'm sorry."

"Heard you not that we were victorious today?" Antony's words were in the mode of his customary boastfulness, but his heart didn't seem to be in it, his tone as passive as his voice. "We turned them back."

For now, for today, Vorenus heard himself adding in his mind. But he said nothing.

"Yes," Caesarion said—his smile proud or sad, Vorenus couldn't tell. "A fine day's work. I should have ordered some feast in celebration. As it was, I sent the wine to the temple of Asclepius, for the wounded."

"A poor choice," Antony muttered, his voice sounding more defeated than defiant at the pharaoh's decision. "Wine is wasted on the dying."

Caesarion's shoulders shrugged in reply.

"But what of my queen?" Antony asked. "Your mother."

"Her Highness has retired to Antirhodos," Khenti said, his eyes unreadable in the dark. "This afternoon."

"And the children?"

Caesarion appeared to take Antony's question to include him. "Still here. All of us."

Antony started to say something more, then stopped and turned to look down the hall to the balcony. After a moment he began to walk, slowly, in that direction. The others followed him out to stand, as Vorenus once had with Pullo, overlooking the palace grounds and the Great Harbor beyond. Antirhodos was a stretch of black against the moving reflections of the water. Antony set his hands against the stone wall and stared out at it as if seeking movement.

"She didn't tell you she was going to the isle?" Vorenus asked from beside him.

"Not today," Antony said quietly, the cooler wind off the ocean brushing through his still-thick curls of hair. "Though we did talk about it coming to this. Someday."

Vorenus agreed, not knowing what else to say.

Caesarion was standing back from the balcony, beside Khenti. "She said the island would be more easily protected than the palaces here," he said. "I disagreed."

"Of course," Antony said, his voice distant. "Good man."

"Thank you, sir," Caesarion said, genuine pride in his voice.

After a minute, Antony spoke again. "Are there priests with her?"

Caesarion took a moment to answer, and when Vorenus looked back at him, he saw that there was confusion in the young man's face. "Priests?"

Antony didn't turn back. "She may want to pray," he said into the night.

"The priests of Isis are at the temple there, as always."

Antony's nod was almost imperceptible. "Isis," he said. "The resurrecting goddess."

The other men said nothing, and Antony just stared out into the harbor, face dark.

"I can call a boat, sir, to take you out to the island," Vorenus said.

"No. No matter. The light's out." Antony's eyes turned to Vorenus, but his gaze seemed somewhere else, somewhere far away. "I'll pass this night at the Timonium," he said.

"As you wish, sir," Vorenus said. "Though the children—"

"The children..." Antony choked off the words, his body tensing for a moment as he froze up, thinking. "No, no," he said, as if responding to a question. "Let them sleep. A peaceful night." He breathed deep of the air. "Sleep."

"Yes, sir," Vorenus said.

Antony nodded, seemed ready to turn away, but then he stopped and refocused his attention on the legionnaire. "Vorenus, I..." The general blinked, appeared uncharacteristically uncertain. "Well, it's been a pleasure having you beside me all these years."

Vorenus, uncertain himself, kept his face stoic. "I've been honored to fight for you, sir."

"I hope ... that is to say..." Antony stammered to a halt, then sighed and smiled in a kind of genuine warmth. He held out his hand. "Thank you, Vorenus."

Vorenus took the offered hand and shook it. "Thank you, sir."

Antony held the grip a few seconds longer than Vorenus would have expected, then let go. "You're a good man. A loyal man. Remember that."

One of the Egyptian guards appeared from the darkness of the main hall and bowed to Caesarion and Antony in turn before whispering a report to Khenti's ear and then hurrying back into the dark.

"What news?" Antony asked, a new softness bordering on humor in his voice. "Octavian has breached the walls?"

"Only Titus Pullo to see Vorenus," Khenti said, his face characteristically stone. "I've ordered him kept at the gate, sir."

Something flashed in Antony's face, but it passed too quickly for Vorenus to read. "No," the general said, waving his hand absently as if brushing his former orders out of the air. "Let him come in. I'm on my way out anyway."

Khenti bowed and then disappeared into the darkness.

Antony watched him go before turning back to Vorenus. "Tell Pullo ... well, give him my regards. He, too, is a good man."

"Of course," Vorenus said, unsure what more he could say.

"Good," Antony said, once again looking out over the harbor. "Good."

"I'll have a guard called to walk you to the Timonium," Caesarion said.

"No, not necessary," Antony replied, taking in the young man with a smile of gratitude. "It isn't far. I'd like to go alone."

"As you wish," Caesarion said.

"You've done well, you know," Antony said. And then, before Caesarion could reply, the general reached out and clasped him by the shoulders, pulling him into an embrace.

Caesarion appeared to be surprised by the gesture, but he was quick to return the embrace, brief though it was. "I was raised well," he said.

"Then we must once again give thanks to Vorenus," Antony said when they parted. "And to Pullo, as well."

Vorenus bowed slightly. "I will tell him as much, sir."

Antony had the look of a man relieved. He inhaled the salty scents of the air. "I should go, then. Khenti no doubt has Pullo waiting in the hall." He glanced one last time toward the harbor. "I think I'll actually walk down by the docks on my way out. It's a good night for it."

Antony looked to them both, smiled, and then was gone into the darkness of the hallway.

"Vorenus," Caesarion said when he was gone, his voice like that of a man waking from a dream. "You don't think he..."

Caesarion didn't have to finish the sentence for Vorenus to know what he was talking about. He was certain Antony had been considering falling on his sword since Actium. "Perhaps. There aren't many options left for us all," Vorenus whispered.

Caesarion took a step toward the hallway. "But if he's really going to ... shouldn't we go and—"

"No," Vorenus said, reaching out to place his hand on the younger man's elbow and hold him back. "We shouldn't. It's his choice, my boy. It'd be more honorable than the Triumph. We cannot deny him that."

Caesarion's face flushed hot, with anger or sorrow, Vorenus couldn't tell.

"Besides," Vorenus said, deciding at last to be open and honest with him, "it could save your mother. Maybe yourself." Vorenus doubted this was so—Octavian would surely parade them all in Rome, and Cleopatra and Caesarion, maybe even the younger children, were too much of a threat to be allowed to live—but he supposed there was at least a chance.

"But the children..." Emotion cracked the young man's voice.

"As he said: let them sleep."

"I can't just let him go."

"You can," Vorenus said. "And you must. Perhaps he's only tired from the day. Perhaps we'll see him again tomorrow." He tried to keep his voice light, whispered as it was, but even so he doubted it himself. He felt certain, in his heart, that he'd seen Mark Antony for the last time in life.

Caesarion's shoulders slumped, and the tension went out of his arm. The resignation was hard for Vorenus to see in one so young, one with so much promise and potential. For a moment he instinctively wanted to curse the gods for giving the young man such a tragic fate, but then he caught himself. No gods meant no fate. It was just open choice and random chance, that was all. That was all anything was. He'd been a fool ever to think differently.

Even as Vorenus thought about him, Pullo came striding out of the darkness toward which they were staring, his head instinctively bowing as he ducked under the final threshold. The big man was smiling. "Why so glum, you two?"

Caesarion seemed distracted for a moment, caught between talking to Pullo and peering back into the dark hallway, but then he, too, smiled, reaching out a hand in greeting. "Oh, nothing, Pullo. It's good to see you."

Pullo took the offered hand, then stepped back to look appraisingly at Caesarion. Vorenus guessed they hadn't seen each other in many months. "You appear well, lad," the big man said.

"And you, old man." Caesarion's mirth seemed genuine as they fell into a familiar banter. A part of Vorenus was surprised how suddenly sure of himself the young man seemed, as if all was right with the world; another part expected it of him.

"Bah," Pullo said, releasing his grip on Caesarion's hand to rub the younger man's head. "Not so old I can't still best you at arms. Your choice of weapon, too."

"Pullo," Vorenus said, coming forward to shake his hand, too. "Glad to see you."

"And I you, Lucius Vorenus. I was able to see some of the fight from the walls. A tough thing."

"Could've used you."

"Yes, you could have." It wasn't a boast, just clear fact, and no one treated it any differently. "I'm glad to find you both, though I didn't expect to find you still up, Caesarion."

"Not just a call on Vorenus, then?" Caesarion asked.

"No. I'm sent for you both."

"Didymus?" Caesarion's voice betrayed something like hope.

"Aye. He sends his regrets for being forced to send a big brute like me in his stead. But he's been busy trying to secure the Library should Octavian take the city."

"*When* he takes the city," Caesarion said, so matter-of-factly that he could have been talking about the weather rather than the destruction of his home, his life.

"As you say, sir," Pullo said, falling into the old habits of a legionnaire.

"Pullo?" asked a girl's voice from the darkness of the hallway.

They all turned, Pullo already grinning despite his effort to look stern. "You ought not be up so late, lady Selene," he said.

The ten-year-old girl melted out of the darkness, a thin shawl over her shoulders. "I couldn't sleep since everybody hadn't come back yet. Did I see my father just now?"

"Yes," Caesarion said, his voice moving toward the fatherly when he spoke to his little half-sister. "He did well today. All the men did. Few losses."

"He was headed down to the docks," Selene said.

"Antony will be retiring to the Timonium tonight," said Vorenus. "He didn't want to disturb anyone."

"Oh," she said as she came forward and wrapped her arms around Pullo's waist. The man bent down to return the embrace, his big hands patting her as gently as if she were a babe. "It's nice to see you, Pullo," the girl said.

"Nice to be seen."

"Things haven't been the same without you."

"I imagine they've been better," Pullo said, smiling as he straightened up and Selene let go of him.

"So the battle went well?" she asked Vorenus.

"It did."

"How could it not with such men to lead it?" Pullo said.

"But what are you doing here?" Selene asked.

"Oh, I came to fetch these two," Pullo replied, nodding his

head toward Vorenus and Caesarion. "Didymus wants to see them."

Vorenus saw that Selene's posture straightened. "A meeting? About the Shards?" she asked.

"I don't know what about," Pullo said.

"At the Library?" Vorenus asked.

"No," Pullo said. "At the temple of Serapis. When I left him he was already preparing to go there to meet you."

"Now?" Vorenus asked.

"Right away if possible. I've probably tarried too long as it is, though it's hard not to do so with company so lovely." He looked down at Selene like a proud father.

"Can I not come?" she asked.

Pullo's face softened toward regret. "I don't think that would be best. We're taking a chance traveling across the city at night as it is. Alexandria isn't as safe for you as it once was."

"Someone needs to stay with Philadelphus and Helios," Caesarion said.

"He's sick again," Selene muttered.

"All the more reason for you to stay," Vorenus said. "With your mother and father gone, Caesarion away, and Helios sick, someone has to keep this place in shape."

"Besides, your father will want to see you first thing in the morning," Pullo said. "Isn't that right, my boy?"

Caesarion smiled, but his face was taut. "I should hope so," he said.

22

The Temple of Serapis

ALEXANDRIA, 30 BCE

When they'd first left the palace, Caesarion had thought Didymus would be meeting them at the old temple of Serapis just west of the Museum, a triangular building raised where the Canopic Way intersected with the wide boulevard that became the Heptastadion and led out to Pharos and the great lighthouse beyond. But, as Pullo soon told them, Didymus wanted to meet them not there, but at the more distant Serapeum, the newer, grander temple of Serapis set high atop a hill in the southwestern, Egyptian quarter of the city. That massive building, the crowning structure of a three-hundred-year-old acropolis, was a destination for pilgrims from across the world, some coming from as far away as distant Rome to pray before its magnificent blue-stone statue of the god who blessed Alexandria. It made sense that Didymus would want to meet there, Caesarion supposed. The Serapeum had become a repository for many books that had not yet found a home in the Great Library. It was just the sort of place to find the librarian.

Besides, despite its sprawling size, the Serapeum would surely be deserted. The Roman siege had turned the once-bustling city into a place whose citizens locked themselves into their homes as best they could—from fear of the Romans and the inevitable chaos that would follow Alexandria's capture. Even the most devout worshipers of Serapis would surely be crowding the older temple in the center of Alexandria rather than the more famous complex along the south wall of the city.

Khenti had not only insisted on going with Vorenus and Caesarion himself, but he'd also insisted on bringing along a second Egyptian guardsman: a bruising braggart named Shushu. Together, the four of them joined Pullo in walking the silent midnight streets of Alexandria, dressed as simple, if well-armed, commoners. Caesarion carried only a dagger, but he could see that the other men were making no efforts to conceal the short swords at their hips. He wondered, as they walked, whether they wore the blades so plainly to send a message to anyone who might consider stopping them. Crime had been on the rise in the city, he knew, especially as the night patrols had grown infrequent due to disease, desertion, and death. As Pullo had told Selene back at the palace, the streets were far more dangerous these days.

Not this night, though: The darkened streets of Alexandria were filled not with roving gangs of thugs, but with a tense emptiness. Even the air of the night, loosely woven with scents of smoke and war, seemed to Caesarion expectant. It was as if the whole of the city was ready and waiting to meet its conqueror. Only when the little party reached the Canopic Way did anything other than an eerie silence greet their passing.

They were walking in a close group, Pullo in the lead, with Vorenus and Shushu to either side of Caesarion, and they had just turned the corner onto the wide and empty main corridor of the city—not far from the tomb of Alexander—when Khenti, trailing behind, abruptly signaled for a halt.

"What is it?" Caesarion whispered after they'd stood still for a moment.

Khenti was looking back down the avenue toward the Sun Gate, body taut like a spring. "I heard something."

"I hear it, too," Vorenus said. "It sounds like—"

"Music," Pullo said, completing his old friend's thought. "I followed a group of legionnaires to the palace, and we all heard it on the way. Seemed to be moving east from the center of the city toward the walls and Octavian's camp."

"Who would be playing music at this hour?" Caesarion asked.

The big man shrugged. "The other men thought it an omen."

Khenti appeared to have relaxed. He looked back at the others. "So what means this omen among Romans?"

"Antony is often likened to Dionysius, god of revelry and debauchery. God of music," Pullo said.

Caesarion frowned. "The music leads out of town. The men think it's a sign that Dionysius has abandoned Antony?"

"Something like that," Pullo admitted.

"Roman omens." Khenti sniffed.

"We should keep moving," Vorenus said. "We're only halfway to the Serapeum, and Didymus will be waiting."

Despite Caesarion's assumptions, the Serapeum complex was not entirely empty. A hundred wide steps led to the hill-crowning temple, and as Caesarion and his small party approached the gate at their foot, two men melted out of the pillared shadows surrounding the barred entrance, their dark cloaks pulled close about their shoulders and hoods drawn to cast their faces into darkness. Whether they were Egyptian or Roman, Caesarion couldn't tell, but they stood with the same physical assurance that he associated with men like Khenti: effective, confident fighters. He'd never seen anyone like them at the Serapeum before.

Pullo, in the lead, drew their party to a halt a few paces from the gate and spread his arms slightly to show his own weapons. "Titus Pullo," he said. "I'm here to see Didymus."

One of the guards stepped forward, hooded head moving up and down them all, as if appraising them. After a few seconds he reached up his hands to pull back his hood.

"Jacob!" Caesarion said, recognizing him at once.

"Pharaoh," Jacob replied, smiling and bowing his head slightly. "I'm glad you could come despite the late hour."

Caesarion considered how to reply but in the end only nodded in return.

Jacob abruptly looked over them. "Were they followed?"

Caesarion and the others turned and saw six more hooded men melt out of the shadows behind them. Four of them were carrying bows of blackened wood, the fletchings of quivered arrows just visible over their shoulders. One slight man, smaller than his fellows, stood in their lead. Caesarion could only barely make out the glinting of his eyes as he shook his hooded head.

"Good," Jacob said, turning toward the temple. "Let's get inside."

"Is it customary to follow your invited guests?" Khenti asked. His voice was steady, not betraying whether he was angry at having been secretly followed, or whether he had known it all along.

Jacob glanced back, and his smile was grim. "Tonight it is. Come. There's only so much time."

The gate was opened, and Jacob led them up the steps to the red-roofed acropolis, the other hooded figures surrounding them as they climbed into the cool night air. At the top of the stairs they passed through a four-columned portico in the thick, high walls that surrounded the temple proper. Their path between the pillars and altars scattered through the main space of the temple was illuminated by a line of lit oil lamps. The priests of Serapis that Caesarion was accustomed to seeing here were noticeable by their absence. There was no scuffling of movement in the distance, no murmurs or chants that might reveal the stone complex for the temple that it was. Instead, there were only the steady lamps under the stars, leading the way deeper into the complex, and the closer sounds of their own passing. Jacob was in the lead, and the six men who had apparently followed them through the streets now fanned out around their little group as it moved from lamp to lamp. The slighter man whom Jacob had addressed walked to the rear of them all, close behind Khenti. All but Jacob kept their hoods drawn low over their heads and faces. Caesarion, feeling frightened and excited all at once, tried to take his cues from the two Romans and two Egyptians surrounding him, all of whom walked as if they had no worries in the world.

Back through several hallways and rooms they walked, before they reached the staircase of stone that wound down into a series of hidden passageways and entrances into the deeper catacombs carved into the rock below. Caesarion had never been into these shadowed spaces—they were the domain of the priests—and he was soon certain that he was completely lost. At last they entered a long and broad room, its walls and pillars hidden by cases filled with scrolls half visible in the dim light of the few burning lamps. A series of simple wooden tables were set in the middle of the room, most of them covered with piled manuscripts. At one sat old Didymus, two more hooded guards to either side of him. When he looked up and saw the approaching party, his face brightened despite the gloom in the room.

"Fine work, Pullo." The scholar stood and rubbed his hands together as if to dissipate his excited energies before he came around the table to greet Caesarion. "I'm glad you could come. I was directing the fortification of the Library when they came for me. I hope they didn't startle you. They did me."

"No," Caesarion said, using his most diplomatic smile. "Though I do wonder what business is so urgent and secretive."

Jacob had taken up a position near Didymus' vacated chair. For his part, the royal tutor remained beside Caesarion as Vorenus, Pullo, and the two Egyptian guards spread out around them. "But you do know why we're here, do you not?" Jacob asked. "You know so much already."

Caesarion instinctively glanced sideways at some of the hooded guards who'd taken up positions in a rough circle around the pool of light in the center of the room. "I understand little."

"So it is too often in life," Jacob said. "We cannot answer all, but circumstances dictate that I answer more than we ever could."

"Circumstances?" Didymus asked, clear expectancy in his voice.

"Octavian's siege, my dear librarian. And his impending victory." The Jew's eyes moved to Caesarion as he spoke, and he nodded his head slightly, as if in apology. "We've waited as long as we could, hoping against hope, but we're certain that Alexandria will fall. Perhaps—in fact, likely—tomorrow."

Caesarion didn't dispute the conclusion, much though he desired to do so. Only Antony's tactical brilliance had bought this night of freedom from the yoke of Rome. That they could count on such results again seemed too much to ask. Even if they somehow staved off Octavian's armies for another day, another night, Alexandria couldn't last. To deny it would be folly, and Caesarion prided himself on not being a foolish man. "If, as you say, my city is about to fall to its enemies, I have precious little time for games," he said coolly. "I'm needed elsewhere."

"You're right that there's little time," Jacob admitted. "But nowhere are you more needed than here. We need your help, Pharaoh. More than this city and this kingdom are at stake. The world is hanging in the balance."

"The Shards," Didymus whispered. "I had hoped so."

"Yes. The Shards." Jacob's tone did not change, making clear the trust in which he held the dozen or so men in the room. "We know without doubt now that Octavian is in possession of the Second Shard. Our spies have seen it. We cannot let him acquire the First."

"The Ark of the Covenant," Caesarion said.

"Yes."

"You told us you knew nothing of its whereabouts," Didymus said.

"This is only partly true," Jacob said. "I know that—like so many other treasures—the Ark is here in Alexandria. But I do not myself know where."

"And you need our help finding it?" the scholar guessed.

Before Jacob could answer, Caesarion shook his head. "I don't think that's what he means," he said. "Jacob may not know where it is, but at least one of these men here does. They don't need help finding the Ark. They need help moving it. Is that right?"

"Close," Jacob said. "We do need your help to move it. But no man here knows where it is." His eyes, as they did on the steps outside, raised to look past them.

Caesarion, like the others, turned to look at the slight guard who had followed them in the night. The guard's hands raised to the cloak's shadowing hood and pulled it back to reveal long dark hair tied back to frame the smiling face of an impossibly beautiful young girl, perhaps sixteen years old. Only his trained impassivity prevented Caesarion from gasping as Pullo and Shushu did. "I do," she said.

"My sister, Hannah," Jacob said from the table.

Vorenus cleared his throat slightly. "*You* know where it is?"

Hannah's brown eyes flashed with something like amusement.

"But you're a girl," Pullo blurted out.

"I thank you for noticing," Hannah said. She raised a hand to her head and shook out her hair as she walked past them to stand beside her brother. Her gait, unlike that of most of the marriageable women Caesarion knew, was easy and practical, not one of seduction. "The prophetess Deborah was a girl, too," Hannah said. She swept back her cloak from her hip, revealing the black hilt of a blade. "It was she who inspired Barak to fight back against the Canaanites. And it was Yael, the tentmaker's wife, who killed the Canaanite general Sisera and ended a war." Caesarion thought her eyes sparkled with something more than amusement now, something more dangerous. "She took a hammer and drove a spike through his temple while he slept. Pinned him to the ground."

Pullo's grin was genuine. "Did she now?"

Hannah nodded. Jacob laughed a little. "So they say anyway," he said. "And if you have not learned by now, it was the queen of Sheba who established this company. It has always been led by a woman."

Caesarion realized he was staring at Hannah and forced himself to look down at the table for a moment.

"Sheba?" Didymus asked. "In Jerusalem?"

Jacob returned to his usual smile, but it was his sister who answered. "We do not have time for history lessons," she said. Her attention turned to Caesarion. "The Ark must be moved. It cannot be allowed to fall into the hands of Octavian—especially when he already controls the Trident. You must help us."

Caesarion closed his eyes, trying to focus against the tide of questions that threatened to engulf him. Octavian was at the gates. His forces were repulsed, but within hours they would be re-gathered and ready for what would undoubtedly be the final assault. Antony was gone—perhaps dead, he thought with a shudder—so where did his own duty lie? Surely it was not here in this place. Surely it was not talking of stories of the lost treasures of angels. No, his duty was to Alexandria. His duty was to his family. He should turn and run back to the palace, to protect the children. That was where he belonged, was it not?

And yet, if the stories were true, if the Shards were real, what could be more important than protecting them? The power of the gods was worth a hundred Alexandrias, a thousand. Vorenus believed he had seen the result of the Trident of Poseidon. But did that make it all true? Was that enough to let go of all that he owed to this city?

"Tell me all of it," he said. "You tell us that there isn't time enough for history lessons. I tell you that without them you'll get nothing from me. I need to know. I need to believe."

"We have killed men for knowing far less than you already know," Hannah said.

Caesarion felt his companions all move slightly closer to him, but his eyes never left those of the girl. "You didn't bring me here to hurt me. You brought me here because you have no other choice. You brought me here because you need me."

Hannah was staring at him, her eyes intense in the lamplight. She was beautiful, but she was deadly. He did not doubt for a minute that she had indeed ordered the deaths of men to protect the secrets of the Ark. At the same time, he knew with equal certainty that she needed them. She needed *him*. What he had that would help them remove the Ark, he did not know, but their desperation was clear.

"We don't have time," Jacob said to his sister. For once, he wasn't smiling.

Vorenus seemed to have sensed the same thing that Caesarion did. "I don't think you have a choice."

"It seems we do not," Hannah said. Her gaze did not leave Caesarion. "But every minute here is a minute that Octavian grows closer."

"Best to talk quickly, then," Caesarion replied.

Hannah turned and nodded to Jacob, who sighed. "You know the truth of what the Ark is—that it's the first of the Shards that fell when the Vested gave up their souls, their free will, in an effort to bring the divine Creator back into the world. You know the threat it can be. What else do you need to know?"

Caesarion let out a breath of his own and turned to Didymus. "Satisfy him and you'll satisfy me."

The scholar blinked back and forth between the people in the room. He had the look of a man screwing up his courage. At last, it seemed, his curiosity got the better of him. "How did it get here? How did the queen of Sheba come to protect it?"

Jacob nodded, thought for a couple seconds. "You know that the man we Jews know as Moses was the crown prince of Egypt before his belief in the one God drew him into conflict with his father, the pharaoh. You know he acquired both the Trident and the Ark, that he took them to the land promised to him by God. What you may not know is that one of his descendants in Judea was a ruler named Solomon, and that some nine centuries ago he was visited by one of Thutmose's descendants in Sheba, a queen who sought after the fate of the Second Shard. She discovered that Solomon had built a great Temple to house the Ark, and that a cult had been built up around the two Shards. Not satisfied of their security, but reluctant to part with them, the queen of Sheba left behind in Jerusalem a family sworn to protect the Shards whatever the cost. Maintained in secret, this family would pass the knowledge of the truth of the Shards from one generation to another and never cease in its sacred duties to protect them. The queen's visit, and her decision to establish this company, could not have been better timed. Before even two generations had passed, Pharaoh Shoshenq invaded Judah, followed by more attacks against Jerusalem and Solomon's Temple. The family protected the Shards through it all."

"Your family," Didymus said. "I knew your father was connected to something."

"Yes," Jacob said. "Our family. Which makes it more difficult to tell you that during the reign of King Hezekiah, almost seven hundred years ago, we failed. The object Octavian knows as the Trident of Poseidon was called by our people Nehushtan back then: the brazen serpent rod of Moses. People had begun to look to it for healing, as the stories said it had healed their ancestors."

"The stories of your people are lies?" Pullo interrupted.

"Not lies. Half-remembered truths, Titus Pullo," Hannah said. "There's a difference."

Pullo exchanged a glance with Vorenus, whose eyes were glaring at him to be silent. "I see," the big man said.

Jacob did not seem distracted by the interruption. "Hezekiah was a true believer in the stories of the Ark: that it not only housed the tablets of the Law given to Moses by God, but that God Himself came to earth to sit upon the Ark and pass judgment through His priests, a distant memory of the fact that the Shards were wrought from the throne of God. Hezekiah believed in the Ark, and he saw the honor given to Nehushtan as an abomination. On one of the great feast days he strode into the Temple, as was his custom, and after honoring the Ark he took the Trident and tried to destroy it."

"Is that possible?" Caesarion asked, trying not to betray the interest in his voice.

"To destroy the Trident itself, yes," Jacob said.

"It's only wood and metal, after all," Hannah agreed. "It is fashioned from the hands of men. He did damage it heavily. But mortal hands cannot unmake the Shard itself, the black stone that actually gives it its power."

"What happened then?" Didymus asked, the look on his

face reminding Caesarion of an anxious cat awaiting its meal. Caesarion imagined the scholar's glee as he incorporated each new piece of information into his already encyclopedic mind.

"Too late to preserve the Trident itself, we still had to protect the Shard," Jacob said. "The guardians split up, with half the family removing the Second Shard from the Temple and fleeing Jerusalem with it."

"How did it get into the hands of this man Juba?" Didymus asked. "Where was it taken?"

"It traveled first to Babylon, though what happened to it next we do not know. We could not maintain contact with them long."

"Your half of the family stayed with the Ark."

In response, Jacob lifted from his shirt a thin silver chain. Hanging upon the necklace was a delicate pendant showing the symbol of a triangle, point down within a perfect circle bisected by a line across its bottom third. "We are the keepers of the Ark," he said.

One by one, the other figures in the room lifted silver chains from around their necks, too, all revealing the same pendant. Hannah was last. "All of us," she said. "And from that day to this we have not failed. From Jerusalem to Elephantine in the time of Manasseh, from Elephantine to Kush in the time of Nebuchadnezzar, and from Kush to here in the time of Alexander, we have kept the Ark safe. We have not failed. And we will not fail now."

"With our help," Caesarion said.

Hannah smiled, and Caesarion's breath caught at the sight. "Yes," she said.

"In the land of Kush, just beyond the borders of Egypt," Didymus muttered. He caught Hannah's eye and raised an eyebrow. "That's not far from the land of Sheba."

As before, it was Jacob who nodded and answered. "The Ark was safe there for almost two hundred years."

Didymus made a slight gasp. "Until Alexander the Great invaded Egypt! Of course!"

The others looked at the scholar, whose smile was near to splitting his ecstatic face. "I don't understand," Caesarion said.

Didymus blinked for a moment, as if watching the pieces fall into place behind his eyes. "When Alexander came up the Nile, the king and queen of Kush met him with an army."

"King Nastasen and Queen Sakhmakh," Jacob said.

"Yes. And for reasons no one has ever understood, the invincible Alexander turned away. He instead came here, to Alexandria, and founded the city." Didymus paused, as if that was all that needed to be said. He only continued when Caesarion still looked confused. "Don't you see? Nastasen and Sakhmakh must have had the Ark. Alexander knew he couldn't win!" Didymus looked back at Jacob for confirmation.

"A true scholar," the Jew said. "But there's more to it. The only reason we allowed Nastasen and Sakhmakh to carry the Ark with them to meet Alexander is that we knew he would recognize it for what it was."

"He'd learned about the Shards?" Caesarion asked. "How?"

"He had one," Hannah answered.

For a few moments, silence settled over the room. It was finally Pullo who spoke. "The Trident?"

"No," Jacob replied. "Another entirely. The Aegis of Zeus."

"Jupiter's armor?" Vorenus asked.

"That's right," Jacob said. "A relatively weak artifact, but useful in that it kept him alive despite wounds that would've killed other men—though it did cause certain changes to his personality."

"Where is it now?" Didymus asked.

"Here," Hannah said. "In Alexander's tomb, as it has been since he died. None has known its power, and we've never wanted to bring attention to it by moving it."

"Wait," Pullo said. "How many Shards are there?"

Jacob shrugged. "We don't know. At least four."

Vorenus shivered. From what he'd told them of the Trident in action, Caesarion could imagine why. "Four? What else?"

"The Palladium of Troy," Jacob said. "It can control wind. It was carried away from Troy by a Greek named Odysseus, though he could not use it. Where it is now we don't know."

"So what of the Ark?" Caesarion asked. "That's why we're here. It's the most powerful Shard, right?"

"The most powerful we know about," Hannah said.

Jacob nodded. "Together with Alexander and the king and queen of Kush, we came to an agreement. Alexander would turn back and not go beyond the borders of Egypt. In return, we would use the Ark to help him realize his dream of creating this city that would bear his name: Alexandria."

"I don't understand," Caesarion said after a moment. "Why would you help him? Surely with the Ark's power you could have defeated him."

"Defeating him was never our goal, Pharaoh. We only want to protect the Shard, and Alexander gave us the chance—we thought—to protect it permanently, to cease moving it."

"Building the new city, you could build a new temple for the Ark," Didymus spoke quietly.

"Yes," Hannah said.

Caesarion nodded. "A Third Temple."

"We built a new home for the Ark in Alexandria," Jacob said, "and it has rested here, undisturbed, ever since." He glanced over toward his sister. "From the day it came to Alexandria until this, only one person has had the knowledge of its exact location."

"So why move it?" Didymus asked. "Wherever it is, surely it is well hidden and will be safe."

"Octavian's man found out about the Second Shard," Jacob said. "Now he searches for the First. You yourselves found out much of the truth, with little effort. Given more time, and Octavian's resources, it would only be a matter of time until he did the same."

"And that's assuming Octavian doesn't just raze the city," Caesarion whispered, the vision of Alexandria in flames managing to push Hannah's image from his mind.

"Yes, but why us?" Vorenus asked. "Why Caesarion?"

Caesarion looked up at the mention of his name, saw that Hannah was staring at him again. "Because only you can help us move it," she said.

23

The Librarian's Choice

ALEXANDRIA, 30 BCE

His mind swirling with too many thoughts, too much new information, Didymus moved away from the main table as the others began discussing their plans to remove the Ark of the Covenant from Alexandria. He sat down at another table, closer to the shadows and the hooded Jewish guards there.

The Ark. The First Shard.

It was here in this temple, Didymus thought. It had to be. The Serapeum had been built by Ptolemy III atop an older acropolis, less than a century after his grandfather, Ptolemy I—Alexander the Great's finest general and closest friend—had first revealed the existence of the god Serapis, an Osiris-Apis-Hades hybrid that could be equally worshiped by Alexandria's Egyptian and Greek inhabitants. Even before he knew of the Shards and the fact of the one God, Didymus had suspected that Ptolemy's divine revelations were nothing more than good administrative policy: a ruler's job was much easier if those he ruled could all honor the same deity, especially if that deity was one that had supposedly given favor to the ruler. Ptolemy had known that Serapis was a lie. Now Didymus wondered if he knew, too, that the acropolis on which his grandson would ultimately build this temple housed perhaps the most powerful object in creation: the Ark of the Covenant.

Didymus closed his eyes for a moment, imagining what it would be like to be so close to such an artifact. It was one thing, after all, to study such an object—and he had, indeed, read all he could about the Ark once he knew it was the object of Juba's desires—but it was something quite different to see it, to touch it.

No, he corrected himself. Not touch it. The stories of the Jews were very specific about what happened when those who were unworthy touched the Ark.

And Didymus had no doubt that he was unworthy. Though he might spend his whole life trying to atone for the mistakes of his youth, he could never undo them.

He opened his eyes and looked around at the rows of scroll-filled shelves surrounding him in the dark. Many of the temple's old passageways and rooms had been used to hold the overflow of thousands of books for which there was no room in the Great Library. A generation earlier, when fires set in the harbor by Caesar had spread to the Museum and actually consumed part of the beloved Great Library itself, it was from copying these hidden stores that the rebuilt shelves were replenished.

How many times had he himself come here, looking for a scroll not yet duplicated? How many times had he been in this very room, wandering this way and that, unaware of how close he stood to such power?

Because it had to be here. It had to be close. There was no reason to meet here otherwise.

Shaking away his own amazement at the past, Didymus tried to focus in on what was going on in the present. They all knew Octavian would take the city, and at the very least he'd search hard for the Ark, torturing whomever he needed to in order to find the information he needed. He'd found out so much already, after all. Even more likely, he would put the city to the torch while he did the torturing. Only later would he search the smoldering remains for it. The Shard itself, after all, could not be harmed. Easier to burn down what stood in the way than to try to look for the secret chambers in which it would be hidden. Fire. It's what his adopted father would have done. It's what his adopted father *had* done when cornered in Alexandria so many years earlier. Alexandria would burn again. And this time the Great Library, and these holdings here, would burn with it.

Didymus felt suddenly nauseated and stood up to try to clear his mind of the vision of books in flame. He walked back over to the main table, where Caesarion, Jacob, and the girl, Hannah, sat in deep discussion about the Ark, surrounded by the others.

"So if we don't move it, Octavian won't ever be stopped," Jacob was saying.

"Then why not use it to stop him?" Vorenus said.

Caesarion looked up from his seat with clear hope in his eyes. "Of course. An object of such power—"

"Cannot possibly be wielded by you," Hannah said. "Not by any of us. It would destroy you. It would destroy me. And even if you could control it, what would you do then? Kill Octavian and claim Rome? You have a right to it. But why stop there? With the Ark you could become a conqueror. Is that your desire, Pharaoh?"

As she spoke Didymus saw it all unfolding in his mind: the power, the possibility. Caesarion was a good man. Surely he would try to be a good and just ruler, and for a long time he no doubt would be. Yet the scholar in Didymus knew that no man was untouched by power. Even those seeking redemption for the many wrought devastation on the few. In the tense silence that had befallen them all, he stepped forward. "With the Ark you could create a greater realm than Alexander ever did," he said, his voice quiet in the lamp-lit chamber. "But remember that even he chose to set it aside."

Caesarion turned to look at him, and Didymus could see his inner struggle in the taut lines of his face, the wideness of his eyes. The world was at his fingertips. How many had faced such temptation? How many could possibly deny it? He opened his mouth as if to speak, but before the words could come Hannah spoke again. "It's God's weapon, Caesarion. Not ours."

It was the first time Didymus had heard the girl say Caesarion's name, and he saw the young man blink as if the word had broken a spell. The boy who might have ruled the world let out his breath with a sigh and a nod. "I'm no conqueror," he said. He looked over to Vorenus with a smile. "You know I don't want to rule other men."

Vorenus gave the curt nod of a military man receiving an order. Didymus wondered at the irony of it even as the room seemed to exhale. After all, wasn't a lack of desire to rule perhaps the finest characteristic to have in a ruler?

"But I don't understand how we can move it," Caesarion continued, turning back to Hannah. "You mentioned a ship, but no vessel can get out of the city. Especially not a royal one. Not just by land are we besieged."

"It's not just any ship we want," Hannah said. Didymus noticed again how sure of herself the girl was. He wondered how long she'd been a leader among this sacred company.

"What then?" Caesarion asked.

In reply, Hannah turned to Vorenus. "He knows."

Vorenus looked confused for a moment before realization swept across his face like the beam from a far-off light. "The trireme," he said, wonder in his voice. "The one we used to escape Actium. It's one of Octavian's own vessels."

"As soon as the city falls," Jacob said, "Octavian's ships will enter the Great Harbor that they only now blockade. There will be chaos. If one of his ships slips out, under the bridges of the Heptastadion and out to the sea beyond, no one will notice. There's no better time for moving the Ark than in the chaos."

"And this trireme," Caesarion asked no one in particular, "it's in the royal harbor?"

Both Jacob and Hannah nodded.

"You could order it released," Vorenus said to Caesarion. "We only need to get the Ark to the palace, to have it ready."

Didymus watched as Caesarion worked things over in his mind. He didn't doubt that the young man was thinking, too, of how he could get his family out of the city the same way. "No," he said at last. "We can't leave from the palace. Anything leaving the royal harbor will be searched, Roman-built or not. We need to bring the trireme to the Ark."

A single pair of hurried footsteps abruptly echoed in the hall, and one of the hooded guards strode into the pool of light around the tables, walking directly to Hannah's side. As he whispered in her ear, the girl's gaze flicked over to Caesarion. She took a deep breath when the guard finished. "Go," she said to him. "See to the others."

"What is it?" Caesarion asked.

"Antony is dead," she said, voice calm and unflinching.

"Dead?" Caesarion croaked. "I ... we saw him, not hours ago."

Hannah nodded, and to Didymus the gesture appeared warmly kind, like that of a mother agreeing with her child that the world was not what either of them would like it to be. "He fell on his own sword. I'm sorry."

"The city will fall," Pullo said, his eyes widening as if he was surprised to have spoken the thought aloud.

"So it will," Jacob said. He stared at Caesarion, the lack of any trace of a smile on his face making him appear disturbingly intent. "Octavian's men will be in the city soon, if they're not already. No more stories. The time to act is upon us."

Caesarion looked down at the table, eyes narrowing.

"The trireme," Jacob said. His voice was urgent. "We need it. The Ark *must* be protected."

Caesarion's head moved up and down absently. Didymus thought he saw the young man's lips moving.

Jacob's shoulders trembled with what appeared to be pent-up rage, and Hannah reached out a hand to grip his arm. "Pharaoh," she whispered. "Please..."

"Khenti," Caesarion said, his head whipping up, eyes clear and voice strong.

The Egyptian guardchief, always rigid, somehow stood even straighter. "Sir."

"I can't go. Octavian will be looking for me most of all. You and Vorenus will return immediately to Lochias without me. Run. Do whatever you need to do to get that trireme in the water and moving. Get the children on board."

"Your mother?" Vorenus asked.

Caesarion shook his head. "She may be dead already. If she isn't, she won't leave, I assure you. And she'll be doing what she can to keep the children by her side. In her pride she'll want us all to meet the same fate."

Vorenus nodded. "I understand, sir."

"Where are we to direct the trireme?" Khenti asked.

Caesarion turned to Hannah. "Well? You wanted my help, and you've got it. Where's the Ark? Here?"

Hannah's face, for the first time since they'd met her, flushed slightly, and she chewed on her lip for a moment. "The map," she finally said.

Jacob unceremoniously pushed aside the stack of scrolls on the desk before them, causing Didymus to wince. Underneath them was a map of the city, already spread out. Hannah leaned over it. "We're here," she said. Then she drew her finger in a line north and west along the angled avenue leading to the Heptastadion, where her finger stopped. "The Ark is in a chamber not far from the water," she said.

Didymus blinked at the map in confusion. "It's not right here?"

Hannah actually smiled. "Not specifically, but the Ark chamber can only be accessed by two tunnels hidden under the city. One starts beneath Alexander's tomb. The other starts here." She turned her attention directly to Vorenus and Khenti. "Bring the trireme up under the first Heptastadion bridge," she said. "There's an access to the canals under the city there."

Khenti glanced for a moment to Caesarion. "Under the bridge. I know of it."

"That's where we'll meet you," Hannah said.

Vorenus nodded for the both of them. "Understood."

"And the rest of us?" Pullo asked.

"The rest of us," Caesarion said, looking across the table at Hannah, "will go get the Ark."

The Jewish girl agreed, and her brother leaned over to roll up the map. At once, the rest of the people in the scroll-filled room began to move. Vorenus turned to Pullo and the two old friends clasped arms firmly before parting. Khenti whispered something to the remaining Egyptian guard—Shushu, Didymus recalled—before the guardchief turned toward one of the hooded guards who was obviously waiting to show them out. Within seconds, they had departed, with several other hooded guards following in their wake. Four of the Jewish guards remained with Jacob and Hannah, who were starting to move away from the tables toward the far end of the room. To light their way, three of the guards retrieved lit lamps from where they hung on pillars.

Didymus remained where he was.

Caesarion, looking back over his shoulder at the departing Vorenus and Khenti, saw him and stopped, too. "Come on, Didymus."

Didymus stood still, a thousand thoughts, a thousand visions, roiling in his mind.

"Didymus?" The voice was Pullo's, though he could not see him. All he could see was the image of the Ark and, behind it, the Great Library in flames.

"We must hurry," Hannah insisted.

Didymus blinked the real world back into focus, saw that the light was dimmer and marred by his own tears. "I'm ... I'm not coming," he said. "I can't. The Library ... I ... I can't."

Caesarion came back, reached out his hand. "A Shard of Heaven, Didymus."

Didymus swallowed hard. "I can't leave it all to the torch."

"You might not be able to stop it," Caesarion said.

Didymus saw how grown the young man looked in the lamplight. Faint stubble marred the smooth skin of his face, and his eyes were unblinking at the beauty and the horror of the world. When, the scholar wondered, had they all gotten so old? "I can try," he said. It was, truly, all he could do now. All he could be good for. "I'm not worthy anyway. We both know it."

Caesarion shook his head. "Oh, Didymus. It's forgiven. If I can forget it, why can't you?"

"It doesn't matter. My place is here. What good is a scholar without his books?"

Caesarion began to say something more, but he seemed to recognize that nothing would change his tutor's mind. Instead he reached out and embraced him warmly. "Thank you, Didymus. For everything."

"The pleasure was mine, my boy." Didymus thought he would have to force himself to smile, but instead it came naturally. He held Caesarion for a moment longer, then pushed him away. "Now go. Save the Ark. Save us all."

24

THE CITY FALLS

ALEXANDRIA, 30 BCE

Selene sat at the head of the boat, trying to appear more serene than she felt. The night-shadowed water of the harbor passing beneath the hull seemed a perfect match for her mood. It was bad enough that Caesarion had left her behind again, but now she and her brothers had been pulled from their beds by their tending nurse to fulfill a summons from their mother on Antirhodos. Kemse, for her part, also seemed ill at ease, the whites of the nurse's eyes more visible than usual, standing out strong on her dark-skinned face against the background of the night. Young Philadelphus was huddled up in Kemse's lap, and she was gently running fingers through the sleeping boy's hair as she made little cooing noises.

Such a baby, Selene thought. She looked over at her twin brother, Helios, to make a face, but he was staring out across the waves with deeply sunken eyes, his skin paper-pale in the light of the moon and the great lighthouse. He'd been sicker than usual these past days.

She had always known her brothers were weak, that she was the strong one, and it usually gave her pleasure to remind herself of the fact. But now and then, in times such as this, a small but persistent voice in her mind wished it wasn't so. She longed, for once, that she could be the one sleeping in Kemse's lap, rather than the one who had to lead them, who had to be strong.

Selene straightened her back, swallowing hard, and watched the royal island getting closer. Small lights bobbed on its shoreline: the men waiting for their little boat. They seemed to be moving around more than usual, and Selene actually turned to look out north to where Pharos stood like a mighty, sleepless sentinel over the mouth of the harbor. She could see the moving lights of Octavian's vessels out there upon the sea, the Roman blockade that had held them trapped in the city. It seemed peaceful, no cause for such anxiety among the servants and guards. Was it only the oddness of the predawn summons that had set them all on edge? Or was it something else, the same deep horror that she felt in her own gut that something had gone very wrong this night?

Their little boat turned to angle into the island's private harbor, and Selene could see that another small boat was anchored there along the dock. It was one of the supply ships, perhaps the same one she'd used to sneak away from the island the previous year, when she walked alone to the Great Library and first learned of the Shards, whose power so thrilled and frightened her.

Selene frowned, thinking it odd to see the supply boat on the island so early. It wasn't due for many hours yet: the goods it would bring typically weren't ready before dawn.

As their silent rowers pulled their own little boat into the harbor she could see that the supply boat was indeed cluttered with empty crates and barrels, evidence that the supplies hadn't been picked up yet. A tarp had been pulled across the haphazardly arrayed containers, and she could see, by the red-yellow light of the Pharos lighthouse, that it was wet.

The guards who met their little boat were nervous. Selene could see it in the shaking of the lamps in their hands, in the way they kept their eyes from looking at anything but her and her brothers as they beckoned them from the royal dock to the island's small palace. What little they spoke was in hoarse whispers, in quick words, and they hurried them as if fearful of being outside. Selene helped Helios along and noticed that he, too, was shaking. From fright or his illness, she couldn't tell.

Once inside the palace, the guards moved them efficiently toward the royal rooms, and Selene felt her heart beating harder. They were going to their mother's chamber. She wasn't meeting them in the hall. She'd summoned them to her private room. Why? What was going on?

Down twisting corridors, from lamp to lamp, they walked in silent parade. Philadelphus was awake now, but he clung to Kemse, sensing the foreboding anxiety in the air. Helios coughed once or twice, the rattling hacks shockingly loud in the tomb-silent halls.

And then they were there. The guard leading them knocked lightly on the door, but Selene didn't need to strain to hear her mother's strong-voiced reply. "Come."

The guard paused for a moment at the threshold before he pushed open the door, his body bowing low and out of their way as he did so.

Kemse gasped and almost violently pulled Philadelphus to her as the little boy cried out in horror. Helios croaked out the word "Father" before his voice was broken off by his sobs.

Selene just stared, disbelieving what she was seeing even as her heart told her she could have expected nothing less. Their mother, Cleopatra, the queen of Egypt, the living embodiment of a god, had obviously been roused from her bed in mid-sleep. Her short-cropped hair was messed, and she was wearing nothing but her night linens. She'd collapsed as soon as she'd stepped from her bed, and she'd fallen back against the cushions at the foot of it, her night linens twisted obscenely by her position, exposing her glistening right breast in the lamplight. Her face was streaked with tears and blood. In her arms, his head dangling lifeless off her elbow, was their father, Mark Antony, once general of Rome. His torn shirt had been pulled closed, but nothing could be done to hide the wide red stain spread out across his abdomen, or the thicker gobs of red that dangled from his fingertips above the pools of blood on the floor and on Cleopatra's naked legs.

Through the gore, their mother's face was serene. She smiled in a look that made something knot in Selene's gut. "Children," Cleopatra said, "our beloved father has left us."

Kemse was trying to turn Philadelphus to look at his divine mother, but the little boy was fighting her in his sobbing urgency to bury his face against the nurse. Helios had slumped against the wall, his eyes staring at everything and nothing all at once.

"Be not sad," Cleopatra continued. Her voice sounded far away. "This is how a king should die. In honor, not in chains. In happiness, not in misery."

Selene saw how their father's face was twisted in the agony of his death. A shiver ran up her spine, tamping down the sobs that welled up in her throat.

"He told me that he loved you all. He asked me to see him buried with full Roman honor before we joined him."

Selene's heart skipped a beat. Philadelphus looked up through Kemse's arms, their mother's words reaching him through his horror. "Join him?" Helios asked, his voice breaking.

Cleopatra looked at him as if he were a far younger child. "Yes, prince of Egypt. None of us are meant for chains."

Something broke in Selene. She wailed. She screamed. She

pulled at Helios, screaming against the insanity of it all, but his gaze would not meet hers, and he shrugged off her touch despite his weakness. She grabbed for Philadelphus, too little, too young to know any better, but Kemse held him tight, and his body was racked with terrible shrieks.

Then she ran. Not looking back, not caring where she was going. Her face streaming tears, she let her legs take her out through the halls, out of the palace, out into the thick night air.

Out of breath and out of tears, she looked up to the uncaring stars, over to the sleeping city, and then across to the glowing lighthouse. At last her gaze fell upon the little supply ship in the small harbor. There were two men nearing it, readying it for a return to the docks.

Selene thought for a moment about going back for her brothers, about shaking them out of whatever it was that held them to that room, but even if she could do it she knew the boat would be gone when she got back. Taking a deep breath to calm her heart, wiping quickly at her eyes to focus her vision, Selene hurried through the shadows to once more steal her way to the mainland.

By the time she'd slipped beneath the tarp covered with her father's blood, she knew what she was going to do. How she would do it, she didn't know, but she was going to kill Octavian.

An hour and a half after stealing away from Antirhodos, as the sun was brightening the sky to the east and melting the stars into a pale blue wash, Selene stood behind one of the pillars flanking the entrance to the Museum. Peering out across the wide main square of the city, ignoring the pain of her blistered feet, she watched as Roman legionnaires that were not her father's marched down the Canopic Way out of the bright dawn, their footsteps hard and angry.

Selene's heart sank, but only for a moment. She'd come too far to turn back now. She'd been halfway across the harbor when she'd realized, through her silent tears of sorrow, rage, and fear, that she had only one hope of killing Octavian: the Shard that she'd seen on Alexander's breastplate.

It had to be a Shard: a black stone, swallowing light, just like the one Jacob had described as being in the Trident. Somehow it had protected Alexander. Somehow it had kept him strong. It could do the same for her.

And no army of Romans was going to keep her from it.

Besides, they surely would think her no threat. She was just a little girl, alone and unarmed. Surely they wouldn't even stop her.

She smoothed out her dirtied linens to wipe the sweat from her palms, then stepped out from the pillar and hurried across the avenues and up the steps to Alexander's tomb. The legionnaires kept marching. No one shouted for her to stop.

The great gallery of pillars detailing Alexander's life was usually dim, but this morning it was dark as night, its lamps all lifeless. Selene moved quickly despite her sudden blindness, trusting her memory and urgency to get her where she was going. Ahead, she could see the light-framed portal between this chamber and the central chamber beyond, which was lit from above by windows. Alexander's crystal coffin glimmered as if beckoning her.

Moving so fast she was near to a run, she had no time to stop when the shape of a man in Roman armor stepped out from the shadows in front of her. In the instant before she ran into him, she tried to dodge aside but only succeeded in bouncing off his hip and leg. She fell forward into the lighted chamber, her ankle twisting badly on the steps. With a sharp cry of pain she struck the dark stone floor, her loose night shift catching in her feet and tearing as she crumpled to the ground.

"By the gods, girl! Are you hurt?"

Selene could not see the Roman, but she could hear that he was coming down to help her. She scrambled to stand, wincing at pains in her ankle and ribs, and tried to get away from him. "Stay back," she gasped.

"I'm not going to hurt you," the man said. His boots made shuffling noises in the chamber as he stopped.

Selene, panting from the pain, managed to limp close to one of the white-marble statues of her mother's ancestors, and she reached out to it, bracing herself. "Just stay back," she said, closing her eyes to swallow the pain and try to think what next she could do. With a Roman soldier here, she couldn't get the Shard. And Octavian's armies were just outside.

"I am," the man said. "I'm sorry. Can I get you some help?"

Selene at last opened her eyes and turned to look back at the Roman. Her ribs wailed at the movement, but it was not pain that made her take in her breath. The man with her in Alexander's tomb was a handsome young man wearing fine leather armor. Emblems of eagles held his white cloak back off his shoulders, and the ornate, burnished helm under his left arm was crowned with a shoulder-to-shoulder red crest: all told, he wore the battle dress of a high-ranking centurion at the least, more likely that of a member of Octavian's most trusted staff. But it was his skin that most captivated her: darker than that of a Roman, dark enough for him to be a Numidian. Selene's eyes widened as there was only one man that he could be: Juba, the adopted son of Caesar who'd sought the Scrolls of Thoth, the man whose messenger had nearly killed both Didymus and Vorenus on that terrible night. "I'm ... I'm fine," she managed to say.

Juba's face softened with relief. Then his gaze fell down along her body. His cheeks darkened. "My lady," he stammered, "your dress..."

Selene looked down, saw that her torn shift was hanging open, exposing much of her just-budding chest to the man. She blushed and grasped the opening shut, thinking despite herself of her mother's bared breast and the way her father's torn shirt had been pulled closed. She tried to say something, but among her fear, horror, and revulsion, no words would come.

"Here," Juba said, his hands quickly working to free his cloak. "Take this."

Head bowed low to avert his gaze, he hesitantly stepped forward, right arm outstretched with the white cloth. Holding her torn dress with one hand, Selene snatched the cloak from him with her other. She wrapped it quickly around her own shoulders, letting it fall around her body like a robe. "Thank you," she managed to say.

Juba nodded, glanced up hesitantly and then smiled. "It's my pleasure. I'm sorry I frightened you."

Selene started to say something more, but one of the doors leading out of the chamber opened loudly, revealing the high priest of Zeus-Ammon in his finest garb. "Lord Juba," he said, "I'm sorry for keeping you waiting."

Juba looked over at him and smiled. "Not at all. I was just talking with one of your anxious acolytes."

The high priest turned to where Selene stood and instinctively spoke her name. Even as the words escaped his lips, he seemed to be trying to swallow them, his eyes wide at both the shock of seeing her and the horror of having given her away.

Juba stared at her, his face unreadable. "Selene?"

Selene backed away like a caged beast, but she could only manage two steps before her back was up against the wall.

Sounds from the great gallery suddenly echoed into the chamber: cheers, salutes, movement. "He's here!" the high priest gasped.

Juba blinked and shook his head as if waking from a dream. Then he rushed forward, quicker than Selene could react, and grabbed her arm. "You've got to hide," he whispered, voice urgent.

Selene agreed, struck dumb with confusion. Was he helping her? Why would he do that?

Juba looked around, his eyes desperate. He spotted the open door behind the high priest and reached down to lift her up with his right arm, as easy as he carried his helm in the other. He hurried her over as the sound of footsteps grew louder. The doorway was a gaping mouth of shadow compared to the prismatic light of the central chamber. Juba's grip was firm but soft, protectively secure over the looseness of the cloak he'd given her to wear. His body was warm through his armor. Selene started to say something as he set her down inside the door, started to ask why he was helping her, but he held a strong finger to his lips. The footsteps were very close.

Selene reached up to touch him, but he was already pushing the door shut, cutting her off from the light of Alexander's tomb. Her hand went forward in the sudden dark and touched only hard wood over-strapped with iron.

She stood in silence and felt a shiver run up her spine from something other than the slightly cooler air in the hallway. There was a small lamp lit a short distance from the closed door, and her eyes quickly adjusted to focus on the door. She leaned forward to rest her ear against the crack between thick boards, and she closed her eyes to listen.

"Lord Octavian," she heard the high priest say. "You grace this place with your presence."

Selene felt her fingers flex against the wood of the door, as if she might tear through it, but she forced the rage down until it was only a tightening in her jaw. She moved her ear away from the door long enough to look around and see that there were no weapons nearby. Perhaps if she went down to some of the other tombs she'd find something, but she was certain she'd have no chance of killing him right now even if she did.

Patience, she told herself. Patience.

Selene put her ear to the door once more. "Juba, you've

lost your cloak," a voice said. A commanding, arrogant voice. Not Juba's. Not the high priest's. Octavian's, she decided.

"Lost it this morning. On the road. A beggar girl was in need of warmth."

"And you gave her royal linen?" The tone of Octavian's voice was mocking. He sighed loudly. "Your too-warm heart will cost me dearly one day, I fear."

"I hope it does not," Juba said. His voice sounded weaker than that of his older adopted brother. Selene imagined him with his head lowered.

"So. This is Alexander."

"Yes, my lord," the high priest stammered. "The Great Conqueror, son of Zeus-Ammon, king of Macedon and Egypt, Persia and—"

"Spare me the list," Octavian interrupted. "I haven't the time."

"As you wish," the high priest said, his voice quiet.

"Don't you think he looks smaller than you expected?" Octavian said.

"I don't know," Juba said. "I suppose we always imagine the men of legend to have been larger than they really were. He was, in the end, just a man."

The high priest of Zeus-Ammon made a coughing noise, but apparently the other two men ignored him. "But a man who did great things," Octavian said.

"Yes. He was that."

There was silence for a moment, then Selene heard someone else approaching the chamber. "Ah, the wreath," Octavian said.

"Wreath, my lord?" the high priest asked.

"Yes, priest. A conqueror, I've come to pay my respects to the man who built that which I've conquered," Octavian said. "Open it up."

"My lord?"

"The coffin. Open it up so I may place a wreath upon him."

"But this ... this is highly irregular," the high priest said. He seemed to gather himself. "I cannot allow it."

"Very well," Octavian said, his voice cold. "Legionnaire?"

"Yes, Imperator," a fourth voice answered.

"Fetch a hammer."

"No!" the high priest blurted out.

"No?" Octavian asked. "Then open it up."

Several seconds passed before Selene heard keys shaking. Boots shuffled on stone. Four locks were unlatched. Then came grunting, followed by the sound of something heavy sliding away.

"Remarkably preserved, isn't he, Juba?" Octavian said.

"So he is. His armor in particular is..." Juba's voice abruptly trailed off. Selene felt her heart pumping hard in her chest. If he was looking at Alexander's armor, he was looking right at the Shard. If he saw it ...

"Is what?" Octavian asked.

Selene strained to hear what was happening, her ear pressed as hard as she could bear against the door.

"Is what, Juba?"

He'd seen it. He had to have seen it.

"What?" Juba said. "Oh, sorry, brother. I was ... just thinking about this. This moment, I mean. It's extraordinary. I'm honored."

Selene let out a breath that she didn't know she'd been holding. Juba had seen the Shard. She knew it. But he hadn't told Octavian. And he had shut her behind this door when he ought to have given her, too, over to him. Her mind reeled with questions enough to make her feel dizzy.

From the other side of the door she heard movements that must have been the sound of Octavian placing a wreath on Alexander's corpse. When he was done, the high priest asked him if he would like to see some of the tombs of the Ptolemies, starting with Alexander's own general. Selene smiled to hear it. She was in the hall where some of the most recent members of her family were entombed. Getting Octavian into another of the halls would perhaps give her a way out of the mausoleum.

"No," Octavian said. "I came to see a king, not dead people."

"Of course," the high priest said, though his voice sounded both hurt and confused.

"Leave me," Octavian said. "I need a few minutes alone. All of you. Not you, Juba. Please, stay."

Selene heard the sounds of many feet moving away. Even after she could hear them no more, neither Juba nor Octavian spoke for perhaps a minute or more.

"You've done it," Juba finally said. She heard his own footsteps now, getting closer until the door beneath her head creaked slightly with the weight of his presumed leaning. She could hear his voice as if it were in her own ear. "Alexandria is yours."

"We both know I could not have won this victory without you, brother," Octavian said.

"It would've been won without me, I'm sure," Juba said.

"Perhaps, perhaps not. But even if so, it would not have gone so well. The Trident was"—Octavian let out a chuckle—"well, a gift of the gods."

"As you say."

"I know this has been hard on you, Juba. We might have done things we aren't proud of, but it was all for the greater good, my brother. You must remember that. It was all for this. Antony is dead. Rome is whole. Our father's dream is alive." Octavian paused for a moment, but Juba remained silent. "Of course, though I'm in your debt, we both know I cannot proclaim this openly."

The door creaked slightly. Selene surmised that Juba was nodding his head. "I wouldn't want you to do so," he said.

"We'll find something suitable, though," Octavian said. "A province for you to govern, perhaps. Titles. A rich woman for your bed. And wealth enough. You needn't worry about that."

"Just a quiet corner with my books," Juba said. Selene felt she could sense the honesty of his response like a flow of warmth through the wood.

"Of course. Perhaps you'll read of more artifacts, more weapons of the gods."

"What of the Trident? You'll keep it, I suppose?"

"For now. For safekeeping, and in the hope it isn't used again."

The door heaved with Juba's sigh of relief. "Never would be too soon," he said.

"For the greater good," Octavian repeated. "Remember that."

"Greater good. Yes." There was a pause for a moment. "And what fate for Cleopatra and her children?"

"Hm? What care do you have for them?"

"No care," Juba said. "Just curiosity."

"Cleopatra will want to commit suicide, of course. Follow Antony out with honor. I'll not have that. She's being arrested to prevent such a rash end, kept alive to be taken to Rome for my Triumph. I'll enjoy that."

"Caesarion?"

"There can only be one son of Caesar, one emperor. I'm told he's gone to ground like a cornered rabbit. But whatever hole he's crawled into, we'll pull him out of it sooner or later, and that will be that."

"Not the other children, though?"

"I haven't decided. Why? Have you a thought?"

"I don't think you should kill them."

"Ah, that weak heart again."

"No, it's not that. It would just show the ... mercy of the son of a god if you spared the children of your enemy."

"Cuts close to you, doesn't it?"

"It does. Caesar had mercy on me after my father fell, and I would have the same done for them. More than that, though, I think it would show your willingness to forgive the sins of the past as you move forward to a new Rome. It would be well received at home, I know, especially since Antony left your own sister to take up with Cleopatra and give rise to these children."

Selene listened hard to the silence. She thought she could hear Octavian pacing. "I suppose Antony's children could be spared," he said. "Perhaps I'll even adopt them. It would go over nicely with the Senate: pardon to those who move forward. I like that very much."

"So you'll spare them, then?"

Octavian laughed. "If it pleases you, yes. I will."

"Thank you. It's for the best anyway."

"I suppose." Octavian sighed. "Well, it's a small matter in the moment. More pressing is the basic security of the city. The palace will be secure shortly, and Delius has put together some excellent plans for the transition of local control. I should see to it."

"Of course. I was hoping I might help to secure the Great Library."

"If you'd like," Octavian said. His voice sounded distracted. "Just be careful. I can't afford to lose you."

"The ... guards you assigned me haven't failed to keep me protected yet." There was something hard and pained in Juba's voice, like resentment.

"Good. And they'll remain with you." If Octavian noticed the tone in Juba's voice, he didn't show it.

"One last favor," Juba asked.

"Yes?"

"Could I have a few minutes here alone?"

"Alone?"

"Without the guards. I just ... I want a few minutes to reflect here."

"So sentimental." Octavian chuckled. "It's all that stands between you and being a great leader of men, Juba. You cannot be sentimental when the survival of the state is at stake."

"I can imagine so."

Selene heard the sound of footsteps, and Octavian's voice was growing quieter. "Very well," he said. "Your guards will wait outside. Leave him in one piece, my brother!"

Once Octavian's voice had receded, Selene leaned back away from the door, expecting it to be opened. What would she say to him? She had so many questions, she didn't know where to begin. He'd been her enemy, had he not? But he'd also hidden her. And the feel of him had been so comforting, so protective. And he'd argued to save her brothers. Why? And what did the tone of his words mean when he spoke of his guards?

Selene stood in the half-dark for long minutes, lost in her thoughts as she watched the door, waiting. When it still hadn't moved, she leaned her ear back to it and heard shuffling sounds of cloth from the other side. Grunts. And then a repeat of the sliding sound she'd heard earlier. Creaks of leather and the quiet ringing of metal. Then, at last, footsteps coming closer.

The door swung open and Selene squinted in the blinding light. Juba was there, filling the frame, back-lit by the rays of sunlight that spun colors around Alexander's closed crystal tomb. As her eyes adjusted she could see that there was a new smile on the Numidian's face. And something more had changed, too: he was wearing Alexander's armor, and its black stone shone like dark fire upon his chest.

25

The Enemy of My Enemy

ALEXANDRIA, 30 BCE

Didymus sat on one of the curving stone benches in the main hall of the Great Library of Alexandria, awaiting the end. The Roman soldiers had given up trying to use their shoulders and axes to break down the barred and reinforced front doors, but he knew that they were only gathering their strength for another assault. Probably the final one.

They were getting a battering ram, he supposed. A massive, iron-capped length of wood that would splinter the locks and the bars, opening up gaps like wounds. He and his fellow scholars would try to fill the openings, to ward off the Romans, but he knew they'd fail. They were librarians, not soldiers. He'd known that before he'd left for the Serapeum, when he'd given the order to barricade the Great Library in his absence. He'd known it when he then decided to leave the Serapeum—and the chance to see a Shard—in order to return here for the end. The Romans would get through, and the low reflecting pool between the ten pillars in the entry hall would be stained first with rivulets of bright red and then, as more of their blood spilled out into its waters, it would mix to a soft, pleasant pink. After that, if history was any indication, the conquering Romans would burn the Library and the bodies of its defenders—some, no doubt, still alive—to ash.

Didymus looked down at the central round pool at his feet, saw the steadily rippling reflection of the light of this new day streaming through the eastern windows of the dome high above him. Closer still he saw the three staircases spiraling round the walls of the six-sided hall, and the doors to the ten halls of knowledge and all the books beyond. The doors were, for the moment, bolted and barred shut, but it didn't matter. Breathing deep, he could still smell the scrolls.

Didymus was glad, at least, to know that he'd probably not live long enough to smell the smoke.

The librarian felt an instinctive chill run up his spine and he stood, hoping movement would get his mind on something other than the thought of fire and screams. He walked around the pool, only to find himself staring back down the pillared entry hall to where half a dozen of his fellow scholars were slumped, in exhaustion, around or against the makeshift barricades they'd pushed up against the front doors. The turned-up desks and boards and bookcases looked obscenely out of place. He'd always thought of the Library as a temple, meant to be kept as orderly as one.

There was a noise from above him: the sound of fast footsteps approaching. He'd stationed a lookout up in his own office, a fine vantage point to the open courtyard in front of the Library, and it seemed that they'd spotted something. The ram, he supposed.

The face that appeared at the railing belonged to Thrasyllus, one of the youngest of the scholars who'd chosen to remain at the Library after he'd told them of Antony's death and the fall of the city and gave them free pass to leave. He had always been a driven young man—a student of astrology, which Didymus found unfortunate—yet his usual confident surety was gone for the moment. He appeared both frightened and confused.

"What is it?" Didymus asked.

"Master," the young astrologer said, stuttering in his haste, "there's a man outside who wishes to talk to you. He calls you by name."

"Who?"

"A dark-skinned man. But he wears the crest and markings of Caesar's own family."

Didymus swallowed hard. "Juba."

"He isn't alone," Thrasyllus said.

Of course not. Juba would bring many soldiers to destroy the Library. He'd have a special interest in its destruction, Didymus imagined. "How many men?"

"No men, master. He's with a young girl." The look of confusion on the astrologer's face deepened. "I ... I think it's the lady Selene."

Didymus was staring out his office window at the encircling Romans when Thrasyllus knocked quietly on his door.

"Please, come in," Didymus said as he turned around, trying to make his voice sound more in control than he felt.

The door opened and the young astrologer bowed out of the way to reveal Selene, who rushed forward quickly. Didymus crouched down to embrace her. He started to tell her how sorry he was for the death of Antony before it struck him how little the words were in comparison to her loss. But he realized, too, that he had nothing more to give. "I'm so sorry," he whispered.

She'd raised her arms around his neck, and he felt them shiver. "Me, too," she said. And then she let him go, stiffening as if she were embarrassed by her sudden show of emotion.

She ran her hands down a simple linen dress that appeared to be slightly too big to be her own. Her eyes were wet as she blinked away from him, looking toward the door.

Didymus stood, his gaze following hers, and he saw, standing in the doorway of his office, the man who was unmistakably Juba, the adopted Numidian son of Julius Caesar himself. He was wearing his finest dress uniform, the helm in the crook of his arm gleaming with fresh polish, though Didymus' attention was drawn quickly to his strange way of wearing his white cloak. Didymus had only seen such cloaks pulled back off both shoulders, but Juba's hung from his right shoulder alone, such that it draped across the front of his chest to hang half over the short sword at his left hip. The thought ran across Didymus' mind that he could later research whether this was a Numidian custom. It wouldn't take him long to do: he knew precisely where he'd find the book he needed, and he knew it was written in familiar Greek. It wouldn't take long at all. But then, as soon as he imagined the halls of scrolls, he pictured them in flames, the little bits of burning papyrus fluttering in the smoky air like bright butterflies.

"My dear Didymus," Juba said, bowing cordially. "I am pleased at last to meet you."

Didymus bowed low in response, feeling a chill against the back of his neck like the wind he imagined preceding an executioner's swing. "Is it to you that I owe thanks for the sparing of this building?"

"It is," Juba said. He smiled diplomatically. "Though the men remain, as you might imagine, most anxious to burn it nevertheless."

"I hope they can be dissuaded, prince of Rome and Numidia."

Juba grinned. "Numidia and Rome," he corrected.

Didymus nodded, though he couldn't imagine what difference it made.

"I was hoping we could talk," Juba said. "All three of us."

"Of course," Didymus said. He motioned to the two chairs he'd placed in front of his desk, distantly remembering Caesarion and Jacob sitting in them as they learned the truth of the Shards. "Please, sit down. Thrasyllus, see that we are not disturbed."

The young astrologer bowed, more deeply than Didymus had ever seen, before he closed the door. Juba held a chair for Selene before settling into his own. Didymus glanced once more out the window, confirming that the Roman army hadn't moved and wasn't yet bearing torches, before he, too, sat down. "Well," he said, "I thank you for sparing the Library so far."

"I wouldn't see it burned," Juba said, the quickness of his response speaking to its honesty. "Though I would do so gladly if it got me what I want."

When he knew Juba was on his way up, Didymus had pulled from its hiding place the letter from that horrible night, the night that brought them all to this place and to the truth of the Shards and a war greater than any battle between men. He lifted it now from the papers strewn atop his desk. Smears of red still stained its surface, marring its inks. Didymus held it gently in his fingers, turning it over twice before he set it down, faceup, on the wood. Amid the stains he could see the Numidian's mark. "I don't have what you're looking for," Didymus said, his eyes still fixed on the letter. "I told the man you sent. The Scrolls of Thoth don't exist. They're not here. Burning this place will reveal nothing."

"I know," Juba said.

Didymus looked up. "You know?"

"It's not the Scrolls that I'm after. It's the Ark. The First Shard."

Didymus felt his heart skip a beat in his chest. A wave of nausea washed over him and he had to swallow the urge to be sick. "Sh-shard?"

Juba smiled. "One of the Shards of Heaven. Like the Trident that my stepbrother Octavian has in his possession. The Ark of the Covenant. I want it. No, I need it. And you're going to get it for me."

"How—?"

"How do I know of the Shards?" Juba looked over to Selene. "I've suspected some of it, but I know more today than I knew yesterday."

"Selene?" Didymus looked at her as if he were seeing her for the first time: young, strong, defiant. "How could you? To the Romans?"

"Not to the Romans," she said quickly. Her cheeks were tinged with red, but her chin was raised. "To Juba. We have to tell him everything."

"What?"

"He's on our side," Selene said, her eyes pleading. "It's our only hope. You've got to tell him about the Serapeum."

Didymus pushed back from his desk and stood, backing away from them and turning toward the window. His hands raised to his head as if he meant to cover his ears. His gaze fell on the surrounding army. The Romans looked anxious, hungry for destruction. "No. No..."

"You've got to tell him whatever you know about the Ark."

Didymus felt his stomach lurch, as if he'd been kicked in the gut. "Oh, Selene," he moaned.

"The lady Selene is right," Juba said, his voice calm and confident. "I want the same things you want. The Library saved. The children of Antony and Cleopatra alive."

Didymus blinked at the Romans and the tense city. He did want that, didn't he? The Library saved? He'd given up the chance to see the Ark to attempt just that, hadn't he? And of course he wanted the children alive. He'd given so much for them, felt like a father ...

The precision of Juba's words suddenly struck him, widening his eyes. "But not Caesarion," he whispered.

It wasn't a question, but Juba treated it as one. "Nothing can be done for that," the Numidian said. "I'm sorry. I did try."

Didymus leaned forward and placed a hand upon the window to keep from falling. Caesarion. He pictured the child, the boy, the man. *Not Caesarion*.

"He did try," Selene said. She sounded close to crying. "I heard him. Octavian wanted to kill us all. Juba talked him out of it."

Didymus closed his eyes on the Roman soldiers, on the suddenly swirling room. He closed his eyes and tried to make dispassionate sense of it all. Of course they couldn't let Caesarion live. He was too much of a threat. He and Antony were destined to die. Cleopatra, too, maybe. It would be a miracle if they didn't kill the other children, too. But why would Juba care? Why would he try to save them? It made no sense. "I don't understand," he finally said. "What are you after?"

"Vengeance," Juba said, his voice cold. It wasn't the kind of reply Didymus expected and he spun away from the window to look at them again. Selene had her head down, but her face was wet. Her arm was outstretched, her hand in Juba's. The Numidian had been looking at her with pity in his eyes, but when he turned his head to Didymus his stare was filled with lethal anger, as if he were in thrall to another power. "I want vengeance. And the Ark can get it for me. Understand that I will stop at nothing. I feel it like a fire in my veins, like a flame in my heart. Vengeance, librarian. I will burn this Library to the ground to get it. I will kill if I need to. I will destroy Octavian—and any who stand in my way before him."

26

The Ark of the Covenant

ALEXANDRIA, 30 BCE

Caesarion had been beneath the city before. Alexandria was a city grown from its public works—from its elaborate watercourses underground to its great temples and palaces above—and it was the responsibility of any good ruler, he believed, both to understand these workings and to see to their upkeep. As a result, he'd often had cause to enter the dark canals beneath the streets, or the deep-cut labyrinths of tombs in the necropolis to the west, especially after his mother had gone north to Actium.

Even so, he'd never seen anything like this. Along with Pullo and Shushu, the Egyptian guard who'd remained with them after Khenti left with Vorenus, he had been following the other guardians of the Ark through a perfectly square underground passage that wound its way northwest from the famed Serapeum toward the Heptastadion like a meandering river: twisting, turning, now and again dropping down cascades of steps that appeared suddenly at the edge of the lantern light.

Indeed, the more he thought of it, the more he wondered if it was meant to replicate the course of the Nile. Were those occasional abrupt steps downward meant to replicate the five tumbling cataracts of the Mother River? And the only other break in the smooth-walled passage had been the merging—quite some time after they had left the temple of Serapis—of an identical passageway from the east; though the Jews had said nothing, Caesarion decided that this must have been the other, shorter passageway that originated beneath Alexander's tomb, perhaps bending back against itself like the eastern branch of the Nile, if his hypothesis about its design was correct. Like the Mother River itself, the longer passage they followed had, from that point on, no branches or doors. There were only two ways in, and it seemed that there was only one way out: to keep moving northward, toward the sea.

His mouth would normally have been filled with questions about it all, but there was simply no opportunity to ask them. The keepers of the Ark were moving with a tense focus that silenced questions. More than once they would signal for a halt and one of their number would move ahead into the darkness for several minutes at a time. The passage was narrow—only two men could walk comfortably abreast—so Caesarion could not see what they did. But from the quiet sounds of their workings, he guessed that they were disabling traps set into the passageway, even if he never saw a sign of the disarmed traps in their wake.

By chance, he was walking beside Pullo, behind Hannah and Jacob, and Caesarion knew that, even if there had been time for questions, he would have had difficulty asking them. The girl had been captivating when they'd spoken back at the temple. She was confident and mysterious, intelligent and strong, so very unlike any of the servant girls he'd known in the confines of the palace. It was only the fact that he couldn't see her face, he supposed, that allowed him to think anything coherent at all as they walked—although, he noted to himself as he watched the back of her, not thinking about *her* was still difficult.

"The masonry work here is different," Pullo whispered, momentarily pulling Caesarion's mind from Hannah's long hair.

"Is it?" Caesarion asked, looking around them at the stone walls and ceiling. They were, he noticed now, more roughly hewn than they had been earlier in the passage.

"A different set of workers," Pullo said. "And the stone is different, too."

"You're perceptive for a Roman," Hannah said without turning.

Caesarion looked over to Pullo, saw even by the dim light of the lantern he was carrying that he was smiling. He clearly appreciated her quick wit and confidence—just as Caesarion did. "Pullo was a mason himself when he was my age, before the wars," he said. He flashed the big man a smile. "That was many, many years ago, of course."

"Is that so?" Hannah said. She glanced only quickly over her shoulder, without breaking stride. "You're quite full of surprises, my big friend. Yes, I believe these passages were built in many different stages, by different crews of workers, using stone cut from different quarries. That way no one could know of its full design or aim. That's also one of the reasons it cannot be straight."

"It must also weave through the other foundations of the city," Pullo said.

"That, too," Hannah agreed.

Before Pullo could say anything more, the passageway abruptly widened out into a larger space. Ten paces more and Hannah signaled for a stop. Their single passage, which they had followed for so long, here divided into three more passages that continued on into the gloomy dark like three deep-throated maws. From somewhere—above, below, or to the side, he couldn't tell—Caesarion could hear a faint splashing. One of the underground canals, perhaps?

Hannah held her lantern forward into the dark and looked back at Caesarion and the others. "Stay close, as the right path can take us to the Ark, while the wrong path will most certainly take us to our deaths."

"More traps?" Shushu asked. The Egyptian guard had been silent for most of their march, but the threat of death clearly focused his attention, and he, too, had apparently guessed the reason for their many time-consuming pauses along the way.

Hannah nodded, then began walking down the passageway on the left. Everyone hurried to catch up.

The passage they followed continued on for perhaps twenty paces, then bent right before turning left again. Ahead, a heavy wooden door loomed in the dark, crossed over with thick iron. For a few seconds they all stared at it, as if surprised to find such a structure in the old passageway. Caesarion could see even from a few paces away that the door was tightly sealed in the frame, with thick bulges of tar pressed into its gaps. He wondered if it was so well sealed that it cut off the air beyond it. Would they open it and enter the Ark chamber breathing the same air as those of its guardians who placed it there so long ago?

To his surprise, Hannah approached not the door, but the wall that he presumed was the western side of the corridor. Reaching out beneath her lantern, she began to run her fingers across the stone, gently rubbing it until, a few silent moments later, she appeared to find what she was looking for and leaned forward, pursing her lips to blow. A fan of dust puffed out of a hidden crack, and she alternatively brushed it back and blew at the seam.

After a minute, Jacob gasped. "There," Hannah said. "I think this is it."

Caesarion saw that she'd revealed a sliver of stone that pulled away. Beneath it was an indentation in the rock that appeared as if it could be used for a handle for a hidden door. "You've never been here before?"

Her gaze flicked up to meet his, excitement dancing in her eyes. "No. My mother was the last to enter. But she told me the secrets before she died. And this seems to be about the right place for Schedia, don't you think?" she asked.

Caesarion didn't know what she meant, but he nodded just the same. Hannah's dark eyes found his and her smile seemed to widen. Amused. Perhaps impressed. It was, he thought, the most remarkable thing he'd ever seen.

"Pullo," Hannah asked, turning in his direction, "would you mind helping here?"

The big man grinned, seemingly glad to be doing something he knew how to do. Handing his lantern to one of the other men, he stepped up to the rock handle that she had exposed and gripped it. After Hannah gave him an encouraging nod, he began to pull.

Pullo strained, gritting his teeth. His thick arms bulged, the veins wrapped round them standing out like tightening ropes. His jaw clenched, and sweat appeared among the thinning gray hairs atop his forehead.

At last, the hidden door began to pull outward. It came slowly at first, groaning as stone rubbed on stone, but then it opened faster as momentum shifted in Pullo's favor. Little tendrils of dust misted down from its edges, scattering on the floor.

Hannah held a lantern through as soon as there was room. "It goes on," she said, barely able to contain her thrill. "I see steps."

Pullo pulled the door open far enough that even he could get through, then stopped. He was panting, his arms looking loose and tired, but he was smiling proudly. Caesarion patted him on the back. "Well done, my friend," he said.

"Thank you, sir," said Pullo. Then he retrieved his own lantern and motioned for Caesarion to follow Hannah and Jacob through the door. Only when everyone was through did the big man pull the door shut behind them. It swung more easily now.

The passage beyond was, as Hannah had seen, very short, quickly encountering a flight of stone stairs that reached up into the darkness. They crept up the steps almost reverently.

"There are no seams," Pullo whispered. "No tool marks. Nothing."

Caesarion looked around. The walls, the ceiling, even the floor—everything was perfectly smooth, yet it appeared to be natural, without signs of the workings of men.

"The power of the Shard," Jacob said in wonderment. "The Ark controls earth above all other things, just as the Trident controls water. This was built by its power. We must be very close."

As he spoke, they reached the end of the stairs, their lantern lights pushing back the darkness of a chamber that appeared to be a perfect, featureless cube, perhaps a dozen paces on a side. In the middle of it, set high upon a three-tiered dais and glinting the light of their feeble oil lamps back to them in shimmers, stood the Ark.

Caesarion had read the stories of the Ark, but whatever his expectations were upon actually seeing it, they were surpassed by the reality before him. The Ark sat broad to them, its acacia-wood sides—angled ever-so-slightly inward from the base to the gold-trimmed top—gleamed as if freshly polished, covered over with ornate twists of metallic vines and leaves. At the center of the side facing them was the very same symbol that was upon the pendants of the guardians: a triangle, pointed downward like a flipped pyramid, set atop a perfect circle cut through by a horizontal line across its bottom third. On each end of its top sat two small statues, one wrought of silver and the other of what appeared to be the same clean gold: elegant beings that knelt facing each other, heads bowed in reverence, the wings sprung from their backs stretched out, feathered tips straining to touch over what appeared to be a black disk beneath them. To Caesarion's eyes they appeared Egyptian in design, embodiments of the goddess Maat. From where he stood their closer wings were lowered, the back ones raised, as if they meant to frame something in the empty space above the Ark—as if, he thought on reflection, they were offering a seat between them.

Hannah, Jacob, and the other guardians instinctively knelt. Caesarion followed suit, and he saw out of the corner of his eye that even Pullo did the same. Bowing his head, Jacob began to chant in a language Caesarion did not know, his voice smooth and strong in devotion. The rest of the guardians joined in his song, a building pulse of ancient and worshipful humility whose power Caesarion could recognize even if he didn't know the words behind it. He closed his eyes and let the chant flow through him like a low hum in his chest. A small, absent part of him noted how *right* it all felt at this moment, as if it tapped into some vestigial part of his own being that had always been there even though he'd known it not, while the greater part of him just swam away on the rising tide of the sound, unthinking of anything but this moment of prayer and the vast, unfathomable power of the One God.

Only when the last note was done did he open his eyes and see that Shushu had not bowed with the rest of them. He'd instead walked forward and mounted the three steps of the dais, moving around the Ark to stand behind it, facing them, his hands reaching out as if he might embrace the twin beings on its top.

Caesarion shouted at him to stop, but it was too late. Smiling, Shushu gripped the Ark and closed his eyes.

For a moment nothing happened. The guardians remained

kneeling, though Caesarion could see that Hannah and Jacob were looking up, watching the Egyptian. Pullo stood as if he might run forward and pull the guard down off the dais, but then he stopped and stared as Shushu began to tremble and shake. His eyes opened, wide in shock, and his face suddenly twisted in voiceless agony. Trickles of red appeared at the corners of his mouth.

Caesarion felt something like a cold wind pulling toward the Ark, and it roused him at last to shake himself from his own paralysis and stand, thinking he might pull Shushu's hands away. Yet even as he stood there was a muted but terrible popping that reminded him, with sickening revulsion, of the sound of a ripe grape being crushed between fingers. The Egyptian's eyes rolled, bulged, and darkened toward black. He vomited a rush of bright blood. Then, before Caesarion could take a step, Shushu was flung back off the Ark with a resounding boom that Caesarion felt in his chest. The Egyptian flew through the air in a blur, striking the far wall of the stone chamber with the sound of shattering twigs before collapsing to the floor in a boneless heap.

Pullo and Caesarion rushed forward to the Egyptian, kneeling to look for any sign of life. There was none. The whole of his body was contorted with the appearance of pain and death. The air that hung about him smelled of blood and bone.

Hannah had stood and walked deliberately across the chamber to look down upon Shushu's remains. Her face was impassive. "It's said among our scriptures that the Ark is death to those who are unworthy," she said. "I think it means that it destroys those unable to control its power."

"But how can anyone know without trying?" Pullo asked, holding one of Shushu's wrists with a look of revulsion that Caesarion would not have imagined him capable of feeling.

Hannah shrugged. "I do not know. If any man had such knowledge of the Shards, it has not been passed on. It's not our place to be tempted with the power of the divine. It has always been thus."

Caesarion looked down at the broken man before them. His stomach churned with anger, grief, and horror. And guilt, too, he decided: guilt because the dead man had been there only because of him, guilt because the Egyptian was dead while he still lived, and guilt because he knew that they would soon walk away from the corpse, moving on to the matters of the living. "What about Shushu?"

"We can do nothing for him now," Jacob said, coming forward to join them. "Only the Ark matters. And we cannot take it back to the Serapeum. Unless your friend has failed, your boat will be close at hand soon."

"Vorenus won't fail," Pullo said.

"I hope not," Hannah said. Behind them, the guards had found two long poles laid out to either side of the dais, and they were fitting them carefully through thick rings at the corners of the Ark's base, in order to move it without touching it.

Caesarion looked around at the featureless chamber. "How will we get the Ark to the sea?"

Hannah looked up from Shushu's corpse to the blank wall of stone. "We go through the door," she said, pointing forward.

Pullo stood and ran his fingers across the smooth surface. "Another hidden door?"

"It is said to be based on the designs of Archimedes," Jacob said. "It can only open from this chamber. Your friend Didymus would've liked to see it, I should think."

"That he would have," Caesarion agreed, at last standing to join them. "I can see nothing. How does it open?"

Hannah set her hand against the wall, leaned against it ever so slightly. "Archimedes was a very clever man," she said. "Just push."

There was a clicking sound from within the stone. Then, a few heartbeats later, it repeated. Then again, faster this time. And again and again, speeding up until they heard the sound of metal gears winding into motion. At last the stone wall vibrated and split vertically along a hidden seam. Tendrils of dust spilled out, and all at once two newly formed halves of a door swung out with smooth precision, folding back into the walls and revealing a passageway that was twice the height of a man and just as wide.

The smell of the sea washed over them all, briny and thick. Then, as the grinding sounds of rock and gear fell silent and the two halves of the door settled into their final positions with an echoing thump, they heard the call of seagulls and the steady beat of waves on a rocky shore.

The passageway before them was clearly made to seem a simple part of the city's freshwater system: it had a trough cut down its center, and it gently ramped downward to what Caesarion immediately recognized as one of the primary water-carrying canals beneath the city, as broad as the avenue above it. The little sliver of its wide surface that he could see at the end of the sloping passage was flashing with the reflected light from some nearby opening to the sun and sea. Looking up, just on the other side of Archimedes' door, Caesarion could see a rock-lined opening in the ceiling that extended up, through the subsurface of Alexandria, to some rainwater collection point far above. There were hundreds of these collection points, which combined to help keep the underground aqueducts full even in the driest months of the year: like roots for trees or veins in flesh, the network of deep canals was the lifeblood of the city. And looking up here from the canal, no one would have a reason to suspect that the stone wall at the upper end of this particular tunnel was actually a most remarkable hidden door—not that it could be opened anyway.

Hannah had passed him by, picking her way down the drier

edges of the sloping tunnel, and Caesarion followed her, marveling at what a brilliant piece of engineering and design it all was.

He had toured this very part of the undercity before, but when he at last reached the edge of the canal he saw it now with fresh eyes. There were walkways running along each side of the canal—just a couple of feet above the surface of the water and meant for maintenance, of course, but also just broad enough, Caesarion now supposed, to safely maneuver the Ark. Looking up here he saw the vaulting ribs of arches that extended out from wall to wall, stretching into shadow as they followed the paved street above, going south. A part of him expected to hear the rhythmic beat of marching footsteps echoing down through the stone—the sound of Octavian's armies overrunning the city—but he doubted that they would have reached so far so soon, and the stone above them was probably too thick to hear such things anyway. Looking in the other direction, to the north, he could see where the wide watercourse ended against the stone wall that marked the edge of the Great Harbor; he could see and smell the ocean through both the access gates at each end of the twin walkways beside the canal and the iron-barred spillway a foot or so above the water between them. Hannah had stopped at the canal's edge, but Caesarion moved along the walkway in the direction of the harbor and the light, feeling eerily like a ghost beneath the city that was—or at least had been—his.

The access gate was locked, as it ought to have been. Between its bars, Caesarion could see that Hannah's directions on the map had been perfectly accurate: the broad street above the canal was the very same road that ran forward along the Heptastadion, the giant causeway that stretched out from Alexandria like a finger pointed northward to the island of Pharos. Huddled just inside each of the locked gates sat four or five large clay jars, big enough to need two men to move them. Explosive pots, he knew. And outside each of the gates sat a square stone platform extending from the harbor wall, perhaps a dozen feet on a side, where the main supports for the Heptastadion's first wooden bridge were rooted into the strong rock a man's height above the tide. That bridge arched over the water, extending forward above Caesarion's head, shadowing the sea directly in front of the spillway. Though he couldn't immediately see them through the access gate, Caesarion knew that even more pots were hidden among the bridge's beams and rails higher above the water: he had ordered them placed there, he remembered, after one of his boat rides with Khenti, on the day he first learned of the Shards. They'd passed under this very same bridge, looking to see that such defensive explosives were in proper position to destroy it if the city were attacked from Pharos. Caesarion felt a strange kind of amazement to have returned to this place, and to see it through such different eyes. Not as a pharaoh now. Not anymore. Just a man in a greater fight to protect the Ark.

Hannah had followed him, and she quickly unlocked the gate using a key that few were meant to have—Caesarion decided not to ask how she had obtained it, instead wondering to himself how he had never noticed how much larger this access gate was than it needed to be—and let it swing open to its small platform beneath the bridge. Below, the harbor waves broke on scattered rocks, and gulls reeled in the cool air of the morning.

"He's not here," Hannah said, looking out at the empty water.

Pullo had come up behind them. "He will be," the big man said. "I know Vorenus. He'll be here. He will."

Caesarion shielded his eyes to look back across the waves toward the Lochian palace and the royal harbor at its base. There were many ships moving in the early light, and his heart sunk to see their Roman colors. With Antony dead, Octavian hadn't hesitated to order the city overrun. All Caesarion's defensive planning—the new walls to the west, these explosives here—had been useless in the end. Alexandria had given herself over to Rome, her citizens too tired to continue the fight. With luck, the capitulation would at least save her from the torch. There would be panic, and there would be killings, Caesarion knew, especially in the first hours as the pent-up rage of the conquering Romans was released in vile and horrific acts—he'd read enough of sieges to know the way of things—but Octavian would see that most of the city's people would go unharmed. What good, after all, was a great city without her people?

Not all would be so lucky, though. For all his mercy, there were those whom Octavian could not allow to live.

Let Vorenus have found the children, he thought. Please.

Just as Caesarion began wondering to whom he was directing his prayer—if it was a prayer—there was a rumble like thunder from beneath them, and the waters of the canal stirred and shook as a whirlpool formed where the passage leading up to the Ark opened into the canal.

The platform, too, shook, the wooden bridge above straining, and it knocked Hannah off balance. She fell into Caesarion, her head coming down against his chest, and strands of her hair brushing up against his face. She looked up, her eyes searching and, Caesarion thought for a moment, hopeful. Her face tilted back as it raised, her lips parting only slightly as she breathed.

Roses, Caesarion thought as the scent and the feel of her filled his world. Red, red roses.

And then, just as her face approached his, the platform shook again, and from the direction of the Ark chamber they heard—unmistakably—the sound of shouting from the other guardians of the Ark.

27

One Fatal Mistake

ALEXANDRIA, 30 BCE

Juba had long since grown to despise the presence of the two praetorian guards that Octavian had assigned to him for his supposed protection, but on this early morning, in the confined space of the dark passageway they'd been following from Alexander's tomb, he was glad for the way in which they went about their business. The square-shaped passage was surprisingly free of traps—or any markings whatsoever—but alone he would have still moved more cautiously than the praetorians did. Despite the fiery desire for vengeance that burned in his chest, an instinct for self-preservation would have seen him walking carefully into the dark. Not so these men. They hurried into the unknown with supreme confidence, one in front and one in back of him and Didymus, the little oil lamps in their hands feebly pushing back the shadows with a warm orange glow and the swords at their hips seemingly ready for use. The detachment of six other Roman legionnaires moved swiftly in their wake, no doubt wondering what they were doing rushing through a tunnel underground rather than pillaging the buildings above them.

Good Romans, though, they'd not voiced their displeasure when Juba had ordered them to accompany him. Nor had they shown anything but quiet, businesslike patience as they followed the tunnel through its twists and turns and occasional stairs.

Not so with Didymus. The Greek scholar was anxious with both concern and excitement. With Juba's assurances that the Library would be spared, and that Selene would immediately be returned to Antirhodos under the most secure guard to prevent anything from happening to her—and that the same guard would take control of her siblings, as well, in order to keep them safe—Didymus had revealed everything he knew about the tunnel on one more condition: that he be allowed to accompany their mission to recover the Ark. Knowing that the scholar was no physical threat to that effort—and that he could, in fact, be of some use either as a hostage or as a source of further information—Juba agreed at once.

It was a decision Juba was glad he'd made, as the scholar had been useful not long after they entered the hidden passage, when they'd encountered another passageway heading off to their left, a branch that Didymus had insisted must lead to the distant Serapeum. And now, as the praetorian in front signaled for a halt in a room with three passageways leading forward, Juba was once more glad he could turn to the man who'd figured out so many of the world's greatest secrets.

"I thought you said this was a single tunnel leading to the Ark."

The librarian's face was part frown and part fascination. "I did," he said. "That's what we were told. Two of these paths must be false leads."

"I'll break up the men, then," Juba said, thinking a simultaneous search would be fast, efficient.

"No, wait." Didymus closed his eyes for a moment in thought. "Two-thirds of them will die."

A quiet murmur passed over the men behind them, but Juba ignored it. "Why?"

"The Ark's guardians would have tried to keep it well protected. Two of these paths are surely traps."

Juba felt impatience rise like heat in his chest, thinking what a small sacrifice two-thirds of these strangers would be when weighed against the destruction of Octavian, but he quickly shook such thoughts away. It was Octavian's kind of thinking, the very thing he wanted to destroy. Such impulses had been coming to him more and more since he had donned the armor of Alexander, the Aegis of Zeus. He resisted the urge to pull away the cloak hiding the armor, the urge to reach out with his mind and embrace the warmth of the black stone mounted at the center of his chest. "Then what do you suggest?" he asked.

The scholar walked forward, past the lead praetorian, and he paced back and forth in front of the three passageways, now and again pausing to look up at the ceiling above one of them, or at the floor at his feet. He wasn't, Juba was certain, looking for signs of the Jews' passage: they'd already learned that the sealed doors to these passages had prevented even the faintest traces of dust from collecting on its floors. What then, Juba wondered, was he looking for?

Didymus abruptly stopped pacing, his head whipping up to nod at each of the passages as if counting them. "How many steps have we gone down?" he asked over his shoulder.

"Steps?" the praetorian asked from behind Juba. "We were supposed to be counting steps?"

The librarian shook his head impatiently as he turned around to face them. "No, no. Not individual steps. Those occasional little sets of stairs. How many? Five? Six?"

Juba had balled his fists to keep them from tearing at his

cloak, but the scholar's question allowed him to relax them as he thought back. "Five, I think."

The praetorian who'd been leading agreed, the light cast by his lantern bobbing over the scholar in front of them. Didymus grinned like a little boy. "Then we go left," he said as he started to walk in that direction, his pace fast with resolution. "Always left."

Juba and the others hurried to catch up to him, the praetorian stepping around him to once more take the lead. "How do you know?" Juba asked. They were quickly moving past a turn in the new passageway. "Are you sure?"

Didymus shrugged, but his face was still beaming as they walked. "It's the Nile. The whole passageway is a model of the river. This must be the start of the delta."

"But how do you know we go left?"

"The Ark is here in Alexandria, and Alexandria is off the Canopic branch of the Nile. The farthest west," the librarian answered.

Juba was starting to ask how he could be so certain that the passageway had anything to do with Egypt's great river when the praetorian in front raised his arm to signal for silence. Juba strained his ears as they crept forward, feet making soft noises on the smooth stone. Another turn, and at last he could hear what the praetorian already had: voices, faintly echoed from the rock around them, too dim to discern their words but clearly near at hand. And then, at the far reach of the light of their lamps, they saw a large wooden entryway at the end of the passage, bolstered with iron.

"They must be on the other side of the door," the praetorian whispered.

At a motion from Juba, the second praetorian joined his fellow in front of the door. They both drew their swords.

For all his experience at war, Juba had been fortunate to take part in few fights. Feeling close to it now, his heart thrilled in both anticipation and fright. He signaled four of the legionnaires to move up front, confident that there was little danger from behind.

He didn't desire a fight. He'd made that order clear enough, he hoped. But if the Jews didn't quickly agree to terms, if they didn't quickly surrender the Ark, Juba knew he wouldn't let them stand in the way of his vengeance. As he'd told Didymus back at the Library, the need for it burned in his veins, burned with a smoldering rage that threatened at any moment to consume him.

The men ahead exchanged nods of readiness as one of the praetorians gripped the door handle. Juba took a deep breath and pulled his own sword. Then he turned to Didymus.

The scholar, he saw, wasn't paying attention to the assault about to happen. He was fingering something on the wall beside him, an indentation just the size of a man's hand, and he was looking at the ground beneath his feet, where faint sweeps of chalky dust—glaringly apparent against the otherwise spotless tunnel—showed that something heavy had recently moved there.

Juba's gaze traced the lines on the ground, and he saw it all for what it was. He reached past Didymus to the stone, gripped what he could see now was a hidden handle in the rock, and began to pull the secret door open. He turned to whisper a warning not to open the wooden door, but his realization had come to him too late.

Time seemed to slow, as if he were moving through thick sand. He saw, in terrible clarity, the handle of the wooden door lifting in the praetorian's hands. He saw him turn to his fellow with a look of final satisfaction as he pulled.

Then time lurched forward, actions speeding into sudden fast motion. Juba found his voice, only to have it drowned out by the splintering boom of the wooden door blasting inward. The world seemed to scream.

The next moments came to Juba in flashes. Blood flinging into the air. A plank hitting the Roman in front of him, grotesquely doubling the man over. Shadows reeling as lanterns flew and clattered. And then the shock of bitter cold as a pent-up tide of water roared forth from the doorway, flooding the passage.

Parts of the door and the men in front of it swept down through the passage, knocking down those still standing and driving them back. Juba felt his own legs being pushed out from beneath him as he fought to hold on to the handle in the stone door. Didymus slammed into him, the older man somehow catching into the folds of Juba's cloak.

The full weight of the water crashed into them then, a buffeting blow that struck like a great hammer in the hands of an unseen and very angry god. The wall of water drove them off the floor, Didymus clinging desperately to Juba, whose grip on the door was the only thing keeping them both from being swept away. Juba's body swung in the passing wave, his eyes closing against the cold and the spin as everything in his being concentrated on holding his straining grip. He felt his body slam up against the scholar's, then the wall, but neither of them let go. For a heartbeat his face found air. Then a second wall descended and they were surrounded by water.

Juba opened his eyes to see only the slightest haze of shapes through the rush of water in the flooding passage. The lamps had all been extinguished by the onslaught, but a dim light reflected down from somewhere beyond the exploded door. It was, Juba thought, a way out.

But there was no way to swim against such a current. And it was not the way to the Ark.

He looked toward his grip, saw that the stone door was already partially ajar. Water was streaming into the crack that he had opened. Willful determination shook him into action. He pulled himself against the current, kicking to pivot his legs against the stone near his hands. His lungs burned, and his mind wailed at the horror of drowning. He fought the emotion down, only to have it replaced by the terrible doubt that he wouldn't be able to open the door further. He would be too weak, or it would be frozen in place, or ...

He pulled. His surroundings grew dimmer, becoming a narrowing circle of light.

He pulled.

In his tunneling vision Juba saw that Didymus had swung himself around, too, to join him. The Greek planted his feet beside Juba's. Juba thought that the stone beneath his grip moved, and he didn't know if it was from the scholar's help or if the rush of the water was actually pushing the crack open.

Together they pulled, straining against oblivion.

The door came free, the current catching it and pulling it wide even as the water slammed them, one after the other, into the void behind it.

Once more he spun and rolled as they rode through churning waves. Juba felt himself pop free of the water into the air and he inhaled instinctively, but just as he did so his ribs crashed against an edge of stone and the air in his lungs was coughed out again. His body bounced upward, vision fading to black, before he at last bobbed out for good, gasping for air.

Juba kicked with what little energy he had left, keeping atop the rising surface. When it ceased pushing him upward, his feet found purchase on the stone of a stair and he scrambled up out of the water in an exhausted push. Didymus came up out of the water beside him, somehow alive. Juba helped pull him up onto the stairs, where the scholar collapsed facedown, coughing.

Juba's ears rung, his vision sparkled with flashes of light, and his lungs felt like they were torn and raw, but he'd made it. He was alive. And the Ark was near. His vengeance was near.

Need pushed him on. He crawled upward, step by agonized

step, light growing around him, until he reached the end of the stair and heaved himself over the top onto the floor of a large chamber. He lay there for a few seconds, panting and spitting what he hoped was water, before he managed the strength to force himself to his knees. He raised his head, water pressing his hair flat against his forehead, and centered his swimming sight on the object of his dreams.

It was there. More beautiful than he would ever have imagined: shining like a new thing, all burnished gold and glory. Twin wooden poles had already been mounted to its sides, preparing it for transport. His heart soared, and for a moment he felt like singing.

Then he saw the four men standing around him. They wore dark hooded cloaks, pulled back from their shoulders to give freedom to their arms as they held notched arrows to their tightened bows, deadly points taking slow and careful aim at the intruder.

"Wait," he croaked, but then the strings were loosed and four arrows buried themselves in his body, finding openings around his armor.

Juba slumped forward, arrows snapping and metal ringing as he struck the stone floor, and silent darkness overtook him.

No.

The thought was so clear, so present in Juba's floating mind that it startled him into a single, strong, undeniable realization. He wasn't dead.

He should be. Juba knew that. He'd very nearly drowned. He'd been shot through with four iron-pointed shafts—any one of which would have killed a man.

But he was alive. Somehow, someway, he was alive. How?

The answer came to him as if from another voice. *The breastplate*, it said. *Alexander's breastplate*.

The memory of it came back to him through the fog of darkness in which he floated. He'd seen it in the tomb this morning and recognized it at once for its potential power, even if he hadn't recognized it for the artifact that it was. Even if he hadn't realized then it was the Aegis of Zeus until Didymus told him. The Aegis. The very armor of the father of the gods.

Not that he believed in the gods. He could no longer remember a time when he had. If what Selene and Didymus had told him was true—and he was certain now that it was—he was right to doubt the divine. There was only one God, and He was gone. All that was left were the Shards.

Despite the coldness of his thoughts, Juba felt a warmth somewhere nearby, like a deep well filled with ready flame. The breastplate again, he realized. With the blacker-than-black stone upon it. He reached out to the Shard in his mind, thinking of the silver and bronze ribbing he'd seen embedded on the inside of the armor and that odd symbol in the middle of it all, directly behind the Shard itself: a six-sided shape in a six-pointed star. Imagining himself pushing out through those metal contacts, through that symbol, he gave himself over to the power of the Shard, just as he had so often with the Trident. Like the feel of those twin snakes beneath his palms, the metal of the breastplate around him seemed to move like a thing alive as the Shard drew him ever deeper even as it pushed back and into him.

Power. He felt it coursing into the body that began to awake around him, filling his veins. Power. Life.

And rage. Deep and raw. Rage only barely contained.

The darkness around him lurched hard. Once. Then twice. Then twice more.

In his mind, Juba felt like laughing. His heart was beating again. Beating and calling for blood.

So this was how Alexander had survived so long, through so many battles, through so many wounds that should have ended his life. This was the power of the Aegis. Power that was now his. Power that would help him avenge his father. And himself. Power that would help him kill Octavian. *Kill.*

Juba's sense of hearing abruptly returned, and he could hear that there was movement around him. Feet on stone, hushed voices.

"Are you sure you're okay?" someone asked.

"I am to see this," Didymus rasped.

"More beautiful than you thought, isn't it?"

"It is," Didymus replied.

In the pause that followed, Juba imagined Didymus staring at the Ark, the object of Juba's own desires. Unprovoked anger shook him to the marrow of his bones, even as another part of his mind—a small, shrinking part—wondered how he could hate the man who'd helped him get this far. What had Didymus ever done to him?

The thought drifted away in the storm of violent anger that swirled up and into him through the Shard upon his chest.

Then came a girl's voice. "We need to go," she said.

He heard the sound of wood bending, and of men grunting under a heavy weight. "Keep it steady," a male voice said. "Slow down the ramp."

Juba cried out in his mind, quaking with ire, but his body, he was certain, did not move.

"So who is your Roman friend?" the girl asked.

"Juba," Didymus said. He sounded distracted, as if he couldn't take his gaze off the retreating Ark.

"This is him?" asked the first voice.

"What's he doing here?" the girl asked.

Getting revenge, Juba screamed back in his mind, and he pictured himself standing, stopping them from taking away his prize, his power, his Ark. His vengeance.

But then, in an instant, he lost the focus of his energies and the pain of his wounds surged over him like a roll of thunder.

His heart still pounding with the strength of the Shard, he fell out of consciousness again.

When he returned to his senses, the pain of his wounds was more manageable. Whether the Shard had partially healed them or his mind had found some means of separating the pain from his mind, he didn't know or care. What mattered was that the voices in the room were gone.

His eyes snapped open, focusing first on the congealed blood that had pooled around his face on the floor and then, as he slowly turned his head, on the empty dais in the middle of the chamber, where the Ark had stood.

No.

They'd taken the Ark. His vengeance. His hope. They'd taken it and left only a few oil lamps flickering hungrily in the dark.

No.

Like a command in his mind, the thought moved muscles in his weakened body. One of his fists balled up.

No.

Rage boiled in his chest, in his mind. He felt it like a wildfire behind his eyes, behind the breastplate. He gritted his teeth and tightened angry muscles to pull himself once more to his knees. Pain shook at his senses, threatened to overwhelm him again, but he dipped down into the surging heat of the Shard and felt a wave of strength push back against the screaming of his body.

No. Vengeance was supposed to be his. By right of his father, who died after Caesar's defeat. By right of the crowds who'd jeered and mocked him when, as a little boy, he was dragged through Rome in Caesar's Triumph.

Vengeance.

By right of the Roman faces mocking his skin, his speech.

By right of the blood on his own hands, blood that he'd spilled by order of Octavian, Caesar's son. The countless men at Actium. The innocent, unknowing sailors off the coast of Italy. Quintus. Even Syphax.

Vengeance. Power.

There was an open door on the other side of the chamber. Juba heard voices, just barely audible, coming from it.

Juba bared his teeth in a smile, and a pulse of strength brought him to his feet.

The Numidian strode, eyes focused and unblinking in his rage, across the stone floor. Ignoring the broken man slumped against the wall, he marched down the ramp. He drew his sword.

The ramp ended at an underground canal. He turned to follow the sounds to the right, moving quickly, making no effort at stealth. They had carried the Ark down through an open gate and onto a platform beside the harbor waters of the city. The hooded men who'd shot him were now standing around the edges of that stone platform, bows ready to fire at any threats from above or without.

Feeling the dull pain of an iron point scraping against his ribs, Juba felt like laughing. Let them shoot, he thought. Let them try.

A girl was among the archers, her hand reaching out to grip that of a man standing beside her, a man of royal complexion and bearing—Caesarion, Juba was sure. Behind the Ark, just inside the open gate, stood another young man who was laughing about something, a massively muscular tall man holding an oil lamp, and Didymus.

Everyone but the Greek was looking out to sea as if they were waiting for something.

Didymus had just turned to look back along the canal when Juba reached them from behind. The librarian's eyes widened in shock, but he could say nothing before Juba tossed him aside like a harmless sack of wheat, his focus on the more threatening men standing between him and his rightful destiny.

As it had in the tunnel, time shifted into slow motion. But now, instead of feeling as if he couldn't move, Juba's movements felt faster than life, faster than he'd ever thought possible. Even as Didymus was smashing against the stone wall beside him, the Numidian was moving past him, to the large man with the lamp, who was instinctively swinging his upper body around to confront the noise behind him.

In one smooth motion, Juba ducked beneath the big man's powerful but slow swing, the short sword in his hand jabbing forward to cut a deep gash across the back of the man's left knee, slicing the tendons there and hamstringing him. The lines on the massive man's face deepened as he screamed in slow time, his body starting to buckle. Juba, grinning like a feral cat, stopped his own lunge when the edge of his blade had run its course through the man's flesh and his own knee was almost touching the ground. Then he kicked himself into a spin that drew his sword back across the man's ripped leg, his reach extending as he spun in order to carve a swath over and through the right knee, too. The big man started to collapse over the other way, sprawling toward a jumble of large clay pots beside the gate.

Blood was hanging in the air like frozen red rain, the big man still falling, as Juba's momentum carried him around and he drove his blade to the hilt up and through the lower back of the young man standing between him and the Ark.

Juba let go of his grip, allowing the young man to crumple, blade protruding from his gut, onto the stones behind the Ark. Juba stepped over him, the wave of power from the Aegis ebbing and time shifting back into proper speed.

He heard screaming and crashing, wet sounds close to his feet. Caesarion and the girl on the other side of the Ark were spinning and preparing to defend themselves. Four bows started to turn in his direction. Too late.

Imagining the power to come, feeling the power that he already had, Juba smiled. Then he reached out and calmly placed a hand on each of the angels atop the Ark.

28

The End of a Kingdom

ALEXANDRIA, 30 BCE

The island of Antirhodos appeared tranquil in the early morning light. The harbor waves still broke on its sandy shores. The palm trees still swayed along its promenades. Its small royal palace still stood, no differently than it had for years.

Vorenus, standing beside Khenti on the foredeck of the Roman trireme they'd taken at Actium, thought the island seemed a perfect, peaceful antithesis to the chaotic fall of the city around it.

He and Khenti had seen the beginnings of that chaos as they'd run, hardly stopping for breath, from the Serapeum across the city to the Lochian palace and its sheltered, royal harbor. Fast-moving Roman scouts had already been riding through the streets on horseback, setting fire to the occasional building and happily racing down the few civilians daring the daylight, trampling them with their hooves. Fires were being set, too, by the Alexandrians themselves; Vorenus had never known a community to fall without some of its citizens turning on each other, beginning the process of looting and execution before the invaders arrived en masse and controls could be put in place by the conquering commanders. He and the Egyptian had been forced to take a long path to reach the palace as a result of the many predawn terrors, and by the time they'd reached the harbor, the sun was rising and the trumpeting calls of the invading army's horns were echoing close indeed.

What chaos was going on in the streets now, Vorenus could only imagine, though he could see the evidence of it in the form of at least a dozen smoke columns threading up into the sky above Alexandria. Buildings were being torched. Stores were being robbed. Women were being raped. People—innocent people—were dying.

He could hear none of it. He could see none of it. But he knew it was so. No matter how often the Romans claimed to be civilized, men were all barbarians in the heat of battle. And never more so than when they won.

Vorenus knew. He'd been one of them.

"The city begins to smoke," Khenti said.

Vorenus was accustomed to the dispassionate, businesslike nature of the Egyptian's voice, but to hear him speak so about the destruction of his home nevertheless made him shiver. "I don't think Octavian will let it all burn."

When Khenti didn't reply immediately, Vorenus looked over to him and saw that the Egyptian was looking to the rear of their ship. "Manu wonders if he may bring us into the docks on the south side of the island. The docks of the royal harbor might be too tight."

Khenti had been efficient in conscripting a crew for their trireme at Lochias. Though they'd been forced to leave a bit shorthanded on the oars—Khenti could find only so many guards in the short time they had—they'd been fortunate to find Manu actually working down in the royal harbor when they'd arrived. There was no more experienced captain in the Egyptian ranks, though Vorenus had never heard him speak a word to anyone. He'd long suspected, in fact, that the captain was a mute. How Khenti and others managed to communicate so well with him despite his apparent silence was a wonder. "The south side is fine," Vorenus said. "Whatever he thinks best."

Khenti nodded back toward the keel, then returned his attention forward. The ship began to turn beneath them, the bow angling off to port. Vorenus closed his eyes to feel the steady beat of the oarsmen rocking them forward through the harbor. He'd never liked riding upon the sea—especially after Actium—but there was nevertheless something soothing about the rowing of a warship, something that reminded him of waves on the shore. Like a mother's heartbeat, he supposed. He'd seen many an angry, crying child comforted upon a parent's breast, lulled to quiet and sleep by that sound and that feeling of home, and perhaps it was the same with men and the sea. He'd never experienced holding a child himself—his duties had left him no time for children of his own, no doubt part of the reason he felt so close to Cleopatra's young family—but he'd seen it often enough to think it similar.

"Some Romans have beaten us to the island," Khenti said.

Vorenus opened his eyes. Manu had steered them around the island, bringing them into line with the docks on its south side, and they could see now that another boat was already docked there: a bigger ship than their own, flying Roman colors. More than that, a golden eagle standard was set at its foredeck. "Not just any Romans," Vorenus said, quickly thinking through their options before deciding that there was nothing to do but carry on with the hope of rescuing the children, the only family he'd ever known. "It's Octavian."

*

A squad of legionnaires was waiting for them on the dock. There was no fight. Facing perhaps two dozen well-armed and coordinated Romans, Vorenus and Khenti knew they were outmatched. Yet Vorenus still believed he might manage to negotiate a peaceful outcome, some way of getting the children out under the pretense of the Roman flag their trireme flew. Besides, he was himself a Roman, was he not? Even after all that had happened, a part of him still clung to that land of his birth. They'd listen to reason, he was sure.

All such hope disappeared once he and Khenti stepped foot on the island. The Roman squad leader, a veteran man Vorenus didn't recognize at first, stepped forward to address him. "Lucius Vorenus," he said.

"Do I know you?"

The Roman smiled. "Too long among the filth and you've forgotten your old comrades. We served together in Gaul."

Vorenus squinted, finally saw behind the wrinkled face and whitened hair the man he'd known. "Galbus?"

The man smiled. "You took my rank, Vorenus. You and that big bastard Pullo, with your nonsense charge against the Nervii in Gaul." His eyes sparkled as his voice took on a formal tone and he stepped back into even rank with his fellows. "You're under arrest by order of the Imperator of Rome, Octavian, son of the god Caesar. Surrender your arms."

"Galbus," Vorenus started to say, "We need—"

"Surrender your arms," Galbus said again.

The rest of the legionnaires came to dangerous attention, and Vorenus felt the threat of the spear points and blades. He felt, too, the tension in Khenti; the Egyptian, he was sure, was going to attack. He was also sure that they'd both be dead in seconds if he did. Not knowing what else to do, he reached slowly for the belt holding his gladius and unbuckled it. "Do as they say," he said to Khenti.

Khenti did so at once, unlimbering the swoop-bladed sword

at his own side and slipping a short, hiltless dagger out from behind his back. At a nod from Galbus, two legionnaires came forward and collected the weapons.

"Good," Galbus said, voice satisfied. "Come, Vorenus. You've an audience with the judge of Rome."

"And the Egyptian, sir?" asked the legionnaire holding Khenti's weapons.

Galbus looked the guardchief up and down. Disgust twisted his face. "No better than beasts, these Egyptians." His face brightened slightly. "Take him down to the end of the dock and gut him like one."

Vorenus jumped forward, the instinct to save Khenti overriding the logic of the odds, but something hard struck the back of his skull and he instead crumpled forward to the flat blocks of stone paving the promenade along the dock.

The last thing he heard before he passed out was Galbus laughing.

He awoke to surges of pain that pounded his skull with every heartbeat. He groaned involuntarily, and someone's fist immediately impacted his ribs. "Quiet, you," a voice growled.

Vorenus coughed air back into his lungs, but he managed not to groan again. And the new input of pain from his side somehow cleared his head enough for him to blink the scene before him into focus.

He was in the throne room of the small royal palace on Antirhodos. Dozens of braziers were lit in and around the pillars supporting the roof, and the air was thick with rich incense that tickled at his nose. Large rectangles of sunlight draped across the floors and walls, the angles of the light revealing that little time had passed: it was still early morning. He'd been here often at this time of day, making one report or another to the throne of Egypt.

Only this time it was not Cleopatra upon the orange-stone chair raised up at the head of the room. It was not the incarnation of the goddess Isis who looked down upon them all, enjoying the breeze from waving palm fronds in the hands of collared slaves on either side of the kingdom's seat. It was Octavian. Older than he was when Vorenus saw him last, and more confident, stronger in shoulder, but undoubtedly the adopted son of Julius Caesar. As Vorenus looked up, the younger man smiled.

"Welcome, Lucius Vorenus," he said. "I'm sorry for your treatment. It seems unfitting for a hero known to my divine father. Then again, it seems too kind for a traitor both to Rome and to his memory."

Vorenus worked to fight down the rising gorge in his throat while trying to formulate a reply, but the sound of a woman struggling in one of the side halls turned Octavian's attention elsewhere.

A moment later, Cleopatra appeared, half-dragged from the family's living chambers between two Roman soldiers. She was wearing what appeared to be her nightclothes, and they were bloodstained and partially rent, leaving the luscious olive skin of one shoulder bare and allowing peeking glimpses of her voluptuous body as she was thrown forward to her knees in front of the throne. Behind her came her two boys, Alexander Helios and Ptolemy Philadelphus. There was blood on their nightclothes, too. More than on their mother's, Vorenus noted. Then, with horror, he saw that no one else was coming from the hallway. Where was Selene?

As if in response, a contingent of Roman soldiers on the other side of the throne room parted, and the young Selene appeared. Unlike the rest of her family, she wore a royal gown. Not the most elaborate dress he'd ever seen her wear, but clearly more formal than anything the others had on. And where their faces were freshly damp with tears and stained with the red of emotion and blood, Selene's was clean and she wore the countenance of a person who was finished with tears. She walked deliberately across the stone floor, her head high and her hips moving in careful rhythm, womanly despite her young age.

She reached her arms out to her brothers, thin bracelets of gold dangling from her wrists, and they came to her as they perhaps had once come to the mother who knelt unmoving, head down against her chest and shoulders rising and falling in slow breaths, in front of them.

"Selene," the young Philadelphus croaked as he embraced his older sister. "Kemse. She's ... they—" The little boy's voice broke and he sobbed into her breast.

"She tried to stop them," Helios managed to say, and then he began to cough in violent, phlegmatic hacks.

Selene just held them, cooing softly. Her gaze, Vorenus saw at last, was fixed not on her brothers, nor on her mother, but past them all. She was staring at Octavian. And Octavian was staring back.

Vorenus stared, too, wondering what was happening. The fact that his head was ringing like an anvil was not helping him figure it out.

"Lord of Rome," Cleopatra said.

Heads turned to the woman who had seduced two of Rome's greatest generals, the woman who had ruled Egypt and, for a moment, almost held the whole of the world in her hand. It was a testament to the striking appearance of her daughter that anyone's eyes had ever left her. She was still, after all, even at the age of forty, the most beautiful woman Vorenus, at least, had ever seen. And if anyone in the room were to say differently, Vorenus would know him a liar.

Octavian's head turned slower than the others, but at last he, too, looked at the queen on her knees before him. "Cleopatra," he said. "I've dreamed of this moment."

Cleopatra rose from her knees slowly, her head still bowed. Vorenus didn't doubt that the top of her gown was hanging open to Octavian's view as she did so. "Antony is dead," she said, as if his death explained everything that needed explaining.

"By his own hand, I know. And from what I've been told you were planning to do the same to yourself and your beautiful, innocent children."

Cleopatra at last straightened her back to look up at him. "You are Rome, and I would do only what Rome wishes."

"Is that so? You were barricaded in that room to do your hair, then?"

Many of the Romans in the room snickered. Cleopatra ignored them. "I was mourning, my lord."

"Ah, yes. For that pig, Antony. A traitor to Rome. I should think you'd be glad to be rid of him."

"Egypt has ever been a friend to Rome," Cleopatra said. Her voice, Vorenus noted, betrayed nothing of the cold hatred that he knew must be in her heart. She increasingly sounded, quite to the contrary, playful and flirtatious.

"And so it will remain," Octavian replied. "Indeed, I think Egypt will be under the direct rule of Rome from now on. The time of the Ptolemies is done. You'll be the last of your family to see the throne."

Cleopatra gasped despite her attempts to keep her calm. She knew, as did they all, the import behind Octavian's words: Caesarion would never rule Egypt. He was a man marked for death, if death hadn't reached him already.

Please let it not have, Vorenus thought.

"I think you should return with me to Rome," Octavian continued. "As a sign of ... the friendship between us."

Something like a shiver made Cleopatra's shoulders tremble, but her voice betrayed nothing as she bowed—longer and lower than necessary—to the throne. "I serve your will, of course," she said.

"Very good," said the Imperator of Rome. Then his gaze turned to Vorenus again. "And so to you, my once-Roman friend. What are we to do with such as you?"

It wasn't really a question, and Vorenus did not treat it as one. He tried only to stand as straight and proud as his throbbing head and aching ribs would allow.

"You were a good man, Vorenus. I even remember you from my youth, if you can believe that. I thought you were a loyal man, then. I'm sad to see I was wrong."

Vorenus thought about replying, about declaring his undying, unceasing devotion to the true spirit of Rome, the Rome that he and Pullo had fought and bled for, the Rome that Julius Caesar had promised them once. But it would serve nothing. He'd fought against Octavian's armies, and Octavian wasn't his adopted father. He was a man of more ambition, of more calculation. And for Octavian, Vorenus knew, he was only a man to be used for an example. He looked over to Selene and her brothers, and he saw the many Roman soldiers around them, how easily Octavian could kill them all. He imagined Caesarion waiting for a ship that would never come, running through the streets of his home like a hunted rabbit.

I'm sorry, he thought. I failed you all.

"Those who beg mercy of Rome shall have it," Octavian announced in a loud voice to the room. "Let it be known to all those who have served under Antony. Turn over arms, submit to the authority of the Imperator, and live. If not, go the way of Lucius Vorenus." His gaze fell on Vorenus, piercing and angry. "His head. Now," he said, dismissing his life with a wave of his hand.

Metal rang from behind Vorenus, and he closed his eyes. This will do for the headache, he thought to himself. It was the sort of thing Pullo would say, and the thought of his old friend made Vorenus both sad and happy at the same time. At least Pullo lived.

"No!" shouted Selene.

Once more the room turned to the girl who for the moment seemed a woman. Her brothers were startled away from their embrace of her, leaving wet marks upon her dress. With Octavian's attention upon her she approached the throne that might one day have been hers, arms loose at her sides as she swayed up next to her mother, who only looked down at her daughter with an unreadable expression upon her face. Selene's jaw was stiffly set, and her gaze did not fall to the ground. She did not bow.

"No?" Octavian sounded amused. "You disagree with the judgment of Rome?"

Cleopatra's hand twitched at her side, as if she thought to reach out to her daughter to protect her from the dangerous game she was playing, but Selene was already speaking, her voice steady and smooth. "Vorenus was more a father to me and my brothers than Antony ever was," she said. "He has been, as you said yourself, a loyal man. Yes, he was loyal to Antony, but it was only because it was his place to be. Antony chose for both of them."

Octavian said nothing, but he stared at the girl for long seconds, seeming deep in thought. "What is his life worth to you?" he finally asked.

"Whatever mine is worth to you," Selene replied. "He is as my father. If I'm to be spared, let him be so." She bowed at last, graceful and smooth, and held herself low and humble before him.

Vorenus saw Octavian swallow hard. "You're as interesting as you are beautiful," the Imperator said. The smile that spread across his face seemed to Vorenus both victorious and devious. "I'll offer you a bargain. A gift to show my goodwill to Egypt and Rome's loyal subjects."

Cleopatra's hand twitched again, but instead of reaching out to her daughter she bowed alongside her.

"I offer Lucius Vorenus of the old Sixth Legion free passage from this room as a wedding gift."

Cleopatra knelt on one knee, then raised her head to address the man upon her throne. "A wedding gift?"

Octavian's face flashed to malice for a moment before it returned to something that might have been kindness. "Yes, my lady. For your daughter, who I will give to a truly loyal man, Juba the Numidian."

"Numidian?" The word was gasped out of Cleopatra's throat.

"A man of my own family," Octavian said, an edge in his voice. He stood from the chair, came down the steps to stand before Selene. "Well? I give you a place in my family, lady Selene. And so to these your brothers."

Selene had remained bowing, but now she raised herself up. "If Juba will have me," she said in a quiet voice.

"He will."

The leering look in Octavian's eyes as he stood so close to the girl and passed his gaze over her body made a heat rise in Vorenus that brushed aside his pains and focused his awareness. His fingers stretched and balled into fists. *I can get to him*, he told himself. *I can do it.*

But then Selene was turning toward him. Her eyes shone with dampness, but the smile on her face seemed genuinely happy. Her mouth shaped in silent speech. *Go*, she seemed to say. *It'll be fine.*

Vorenus felt her love, her devotion, her kindness. He relaxed his fists and returned her smile with his own. *Be strong*, he tried to tell her. *Be strong and live.*

Hands were pulling him away, out of the chamber. He nodded to the girl who thought she'd saved his life, and then he turned and let Galbus lead him out of the palace and into the sunlight. For Selene's sake, he walked as if he had no care in the world.

Three legionnaires formed around him and Galbus. None of them returned his weapons to him. None said a word.

Not that anything needed to be said. Vorenus knew Octavian could never let him live. He'd only promised free passage from the throne room, not from the island. Selene would learn such nuances in time. She'd learn to play the game. And she'd be good at it in the end. Vorenus was certain of that, too. She was stronger than anyone ever gave her credit for. And she and her brothers would live. That was the important thing now. If it took his death to ensure that, he couldn't complain.

Vorenus took a deep breath of the salty air, feeling the shadow and light pass over his face as they walked beside the palm trees that grew along the promenade. They were taking him to the end of the long dock, past the ships. The better to dispose of his body, he supposed. Let him float to the deep with whatever was left of Khenti.

They passed the royal barge and then, as Vorenus expected, the smaller trireme that he'd arrived on. There were, he saw, a handful of Roman guards on its deck, keeping an eye on the trap that led to the oarsmen below. Vorenus could hear that the Egyptians he and Khenti had conscripted to that duty were still inside the boat, their fate yet to be determined.

Not far beyond, the paved quay ended at the southern point of Antirhodos, an area that couldn't be seen from the rest of the island, hidden behind piles of crates and barrels. The channel separating them from the city was deep and fast with strong current. All the better to kill him quietly and have him swept away.

Galbus stepped aside, motioning Vorenus toward the edge. Vorenus sensed the other three legionnaires slowing and taking positions behind him. Their movements were so scripted, executed so silently, that a part of him wondered how many men they'd executed as a group. Not that it mattered. Not now.

The waves moved up and back among the rocks below him. Instead of looking down at them, he looked off at the sea and tried to remember his mother.

He could see a body rising out there, floating up with the tide before falling away again amid the waves. Khenti, Vorenus thought. I failed him, too.

"You'll meet your Egyptian friend in the afterlife," Galbus said.

Vorenus doubted that was so. "Be quick," he said. It seemed the sort of thing he ought to say, though he didn't really know if it mattered.

Vorenus fixed his gaze on that faraway body. He heard, for the second time in minutes, the sound of a blade being pulled from its scabbard. The body on the water rose on a high wave, rolling over. Vorenus, through his tired eyes, at last saw it clearly. Blond-haired, wearing the uniform of a legionnaire.

A gladius, still in its sheath, suddenly flew up from the shoreline rocks below him, hanging for a moment point down in the air before him. Only in that moment did his mind catch up to the reality of what was going on.

Though no longer the young man that he'd once been, Vorenus could still move with speed when it was necessary. He reached out and snapped his hand around the grip of the gladius even as he spun on his toes and brought the weapon around in an arc. For a fleeting instant he saw the dark shape of Khenti leaping up over the wall, swoop-bladed Egyptian sword in hand, but then Vorenus lost sight of him as he came around and his swing landed solidly against the edge of the blade that had been meant for his neck.

Galbus' eyes widened in shock as his blade sank into Vorenus' sheathed gladius. Their arms reverberated for a second, and then Vorenus lunged forward, slamming his forehead into the Roman's nose.

Vorenus felt wet splatter his face as he drove into the man.

Galbus fell backward, dropping his sword as his hands flew to his broken face, and Vorenus scrambled over him, skittering to stay on his feet and turn toward the legionnaries even as he unsheathed the gladius in his hand.

Khenti had two of the remaining legionnaires engaged, his curved blade already dripping with blood from the third, who was down on the ground, the hilt of a dagger protruding from beneath his jaw. The man's legs were jerking in short spasms.

The Egyptian danced around to his left, face dispassionate, almost curious as he kept their attention. Vorenus took the opportunity to rush at the back of the Romans, his arm rocking backward and forward in a perfect gladius thrust, the kind he'd tried to teach Caesarion when the boy was younger. He aimed the strike for the open side in one legionnaire's armor, and it slipped just below the man's ribs and into his body with fluid, seamless ease, right down into the man's pelvis.

The dying man slid off his blade, and Vorenus turned to see Khenti dispatch the one remaining soldier with a flash of metal that passed across his neck. The Egyptian twirled his sword and sheathed it, face as still as stone, before another dead Roman fell to the pavement.

Khenti motioned to the sprawled and gasping Galbus before Vorenus could say anything. "I can finish him quickly," the Egyptian said.

Vorenus looked down at the man. His face was smashed and bloodied, his eyes wild. "Let him be," Vorenus said.

The Egyptian just looked up, as if the answer didn't matter one way or another. "Then we should leave," he said.

Vorenus strapped on the gladius belt with practiced speed before they ran back to the trireme. The alarm had not yet been raised, and they had no difficulty dispatching the few Roman guards and readying the ship for sail based on Manu's hand signals.

The oarsmen below were only too happy to set their backs into their strokes, and they'd already pulled them away from the dock and against the current by the time Romans began to spill out of the palace. They ran down the docks, sprinting up planks and onto Octavian's bigger royal barge. Oars began to appear through the holes in its sides, extending out like hundreds of thin legs. With so many experienced men below its decks, the royal barge would easily overtake their poorly crewed boat.

"They'll catch us," Vorenus said, pointing out the obvious.

"Yes, they will," Khenti replied.

The deck beneath them shook slightly as the oarsmen ceased rowing backward and began to drive forward with the current through the channel. Manu's bearing was the fastest way to escape the island and would carry them directly toward the Heptastadion, but it would also take them right past the royal barge as it readied for the water. Already Vorenus could see legionnaires pulling bows on its deck. "We won't even reach the bridge," he said.

"I think perhaps we will," Khenti said. Vorenus looked over at him, and he saw that the Egyptian was looking back toward Manu, who was just completing a series of signs. The captain's face was beaming like a kid's.

The trireme began to drive hard through the water, the oarsmen stroking with everything they had. Vorenus felt the current rolling beneath them, pushing them faster and faster. Manu turned the tiller slightly, grinning, and pointed forward.

Vorenus turned, saw the surprise on the Roman faces even before he realized what was happening. A few of them hurriedly released their drawn arrows before they dropped their bows and began to brace for impact. Most did not.

The thick metal ram at the head of their trireme, which had once split the side of Antony's flagship at Actium, now slammed into the keel of Octavian's barge, shuddering the full length of the bigger ship as it broke through the back end of it. Vorenus, who'd had no time to brace himself, rolled forward across the trireme's deck amid a hail of fractured planks.

A few oarsmen and two legionnaires fell down onto their deck from the impact, which cut a gaping wound into the barge, as the trireme's momentum barreled them onward and they tore the hole open even further. Vorenus heard the telltale roar of water beginning to rush into the larger ship's hold even as he watched Khenti dancing through the rain of debris, sword spinning, efficiently dispatching the Romans who'd fallen onto the trireme's deck and didn't dive overboard fast enough.

By the time Vorenus had staggered to his feet, the decks were cleared and the barge was starting to sink in their wake. A few desperate arrows were falling into the water behind them, but the oarsmen already had them out of range. Khenti was walking toward him, sword put away, as calm as a man out for a stroll.

Vorenus smiled, feeling at last like maybe, just maybe, they might pull this off. Then he turned toward the first bridge of the Heptastadion looming ahead, just in time to see their destination erupt upward into the morning sky in a fiery roar of black-billowing smoke, broken wood, and shattered stone.

29

The Power of a Shard

ALEXANDRIA, 30 BCE

Out on the water ships were moving in so many directions it was dizzying. But none of them, for the moment, appeared to be heading toward the Heptastadion and the eight men and one woman huddled around the Ark of the Covenant in the quiet beneath its first bridge.

Caesarion watched it all with anxious anticipation. "He'll come," he said, more to himself than to anyone else. "I know Vorenus. He won't fail."

"Aye," Pullo said. Caesarion looked over his shoulder at the big man, who was standing with Jacob and Didymus on the other side of the Ark, just inside the gate to the underground canal. "I'd bet my life on him."

"We don't doubt your friend, but faster would be better," Jacob said, a touch of his typical amusement in his voice.

"Oh, I don't deny that," Pullo said with a grin.

"We can only wait so long," one of the four guards ringing the edge of the platform whispered to Hannah. Like his fellows, he had an arrow nocked on his bow as he scanned the water and turned to aim at every sound.

"Oh, I don't think we've anything to fear at the moment," Pullo said. "No one knows we're here."

"Meaning no disrespect, Titus Pullo, but that's what we thought before," Hannah said. "Before Didymus and his friend showed up."

"He wasn't my friend," Didymus said.

"As you told us," said the guard.

"You—you don't think I'm lying, do you?"

"We do not," Hannah said before the guard could respond. "But you did say that there were more Romans with you. Though I doubt anyone could have survived the trap, we'd rather not take the chance that someone got away and is bringing more Romans to find us. So haste would be best."

"He'll come," Caesarion said, looking back to the sea. His voice sounded quieter than he intended, and he wondered if it showed the doubt in his heart. What if Vorenus didn't come? What if they'd been arrested at the palace? Or even in the streets? What if they couldn't crew the ship? God, he hadn't even thought about—

Hannah's hand brushed his, breaking his train of thought. He felt her fingertips, light as feathers, interweaving between his own—tentatively at first, but then more solidly confident as he started to respond. He didn't dare to look over at her as they held hands. He was just happy to feel her close warmth, reassured by her flesh in his.

"I hope your friend's boat has a private room," Jacob said, laughing.

Caesarion felt his cheeks blush hot. He felt Hannah's hand squeeze his. And then, before he could turn to say something to her brother, time slowed into a rush of sound from behind them: something cracking against stone, rapid movements of cloth and leather, the sliding sounds of metal, and then the piercing screams of first Pullo and then Jacob.

The scene behind him finally came into view, and Caesarion pulled Hannah behind him. His eyes took the horror in all at once. Didymus was crumpled and unmoving against the stone wall inside the canal. Pullo was collapsing like a timbered tree against the big pots of oil, the lamp dropped from his hand rocking on the stones and flashing light on and off of the red spraying from the back of his legs. And closer, right behind the Ark itself, Jacob stared down, eyes glazed and face frozen in an expression caught between amusement and disbelief. The point of the blade protruding from his stomach was shockingly bright. A trickle of blood bubbled from his mouth, and then he was falling away, lifeless. Behind him, eyes shining as if lit from within, stood one of the adopted sons of Julius Caesar. His clothes were ripped and stained, his face smeared with red. The shafts of broken arrows still angled from behind the thick golden breastplate on his chest. The black stone at its center seemed to glow like cold dark liquid fire.

Juba smiled—at him or at something else, Caesarion couldn't tell—and then the Numidian reached forward, his hands glazed with gore, and grabbed hold of the two angels atop the Ark of the Covenant. In response, a surge of power expanded from the Shard within its casing, flattening everyone else on the platform and leaving Juba standing alone.

Like Shushu, Juba trembled and shook when his hands tensed upon the metal. But where the hapless Egyptian had been racked with pain, the Numidian appeared to stand taller, his smile widening.

Hannah had fallen to her back with the others, Caesarion draped protectively over her body. "Shoot him!" she shouted.

The four archers had already regained firing positions on their knees, and four arrows were loosed, point-blank, to join their old mates in the Numidian's body.

The arrows never made it. One instant they were flying from their bows, hard and fast, and the next instant they were floating peacefully, improbably, in the air.

Juba looked down upon them, and his eyes were aglow with an inner fire. The air around the Ark grew cold and shimmered with blue, like spinning, thin wisps of flame. At once the arrow points crumpled in on themselves, the iron snapping and cracking as if wadded up by unseen hands. The little rough balls of material that were left fell limp to the ground.

"Oh, God," one of the archers said. "I didn't—" Juba's fiery gaze turned to the man, and his words were cut off as he arched his back and screamed in a horrible gurgle of anguish, blood geysering from his body behind a cracking sound not unlike the grinding of stones.

Juba's head turned, eyes finding the next archer. Even as the first one fell, the second began to scream, too.

It had only been a matter of heartbeats since Juba's attack. Hannah was trying to push herself off her back, to get to her feet, and Caesarion was doing the same, trying to keep himself between her and the Ark. They were no longer holding hands. She was only a few feet away, but he had to shout to be heard over the horrible screams of the dying archers. "Jump!"

Even as he said it, he knew she'd never go. Her family had been entrusted with the Ark. For generations they'd kept it safe. At what cost of life, he didn't know, but he was certain that she would face the addition of her own without a second thought. Even the other archers didn't flee. While their comrades were ripped apart from within, one was notching another arrow while the other was unsheathing his sword. As Caesarion watched, Juba's eyes began to turn—slowly and patiently— to the two of them. The screaming on the platform increased, and the sword and last arrow dropped unused to the ground.

It seemed then to Caesarion that the whole world was screaming: the four archers around him wailed in agony, and

Caesarion could see behind the Ark that Pullo was roiling on his back beside the oil pots in contorted terror, his hands gripping the backs of his legs as if he might pull his rolled-up hamstrings back down to his knees.

Hannah is next, Caesarion thought. God, he'll take Hannah next.

Caesarion, the man who once might have inherited the world, made a decision. He scrambled to his feet, turning his back on the girl whom he might one day have loved, and lunged forward through the cold blue twists of wind to place his hands, too, upon the Ark.

Caesarion had dreamed once that he was riding the Nile through the mighty cataracts, helpless while the boat beneath him forever fell away along the torrent beneath him even as it threw him roughly side to side and threatened, at every turn, to cast him out into the crags and froth and all-encompassing roar.

In the instant that Caesarion placed his hands upon the two statues atop the Ark, the same sensations overtook him. He was tumbling and sliding downward, unable to control the river of power that pulled him out of the world of light, of metal beneath his hands and stone beneath his feet, toward a world of deeper and deeper darkness.

Without thinking, he tried to throw out his arms as if he might scrabble for a hold on the fast-fading reality, but there was nothing to grab, and he had nothing to grab it with. His arms and his hands were things he'd left behind. He imagined them back behind him, shaking more and more violently as his fingers pressed into metal that wouldn't give way.

Pressure built around him as he descended and the shadows grew stronger. Had Shushu felt this just before he'd died?

Or was Caesarion already dead?

Am I?

Hannah. God, Hannah. The children. Helios. Philadelphus. Selene.

The images came to him in a rush of emotion, hanging in front of his mind's eye only for a moment before they, too, threatened to fade away.

He screamed into the black, trying to bring them back, but the more he fought against it, the more they fell into shadow. As the increasing pressure threatened to crush him at last, the final glimmers of their faces disappearing, Caesarion's mind screamed against the power of a God whose existence he doubted more than ever. How could it be so cruel?

It couldn't, his heart replied. God isn't cruel. And God isn't dead.

Caesarion ceased fighting the dark. He ceased trying to hold on to the world and instead let go of it all, opening himself up to the power sweeping around and—he now knew—through him. Like a man at last coming up for air, the pressure that had been building released like a burst bubble. He opened eyes he didn't know he'd closed.

He stood beside the Ark, his hands beside Juba's on the golden angels. The Numidian's eyes still burned with the power that was coursing through him—Caesarion didn't doubt that his own were alight, too—but there was another flame there now: jealousy, rage, and fear. Despite the power that Juba had unleashed, there was something fighting against the other man. Like a ship dragging an anchor, the Numidian was being held back from unleashing the full potential within the Shard. Caesarion felt it through the Ark, like a tremor in the wind, a rock breaking the pulse of waves. What it was, where it came from, Caesarion didn't know. But it gave him the opening he needed.

Reaching down into the darkness within himself, that inner place that the world couldn't touch—that river of coursing power that he knew had been there all along, needing only the bridge of a Shard to be reached and only the faith of his spirit to be controlled—Caesarion pulled up currents of the energy and unleashed them at Juba.

The Numidian recoiled as if he'd been slapped, and he staggered backward, his grip on the Ark breaking.

I've got to keep him back, Caesarion thought. I've got to keep him from the Ark.

Debris twirled between them in a green glow. Dust, small rocks. Caesarion remembered Juba crushing the iron points on the arrows. The Shard of the Ark controls earth, he remembered. Earth.

He focused in on the stones between them, the stones all around him. He *felt* them, sensing weak cracks, stronger veins. He recognized metals and, like a magnet, began to pull them toward him, particle by particle.

An iron wall began to form between Juba and the Ark, a solidifying fog of gray growing up from the floor. A foot high, then two. Three. Four.

Bigger. It needed to be bigger.

Caesarion tried to bring up more power, to draw more metals to him, but he felt suddenly dizzy and his vision swam.

I'm fainting, he thought, wondering how he could be so objective even as his body rejected his mind. I can't take it. I'm not ready. No one should ever be.

But he had to stop Juba. If he didn't, they all were dead. And what would this power be in the hands of such a man? What would it be in the hands of any man?

He'd surprised the Numidian, but he knew it wasn't enough. If Juba accessed the Shard again, it would be the end of them all. He wouldn't be able to stop him.

By sheer force of will, Caesarion's vision cleared. He saw Juba was stepping over the waist-high wall, his hands already reaching out for the Ark.

"No," he said.

Praying that Hannah would live out the day, that the Ark would be safe, that it would all, in the end, be worth it, Caesarion dove into the depths like a man seeking the bottom of the sea. Only when he thought he could take no more did he rise up and throw it all—the power, his heart, the last moment of his consciousness—into Juba's stomach.

As his limp body let go of the Ark, through a pulse of bright green fire, Caesarion saw the Numidian doubled over, flying backward into the darkness beneath the city. Then the fire was gone and he saw the side of the Ark rising in his vision. He saw the arching supports of the bridge above him. And, just as the light behind his own eyes went out, he saw the face of Hannah, like an angel's in sunlight.

30

The Lies of a Scholar

ALEXANDRIA, 30 BCE

Didymus was, first and foremost, a scholar. Long before he'd traded his morality for Octavian's support of his candidacy to lead the Great Library at Alexandria, before he'd even begun to tutor the children of Cleopatra, he'd been fascinated with knowledge. As a child his thirst for learning was insatiable. He'd read anything and everything he could get his hands on, forgetting nothing his eyes passed over, and he prided himself on his observational skills.

It was perhaps to be expected, then, that when he awoke to screaming in the half-darkness beneath the streets of Alexandria, he was driven first by intellectual curiosity to look around. Even after he remembered what had happened—he'd seen Juba, impossibly still alive, coming down the walkway beside the underground canal toward the Ark, and the Numidian had flung him aside into the hard stone wall—and realized what was currently happening—men were dying, screaming out the end of their lives in horrifyingly pitched wails of excruciating pain—he couldn't run. He couldn't move. He had to stay, to try and watch, in increasing shock, what was unfolding.

Slumped over against the wall, he saw first his own blood glistening on the moss that grew in the gaps between its stones. Next he saw flashing light—blue light, he thought—and he felt a bitter cold wind coming down the canal, as if the city were breathing out, or the sea was breathing in.

Something rattled into his side, and Didymus rolled to see what it was, trying to ignore the pain that threatened to split his potentially cracked skull. Pullo's lamp, he saw, still lit. By its light, he saw the long spray of blood on the ground beside him, leading to good, loyal Pullo, who was writhing on his side facing him, his head jerking backward with pained gasps, again and again, into the big oil pots behind him. Didymus started to reach out toward his old friend, his stomach twisting, when he saw that for all Pullo's pain, he wasn't one of the men being torn apart. His gaze moved past Pullo and the pots, past the still form of Jacob, impaled on a sword, to where Juba, the man he'd led to this place, stood with his hands on the First Shard, the Ark of the Covenant.

A thin veil of what looked like luminous blue smoke curled about the Numidian like a tornado, sucking the air out of the tunnels. In front of him, the four archers assigned to help protect the Ark were in various states of torture: each of them was screaming in a rain of his own blood, the worst of them shrunken down and in on himself as if his skeleton was being crushed within his body.

Just then Caesarion jumped into view on the other side of the Ark, and his hands gripped the two angels on its top. His shoulders began to shake, and his eyes shut. The twisting clouds spinning about the two men and the Ark between them began to turn faster and faster.

"Did-mus," Pullo croaked through clenched teeth.

Didymus managed to pull his attention away from the Shard-driven storm of power on the platform. He looked down at Pullo, who'd pushed his back up against the pots and was shaking and jerking like a man in seizures. The big man's eyes seemed to be going in and out of focus, as if he couldn't keep the world in sight.

"Pullo," Didymus said. "I ... what can I do?"

"Vorenus," Pullo whispered. "Vorenus."

"It's Didymus. I'm here." The air around them seemed to groan, but Didymus didn't look. He wanted to see, to understand, but he wanted more to help the man who'd been his friend even when he didn't deserve to have one.

"Vorenus," the big man repeated. "Save ... Ark. Caes-ion."

Didymus started to ask what Pullo wanted Vorenus for, if that's what he was wanting, but an exhalation of wind jerked his gaze upward. The storm around the Ark had calmed slightly, and it seemed to his eyes more green than blue now. Juba had staggered back toward him and Pullo, only a few steps away, and Didymus thought for a moment about reaching out and grabbing his feet out from under him, about doing something to help Caesarion, even if he could save no one else. But he knew, deep down inside, that he was a coward. He was weak. Why else had he gone along with Octavian's plan to kill Caesarion so many years ago? Why else had he led Juba here now? Had there really been no choice? And he could do nothing against a man such as Juba, he rationalized. He was a librarian, not a warrior. Not a man like Pullo.

A high-pitched tinkling sound came to the scholar's ears. The surface of the platform shimmered as a haze of dust formed upward and swept across it. Didymus watched it slide past them, past Juba, gathering between the Numidian and the Ark, a swirl of debris that took the shape of a wall. Inch by inch, up from the platform, it grew more and more solid.

An iron wall, his scholar's mind noted. An iron wall that

will seal Juba away from the Ark. And us with him. That's interesting.

The wall ceased forming for a moment, the storm abating slightly. Juba stepped back toward the Ark, one leg coming up over the low half of the wall. His arms were reaching out.

"No," Caesarion said, his voice booming with otherworldly power.

Didymus, without thinking, dove atop Pullo, protecting him with his body an instant before the storm exploded outward in a flash of green fire, scattering debris that pounded bruises into the librarian's back. He felt but did not see as Juba soared over them, and he heard his body skittering across the paved walkway into the deeper dark.

The silence that fell around him next was so sudden that the librarian thought for a moment that the concussive force of the energy burst had deafened him. But then he heard the rasp of Pullo's quick and shallow breaths beneath him, and the call of frightened seagulls out below the bridge.

"Caesarion," he heard Hannah say from somewhere on the platform beyond the Ark. "Stay with me. I see it, Caesarion. I see the boat."

Didymus pulled himself off Pullo, his face excited. "Do you hear, Pullo? Vorenus is coming. We'll get you—"

Pullo wasn't looking at him. His gaze was fixed on a point behind him, up the walkway toward the Ark chamber.

"Didymus," he said, his voice a whisper of concentration. The big man wasn't shaking anymore, and he seemed extraordinarily calm. "Get me the lamp."

The librarian complied without thinking, turning and picking up the lamp before he looked up and saw Juba, walking slowly toward them.

Pullo reached out and took the lamp from his hands. "Tell Vorenus I'll miss him," the big man said. "And he may be right about the gods. I'll know soon. Now go."

Didymus gathered himself to his feet, looking from his friend to the Numidian, who was walking like a man possessed, ignoring everything but the Ark in front of him.

"Go," Pullo repeated.

The librarian looked once more to the man on the ground. Pullo was still staring at Juba, the lamp hot in his hands. "But Pullo—"

"Go."

Didymus backed away, tripping over the big man's useless legs and staggering to keep his feet. Juba was very close.

"Vorenus always said there'd be judgment in death," Pullo said, his voice deceptively strong.

Juba stopped walking, turning his attention toward the big man. Didymus stumbled two steps, three, to the edge of the canal. He leaned out into the cold, momentarily still air.

"If so, I'll see you in Hell," Pullo said, and Didymus, turning for one last look at his old friend, already jumping for the water, saw him toss the lamp over his shoulder into the oil pots behind him.

The librarian broke the surface of the canal a moment before the churning fire of the explosion tore through the air behind him. The water around him shook violently, tumbling him like a stone for the second time this day. He dove deep before kicking his way up, feeling for the direction of the air as concussive blasts rocked the canal in waves, one after another. And then, just as he reached the surface, the ceiling between Didymus and the new wall beside the Ark fell into darkness as the stones of the collapsing tunnel sealed him inside, shutting out the sun.

Didymus heaved himself, dripping wet and more exhausted than he'd ever been in his life, up out of the canal and onto the fractured stones of the walkway. Dust glowed like sprinkling, slow-falling rain in the slivers of light that shone through the few gaps in the wall of rubble that had come down across the end of the canal where Pullo had lain. Light shone, too, like thin drapes hanging down from cracks that the quaking explosion had torn in the ceiling above. The librarian groaned, aching in seemingly every part of his body. The sound of small rocks rattling down through the rubble, or calving off the ceiling to splash into the canal, echoed loudly in the cavernous space.

The scholar hobbled painfully toward the ruinous wall of collapsed stone. From beyond it he heard the muted sound of movement. His first thought was of Pullo, but the big man had to be dead. No one could have survived that.

There was one gap, perhaps a few inches wide, near eye level, and he approached it first, leaning forward to put his eye to it. There were clouds of dust outside, but through spaces in the drifting haze he could see the Ark, littered with dust and small bits of shattered rock but protected from the force of the blast and the collapsing tunnel by the short metal wall that had formed up beside it. Hannah stood behind the Ark, her garments singed, her long hair grayed with chalky dust, but otherwise seeming unharmed. She was waving at someone, and as Didymus watched, the prow of a trireme glided into view, pushing through the debris-littered sea. The sun shone brightly on its decks and on the platform, and the librarian realized that the bridge that ought to have sheltered them must have been destroyed in the blast.

The trireme slowed and stopped. Didymus heard the thump of a plank falling on stone, and then his heart leaped to see Vorenus run into the line of his sight. Pullo's friend—God, he thought, *Pullo's* friend—knelt behind the Ark, Hannah bent down, too, and when they stood, Vorenus had Caesarion in his arms like he was cradling a child. Caesarion's chest rose and fell. He was alive.

Vorenus and Hannah moved away, out of sight. Egyptians came, six or seven of them, and they lifted the long poles on the sides of the Ark between them, carrying it down to the trireme.

Didymus smiled to himself tiredly. It was gone. Pullo had done it. The Shard would be safe now. Caesarion would be safe now.

Vorenus came back to the wall, began throwing rocks out of the way, fist by fist, as if he meant to tear his hands to stumps on his way through the rubble.

Didymus felt his throat catch before he managed to speak. "Vorenus," he croaked. "Stop."

Vorenus looked up, eyes searching the wall. "Pullo?"

"It's Didymus."

"Didymus? Where's Pullo?"

Didymus had to close his eyes. He couldn't bear to look at him. "He's gone, Vorenus."

"Gone?"

"He's ... dead, Vorenus. He ... he saved us," Didymus said, trying but failing to be strong. "He was hurt. He ... told me to tell you—"

The librarian's voice finally gave out and his words choked off in a sob. When he finally had control of himself, he opened his eyes and saw that there were tears on the face of the Roman, his jaw tight with emotion. "What did he say?"

"He said to tell you ... he said you were right. About the gods. You were right all along. He said he'd see you soon."

Vorenus coughed out something between a laugh and a sob. "Always was a lying bastard," he said. Then he swallowed and his face grew hard. "Thank you, Didymus. I ... I—"

"Just go," Didymus said. "Hurry. Go." His own words made him think of Pullo, but he managed to set that memory aside for the moment. "Get out of here, all of you."

Vorenus seemed about to say something more, then only nodded. But he didn't move, and his eyes remained downcast.

The sound of shuffling and a grunt of pain came to Didymus out of the dark behind him. He turned and saw in a distant ray of light that Juba was limping toward him along the walkway. No longer a man possessed, he seemed instead a man defeated. As Didymus watched, he fell over against the wall to rest for a moment, his hands gripping the broken end of an arrow protruding from his side. With a jerk and a gasp he ripped it from his body and dropped it, the wooden shaft clattering on the ground.

The scholar turned back to the wall. Vorenus was still there. "Go," he said again, voice stronger with desperation. "Take care of him. See that he reads his books, okay?"

The Roman's smile was grim when he looked up. "Good-bye," he said.

Didymus didn't know who Vorenus was addressing, but he decided to speak for both of them. "Good-bye," he whispered.

Vorenus started to go, shouting something to the trireme even before his back was turned. Didymus heard oars hitting the water, and the ship began to move. Vorenus took one last look at the wall, face hard as its stone, and then all Didymus could see was the sea.

The shuffling of Juba's feet was louder now. Didymus turned and watched the Numidian approach, close enough for the librarian to tell that the man's clothes had been ripped and torn to tatters by the force of the explosion, that his dark skin was sooty with streaks of black. He'd pulled all the arrows from his body while Didymus had said his good-bye to Vorenus, and now damp streaks of red spotted his sides. Only his breastplate seemed untouched. He looked tired beyond exhaustion, like a broken man, and there was both confusion and acceptance on his face. "It's gone, isn't it?" he asked, voice hoarse.

The scholar didn't need to ask what it was that was gone. Not knowing what else to do, he helped the Numidian hobble painfully over to the wall. There was nothing more to be seen through the gap, but the stones there gave the Numidian a temporary place to rest his weight.

Didymus wondered, absently, if this adopted son of Caesar would kill him for helping his friends. Or perhaps he'd simply turn him over to the other adopted son of Caesar as some kind of peace offering. He didn't even know if that made sense, and he himself was far too tired to care.

A cascade of stones scattered down off the ceiling nearby. Didymus didn't flinch, but he recognized the danger in an academic way. "We should go," he said.

The Numidian had sat down on the pile of rubble beside him. He bowed his head. He was looking at his hands, as if he expected to see something more upon them than scrapes and dirt. "I think I killed men today," Juba said quietly. "I don't ... remember clearly." He sounded more tired than even Didymus felt.

The librarian took a deep breath, thinking about what to say. "I don't know," he finally said. "It all happened so quick. I don't understand even what I think I saw." It was true, he decided, after a fashion.

"And this man?" Juba asked.

Man? Didymus looked down at the ground and saw, after his eyes adjusted, first the torn and half-burnt clothes and then the shape of the man beneath them.

"Caesarion was here," Juba said weakly. "I think we fought. Is it him?"

The librarian had to step around the body and kneel in order to get a look at the dead man's face. It was an act that would have turned his stomach once, but it seemed a small thing after what he'd already seen this day.

Jacob was badly burned, his hair gone, but Didymus could still recognize him. And the blackened sword still protruding from his stomach was all the confirmation he needed.

"Is it Caesarion?" Juba asked again.

Didymus stared into Jacob's lifeless eyes, but it wasn't the dead Jew that he saw. It was his old friend, Titus Pullo, who'd given the last of his life to let Caesarion escape with the Shard. Pullo, the bravest, strongest man he'd ever met. Didymus felt tears upon his cheeks, tracing through the numbness of his emotions.

"Well?"

Didymus blinked up at Juba, who looked down through sunken eyes, his shoulders hunched with exhaustion. Didymus swallowed hard, stood, and then did the bravest thing he could think to do, just the sort of thing he thought Pullo would do if he were still alive: he lied. "It is," he said, letting his emotions quake his voice. "Burned badly, but it's him."

Juba let out a sigh that seemed mixed with both relief and sadness. "I thought it was."

The two of them stared down at the dead man in silence, each lost in his own thoughts. A minute passed, perhaps two. More rocks fell, splashing into the water not far away.

"We should move him," Juba said at last. "Octavian will want to see—"

"No," Didymus interrupted. "Leave him. Let the world remember him for what he was. Not this. Don't let him be paraded in front of his family."

"But he'll want to know ... to confirm it."

"We'll both tell him," the librarian said. "There was a fire, in a building. The body burned."

Juba opened his mouth to object, his eyes still downcast at the body, but no words came. After a few seconds he agreed tiredly. "We could do that," he said. "We could lie."

"I'll keep the secret until the day I die," Didymus said, meaning every word.

"Yes," Juba finally said. "Died in a fire."

More rocks fell, only a few feet from where they stood.

Didymus reached out and pulled on what was left of the Numidian's sleeve. "Come on," he said. "Let's go."

Juba lingered for a moment longer, then allowed the scholar to help him up and lead him from the wall and the body. Together the two men limped away slowly, each leaning on the other for support, up the pathway beside the canal, looking for a way up out of the darkness to the world of light above.

Epilogue

The Girl Who Would Fight the World

ALEXANDRIA, 30 BCE

Cleopatra Selene, the ten-year-old daughter of the queen of Egypt and Mark Antony, stood on the steps of the royal palace on Antirhodos, holding a fruit basket and watching the lingering smoke rising up from the smoldering ashes of a funeral pyre on the pavement below. Servants and slaves were sweeping chalky dust off the stones, back toward the charred pile of burned wood. Here and there amid the gray and the black she caught glimpses of white, and she had to look away, over the waters of the harbor toward Alexandria.

Less than two weeks since Antony's suicide, a few days since Octavian had formally declared his sovereignty over the city with a grand parade of his troops down the Canopic Way, and plumes of smoke still dotted Alexandria's storied skyline. From more burning buildings, she supposed. Octavian had issued reprimands against his army's looting, but he deemed most of the damage they caused unimportant. Dozens of civilians continued to be raped or beaten or murdered each day, but these as well were not considered great outrages. The official reports being sent back to Rome, she knew, spoke only of success and glory, nothing of the chaos and the death that spread in the Imperator's wake.

Imperator. Already there was talk that he'd refuse to give up the title should the Senate ask it of him. There was talk that the self-proclaimed son of the god Caesar would follow in his adopted father's footsteps and hold all the power of Rome—unified now, after so many years of war—in his hands. In private, the rumors said, he already called himself by a new name: Augustus Caesar, the greatest Caesar. And this month in which he conquered Egypt, they said, he would order renamed August, in his own honor.

From everything she'd come to know of Octavian, Selene expected that the whispers were all true.

Octavian. Imperator. Son of god. Augustus Caesar. Selene wasn't going to rest until he was dead. It didn't matter what his name was.

She looked down to the basket in her hands once again, taking a deep breath and trying not to think about the taste of the ashes in the air.

Then she began to climb the steps to the palace and her waiting mother.

The men guarding the door of Cleopatra's chamber were adamant that they couldn't allow Selene inside. "You can't go in," one of them kept repeating. Before Octavian had reached the royal island, her mother had sent Antony's body to the priests with orders that it be embalmed like those of the pharaohs of old. She'd then moved the family's finest treasures into her room in the palace, intending to barricade herself inside as she prepared for the end. Only the speed of Octavian's arrival had prevented her from carrying out her plans to follow Antony into the embrace of death. Since then the queen had been kept under arrest in her own chamber, surrounded by now-useless gold.

"But I need to see her," she insisted.

"Orders of the Imperator of Rome."

Rather than spit, Selene looked sheepish and childlike. "I'm a girl with a fruit basket," she said. "What harm could I be?"

"I'm sorry. You can't go in."

Selene pouted, pushed her weight to one hip. "I want to see my mother," she said.

Before the guard could repeat his denial, another voice came from down the hall. "What's this, legionnaire?"

The Roman guards came to attention and saluted, and Selene turned to see that Juba was walking toward them slowly, still limping from the wounds he'd sustained in the battle that had killed Caesarion. Her brother's death had been an accident, Didymus told her, and the Numidian himself had never taken credit for his killing, despite the honors he might have received from Octavian for it. She still blamed him, though, and she hated him for it. She'd trusted him to get the Ark, to help her brother. Not lose them both.

"The lady Selene wishes admittance to deliver fruit to her mother," one of the guards reported.

"I can see that," the Numidian said. Selene noticed now that Juba was carrying a book. From the Great Library, she supposed. He'd been spending most of his time there since the fall of the city, his readings guided by Didymus himself. She'd often wondered if they were still looking for the Ark, which Didymus told her had been taken by the Jews. If such things were on his mind, he showed no indication of it now. "And why won't you let her in?"

"Orders of Octavian, sir."

Juba at last stood beside them. He looked down at her with

a warm smile, and she remembered the feel of him when he'd held her back at the tomb of Alexander the Great. "She doesn't look like a threat to me," he said.

Selene did her best to appear even more innocent. The guard frowned. "The fruit, sir. It could be ... poisoned."

"Ah," Juba said. "I suppose so. May I?"

"Of course," Selene said, realizing that these were the first words she'd spoken to him since he and Didymus had left her at the Great Library, since she'd stood defiant before Octavian and been promised to the Numidian in marriage in exchange for the life of Vorenus. She'd heard that he'd been surprised by the news when he'd been told, but that he hadn't objected to it. She was pretty sure she hated him for that, too.

Juba reached down, his darker-skinned hand brushing hers on its way to grabbing an apple off the top of the basket. He held it up, and their eyes met. He paused, as if waiting for something, then raised the apple to his mouth and bit off a chunk and began to chew. He closed his eyes, savoring it for a moment, but a second later his eyes shot open and he seemed to gag and convulse.

The guards gasped, and even Selene was taken aback in shock, but then the Numidian began to laugh. "Just let her in," he said, tossing the apple to one of them. "And don't bother her again."

"Yes, sir," one of the guards said as they parted and unbolted the door to her mother's chamber.

Selene bowed her head to them, then turned to Juba. He was smiling still, but there was something other than amusement in his eyes. She thought it might be hope. "Selene," he said. "I ... I would hope we might speak before the voyage to Rome. I ... well, I would like it if we could know one another better. We have much in common, I know."

His voice had grown more assured as he spoke, and she

recognized in his final words the same deadly seriousness she'd heard from him as he sat in the Great Library on the day of the fall of Alexandria and told Didymus that he wanted Octavian dead. Yes, she thought. They did have that in common. "I think I would like that," she said, not yet certain if she meant it, but certain it was the right thing to say, the sort of thing her mother had taught her to say.

Juba's face, which had seemed so tired, brightened. "I'll look forward to it," he said, and he bowed to her, a hitch in his side revealing a pain his happy face denied.

She returned his bow with a nod of her own, and he turned and walked away down the hallway, humming quietly to himself.

When he was gone, the guards opened the door and Selene entered the chambers that had become Cleopatra's prison. The door shut behind her and she passed through the drapes of the antechamber in the bedroom.

Her mother, she saw, sat on a gilded chair that had been placed at the foot of her bed, the very spot where Selene had seen her holding Antony's body. Since that fateful morning, the whole of the room had been rearranged, the linens drawn up and cleaned, the furnishings pushed away from the bed to the corners in order to keep the focus on that single, solitary chair at its foot. Everything was covered with the most wondrous decorations at the imprisoned queen of Egypt's disposal, all fine metals and polished acacia wood. The most glorious chests from her royal treasury sat around the room, opened to reveal their glittering holdings. Cleopatra had, her daughter saw, spared no effort to make her bedroom into a throne room.

Nor had the queen failed to adorn herself with all the wonder and riches befitting a woman who had ruled, for almost the entirety of her life, as the goddess Isis incarnate. She wore a resplendent dress, her most expensive gems and pearls wrapped around the oiled skin of her graceful neck. The bracelets on her wrists, draped languidly over the arms of her chair, were thick gold, and the woven hairs of her finest wig framed a face painted in accordance with formal Egyptian rite. Her mother was, Selene thought, as beautiful as she'd ever seen her. Even the two chambermaids standing by her side were incredible to behold.

Cleopatra's face was impassive, and her eyes did not move to acknowledge her daughter. "Selene," she said, voice smooth and formal.

Selene knelt and bowed low, as was custom before the queen. "Mother," she said, pushing the basket before her. "I have what you requested."

"I am pleased," Cleopatra said.

The chambermaids came forward slowly, their linen skirts making swooshing sounds in the tomb-like silence of the room. Selene saw the feet of the two girls move into view before her face. She saw them shift as they bowed to her offering, before picking it up between them and slowly retreating the way they'd come.

Selene at last lifted herself from the floor to stand in front of her mother. The chambermaids had brought the basket to Cleopatra and set it in her lap. The queen's eyes remained fixed forward on the same distant, unknown point far beyond the walls of the room. Selene knew the look well. She'd practiced it herself.

Cleopatra's hands remained unmoving on the arms of her gleaming chair as the chambermaids carefully, deliberately, removed each piece of fruit and set it aside. It only took them a minute or so of work to uncover the venomous little black snake that had curled up so peacefully beneath it all. Selene couldn't see it, but she heard it hiss at being disturbed, and she saw the eyes of the chambermaids widen with fright despite their best efforts to appear calm and otherworldly. The two bowed once to the basket, once to the queen, and then backed away to stand once more beside her. Selene could see the glimmer of sweat on their foreheads.

After another minute of silence, Cleopatra's head tilted ever so slightly downward, her gaze finally falling to the asp in the basket upon her lap. They widened only slightly, but Selene could see that her chest rose and fell in deeper breaths.

"You don't have to do this," Selene said.

Her mother's eyes at last looked up at her. "You should know enough not to say that."

"You know I won't follow you," Selene said.

"Then you will be led in the Triumph of Rome, while I join your father in reigning eternal among the stars."

Cleopatra's voice was disapproving, but there was something recognizably maternal in it, too. Selene held on to that. "I won't rest until we are avenged," she said. "I swear it."

The queen of Egypt smiled. "I'm glad to hear of it, my daughter. You've much to learn of love and life, but hatred and vengeance is a lesson best learned early. I hope it will serve you well."

"I remember all your lessons, Mother. I ... I love you."

"And I you." Cleopatra smiled once more, gently, lovingly, and then her eyes moved again to the contents of the basket. The asp, as if it knew it was being watched, hissed loudly, and Selene heard it moving around the woven reeds. "You should go, Selene. My time grows short."

Selene took one last look at her mother, whose countenance was returning to the stoic dispassion with which she hoped to face eternity. Already Cleopatra was raising her arm, the bracelets falling away from her wrist and the thick veins beneath it.

Ten years old and only minutes away from being an orphan, Cleopatra Selene bowed once more to the queen of Egypt and then left the room, closing the door quietly behind her. The past was done, and she had a future to plan.

Glossary of Characters

Alexander Helios: Son of Mark Antony and Cleopatra VII, twin brother of Cleopatra Selene, he was likely born in the year 40 BCE. He disappears from reliable historical records after the fall of Alexandria in 30 BCE.

Alexander the Great: Alexander III, born in Macedon in 356 BCE, succeeded his father as king in 336. In his youth he led a number of Greek city-states to revolt against what had been a Macedonian-led alliance, and Alexander quickly set in motion a series of campaigns that led him as far north as the Danube and solidified his position as ruler of a united Greek state. Alexander subsequently moved his armies east against the Persian Empire, then the largest and most powerful state in the known world. He led his men to conquer Asia Minor and Syria, routing the Persian armies and defeating city after city. In 332 he entered Egypt, where he was declared to be the son of Ammon, an Egyptian deity. For reasons unknown, he faced off with the armies of the Kush but refused to fight them. Instead of continuing his campaign south into Africa, he moved north and founded the famed city of Alexandria, which subsequently became the capital of Egypt. Returning east, he captured Babylon and put an end to the Persian Empire before entering central Asia and defeating several states. Alexander then journeyed toward India, where his armies, though successful, finally balked at fighting farther from their Greek homes. Throughout his long career, he is said never to have lost a battle, and though severely wounded on several occasions, he was still reportedly vigorously strong. Nevertheless, he died under uncertain circumstances shortly after returning to Babylon in 323 BCE. After his death, he was placed in a golden sarcophagus, which made its way to Alexandria, and his world-spanning empire soon broke into rival states. His golden sarcophagus was melted down around 81 BCE by Pharaoh Ptolemy IX Lathyros when he was short of money (an act for which the angry citizens of Alexandria soon killed him). Alexander's miraculously preserved body was at that time transferred to a crystal sarcophagus, which remained on display in the city until its disappearance around 400 CE.

Caesarion: Caesarion, whose full name was Ptolemy XV Philopator Philometor Caesar, was born to Cleopatra VII in 47 BCE. According to Plutarch, he was rumored to have been executed by Octavian after the fall of Alexandria in 30 BCE, though his exact fate is strikingly unknown. While later Roman writers questioned his paternity, there is little reason to question the claim made by Cleopatra that he was the son of Julius Caesar.

Cleomedes: Very little is known of Cleomedes, a Stoic Greek astronomer active at some point between the middle of the first century BCE and the fourth century CE. His elementary astronomy textbook *On the Circular Motions of the Celestial Bodies* is widely regarded as poorly written and full of errors, yet it is also important for preserving the otherwise lost works of the earlier astronomers Posidonius of Rhodes and Eratosthenes.

Cleopatra Selene: Daughter of Mark Antony and Cleopatra VII, twin sister of Alexander Helios, she was likely born in the year 40 BCE. After the fall of Alexandria in 30 BCE she was placed under the guardianship of Octavia, the sister of Octavian, before being married to Juba II sometime between 25 and 20 BCE.

Cleopatra VII: The last pharaoh of the Ptolemaic dynasty, Cleopatra VII ruled Egypt from 51 BCE until her suicide at the age of thirty-nine after the fall of Alexandria in 30 BCE. As pharaoh she had an affair with Julius Caesar, to whom she bore his only known son, Caesarion. After Caesar's assassination in 44 BCE, Cleopatra took the side of Mark Antony in the civil war against Octavian and eventually bore him three children: Ptolemy Philadelphus and the twins Cleopatra Selene and Alexander Helios.

Delius: One of Mark Antony's leading generals, he defected to the side of Octavian just prior to the Battle of Actium in 31 BCE, reportedly bringing with him Antony's plans for the fight.

Didymus Chalcenterus: Born around 63 BCE, he wrote an astounding number of books in his lifetime on a wide variety of subjects, though he is now primarily known as an editor and grammarian of Homer. One of the chief librarians of the Great Library in Alexandria, his name Chalcenterus means "bronze guts," supposedly a statement about his indefatigability as a scholar.

Galbus: Unknown to history.

Juba I: King of Numidia, he allied himself against Julius Caesar in the Great Roman Civil War. After being defeated by Caesar's forces at the battle of Thapsus in 46 BCE, he fled the field with the Roman general Marcus Petreius. Trapped, they took their own lives by duel, with the survivor being aided in his suicide by a waiting slave.

Juba II: Probably born in 48 BCE, he was left an orphan by the suicide of his father in 46 BCE. Adopted by Julius Caesar, the man who'd caused his father's death, Juba was raised as a Roman citizen and ultimately joined his adopted stepbrother Octavian in the war against Mark Antony and

Cleopatra. He was restored to the throne of Numidia after the fall of Alexandria in 30 BCE, and around the year 25 BCE he was married to Cleopatra Selene. Some years later he was given the throne of Mauretania. Juba was a lifelong scholar who wrote several books before he died in 23 CE.

Julius Caesar: Born in 100 BCE to a noble Roman family of comparatively little significance, Julius Caesar achieved a position of unparalleled power within the Roman state and thereby laid the stage for the end of the Republic under his adopted son Octavian. A well-regarded orator and savvy politician, Caesar rose to prominence first as a military leader in the field, whose reputation won him election, in 63 BCE, as the religious leader of the Roman Republic. Returning to the military sphere in subsequent years, his extraordinary abilities were proved in successful campaigns in Hispania, Gaul, and Britain. His power and popular appeal eventually led to the Great Roman Civil War when he crossed the Rubicon with an armed legion in 49 BCE. Victorious in the civil war, Caesar voyaged to Alexandria, where a civil war had broken out between Cleopatra VII and her brother-husband Ptolemy XIII. Caesar supported Cleopatra, defeating Ptolemy and making her sole pharaoh of Egypt, and she, in turn, became Caesar's lover, bearing him his only known biological son: Caesarion. Returning to Rome, Caesar took solitary control of the state as a popularly supported dictator, effectively ending the Roman Republic. From this position of authority he instituted significant reforms to the Roman calendar, the workings of its government, and the architecture of its capital. Caesar was assassinated in 44 BCE by a group of at least sixty Roman senators, who reportedly stabbed him twenty-three times before he died. His popularity among the common people at the time of his death was so great that two years after the assassination he was officially deified. Though his murder had been intended to restore the Roman Republic to order, it served only to set off another series of civil wars. These conflicts culminated in the struggle between his adopted son Octavian, to whom Caesar had bequeathed the whole of his state and his powerful name, and his popular former general, Mark Antony, who had taken residence in Alexandria with Caesar's former lover, Cleopatra VII.

Kemse: Unknown to history.

Khenti: Unknown to history.

Laenas: Unknown to history.

Lucius Vorenus: Along with Titus Pullo, Vorenus is mentioned only once in the existing record: in Julius Caesar's *Commentary on the Gallic Wars*, where their inspiring actions in battle are reported. His birth and death dates are unknown.

Manu: Unknown to history.

Marcus Petreius: A Roman general, he allied himself against Julius Caesar in the Great Roman Civil War. After being defeated by Caesar's forces at the battle of Thapsus in 46 BCE, he fled the field with Juba I, king of Numidia. Trapped, they took their own lives by duel, with the survivor being aided in his suicide by a waiting slave.

Mark Antony: A Roman politician, he was Julius Caesar's good friend and perhaps his finest general. In the years following Caesar's assassination, Antony struggled with Octavian for control of the Roman Republic, though an uneasy peace was reached in 41 BCE when Antony married Octavian's sister. The following year he had an affair with Cleopatra VII, resulting in the births of the twins Cleopatra Selene and Alexander Helios, and soon he was making his home with her in Alexandria, where she gave birth to another son, Ptolemy Philadelphus, in 36 BCE. Open war broke out between Antony and Octavian in 32 BCE, with their two great armies facing off at the Battle of Actium one year later. Defeated, Antony returned with Cleopatra to Alexandria, where he committed suicide after the fall of the city.

Octavian: Born in 63 BCE, he was adopted by his great-uncle Julius Caesar just prior to his assassination in 44 BCE. Though he originally joined forces with Mark Antony to rule the Republic, their ambitions would not allow the peace to last, and the war between them tore the Roman world in two. His eventual defeat of Antony made him sole ruler of Rome, giving him the power to remake the Republic into the Roman Empire. Known most popularly as Augustus Caesar, the name he adopted in 27 BCE, he is rightly regarded along with his adopted father as one of the most influential men in history.

Ptolemy Philadelphus: Born in 36 BCE, he was the youngest son of Mark Antony and Cleopatra VII. He disappears from the record after the fall of Alexandria in 30 BCE, his fate unknown.

Quintus: Unknown to history.

Syphax: Unknown to history, though it is reasonably certain in the records that an unnamed slave aided in the suicides of Juba I and Marcus Petreius.

Titus Pullo: Along with Lucius Vorenus, Pullo is mentioned only once in the existing record: in Julius Caesar's *Commentary on the Gallic Wars*, where their inspiring actions in battle are reported. His birth and death dates are unknown.

Varro: Marcus Terentius Varro (116–27 BCE) was a Roman scholar of great renown.

Acknowledgements

There are countless people I need to thank for making this book happen, beginning with the love and support that the Livingston family has shown me over the years: Russ, Anita, Lance, Sherry, Samuel, and Elanor, as well as the extended branches of our tree. I am truly blessed to have such wonderful people surrounding me. Saying thank-you may not be enough, but it's a start.

This book took a long time to see the light of day, and I am grateful to those friends who read it before the dawn, including Catherine Bollinger, Mary Robinette Kowal, David Goldman, and Laurel Amberdine. Thanks are due also to Luc Reid, for building Codex and thereby putting me in touch with such fine people. My colleague and friend Kelly DeVries also read the manuscript and gave me encouragement while also helping me to avoid a historical error or two. The incomparable Harriet McDougal gave me far more than I can ever return. And I would be much remiss if I didn't thank graduate school friends A. Keith Kelly and Fred Bush for telling me—years apart—that I just might be a writer.

Among those people most directly responsible for what you have in your hands, I want to thank my agent, Evan Gregory, my editors, Paul Stevens and Claire Eddy, and the many talents at Tor who have made this book—from cover to copy—better than I ever could have imagined.

Last but hardly least, I wish to thank the many teachers who have shaped whatever successes I have managed. In particular, I want to thank Miss Brockman, from Belmont Elementary School. I still remember when you asked to see the story I wrote about the government's supersecret automosubmajet. I still remember when you read it to the class, and I still remember when you smiled and said you liked it.

I hope you like this one, too.

Books rarely get a second chance at life, so writers rarely get a second chance at acknowledgments. Yet here this book is, and here I am.

The original release of this book (then titled *The Shards of Heaven*) came at a pivotal moment in my life. It was a magical gift, and the years since have only deepened the gratitude I expressed back then. This second chance widens my thanks, bringing in new names like my agent, Georgina Capel, and of course to the amazingly talented staff at Head of Zeus who have turned a dream into a splendid reality: Nicolas Cheetham, Charlie Hiscox, and Simon Michele, who created this mind-blowing cover (and the astonishing covers for my Seaborn novels, too!).

But above all, I want to express my gratitude to the many readers who loved my books from the start and continued to beat the drum for me all these years. Whether it was Brian's 'fan club' goodies, Eilonwy's 'Livingstans' group, JordanCon's award, or just a kind word or review from a relative stranger, your collective support has truly meant the world to me. Thank you.

THE AEGIS AND THE OASIS

A SHARDS NOVELLA

For Kayla,
who kept me sane

A Note to Readers

An earlier version of this story, then titled "The Temples of the Ark," appeared a number of years ago as a prequel/tie-in to my Shards trilogy of novels. I was thrilled when my publisher gave me a chance to revisit and rewrite it under this new title. Some of that work, I hope, is due to my improvement as a writer. But just as much or more is due to the latest archaeological finds in the two primary locations of the story—the Bahariya Oasis, where it begins, and the Kharga Oasis, where it ends—as well as the latest historical studies of the land of Kush and its rulers.

Engaging in this kind of research was necessary because this tale, like the larger Shards series into which it fits, falls within the genre of Historical Fantasy. Even more particularly, it is what is often called a "Secret History": its characters and events are intended to fit within the bounds of known history to the highest degree possible. So I've done what I can to (mostly) get it right.

As but one instance, efforts are currently underway to preserve and restore the ruins of the Temple of Hibis in the Kharga Oasis. Among the discoveries that have been made there is a line of battered stone sphinxes that line the road leading to the temple—not all of which are aligned as they should be.

The Citadel
March 11, 2025

I do not know whether there are gods, but there ought to be.

— *Diogenes of Sinope (4th century, BC)*

I

The Aegis

Stirred from dreams of home, Hephaestion awoke in the arms of his king.

In the corner of the tent, the oil lamp that he and Alexander had lit before crawling under the blankets was still burning. Its steady flame pushed feebly against the shadows, and most soldiers in the army would have doused it to save the oil. But not here. For all of Alexander's rage upon the field, for all that he had walked the earth from Greece to Persia as a mighty leader and killer of men, the strange truth was that their strong-shouldered king was afraid of the dark. Not for the first time, Hephaestion smiled at that.

The air in the tent was dry and calm, and Hephaestion could feel the heavy scents of the worn canvas around them— the dust and the sweat, the rain and the blood of two years of campaigning. He couldn't smell them, though. The sweeter scents of the balms and oils he'd worked into Alexander's skin were far closer, and he was glad for them.

There was a reason for the dreams, he knew. He clearly missed what they'd left behind in Macedon. The memories. The familiarities. The comforts. Dreams might be fantasy, but they pointed to that truth, at least. He knew he wouldn't trade this waking reality for them, though. The greater truth was that this, here, now, was home. In the arms of a conqueror. *His* conqueror.

Alexander's tawny hair had grown longer since they'd arrived in Egypt, and Hephaestion gently blew at a loose strand that curled up and threatened to tickle his nose.

The hair swayed away, and Alexander stirred in response. Then the corded muscles of his arm flexed and began to lift. Hephaestion knew the motion. He'd felt it enough over the years. Alexander was at peace, in body and in spirit, and in that serenity he would turn away, would roll over to face the outer wall of the tent. To look away.

That turned back had bothered Hephaestion when they were younger. He'd thought it meant Alexander was ashamed of him, ashamed of what they shared.

He knew different now. It was Alexander's secret challenge to the world. In his sleep, in that weakest of times, the king would expose his broad, naked back to the door as a ready target to any who might wish him harm. And every night he wasn't killed in his sleep would mean another night with the full trust of the men who'd sworn to follow him to the ends of the earth.

Which meant, of course, that he trusted Hephaestion most of all.

Hephaestion lifted his weight off, giving Alexander the space to sigh over to his side. That familiar back rolled into view, and his oiled skin shone in the dim light, bringing the darkness of the thick scar upon his shoulder into sharp relief. It had only been a few months since the king had taken the spear-wound at Gazza, but already it was fully healed. It looked as if it were years old.

One more sign of his divine birth, many said. One more proof.

None of them knew the truth as Hephaestion did. Alexander was as human as any other man. Divinity wasn't how the few blows that ever reached him healed with such inhuman speed. Ichor didn't run through his veins. And the fates didn't explain why nothing could slow his onslaught when he donned his armor and the battle-rage boiled over him, why he could press ever forward, scything men like dry stalks of wheat.

Hephaestion eased himself free of the blankets, stood, and stretched. Retrieving his simple linen tunic from the floor, he pulled it over his head. Though the desert would be miserably hot in a few hours, it would still be cold before the dawn, so he found his wool cloak on a stool nearby and put it on, too. Then he sat on the bare stool to bind his sandals. After one last look at Alexander's back, he slipped out of the tent as quietly as he could.

The guard outside came to attention as he exited and acknowledged him. "Lord Hephaestion."

For a few moments the man was invisible in the changed light, but Hephaestion knew the voice. He knew all the men assigned to keep Alexander safe. "Eustathios," he said, blinking towards the big, reliable man who'd drawn the duty this night.

The guard melted into view out of the darkness. He'd been leaning against one of the tall palms that shaded the entrance of Alexander's tent, one the many that lined the edge of the oasis where they'd encamped. "Couldn't sleep, sir?"

"Don't think I've slept well in Egypt yet." Hephaestion admitted. He yawned, and though the clear desert air that filled his lungs was crisp, it was welcome. Like cold water on sore limbs, it helped him wake up. And it had the pleasant taste of slowing watch-fires and dates.

"Me, neither," Eustathios said. "It's the sand that does it, I think. Got Egypt between my toes. And by the gods it's forever itching in my crotch."

Hephaestion grinned as he shook his head in shared grief. Then he turned his eyes to the sky, tracing the lines of constellations in the great dome. He'd managed a few hours of rest, he could see. A decent respite, though nothing like he needed. Nothing like what he and Alexander would have shared in a palace bed back home. "Can't get out of Egypt fast enough," he said. "The oasis is better than the desert, but not by much."

Eustathios didn't respond right away. And though Hephaestion was still gazing at the wide stretch of the stars above, he could feel the man looking at him.

"You want to ask me something, Eustathios."

The guard chewed on his thought before he answered. "Did the Oracle really say he's the son of God?"

Ah. The Oracle. Ever since they'd left Siwa Oasis it had been the one thing on everyone's minds. And not just among the Greeks. Word had traveled so fast ahead of them that the priest of Amun who oversaw this next little oasis had been waiting for them when they arrived—dressed in his finery and bowing so deep it hurt Hephaestion's back just to watch. The priest had insisted that he'd build a temple to honor Alexander, the king become a pharaoh, right here in this very spot.

Even Alexander, who thought a great deal of himself, had found it a bit much.

"Oracles never really say anything," Hephaestion said. He shrugged into the expanse of the night. "It's all riddles and maybes and whatever you want to make of it. You know that."

"Men are saying it's true, though. The Oracle confirmed it. And after Gazza, well . . ."

Gazza. The spear. That scar. Hephaestion knew it would have killed him had *he* been the one hit by it—and the same was true for Eustathios or any other man in camp—but Alexander had only switched hands on his blade and fought on, like a lion in the midst of the chaos. Even his enemies had marveled at it.

When they'd set out from Macedon, some of the king's counsellors had advised against him leading such charges personally, but they didn't understand the way of war. Alexander had veteran leaders enough to take command of the lines, but that wasn't all his men needed. They fought more bravely when their king was by their side. And when they died—which so many did—they did that more bravely, too.

"Besides," Alexander had laughed back then in the court, "what danger could there be? No blow from a man can kill the son of a god."

It had been a joke. He and the other soldiers in the court had all laughed about it. By the stars, they'd grown up with Alexander. They'd seen him shit. He wasn't a god, even if he did have a god's own luck. It was easy enough to joke that no mortal could kill him.

But now, after Gazza, after the Oracle, so many were like Eustathios, wondering if the joke had revealed some kind of hidden truth after all.

Hephaestion wanted to tell them all how preposterous it was. He wanted to tell them that he knew the truth of Alexander, how he'd become what he had become. No matter what some drugged desert hermit said, a man wasn't a god, and Gazza hadn't changed that. The Oracle hadn't changed that.

But Hephaestion knew, too, the sacrifice that so many were willing to make for Alexander the man. He knew how much they had managed to achieve. What more could be done for Alexander the god, he wondered. Could they conquer it all, bring lasting peace to a world of war?

"Alexander is of hearty stock," he finally said. "The same was true of his father, remember?"

Eustathios scoffed. "I knew Philip. Strong as he was, that blow would have slain him. Sure as we stand here, I know it."

"Perhaps so."

"So do you believe it?"

The stars, Hephaestion suddenly thought. They might well put his friend there in the end. Another Hercules. "Maybe the gods are what we make of ourselves," he mused. "Maybe the question isn't whether Alexander is a god, but whether the gods are men like Alexander."

He looked back to the guard, genuinely interested in the big man's reply, but the sound of a horse pounding the earth turned their attentions away. Down the line of tents, a rider was driving hard, his face flashing red as he passed the night fires.

"Hippolytos," Eustathios whispered when the rider got near enough to recognize. "One of the scouts."

Hephaestion walked forward from the tent to meet him, trying to get the noise of the horse and rider further from their sleeping king.

Hippolytos pulled up short in a rush of sandy dirt. Dismounting with speed, he saluted as his sandals touched the sandy earth. "Lord Hephaestion."

"Is it the Persians?" Eustathios spoke first, but it was the very question that Hephaestion would have asked. The Persian governor of Egypt had submitted to Alexander almost the moment that they'd crossed into these lands, but one of the Persian generals—a respected leader named Masistes—had refused to bow to Greek authority. He'd raced ahead of them up the Nile, gathering men into a small force of resistance. Alexander's scouts were sure Masistes had been tracking them as they'd crossed the desert to reach Siwa, but they'd never managed to confirm the location or the size of the Persian threat.

The young man shook his head as he caught his breath. "Kushites," he said, and his voice betrayed the same surprise that Hephaestion had at the word. "Coming from the east. An army of them. Tens of thousands strong."

*

The Macedonian phalanx stretched out under the hot, desert sun: a wall of men whose long spears made them seem a living forest—an extension of the oasis at their backs. Riding up from the far end of its lines, Hephaestion had been taking note that the men were as ready as possible. Hardly a difficult task, and probably not even a necessary one. The men knew their places. They knew their roles. But Alexander had always understood the necessary ritual of such things. So Hephaestion had gone out, as he'd always done, and returned to report.

Their king was easy to spot at the front of the elite cavalry. His colorful banners were clear enough, of course, as was the tall horse upon which he sat, but there was also the sharp gleam of his bronze breastplate in the morning light. The armor—somehow brighter than those upon the men surrounding him—shone through the waves of heat that were already shimmering up from the sands like phantom snakes.

Alexander welcomed him with a nod when he got close. "All is well, Heph?"

Hephaestion reined his own horse into a position alongside him. "As ever."

"Good."

Their army had numbered some 30,000 when they'd crossed into Egypt, but it was smaller than that now. Some of the men had been left in the cities of the Nile, but far more were working upon the edge of the sea, laying the foundations for a new city that would come to bear Alexander's name. Looking out at the stretching expanse of exotic men that had arrayed against them—a sea of color and noise that undulated in its lines like pent-up waves ready to surge free—Hephaestion found himself wishing they had those missing comrades with them again.

For a fifth time this morning, he counted the opposing banners and multiplied them. Even if they'd had *all* their distant countrymen at hand, he could see, they'd still be greatly outnumbered. But at least the odds would be improved.

"I don't care for the heat," Alexander said in an off-hand voice, as if this was just another day, just another duty to be performed. "Though I must say I've never slept better."

Eustathios, whose horse was just behind them, chuckled. Several other men followed suit.

"I'm counting it four to one," said one of other generals. Hephaestion clearly wasn't the only one counting and doing the math. "Maybe five."

There was no tremor of fear in the man's voice. It was only a statement of fact. They all knew they'd fought at such odds before, and it had mattered little. The Thracians, the Syrians, the Persians . . . no matter their numbers, none had stood against the power of their Macedonian arms. None had seen anything like their core phalanx and their agile sweeps of cavalry.

Good tactics, Alexander had once said, could grind great numbers to dust.

So they could. But they themselves had never seen anything like the Kushites before. What tactics would *they* have?

The local priest of Amun—Horhetep was his name—sat on a camel on the other side of the man he thought the son of his god. He didn't speak Greek, but his Persian was as passable as theirs had become. It was enough for him to act as an interpreter through that language. This, along with the fact that he'd said he'd met Kushites before, was more than enough reason for Alexander to insist he be up front with them. "They are an army of lion," the Egyptian said.

A statement of their ferocity, Hephaestion was sure, and one that the Kushites clearly wanted to inspire. Many of the warriors were wearing leather armor over their dark-skin—little different, it appeared, from what so many of the Macedonian fighters were wearing—but over this the Kushites had sashes of fur. And here and there stood men who seemed to wear the full skins of wild beasts. Hephaestion, noting how they were interspersed within the whole, wondered if they were officers. If so, they'd be key targets in the fight.

"Only the leaders matter," Alexander said, answering the priest in Persian. "I'd rather face an army of lion led by sheep than an army of sheep led by a lion."

"And you, pharaoh, are the lion of the sun," Horhetep said.

It wasn't a mistaken image. As was his custom, Alexander wore a golden helm in the form of a lion's head. But the Egyptian's voice somehow managed to be both reverent and flattering. It left Hephaestion uncertain whether the man truly believed Alexander the son of a god or whether he believed that pretending it to be true would benefit him for now.

Both could be so, he supposed.

To believe in the gods was to want something from them.

Hephaestion purposely kept from looking at Alexander's gleaming breastplate, though he was well aware of what it meant for their enemies that he was wearing it. Soon enough, the rage would burn through him. The power and the possibility.

"Riders coming out," Eustathios said in their native Greek.

Beyond the dirty plain of sand between the armies, a small contingent had broken away from the Kushite lines. Four people were moving forward on resplendent camels, golden metal flashing from their flanks. They were making a slow pace, and four other men were surrounding them on foot, each holding a long pole aloft. A dark silken cloth was held taut between them, allowing the riders to remain in shaded comfort.

"Why don't we have that?" Eustathios asked, shading his eyes to watch.

"You know why," Alexander replied.

Eustathios stammered for a moment, clearly at a loss. The conqueror grinned.

"Because they couldn't keep up," Hephaestion said.

Alexander let out a light laugh. "Shall we, Heph?"

"I go as the king goes."

Alexander nodded, then switched to Persian to address Horhetep. "Come with us, priest," he ordered.

And then, without waiting for a reply, he kicked his horse forward to meet the Kushite emissaries. Hephaestion and the Egyptian followed, chasing the king across the hot Egyptian sands.

He'd known Alexander since they were children. He'd laughed with him. He'd loved with him. He'd shed blood with him. But it occurred to Hephaestion, as they came up to the place between the armies where the Kushite emissaries awaited in their artificial shade, that he'd never seen him as relaxed as he had been these past few days.

"One soul in two bodies," Aristotle had once said, chiding them for one of the many tricks they'd played upon their tutor. True enough in its way, Hephaestion had long supposed. He was the king's right hand, acting his will without the awareness of his thought. He was, as Alexander so often said, his second self.

But there was at least one difference between them: Hephaestion hated this country.

In part it was the damnable sand, of course. The winds raised it up as dust, pushed it in great billowing clouds that scratched like insects at their eyes, blinding them as it blotted out the sun and erased their tracks. It was a monstrous beast, this desert, and it wanted to consume them.

Even when it wasn't raised in storm, the sand simply clung to everything. It would grind in their teeth, grate in their sheets, and he simply couldn't imagine how anyone could be at peace with it.

But more than that he felt an indescribable tension in the air here. A dangerous uneasiness in the foreign, hostile landscape. It felt as if the whole of the desert was waiting, and he didn't know what for.

Alexander, though, had welcomed Egypt into his heart. He'd founded what would be his greatest city here: his Alexandria, drawn up from the earth on the edge of the sea. And he'd taken them a thousand miles across the desert to visit its Oracle at Siwa, to be told that he was the true pharaoh, the son of the Egyptian god, Amun. He loved this land. And he wasn't lying when he said that he hadn't slept better. Hephaestion was in a position to know.

A second self he might be, but Hephaestion couldn't understand these things. And he couldn't help but wonder if this would be the day that his sense of foreboding would come to pass.

When they got close, he and Alexander quickly realized that only three of the four emissaries waiting for them appeared to be from Kush. Two of these, judging from their gilded clothes and high bearing, were the king and the queen of their country up the Nile. A young couple, Hephaestion noted, and they seemed little troubled by inexperience or worry. He and Alexander had seen enough leaders to know fear on sight, and this king and queen had nothing of it. They seemed as relaxed as Alexander himself—an accomplishment that was either worthy of respect or mockery. Time would tell which.

The third Kushite rider dressed much as Horhetep did. He had a shaved head and wore a wide golden collar over his white robes. In one hand he held a long thin scepter of black wood decorated with still more gold. A priest, Hephaestion assumed, probably brought along for the very same reason they'd brought the Egyptian along on their side: if the kings couldn't speak to each other, the religious men could.

Though the three Kushites were foreign to his eyes, they were what Hephaestion expected. This was hardly the first time he and Alexander had held parlay with royalty and an interpreter. But the fourth rider under the artificial shade was something he didn't expect: a man who was striking not for his strangeness, but for his familiarity. A much older man, he had the paler skin of the people of the Levant. And he was wearing only the simplest of hooded desert robes. His nervousness on seeing Alexander before him only emphasized how entirely out of place he was in the gathering.

Alexander had brought his horse up just outside the square of their shade. A subtle point, Hephaestion knew: the Greeks, Alexander was proclaiming, had no need of comfort.

As they had among the lines, Hephaestion and the Egyptian took position on either side of Alexander. His own steed shook his mane against the heat, the metals of his harness clattering loudly, and Hephaestion steadied it with a reassuring pat upon its neck.

After a moment, Alexander reached up to unclasp his golden lion helm and set it in front of him on his saddle. Hephaestion followed suit.

The man he assumed to be the king of Kush leaned over to the queen. He whispered something, and she smiled warmly.

The king nodded, but it was the third Kushite who spoke—the one Hephaestion figured for a priest. The words, he assumed, were in Egyptian. He caught nothing of their meaning.

Horhetep understood, though. The priest of Amun nodded sagely, then seemed to clarify some points in the same language before at last translating the message in Persian. "This man is the high priest of a great temple of Amun in Kush, a land up the Nile."

Something about the Egyptian's tone made Hephaestion wonder if there was animosity between the two men. Alexander caught it, too. "Are you at war?" the conqueror asked.

Horhetep seemed to think how best to answer. "We both honor your father," he said.

Hephaestion felt Alexander swallow a tired sigh. "Rivals for influence, then," he said to Hephaestion in Greek. Then, returning to Persian, he asked Horhetep if they'd said anything more.

The priest stammered for a moment, apparently worried that he'd misstepped, but he recovered enough to continue. "He introduces the *qore* of Kush, Nastasene," he announced, referring to the king. Then he gestured to the queen. "And the *kandake*, Sekhmakh. They greet you, Alexander, conqueror of many."

Alexander gave the king and queen—the *qore* and the *kandake*—the slightest of bows in turn. "I am Alexander of Macedon, king of Greece and king of all Asia," he said, speaking relatively slowly so that Horhetep could translate his words. "I have taken this land of Egypt by arms and assent, and I have been rightfully declared by its Oracle to be its pharaoh. This is my land, and I will defend it."

After an exchange with his rival priest, Horhetep dutifully interpreted what had been said. "Their majesties do not desire war."

Alexander cracked his neck. "War there will be if you stay."

The *qore*, Nastasene, smiled when the message was relayed to him. His answer was brief.

"Their king says the numbers are on their side," Horhetep reported.

"And I am Alexander."

"On this they agree."

For a full half-minute Alexander and Nastasene simply

stared at one another. This, too, was a familiar game for Hephaestion, and he found himself looking to the *kandake*—the queen—to see her response to it. She was staring at Alexander. That wasn't unusual. But she wasn't looking at him in fear or apprehension. She seemed to be judging him. Like a merchant appraising goods.

Not wanting to be caught staring at her, Hephaestion then turned to look at the fourth, lighter-skinned man. Perhaps alone among the many tens of thousands on the plain, the man wasn't looking at Alexander. Not at the *man* Alexander, anyway. Hephaestion could trace the line of his eyes. He was looking at the conqueror's armor, at the gleaming bronze of the breastplate that Alexander alone was allowed to handle. And he was staring most especially, Hephaestion realized with mounting horror, at the blacker-than-black stone that was locked into its center. He was staring at the thing that had made Alexander a god, and he was smiling.

"As their majesties have said," Horhetep repeated, "there is no desire for war here."

"Their army speaks otherwise," Alexander replied, casually leaning in his saddle to look past them at the great masses. The warriors were chanting and rocking in a frenetic anxiety. "And it seems to think otherwise."

The two priests engaged in more back and forth before the Egyptian priest translated what had been said into Persian. "The army will stay or go as the *qore* wishes. He felt it was necessary for their protection."

"From what?"

"From you, Alexander king."

"I have no wish to conquer the land of Kush or its people. I came for Egypt. I will return to Persia from here. Tell them."

Horhetep nodded and once more talked with them. "It is not your armies they fear," he finally said.

Alexander raised an eyebrow. "Then what?" he asked.

This time it was not one of the Kushites who replied. It was the fourth man, who'd at last stopped staring at Alexander's armor. And he spoke not in Egyptian or in Persian, but in common Greek. "Your rage, god among men," he said.

Alexander turned to him, his eyes narrowing. "My what?"

"Your rage," the man repeated, and he nodded toward the breastplate. "Like the rage of Achilles. It sits upon you even now as a flame ready to alight."

As far as Hephaestion knew, none but he and Alexander knew the secret of what they'd found in the sanctuary of Athena at Delphi. No one else could be trusted. So when Alexander turned his eyes in Hephaestion's direction, he had nothing to give him but his own wide-eyed bewilderment.

"We know something of what you carry," the pale-skinned man continued. "Which is why we would speak with you."

To cover his concern, Hephaestion scoffed. "What do you think you know of Alexander?"

This time, it was the queen—the *kandake*—who suddenly spoke. "We know enough," she said.

"You speak Greek." Alexander made no effort to hide his surprise.

She grinned. "Better than you speak Persian."

Alexander laughed at that. "I admit I was a terrible student. Too busy getting into trouble with Heph here. If I am to be Achilles, he is my Patroclus."

Sekhmakh turned her eyes to Hephaestion and nodded. She understood the unspoken message: he was Alexander's closest confidant.

Horhetep, clearly confused about being cut out from what was being said, started to say something in Persian. Alexander cut him off with a raised hand before turning back to the *kandake* and continuing in Greek. "What do you want?" he asked.

"We come to ask a great favor from a great king," she replied.

"A favor?"

"We want to give you a gift," she said. "A gift that must never be used. A treasure that must always be protected. Something perhaps only you can protect."

Hephaestion exchanged a glance with Alexander, then spread his arm across the sand before them.

"No," Sekhmakh continued. "We cannot give it to you here. We dared not bring it. But we will take you to it."

"Take us?" Alexander asked.

"Just you," the *kandake* said, before turning to once more acknowledge Hephaestion. "And your companion, if you will. In good faith only myself and Terach will accompany you."

The pale-skinned man smiled. Hephaestion assumed he must be Terach.

Alexander frowned. "Take us where?"

"We marched here from the Nile," Sekhmakh answered. "Our fleet awaits us there, at the old city of the fallen sun god. We will return there, and then we sail up the river to the city of wolves. There we alone will take a path long-traveled by the caravans. The Way of Forty Days it is called, though we travel only to its first oasis. What we would give you is there. And when you have it, we will return to the great river. We will grant you with a ship to travel back down the great river."

Hephaestion wanted to laugh at the absurdity of the two of them leaving their own army to go alone into the desert, but he could see the look of consideration on Alexander's face. "You expect us to go with you," he clarified, hoping to make the foolishness of it plain to his king. "To go with your people, surrounded by your thousands, back toward the heart of Kush?"

"Our thousands," Sekhmakh replied, talking not to Hephaestion but to the conqueror. "And you are Alexander. If we are right, if you have what we believe you have, do you think such numbers really matter?"

"The Aegis of Zeus protected Troy from all Greece," Terach abruptly put in, and he was once more looking at the king's breastplate. "I'm certain it will protect you from us, great son of Macedon."

He thought it foolish, but Hephaestion also knew better than to argue with Alexander when his friend's mind was made up. And it was clear that curiosity had gotten the better of him. The oracle at Siwa had declared him the son of a god. He needed to know what else might be waiting for him in the vast desert.

The real question was how to convince Horhetep that there was no danger. Whether it was out of jealousy or fear, the Egyptian priest was aghast that Alexander planned to head up the river with the Kushites, and his concern was rubbing off on the men. In the end, Alexander recalled that the man had asked to have a temple built in his oasis—a temple that would honor the pharaoh and no doubt better secure his own power. It would be so, the king-turned-pharaoh agreed. Greek money would help pay for it, and the strong backs of the Greek army would help build it. What's more, Alexander insisted that at least one of the carvings would highlight Horhetep welcoming Alexander himself, the two of them paired in stone for eternity. It delighted the Egyptian. It also gave the Greek army something to do while they were away.

And so the next day, when the army of Kush began its march back to the Nile, Hephaestion and Alexander rode with them, alongside the *qore* and the *kandake* in the artificial shade at its lead.

Though Alexander wore his armor as they rode, there were no surprises. The people of Kush held no plans of assassination. What they'd said was true. They only wanted to bring

Alexander to the place where he could take the gift they were offering.

As soon as they departed, Terach rode apart from them. He seemed lost in his own thoughts. Sekhmakh reassured them that his distance was no cause for concern. He was, she explained, a Jewish priest, who'd come to the land of Kush from Jerusalem, and the gift was particularly important to him.

What that gift was, she patiently refused to say. The *kandake* and Terach alone spoke Greek, and from what Hephaestion could ascertain, they alone knew the truth. At first he couldn't imagine how a king could allow his queen such secrets, but the *qore* seemed happy not only to allow it but to support it: he'd brought his army for nothing less than her protection in meeting with Alexander, and he was content to let her go alone with him into the sands.

The more time they spent with Sekhmakh, though, the more Hephaestion thought he might understand the *qore*'s unflinching trust in his wife. The *kandake* was captivating.

She wore white linens, trimmed with gold, that draped over her shoulder and breast, bound about her waist with a beaded and jeweled sash. The gown was cut so loose that it moved in waves about her as she rode, and more than once Hepaestion had found himself avoiding the hints it made about the body beneath. Her skin, like her husband's, was the color of rich cinnamon, dark against the brightness of the sands, yet it radiated an inner warmth in the light of the sun. Without doubt she was beautiful in her way, but many queens were. It wasn't this that made it difficult to deny or turn away from her.

She fascinated Hephaestion—and Alexander, too, he was sure—because of how free she seemed. She rode as straight-backed as any Persian princess they'd ever seen, her head held high on her slender neck, but there was an honest readiness to her smile, an unbidden laughter in her dark eyes, that was entirely unbound by regal customs. She seemed as comfortable on her gilded camel as many of the Greeks were on their horses. And perhaps strangest of all, she showed not the slightest concern that she'd soon be alone in the desert with three men, one of them the greatest conqueror the world had known.

She was also profoundly and ceaselessly curious. She asked question after question about their travels, confirming and reconfirming the truth behind the stories she'd heard about Alexander. And she asked not in worship but in wonder. She simply wanted to know of the world, of what lay beyond her borders. Had she not been a queen in her lands, Hephaestion felt certain that she would have been a restless traveler.

With Terach keeping to himself, Sekhmakh became their near-constant companion and guide on the journey to the little village on the West bank of the Nile where the Kushite fleet was waiting. And even once they arrived she stayed close, explaining in patient Greek what they were seeing as the army loaded and boarded the ships docked in the harbor or pulled up among the reedy banks.

Alexander was stunned by how many ships there were, and as they stood on the busy docks he said as much.

Sekhmakh, who'd been watching some men load a particularly large bundle of crates onto a nearby ship, seemed genuinely pleased.

"A few years ago," she explained, "a man named Kambasuten controlled lands and the river south of here, closer to my *qore*'s lands. He fought against the Persians. My husband also has no love of the Persians. They do not belong here. They do not respect our ways. They do not know the song of the Nile or the cries of the sands. When they took the lands of Egypt, they took much that was ours, too. So we helped Kambasuten fight them for a time. But he grew greedy. He sailed his army into our lands, and my husband fought him on the banks of the great river. These are Kambasuten's ships. They now belong to the *qore*."

It was Alexander's turn to be pleased. "Nastasene destroyed him."

The *kandake* thought for a moment. "Yes, though I think my husband would better say that Kambasuten destroyed himself. He did not need to attack our lands. But when he did so it was necessary to destroy him." She paused, smiled as if embarrassed to have spoken so long. "But you, Alexander, have done far greater. They tell me you conquered mighty Tyre upon the sea."

"He did," Hephaestion said, happy to boast of his friend's greatness. "The city could not be taken, it was said, because it was built upon an island, encircled by the sea. Siege engines could not be brought to bear upon its walls. Yet Alexander broke them."

"How?" Sekhmakh asked. "Would you not need the engines?"

"Of course," Alexander said.

She looked back and forth between them. "But you said the city was surrounded by water?"

"It *was*, yes," Alexander said. "My men built a causeway to the city. It is no longer an island."

Sekhmakh's eyes were wide. Yes, Hephaestion thought. Alexander bent even the earth to his will.

Before she could say anything more, one of the Kushite laborers nearby stumbled. The bundle of crates nearly tipped over. Apologizing, Sekhmakh took her leave of them and hurried off to help.

When the *kandake* was gone, Hephaestion looked out across the Nile. Its waters rippled in the sun. Across from them, on the far bank, stone pillars and broken walls stuck out from the dirt and sand like the broken, bleached bones of a buried giant. The city of the fallen sun god, Sekhmakh called it. Built for a religion that long before had briefly burst across this ancient landscape like a shooting star—flashed, and then been forgotten and abandoned.

After a minute, he took a deep breath and decided to ask what he'd been wanting to ask ever since they'd left their encampment. "Why are we really going with them?"

"I think you know why, Heph." Alexander said. "Because I need to know."

"To know what it is they are offering?"

Alexander shrugged, a toss of his hair in the sun. "Or what it isn't."

Hephaestion shook his head. "You've more gold than Midas, more jewels than any man can dream of. What use is more treasure?"

Alexander frowned for a moment, before a lightness struck upon his face. "Do you remember when we went to Corinth all those years ago? Do you remember when we met Diogenes?"

Hephaestion grinned at the memory. "Of course I do. How could I forget? The philosopher himself, living in that hovel that everyone called a clay pot. Aristotle warned us not to bother with Diogenes. But of course we took that as a challenge."

Alexander chuckled. "So we did."

"And there he was," Hephaestion recalled. "I remember you walked up and told him that you were the son of Philip of Macedon, the student of Aristotle, and that one day you would conquer all of Greece. You asked him if there was anything he would ask of you. Gods, I remember it as if it was yesterday morning. He blinked up at you, studying you, and then —"

Alexander's voice cracked with feigned age. "'Stand a little out of my sun.'"

Hephaestion laughed, just as he'd laughed then. He knew at some level, for all that had come upon them, they were still those two young men standing before Diogenes, blocking the old man's light.

Alexander laughed, too, but not for long. "When I say we're going with them because I need to know, Heph, I guess it's really because Diogenes was right. He saw the truth of me. He saw the truth of all of us. Glory fades. *Life* fades. We're all mortal."

Hephaestion gave him a sidelong look. "Maybe not all of us."

Alexander rolled his eyes. "Yes. Me, too, my friend. Whatever else this armor is, whatever else it does, it is no shield against time. Death will find me one way or another. Even Achilles had his heel."

"Still doesn't explain why we're riding into the desert. The Aegis of Zeus—if that's what it is—may protect you. But if this is still some kind of trap, it won't protect me."

Alexander reached over and squeezed his shoulder. The grip was strong, and it lingered. "It's a chance to know more, to understand more, Heph. About this armor, for certain, but also about us. About them."

Closer to the water, the *kandake* had the crates safely aboard. When the tired laborer bowed low in apology she smiled and returned the gesture.

"She moves so easily among her people," Hephaestion observed. "As if she is one of them."

Alexander, too, was gazing at her. "A good leader must be, even when his men don't want him to be."

Hephaestion nodded. It was that reason Alexander fought in the lines, and it brought his mind back to his conversation with Eustathios, and how the men thought of Alexander more and more as a god. "But surely a leader must be feared to be obeyed," he said.

"Obedience isn't everything," Alexander replied. "I assure you I would far rather excel others in the knowledge of what is excellent than in the excellence of my power and dominion."

Hephaestion felt his friend's eyes upon him. When he turned, he saw that Alexander was looking at him with a smile of genuine affection. He saw, too, the wrinkles at his eyes, the creases in flesh once smooth. "So Diogenes was right?"

"I think he was," Alexander said, "though there's time enough to live still, you and I."

"Life with a god-man has been good so far," Hephaestion said. "Though I'd rather like to get out of Egypt, if you please."

Alexander let out another chuckle. "Soon enough. And you know, Heph, perhaps I won't always be Alexander."

"If not Alexander, then who?"

"Well," he said, "truly, I tell you, if I were not Alexander, I would be Diogenes."

2

The Oasis

It took some time to sail up the river from the city of the fallen sun god to what Sekhmakh called the city of wolves—a far larger and busier port than the one they'd left behind. From there, though the army of Kush continued on, two crewed ships stayed behind. And four people, riding camels, left those behind in turn. With Alexander and Hephaestion following, Sekhmakh and Terach led them into the desert on the caravan route. No artificial shade now, and once they crossed out of the sight of the river, no natural shade, either. Just the barren desert and the plodding of their hooves for company.

The Way of Forty Days was no road such as those that crossed Greece and Persia. It was instead a wide band of lighter colored earth, beaten down by the passing of countless camels and numberless wagons, marked only in the most barren stretches by piled rock cairns that stood sentinel amid the shifting sands.

With only the four of them present, Terach spoke more as they rode. Whatever thoughts he'd had before, he showed no hints of concern now. And to Hephaestion's relief, he largely kept his gaze from the black stone at the center of Alexander's bronze breastplate.

The number forty, the Jew told them a couple days into their ride, was a lie. It was meant to refer to the total journey it would take to reach the distant heart of the continent, where the great desert gave way to impenetrable forests. But most caravans took twice as long to reach that place. No one knew where the number forty had actually come from, he said. His own guess was that it simply meant a large number, not a specific number. After all, the stories of his people told of rains falling for forty days and flooding the earth entire—and looking around them at the desert this seemed not nearly enough rain to manage it.

The way he said it, Hephaestion wasn't sure sure if the man was joking or if it was some kind of test of their faith. If they laughed, would he find them guilty of some crime against his gods?

One god, Hephaestion reminded himself. He didn't know a great deal about the Jews, but he knew they only believed in one.

Alexander, too, seemed uncertain what to make of Terach's point. He at last opened his mouth to try to say something in reply, but he was clearly relieved when Sekhmakh spoke first.

"Along the Nile," she put in, "it can seem as if the river is all there is of the world. Little survives away from its waters. Forty days of rain would be more than enough to flood over its banks and all that is built upon them. Perhaps this is all it means to flood the world: to destroy the things that give us life."

Terach nodded thoughtfully. "An intriguing interpretation, *kandake*."

Sekhmakh shrugged. "As for the Way of Forty Days, I think perhaps four people first rode it, just as we are now, and after forty days they simply ran out of fingers to keep counting."

She laughed at that, and none of them could help but laugh along with her.

When their cheer slowed, the *kandake* pointed forward

into the distance. "Thankfully, that's as far as we need to go," she said.

A line of green ran along the edge of the horizon ahead, bright against the desert's palette of muted browns and dusty reds. Minute by minute, the line grew taller and more defined: it was a line of treetops, they could see now, and it was far closer than it had first appeared.

Within an hour, they had crossed over a final ridge and dropped down into the oasis itself: a wide bowl in the desert whose bottom had filled with a shallow lake ringed with lush greenery and the scattered blocks of homes and farms. It was only here that the worn path they'd been following became something more akin to what Hephaestion knew elsewhere in the world: a defined road that wound between date orchards, small brick buildings, and caravan tents.

The people in the oasis smiled and waved at their party of four as it passed. Some looked Egyptian, others Kushite, and others might well have been Persian. None seemed concerned at the appearance of the newcomers. None seemed at odds with one another. It was, Hephaestion thought, as if the hostilities of the outside world had no place in this refuge in the desert.

As the road they followed made its way around the lake, the *kandake* began to tell them a story. Two hundred years earlier, she said, a tired band of Jewish exiles had come to the lands of Kush, seeking asylum. They had with them a most powerful weapon: a box that contained a stone holding the power of their God. The *qore* and the *kandake* of Kush had welcomed them, had granted them sanctuary, and had given them the peace to continue their worship as they saw fit. The only price the Kushited asked in return was that the Jews would promise to use the weapon to defend them if ever they were attacked. It had been this way for two centuries, she insisted. But the time had come for the Ark, as the Jews called the weapon, to find it a safer home. So they had moved it to this desert oasis, and here they hoped to give it to Alexander.

As she spoke, a great temple came into view, perched on the western side of the lake. Like many other temples they'd seen since coming to Egypt, it sat within a walled enclosure, built of pale blocks of stone. Visible over the top of that enclosure—and tantalizingly seen through a great archway at its center—rose the tall, square shape of the temple itself. Its walls and columned portico were covered with carved symbols and hieroglyphics, all illuminated with bright colors of paint. Extending out from the temple's entrance was a wide, paved avenue, guarded on either side by a line of a dozen or more sphinxes, each as large as a man. The avenue ended at a stone quay upon the lake, and as impressive as the temple was from the view of their shoreline road, Hephaestion couldn't help but think how much more remarkable it would be to approach the complex by boat.

After a few minutes of staring at the temple, Hephaestion returned his thoughts to Sekhmakh's story and the weapon she called an Ark. "Why move it now?" he asked. "Why Alexander?"

Sekhmakh had been looking at the temple, too. There was pride on her face. "Because the one who leads the Jews asks that it be so."

Alexander turned to Terach. "You are descended from those who brought this Ark to Kush?"

For a moment the Jew looked back and forth between the *kandake* and the conqueror, seemingly confused. In reply she made a gesture giving him leave to speak. "I am," he said. "Though I'm not the only one. From Jerusalem to Elephantine in the time of Manasseh, from Elephantine to Kush in the time of Nebuchadnezzar, from that time to this, my family has been among those who kept the Ark safe." He reached into his robes and pulled out a thin chain clasped around his neck.

Hanging from it was the symbol of a circle inscribed upon an inverted pyramid, a single horizontal line cutting through its bottom. "This is the mark held by those who protect the Ark. It is carried by all who watch over it."

Hephaestion didn't recognize the symbol, and he doubted his friend did, either. "This doesn't answer the question," he said. "If it has been safe for so long, why move it?"

"It has been kept safe," Terach said, "but often at the cost of lives. It was only with God's grace that we brought the Ark out of its temple in Jerusalem. It was a further miracle still that it escaped Nebuchadnezzar's reach."

In the shallows by the side of the road, a young Egyptian woman was washing clothes in the water. Terach nodded to her, and she smiled in return. Turning back to the king of Macedon, he shrugged. "And Kush has been safe, it is true, but not without peril. As with Egypt, that kingdom will surely not stand forever."

Hephaestion blinked at the boldness of it. Alexander's back stiffened in his own shock. The *kandake*, however, was strangely unaffected. She was simply minding her camel as it climbed past one of the sphinxes and turned onto the paved avenue. There was a vague smile on her face, as if this wasn't the first time she'd heard Terach casually predict the end of her throne.

"Is there a threat?" Alexander managed to ask.

"Just one," Terach said. He, too, was turning toward the temple now.

A man had appeared at the archway of the enclosure. He held up a brown hand to shield his eyes as they approached. Hephaestion was relieved to see that he appeared unarmed.

"What is the threat?" Alexander asked.

Sekhmakh stopped her camel beside the entrance, and the man on the ground reached out to hold its reins. She said something to him in a language that was not Greek, and he nodded deeply before beginning to gather the rest of their reins. The *kandake* stretched and then swung herself down to the ground. As she settled her feet onto the earth, she looked up at Alexander. "The threat is you," she said. "Only you. Come. It awaits."

On foot now, they passed through the archway, Terach and Sekhmakh in the lead. There were other people coming and going upon the swept stones of the temple. Many wore hooded robes like Terach's. Hephaestion couldn't see their faces, but they seemed to be pilgrims of one sort or another, standing and praying before the little shrines that were scattered inside the walled grounds.

At first it seemed that no one had noticed them, but as they closed in on the main building of the temple Hephaestion was aware that many of the hoods were turning to follow. Glancing to either side, he could see at least two men who had begun to pace their advance watchfully.

As they passed through the off-and-on shadows of the columned portico, Hephaestion let his hand casually brush the grip of the blade at his hip, reassuring himself that it was there. "Alexander," he whispered.

"I see them, Heph."

Alexander was wearing his armor, Hephaestion reminded himself. Come what may, he had the Aegis.

The great wooden doors of the temple were open, and Sekhmakh and Terach disappeared into the darkness. Alexander and Hephaestion stepped into the shadows behind them.

Oil lamps burned atop bronze tripods just inside the doorway, but their flickering flames were feeble compared to the glare of the sun and stone outside. Only when the doors were shut behind them did Hephaestion's eyes truly begin to adjust. He saw that the inside walls of the temple were engraved with images of myth and legend, the shapes and symbols of gods and men etched into the surface of the stone.

Layers of paint brought the figures into sharp vitality. The air was thick and sweet with years of incense.

They were also, he could see, no longer alone. Terach and Sekhmakh had been joined by two more hooded figures. The four of them were talking quietly in front of a doorway that led further into the complex.

It was Terach who finally pulled away from them to turn to the two Greeks. He bowed to Alexander, more solemnly than he'd ever done before. "I hope you will forgive us," he said, "but you cannot pass further wearing the Aegis of Zeus."

Alexander's shoulders tensed up. Hephaestion saw a tightness in his jaw, too, though he was quick to relax it. Even in the little light of the lamps the polished armor shone beautifully. All except the stone. It was a dark pit in the center of his friend's chest. "You truly believe that this is the Aegis?" Alexander asked.

"Others believe it to be so," Terach said. "As for what it is, what it truly is, that is a much longer tale indeed. What is important now is that it is of a kind with the Ark, though their powers are different. What the Aegis does for your life, the Ark does for the earth."

Alexander half-cocked his head. "You fear me possessing both?"

Terach chewed on this a moment before he answered. "To the contrary, Alexander, we *expect* you to possess both. That is why you are here. But we first want you to understand what they are. And we want you ... unstressed, conqueror of kingdoms."

"The rage."

Terach nodded. "Just so. It would be best to have a most level head in these matters. I assure you we mean no harm at all."

"Alexander," Hephaestion started to say.

His friend didn't look in his direction. He simply held up his hand to end the matter. "Very well," he said. "Heph, can you help me?"

The king turned his back, and for a moment Hephaestion was back in their tent, their sweat upon him, watching that same back turned toward sleep. The ultimate trust.

"I need to know," Alexander whispered when he got close. "It'll be alright."

Hephaestion nodded, for there was nothing he could say. Then buckle by buckle, strap by strap, he undid the breastplate.

As the last of it came undone and he began to pull himself free of the armor, Alexander let out a long, tired sigh. It wasn't the weight of the plate, Hephaestion knew. It was the power. It fed on him somehow, even as it kept him alive. Neither of them understood it, and Hephaestion wondered if it was the answer to this that Alexander sought above all.

Terach watched as Alexander disencumbered himself of the Aegis. When the king noticed, he smiled. "You know, you didn't answer the rest of my question."

"What is that?"

Alexander slipped his forearm through the shoulders of the armor, holding it up. "Why me?"

"That's best asked of the one who leads us."

Alexander blinked. "That's not you?"

"Hardly so," Terach said. He turned toward Sekhmakh, who had at last finished her conversation with the other figures and walked up to join them. "It's her."

As Alexander stared, Hephaestion found the words for them both. "You're in charge," he said.

"I am," she said.

"But you're the *kandake* of Kush."

When she smiled in return, Hephaestion felt more ashamed than a scolded child. "A woman can do many things," she pointed out.

"You don't look like a Jew," Alexander said.

"But like my mother before me, I believe as one, little though it is known among our people. Are you also surprised that a woman could be in command of such a company? This does not seem the way of things among your people."

Alexander's smile was fast and genuine. "Oh, you've never met my mother."

"Quite a woman, I imagine."

"You've no idea," Hephaestion said, interrupting.

Sekhmakh raised a mischievous eyebrow, but she decided not to question the matter further. "Very well," she said. "Terach, carry the Aegis. Keep it close, but do not touch its stone. Now come, son of a great woman. It's time for you to see the Ark."

The ark of the covenant, as the Jews called it, rested in a small side room within the temple. The surrounding structure, Sekhmakh explained, was largely a Persian construction, built to honor the three gods of Thebes: Hephaestion even recognized the figure of Darius carved into one of the walls just outside the doorway to the chamber housing the Ark. The Persian king was holding forth an offering bowl to the gods, the tall crown of the pharaohs perched upon his head.

That crown, Hephaestion mused to himself, belonged to Alexander now. And though he refused to wear it, there was a good chance that the temple even now being built in his honor would depict him doing so.

The Ark had been described as a wooden box, and so it was—but a most remarkable one. It sat at the far end of the chamber, its broad side facing them. It was wrought of rich acacia, and the polished grains of the wood gleamed in the light. The base was wider than the top, and long carrying poles had been mounted into metal rings at its sides, so that it could be lifted without fingers touching the Ark itselfto ease. Thin filaments of metal wove around and about its wooden surfaces like vines, and on its broad face they wove into the same symbol that Terach wore around his neck: the pyramid flipped within a circle, a line cutting through its bottom third. More remarkable than all this was the Ark's gold-trimmed top, which was crowned with the statues of two winged beings who appeared to be knelt in prayer toward one another: one fashioned of silver, the other of gold. Their wings swept forward before them, the feathered tips nearly touching each other. Beneath that, between them, Hephaestion caught a hint of deepest black, something built flush into the surface of the top of the Ark.

"By the gods," Alexander whispered.

"By the *one* God," Terach corrected, his voice was striking for its seriousness.

"Whether you believe in the God of the Jews or not doesn't matter," Sekhmakh said. She walked around in front of them, staring at the Ark with her own obvious sense of wonder. Then she took a deep breath and turned to face them. "But you must believe in this: the Ark contains a part of the power of God, far more powerful than that within the Aegis you wear. Because it is a part of God, it is a part of creation itself. But it does not truly belong here. It must not be used."

Alexander took a step toward the Ark, then stopped. Hephaestion saw him chewing on the inside of his cheek, a habit he'd long since given up trying to relieve. "Part of a god's power. Even greater than my armor. I could do so much with it."

Hephaestion felt movement in the room, and he turned to see that there were now four hooded figures behind them. They were close to his king's back. He was certain that they were armed.

"You could," the *kandake* admitted. "The temptation is a danger no matter who possesses the Ark."

Alexander still stared at the Ark for a long minute before he at last turned to face her. "So what is the answer to my question, *Kandake* Sekhmakh, keeper of the Ark? Why me?"

"Because you know enough not to use it."

His eyes narrowed. "Because of the Aegis."

Sekhmakh gave the slightest of nods, an acknowledgement of respect between sovereigns. "You've controlled it, but we both know it has been difficult. The Ark is far greater. It would destroy you. As it would destroy me. Even when Kambasuten came with against us we dared not touch it. We defeated him with blade and blood."

Alexander swallowed hard. Hephaestion knew how little he liked to admit weakness. But they both knew the truth when they heard it. "Agreed."

"You can also protect it in ways we cannot," Terach said.

Alexander turned to the voice, but he quickly shifted his focus back to the *kandake*. "I cannot carry it with me," he said. "I'm on a campaign. My army marches deeper into Persia, to find Darius and hunt him down like the wild dog that he is."

Sekhmakh blinked, and for a moment Hephaestion worried that she might be surprised by his sudden turn toward bloodlust. But she shouldn't have been. Alexander was a conqueror. "I agree that you should not march west with it."

"What then? How can I protect it?"

"By giving it a new home," Terach explained. "In a new city. A temple that is a tomb, buried beneath the ground, unknown to all but a chosen few."

"A new city?" There was confusion on Alexander's face.

Hephaestion, though, could see the perfection of what they hoped to achieve, the fortuitousness of the coming of the Greeks. "Alexandria," he said. "They want you to hide the Ark in Alexandria."

Sekhmakh smiled gratefully. "That is precisely what we wish to happen: for the Ark to be made safe and secure."

Alexander nodded, his eyes narrowed in thought as he studied the Ark. The flickering of the lamp flames shifted the shadows of feathers on the winged creatures, made them seem to ripple with life. It imparted an expectation of movement, as if the kneeling figures were prepared to burst up from their knees, stretching themselves out and letting their strong wings beat a steady rise into the heavens.

"Very well," Alexander finally said. His voice was quiet, almost reverent. "We will take the Ark to Alexandria. We will build it a new temple there."

The ark left the temple in something like a processional. The hooded figures who'd been watching them—all of them, like Sekhmakh and Terach, members of the secret group of Jews sworn to protect their sacred treasure—had taken positions along the poles that held the Ark between them. As Sekmakh and the Greeks stood to either side of the temple's entrance, they carefully maneuvered the Ark out into the shelter of the columned portico to await the cart that had been summoned. Terach walked behind, still carefully holding the Aegis before him as if it was a relic.

The brightness of midday was gone. The dusky shadows of evening had fallen over the oasis. Through the open stone archway, at the end of the avenue with its long line of sphinxes, the wide lake echoed the deepening red of the sky.

Shouts suddenly broke over the quiet. Cries of panic from the shoreline beyond the temple walls. The sound of rushing feet. The ring of weapons being drawn.

Hephaestion and Alexander instinctively drew their swords.

"Treachery," Hephaestion said, turning to Sekhmakh.

The *kandake* of Kush shook her head in response, then began barking commands in her native tongue. The men holding the poles of the Ark lowered it to the ground as quickly but carefully as they could, then they fanned out in a rush, ducking behind stone pillars or retreating back into the temple. Many were drawing swords from beneath their cloaks. And those who hurried into the temple were back just as quickly, carrying bows and sheaves of black arrows.

With a sinuous grace, Sekhmakh slid forward to stand in front of the Ark. She gripped two thin daggers in her hands, their twin blades—each as long as her forearm—sharpened to wicked points. Where she'd hidden them under her clothing, Hephaestion couldn't fathom, but he could see that she held them like an extension of herself. She swayed ever so slightly between the balls of her feet, like a cobra ready to strike.

Hephaestion exchanged a quick glance with Alexander. If it wasn't the Jews or the Kushites attacking, then who?

A high whistle pierced the night, slicing in from the line of sphinxes beyond the stone arch of the entrance. Then another and another. One again their instincts took over, and Hephaestion and Alexander tucked themselves behind a stone pillar. Around them, the rest of the Jews took cover, too.

All but Sekhmakh. The *kandake* refused to move from the front of the Ark. It was as if she intended to shield it with her own flesh.

The arrows streaked in the dim air, then clattered off the stones with a noise like hail.

When the volley stopped for a moment, Hephaestion stooped down and retrieved a broken missile that had fallen near his feet.

"Greek?" Sekhmakh asked. She still hadn't moved. It was a miracle, Hephaestion thought, that none of the shafts had struck her.

Turning the arrow over in his fingers, he knew at a glance that it wasn't Greek. And he doubted it was from Kush, either. He'd seen its like more times than he could count. "Persian," he said, holding it out to his friend.

Alexander took it, nodded, then tossed it into the shadows. "Masistes," he said. "Bastard found us."

At a shout from Sekhmakh, the defenders with bows launched their own volleys in return. The missiles shot out through the archway, but Hephaestion could see that fewer arrows were going out than had been coming in.

"Persians?" Sekhmakh asked.

"How many I don't know," Alexander admitted. "They were in the desert. Don't know how they found us here."

"Spies," the *kandake* said. "You are a most recognizable man, Alexander."

Another volley of arrows whistled into the courtyard, and once more everyone but Sekhmakh tucked into the shelter of the tall columns. Some arrows nevertheless found their marks. Screams echoed through the temple.

Behind the shots, a first wave of Persians rolled through the archway, bursting into the inner complex. More archers were among them, and as they spread out they were finding new angles of killing.

"Right flank, Heph!" Alexander shouted. "Down!" The king threw himself into Hephaestion's back, and they tumbled forward onto the stone pavement a heartbeat before an arrow meant to tear into him ripped through open air instead.

"Terach!"

At Sekhmakh's shout, Hephaestion turned and saw that the old man had been hit. The arrow stuck out from his shoulder like a terrible barb, and he was kicking himself across the ground in the panicked shock of a wounded animal. The Aegis had fallen from his hands, not three strides away.

"Alexander," Hephaestion called out. "The armor!"

Even as he said it, he knew it was too late. Beyond the Aegis, beyond Terach's kicking legs, he could see the Persians streaming around the pillars to flank them from either side. It was only a dozen men at this point, but they were coming fast. The setting sun was casting a red light like fresh blood upon the blades in their hands.

"To me, Heph!" Alexander rolled to his feet, and Hephaestion kicked himself up onto his own.

Together, like the young and foolish warriors they'd once been, they ran forward past the Ark, leaping Terach and leaving behind the Aegis to meet the enemy with a roar like mighty lions.

Slowly retreating over the blood-splattered stones, still fighting to survive the first wave of Persians, Hephaestion saw a second wave coming through the archway of the main gate. It was, he thought, the coming of the end.

He tripped over something, stumbled, and recognized that it was Alexander's armor, still uselessly strewn upon the pavement amid the blood and the detritus of battle. The Aegis of Zeus, which had brought Alexander life at Gazza, which had turned aside the arrows at Issus, was in the end unused and useless.

One of the Persians pressed his advantage at the stumble, and Hephaestion only barely managed to get his blade up in time to stop the strike. The ring of the metal rattled his bones, made his teeth grind. He tasted blood in his mouth, and he didn't know whether he'd bit open his tongue or his cheek or both.

The blow nearly took him to a knee, but he pushed himself up against his enemy's weight, reaching out with his left hand as he do so and catching the wrist of the Persian's sword-bearing hand. It was a move of desperation, he knew. It exposed the entire side of his body. If the man had any kind of blade in his other hand, he would open up his Greek gut.

But he didn't. Or he forgot that he did. So Hephaestion had a heartbeat to push the threatening strike back and then plunge the tip of his own blade through the sweat of the man's arm pit and into his body.

Gore sprayed as he kicked the Persian away, and Hephaestion took what small satisfaction he could that the blood of the helplessly writhing man would serve as one more obstacle for the remaining Persians who'd swept around to this side of the temple. It bought him a few more precious seconds.

Not far away, Alexander pulled back from his own latest victim, then ran to the side of Sekhmakh. There were many corpses in front of the Ark—a few of her fellow Jews, far more of the Persians—and the knives of the *kandake* were dripping. Ahead, amid the sphinxes outside the open archway, what looked like a hundred more Persians were gathering to rush in upon them.

Alexander and Sekhmakh gave the slightest nods to each other. They smiled, and then they turned toward the onslaught, two against them all.

Like Leonidas at the Hot Gates, Hephaestion thought.

On his own side, another Persian rushed forward around a pillar, but the man was tired, and Hephaestion dispatched him quickly. Only a handful still faced him, but they were holding back now. They seemed content to let the next wave come in and finish him off.

In the space they afforded him, Hephaestion decided that if he was going to die, he was going to do it standing beside Alexander. He began to back slowly in that direction, determined not to be cut down from behind before he could get there.

There were streaks and pools of blood where wounded men had tried to drag themselves away from death. Hephaestion stepped through it carefully, keeping his sword up between himself and the enemy. They continued to hold back, but they were like circling sharks, watching for any chance to move in for the kill.

His heel struck wood. It thumped like a hollow drum, deep and resonant.

The Ark.

In his mind's eye Hephaestion could see its surface at his back. He could see the two winged figures—still gleaming silver and gold, still freshly shined despite the horror that had been strewn upon the pillars and the ground all around them—and the circle of a flat stone that lay between them. It was a stone that was blacker than black, he knew. It swallowed the light just as the one within the Aegis did.

Alexander had often enough described what it was like to use the armor. This power was greater, Sekhmakh had said. But it was of the same kind.

Hephaestion looked to the men before him, then he glanced over and saw the next wave of the Persians shout a battle-cry and hurl forward at the *kandake* and Alexander.

Without another thought, without hesitation, Hephaestion threw down his sword, turned, and placed both of his hands upon the black stone atop the Ark.

The surge of power that erupted against his skin was so instant, so powerful, that he had to close his eyes and cry out. Hotter than fire, brighter than the sun, inch by inch it enveloped him, consumed him, as if he was leaning deeper and deeper into rock molten in the forges of his namesake god. Hephaestus. Whether the world yawned up to him or he caved down upon it, he couldn't tell.

And then abruptly the heat turned to cold, into a deep void of swirling darkness that loomed up and beckoned him down. He fell, slid, tumbled into a night dark as pitch, and in his mind he screamed down a hurtling abyss, though whether in truth his throat had air enough to make a sound he no longer knew.

Heartbeats had passed. Mere seconds. But it felt like years of his life were being stripped away, burned to a bitter ash carried away by a dark and terrible wind. In desperation he tried to pull back, to swim up against the pull of the bottomless pit that was drawing him on and on into oblivion.

Something jolted him as he fought against that rushing force, and somewhere in the distance he felt the bones of his arms snapping, like twigs shattered in the mouth of an angry beast. But the pain washed away. Everything washed away. His body. The temple. The damnable sand. Even Alexander.

Alexander!

The memory of him rolled into his mind, like the form of him rolling over in bed. The trust. The love. All stripped away. All passing into void, into nothing, into the darkness of death and eternal quiet.

No.

It was a whisper in his mind, but it fought to be heard.

No!

Hephaestion fixed his mind upon Alexander. The man. The memory.

No!

The world stopped. The swirling and sliding abruptly ended, and the power that had been surging over him was suddenly, unmistakably, pulsing *within* him.

He opened his eyes. Alexander and Sekhmakh were there, dancing with death. The next wave of the Persians was upon them, and in a frozen instant he could see the hatred and the rage upon those foreign faces. He could see his king's impending death. Only seconds remained.

Closer, he could see how his fingers were curled and tensed, as if he intended to claw open wounds in the terrible, beautiful black stone. There was blood slashed across the darkness there, like red grooves, but the pain was something he couldn't feel.

Unlike the power.

That was something he felt very deeply.

So as he watched the wall of Persians coming, as he watched the wave breaking over and upon those two figures framed by the frozen spray of blood and spit and sand that hung in the strangely calm light, Hephaestion knew what he had to do.

What the Aegis did for life, the Ark did for the earth.

The rock. The stone. He could feel the elements all around him. Under his feet. In the columns. Waiting. Ready.

He drew the power of the Ark up through his palms. He let it wick up into his flesh, higher and higher, and then he reached out to the paving stones that marked the path between the long line of sphinxes. The feet of the men who'd been running upon them were, for the moment, stilled.

The power had come into him like oil rising into cloth. Now, with the spark of a thought, it ignited.

The world exploded. Time returned. Feet fell once again. But the surge Hephaestion had released was a roar, and behind it came the scream of the earth.

Like a wave passing beneath their surfaces, the power lifted the wide paving stones. As it rolled forward the attackers were toppled and thrown, scattered like cut stalks of wheat upon a winter wind.

Then another thought, another spark of flame in his mind. His hands scraped the stone in a tortured agony and the awful fire of its power burned and poured forth. In response, down the length of the shattered stone avenue, the sphinxes that lined it rose up. With a thunderous crack of rock, they shook off the chains of their makers and hungrily looked down upon their prey. As one, they slouched forward in birth and destruction.

In his mind Hephaestion saw the carnage, but he no longer knew what was real and what was imagination. Already his vision was fading into darkness.

Then the world shook, and a black sheet of darkness seemed to lift from him.

Hephaestion's eyes were open, but when he tried to blink, they did not respond. The air had the sick-sweet scent of blood, but it did not fill his lungs. The sun was a fading memory. He was cold to his bones, cold to his soul, and he was certain he would never again be warm.

Dead.

Dying, at least.

Someone was speaking, a voice that was at once close and far, far away.

It was Alexander, he realized. A voice he would know anywhere. Even in death, it seemed.

Abruptly he was moving again. The new stars in the heavens shook before his eyes.

Then everything stopped and his friend's face was rising up over him. Tears had run clean rivers through the dirty soil upon Alexander's skin. "Hold on, Heph," he was saying. "Hold on."

The shaking came again, and the face and the stars swept lazily to left and right. Alexander was moving his body, Hephaestion thought. He was doing something.

Whatever it was, it was too late. If he'd had air, Hephaestion would have made sure to breathe his last giving a name to his heart.

But he knew it wasn't needed. They'd always known. There was solace in that.

His vision stilled again, and Hephaestion saw that Alexander was lifting something up against the background of stars before bringing it down to his frozen chest. Only then did Hephaestion know what it was.

The stars dimmed. The Aegis descended.

It touched his flesh. And then the darkness became a searing light that carried him away into sleep.

The sun danced upon the nile. Sekhmakh was standing beside them on the riverbank as Terach and the others carefully loaded the crate containing the Ark onto one of the ships that the army of Kush had left behind.

Not for the first time, Hephaestion wanted to call it a miracle that he and Terach had survived, but he knew only too well the power that preserved. He knew the darkness that had made them whole.

"It will be hidden where none will find it," Alexander was promising the *kandake*. Whatever thoughts he might have entertained for using the Ark, he'd told them, they were ended when he'd seen what it had done to Hephaestion that night.

And what Hephaestion had done through it.

Even now, days later, they were certain that the desert carrion were still glutted on the carnage they'd left behind, the horror whose end Hephaestion didn't remember.

His inability to recall what happened did nothing to alleviate his guilt. Somehow it made it even worse.

"I know you will see that it is so," Sekhmakh said, and she kissed the king on the cheek. Alexander, for all his conquests, blushed. Next she turned her smile to Hephaestion. "You are owed much, too. We would not be here if not for you."

Hephaestion tried to smile without worry, but he doubted it was convincing. Though he couldn't remember what had happened in the end, he could still remember how that initial surge of divine power had coursed into his muscles, into his bones. A part of him wanted to feel it again, even as another part of him wanted to throw up at the memory. "I'm glad we survived," he managed to say.

The *kandake* of Kush kissed him, too, in her gratitude.

Within minutes, the Ark was aboard the boat. Terach and three other survivors of the temple got in, too. Alexander had insisted they take charge of the construction and design of the new temple for the Ark in Alexandria: his new city that would soon have the greatest of ancient secrets beneath its streets.

And then, with a final exchange of thanks, he and Alexander boarded the ship, and they set off upon the Nile. The man at the tiller used a pole to push them closer and closer to the main flow of the mighty river, and before long its steady roll had lifted their weight and begun to carry them downstream. It was a great beast, that river, more powerful than any Hephaestion had ever seen. But it was nothing like the power that had flowed in him, and he knew he would never forget that horrible, tantalizing truth. The power, he thought, seemed as if it could have broken the world.

Hephaestion stood at the prow, watching as the waves slipped beneath the boat. The banks rose and fell. Trees and fields appeared and disappeared. He saw it all without seeing, lost in his own thoughts.

"You're quiet, Heph."

Alexander. He'd walked up to stand alongside him. How long he'd been there, Hephaestion wasn't sure, but he knew there was nothing he could hide from him. "I was just wondering," he said after a moment. "What next? Will you keep the Aegis?"

The great king chewed on his lip—gods, what a terrible habit—and he watched a small farm pass by along the closer shoreline. "I've thought about that a lot," he admitted. "I think I must. There may still be more for it to do. And my dream is still alive. They can bury it with me."

Hephaestion nodded. He'd expected as much. At last he looked up from the waters of the Nile to the high Egyptian sun. "And after the Ark is in Alexandria? What then?"

Alexander smiled. "Then we'll leave this country," he said. When that brought Hephaestion's gaze to him, his friend's eyes glinted mischievously. "And maybe you'll start sleeping through the night."

"Out of Egypt," Hephaestion whispered. At once he thought of green vineyards, of peace and home. And then, as if on cue, he was aware of sandy grit in his hair and between his thighs. The thought of it made him let out a tired sigh that became a laugh. "Can't happen fast enough."

"By the gods, Heph, I've missed that sound."

Hephaestion smiled. And beneath them, unaware of its burdens, the great river carried them on.

About the Author

MICHAEL LIVINGSTON is the author of the bestselling audiobook *Black Crow, White Snow* and the Seaborn series of novels it inspired, as well as The Shards historical fantasy series. An acclaimed conflict analyst in his day job, he has twice won the Distinguished Book Prize from the international Society for Military History (2017, 2020) and is the author of numerous popular histories, including *Never Greater Slaughter*, *Agincourt* and *The Two Hundred Years War*. At present, he serves as the Citadel Distinguished Professor at The Citadel. You can find Michael at www.michaellivingston.com.